PENGUIN

Lu

Roald Dahl is best known for his stories for children. But throughout his life he was also a prolific and acclaimed writer of stories for adults. These sinister, surprising tales continue to entertain, amuse and shock generations of readers even today.

Lust

ROALD DAHL

PENGUIN BOOKS

PENGUIN BOOKS

UK | USA | Canada | Ireland | Australia
India | New Zealand | South Africa

Penguin Books is part of the Penguin Random House group of companies
whose addresses can be found at global.penguinrandomhouse.com.

These stories have been previously published in a variety of publications.
Details of each story's original publication are provided at the start of
each chapter and constitute an extension of this copyright page.
This collection first published in Penguin Books 2016

001

Set in 12.5/14.75pt Garamond MT Std
Typeset by Jouve (UK), Milton Keynes
Printed in Great Britain by Clays Ltd, St Ives plc

A CIP catalogue record for this book is available from the British Library

ISBN: 978-0-718-18561-9

www.greenpenguin.co.uk

MIX
Paper from
responsible sources
FSC® C018179

Penguin Random House is committed to a
sustainable future for our business, our readers
and our planet. This book is made from Forest
Stewardship Council® certified paper.

Contents

Madame Rosette

First published in *Harper's* (August 1945)

'Oh Jesus, this is wonderful,' said the Stag.

He was lying back in the bath with a scotch and soda in one hand and a cigarette in the other. The water was right up to the brim and he was keeping it warm by turning the tap with his toes.

He raised his head and took a little sip of his whisky, then he lay back and closed his eyes.

'For God's sake, get out,' said a voice from the next room. 'Come on, Stag, you've had over an hour.' Stuffy was sitting on the edge of the bed with no clothes on, drinking slowly and waiting his turn.

The Stag said, 'All right. I'm letting the water out now,' and he stretched out a leg and flipped up the plug with his toes.

Stuffy stood up and wandered into the bathroom, holding his drink in his hand. The Stag lay in the bath for a few moments more, then, balancing his glass carefully on the soap rack, he stood up and reached for a towel. His body was short and square, with strong thick legs and exaggerated calf muscles. He had coarse curly ginger hair and a thin, rather pointed face covered with freckles. There was a layer of pale-ginger hair on his chest.

'Jesus,' he said, looking down into the bath tub, 'I've brought half the desert with me.'

Stuffy said, 'Wash it out and let me get in. I haven't had a bath for five months.'

This was back in the early days when we were fighting the Italians in Libya. One flew very hard in those days because there were not many pilots. They certainly could not send any out from England because there they were fighting the Battle of Britain. So one remained for long periods out in the desert, living the strange unnatural life of the desert, living in the same dirty little tent, washing and shaving every day in a mugful of one's own spat-out tooth water, all the time picking flies out of one's tea and out of one's food, having sandstorms which were as much in the tents as outside them so that placid men became bloody-minded and lost their tempers with their friends and with themselves; having dysentery and gippy tummy and mastoid and desert sores, having some bombs from the Italian S-79s, having no water and no women; having no flowers growing out of the ground; having very little except sand sand sand. One flew old Gloster Gladiators against the Italian CR42s, and when one was not flying, it was difficult to know what to do.

Occasionally one would catch scorpions, put them in empty petrol cans and match them against each other in fierce mortal combat. Always there would be a champion scorpion in the squadron, a sort of Joe Louis who was invincible and won all his fights. He would have a name; he would become famous and his training diet would be a great secret known only to the owner. Training diet was considered very important with scorpions. Some were trained on corned beef, some on a thing called

Machonachies, which is an unpleasant canned meat stew, some on live beetles, and there were others who were persuaded to take a little beer just before the fight, on the premise that it made the scorpion happy and gave him confidence. These last ones always lost. But there were great battles and great champions, and in the afternoons when the flying was over, one could often see a group of pilots and airmen standing around in a circle on the sand, bending over with their hands on their knees, watching the fight, exhorting the scorpions and shouting at them as people shout at boxers or wrestlers in a ring. Then there would be a victory, and the man who owned the winner would become excited. He would dance around in the sand, yelling, waving his arms in the air and extolling in a loud voice the virtues of the victorious animal. The greatest scorpion of all was owned by a sergeant called Wishful who fed him only on marmalade. The animal had an unmentionable name, but he won forty-two consecutive fights and then died quietly in training just when Wishful was considering the problem of retiring him to stud.

So you can see that because there were no great pleasures while living in the desert, the small pleasures became great pleasures and the pleasures of children became the pleasures of grown men. That was true for everyone; for the pilots, the fitters, the riggers, the corporals who cooked the food and the men who kept the stores. It was true for the Stag and for Stuffy, so true that when the two of them wangled a forty-eight-hour pass and a lift by air into Cairo, and when they got to the hotel, they were feeling about having a bath rather as you would feel on the first night of your honeymoon.

The Stag had dried himself and was lying on the bed with a towel round his waist, with his hands up behind his head, and Stuffy was in the bath, lying with his head against the back of the bath, groaning and sighing with ecstasy.

The Stag said, 'Stuffy.'

'Yes.'

'What are we going to do now?'

'Women,' said Stuffy. 'We must find some women to take out to supper.'

The Stag said, 'Later. That can wait till later.' It was early afternoon.

'I don't think it can wait,' said Stuffy.

'Yes,' said the Stag, 'it can wait.'

The Stag was very old and wise; he never rushed any fences. He was twenty-seven, much older than anyone else in the squadron, including the CO, and his judgement was much respected by the others.

'Let's do a little shopping first,' he said.

'Then what?' said the voice from the bathroom.

'Then we can consider the other situation.'

There was a pause.

'Stag?'

'Yes.'

'Do you know any women here?'

'I used to. I used to know a Turkish girl with very white skin called Wenka, and a Yugoslav girl who was six inches taller than I, called Kiki, and another who I think was Syrian. I can't remember her name.'

'Ring them up,' said Stuffy.

'I've done it. I did it while you were getting the whisky. They've all gone. It isn't any good.'

'It's never any good,' Stuffy said.

The Stag said, 'We'll go shopping first. There is plenty of time.'

In an hour Stuffy got out of the bath. They both dressed themselves in clean khaki shorts and shirts and wandered downstairs, through the lobby of the hotel and out into the bright hot street. The Stag put on his sunglasses.

Stuffy said, 'I know. I want a pair of sunglasses.'

'All right. We'll go and buy some.'

They stopped a gharri, got in and told the driver to go to Cicurel. Stuffy bought his sunglasses and the Stag bought some poker dice, then they wandered out again on to the hot crowded street.

'Did you see that girl?' said Stuffy.

'The one that sold us the sunglasses?'

'Yes. That dark one.'

'Probably Turkish,' said Stag.

Stuffy said, 'I don't care what she was. She was terrific. Didn't you think she was terrific?'

They were walking along the Sharia Kasr-el-Nil with their hands in their pockets, and Stuffy was wearing the sunglasses which he had just bought. It was a hot dusty afternoon, and the sidewalk was crowded with Egyptians and Arabs and small boys with bare feet. The flies followed the small boys and buzzed around their eyes, trying to get at the inflammation which was in them, which was there because their mothers had done something terrible to those eyes when the boys were young, so that they would not be eligible for military conscription when they grew older. The small boys pattered along beside the Stag and Stuffy shouting, 'Baksheesh, baksheesh,' in shrill insistent voices, and the flies followed the small boys. There was the smell of Cairo, which is not like the smell of any other city. It comes not from any one thing or from any one place; it comes from everything everywhere; from the gutters and the sidewalks, from the houses and the shops and the things in the shops and the food cooking in the shops, from the horses and the dung of the horses in the streets and from the drains; it comes from the people and the way the sun bears down upon the people and from the way the sun bears down upon the gutters and the drains and the horses and the food and the refuse in the streets. It is a rare, pungent smell, like something which is sweet and rotting and hot and salty and bitter all at the same time, and it is never absent, even in the cool of the early morning.

The two pilots walked slowly among the crowd.

'Didn't you think she was terrific?' said Stuffy. He wanted to know what the Stag thought.

'She was all right.'

'Certainly she was all right. You know what, Stag?'

'What?'

'I would like to take that girl out tonight.'

They crossed over a street and walked on a little farther.

The Stag said, 'Well, why don't you? Why don't you ring up Rosette?'

'Who in the hell's Rosette?'

'Madame Rosette,' said the Stag. 'She is a great woman.'

They were passing a place called Tim's Bar. It was run by an Englishman called Tim Gilfillan who had been a quartermaster sergeant in the last war and who had somehow managed to get left behind in Cairo when the Army went home.

'Tim's,' said the Stag. 'Let's go in.'

There was no one inside except for Tim, who was arranging his bottles on shelves behind the bar.

'Well, well, well,' he said, turning around. 'Where you boys been all this time?'

'Hello, Tim.'

He did not remember them, but he knew by their looks that they were in from the desert.

'How's my old friend Graziani?' he said, turning round and leaning his elbows on the counter.

'He's bloody close,' said the Stag. 'He's outside Mersah.'

'What you flying now?'

'Gladiators.'

'Hell, they had those here eight years ago.'

'Same ones still here,' said the Stag. 'They're clapped out.'

They got their whisky and carried the glasses over to a table in the corner.

Stuffy said, 'Who's this Rosette?'

The Stag took a long drink and put down the glass.

'She's a great woman,' he said.

'Who is she?'

'She's a filthy old whore.'

'All right,' said Stuffy, 'all right, but what about her?'

'Well,' said Stag, 'I'll tell you. Madame Rosette runs the biggest brothel in the world. It is said that she can get you any girl that you want in the whole of Cairo.'

'Bullshit.'

'No, it's true. You just ring her up and tell her where you saw the woman, where she was working, what shop and at which counter, together with an accurate description, and she will do the rest.'

'Don't be such a bloody fool,' said Stuffy.

'It's true. It's absolutely true. Thirty-three Squadron told me about her.'

'They were pulling your leg.'

'All right. You go and look her up in the phone book.'

'She wouldn't be in the phone book under that name.'

'I'm telling you she is,' said Stag. 'Go and look her up under Rosette. You'll see I'm right.'

Stuffy did not believe him, but he went over to Tim and asked him for a telephone directory and brought it back to the table. He opened it and turned the pages until he came to R-o-s. He ran his finger down the column. Roseppi . . . Rosery . . . Rosette. There it was, Rosette, Madame, and the address and number, clearly printed in the book. The Stag was watching him.

'Got it?' he said.

'Yes, here it is. Madame Rosette.'

'Well, why don't you go and ring her up?'

'What shall I say?'

The Stag looked down into his glass and poked the ice with his finger.

'Tell her you are a colonel,' he said. 'Colonel Higgins; she mistrusts pilot officers. And tell her that you have seen a beautiful dark girl selling sunglasses at Cicurel's and that you would like, as you put it, to take her out to dinner.'

'There isn't a telephone here.'

'Oh yes there is. There's one over there.'

Stuffy looked around and saw the telephone on the wall at the end of the bar.

'I haven't got a piastre piece.'

'Well, I have,' said Stag. He fished in his pocket and put a piastre on the table.

'Tim will hear everything I say.'

'What the hell does that matter? He probably rings her up himself. You're windy,' he added.

'You're a shit,' said Stuffy.

Stuffy was just a child. He was nineteen; seven whole years younger than the Stag. He was fairly tall and he was thin, with a lot of black hair and a handsome wide-mouthed face which was coffee brown from the sun of the desert. He was unquestionably the finest pilot in the squadron, and already in these early days his score was fourteen Italians confirmed destroyed. On the ground he moved slowly and lazily like a tired person and he thought slowly and lazily like a sleepy child, but when he was up in the air his mind was quick and his movements were quick, so quick that they were like reflex actions. It seemed, when he was on the ground, almost as though he was resting, as though he was dozing a little in order to make sure that when he got into the cockpit he would wake up fresh and quick, ready for that two hours of high concentration. But Stuffy was away from the aerodrome now and he had something on his mind which had waked him up almost like flying. It might not last, but for the moment anyway, he was concentrating.

He looked again in the book for the number, got up and walked slowly over to the telephone. He put in the piastre, dialled the number and heard it ringing at the other end. The Stag was sitting at the table looking at him and Tim was still behind the bar arranging his bottles. Tim was only about five yards away and he was obviously going to listen to everything that was said. Stuffy felt rather foolish. He leaned against the bar and waited, hoping that no one would answer.

Then click, the receiver was lifted at the other end and he heard a woman's voice saying, 'Allo.'

He said, 'Hello, is Madame Rosette there?' He was watching Tim. Tim went on arranging his bottles, pretending to take no notice, but Stuffy knew that he was listening.

'This ees Madame Rosette. Oo ees it?' Her voice was petulant and gritty. She sounded as if she did not want to be bothered with anyone just then.

Stuffy tried to sound casual. 'This is Colonel Higgins.'

'Colonel oo?'

'Colonel Higgins.' He spelled it.

'Yes, Colonel. What do you want?' She sounded impatient. Obviously this was a woman who stood no nonsense. He still tried to sound casual.

'Well, Madame Rosette, I was wondering if you could help me over a little matter.'

Stuffy was watching Tim. He was listening all right. You can always tell if someone is listening when he is pretending not to. He is careful not to make any noise about what he is doing and he pretends that he is concentrating very hard upon his job. Tim was like that now, moving the bottles quickly from one shelf to another, watching the bottles, making no noise, never looking around into the room. Over in the far corner the Stag was leaning forward with his elbows on the table, smoking a cigarette. He was watching Stuffy, enjoying the whole business and knowing that Stuffy was embarrassed because of Tim. Stuffy had to go on.

'I was wondering if you could help me,' he said. 'I was in Cicurel's today buying a pair of sunglasses and I saw a girl there whom I would very much like to take out to dinner.'

'What's 'er name?' The hard, rasping voice was more businesslike than ever.

'I don't know,' he said sheepishly.

'What's she look like?'

'Well, she's got dark hair, and tall and, well, she's very beautiful.'

'What sort of a dress was she wearing?'

'Er, let me see. I think it was a kind of white dress with red flowers printed all over it.' Then, as a brilliant afterthought, he added, 'She had a red belt.' He remembered that she had been wearing a shiny red belt.

There was a pause. Stuffy watched Tim, who wasn't making any noise with the bottles; he was picking them up carefully and putting them down carefully.

Then the loud gritty voice again, 'It may cost you a lot.'

'That's all right.' Suddenly he didn't like the conversation any more. He wanted to finish it and get away.

'Might cost you six pounds, might cost you eight or ten. I don't know till I've seen her. That all right?'

'Yes yes, that's all right.'

'Where you living, Colonel?'

'Metropolitan Hotel,' he said without thinking.

'All right, I give you a ring later.' And she put down the receiver, bang.

Stuffy hung up, went slowly back to the table and sat down.

'Well,' said Stag, 'that was all right, wasn't it?'

'Yes, I suppose so.'

'What did she say?'

'She said that she would call me back at the hotel.'

'You mean she'll call Colonel Higgins at the hotel.'

Stuffy said, 'Oh Christ.'

Stag said, 'It's all right. We'll tell the desk that the Colonel is in our room and put his calls through to us. What else did she say?'

'She said it may cost me a lot, six or ten pounds.'

'Rosette will take ninety per cent of it,' said Stag. 'She's a filthy old whore.'

'How will she work it?' Stuffy said.

He was really a gentle person and now he was feeling worried about having started something which might become complicated.

'Well,' said Stag, 'she'll dispatch one of her pimps to locate the girl and find out who she is. If she's already on the books, then it's easy. If she isn't, the pimp will proposition her there and then over the counter at Cicurel's. If the girl tells him to go to hell, he'll up the price, and if she still tells him to go to hell, he'll up the price still more, and in the end she'll be tempted by the cash and probably agree. Then Rosette quotes you a price three times as high and takes the balance herself. You have to pay her, not the girl. Of course after that the girl goes on Rosette's books, and once she's in her clutches, she's finished. Next time Rosette will dictate the price and the girl will not be in a position to argue.'

'Why?'

'Because if she refuses, Rosette will say, "All right, my girl, I shall see that your employers, that's Cicurel's, are told about what you did last time, how you've been working for me and using their shop as a market place. Then they'll fire you." That's what Rosette will say, and the wretched girl will be frightened and do what she's told.'

Stuffy said, 'Sounds like a nice person.'

'Who?'

'Madame Rosette.'

'Charming,' said Stag. 'She's a charming person.'

It was hot. Stuffy wiped his face with his handkerchief.

'More whisky,' said Stag. 'Hi, Tim, two more of those.'

Tim brought the glasses over and put them on the table without saying anything. He picked up the empty glasses and went away at once. To Stuffy it seemed as though he was different from what he had been when they first came in. He wasn't cheery any more, he was quiet and offhand. There wasn't any more 'Hi, you fellows, where you been all this time' about him now, and when he got back behind the counter, he turned his back and went on arranging the bottles.

The Stag said, 'How much money you got?'

'Nine pounds, I think.'

'May not be enough. You gave her a free hand, you know. You ought to have set a limit. She'll sting you now.'

'I know,' Stuffy said.

They went on drinking for a little while without talking. Then Stag said, 'What you worrying about, Stuffy?'

'Nothing,' he answered. 'Nothing at all. Let's go back to the hotel. She may ring up.'

They paid for their drinks and said good-bye to Tim, who nodded but didn't say anything. They went back to the Metropolitan and as they went past the desk, the Stag said to the clerk, 'If a call comes in for Colonel Higgins, put it through to our room. He'll be there.' The Egyptian said, 'Yes, sir,' and made a note of it.

In the bedroom, the Stag lay down on his bed and lit a cigarette. 'And what am I going to do tonight?' he said.

Stuffy had been quiet all the way back to the hotel. He hadn't said a word. Now he sat down on the edge of the other bed with his hands still in his pockets and said, 'Look, Stag, I'm not very keen on this Rosette deal any more. It may cost too much. Can't we put it off?'

The Stag sat up. 'Hell no,' he said. 'You're committed. You can't fool about with Rosette like that. She's probably working on it at this moment. You can't back out now.'

'I may not be able to afford it,' Stuffy said.

'Well, wait and see.'

Stuffy got up, went over to the parachute bag and took out the bottle of whisky. He poured out two, filled the glasses with water from the tap in the bathroom, came back and gave one to the Stag.

'Stag,' he said. 'Ring up Rosette and tell her that Colonel Higgins has had to leave town urgently, to rejoin his regiment in the desert. Ring her up and tell her that. Say the colonel asked you to deliver the message because he didn't have time.'

'Ring her up yourself.'

'She'd recognize my voice. Come on, Stag, you ring her.'

'No,' he said, 'I won't.'

'Listen,' said Stuffy suddenly. It was the child Stuffy speaking. 'I don't want to go out with that woman and I don't want to have any dealings with Madame Rosette tonight. We can think of something else.'

The Stag looked up quickly. Then he said, 'All right. I'll ring her.'

He reached for the phone book, looked up her number and spoke it into the telephone. Stuffy heard him get her on the line and he heard him giving her the message from the colonel. There was a pause, then the Stag said, 'I'm sorry, Madame Rosette, but it's nothing to do with me. I'm merely delivering a message.' Another pause; then the Stag said the same thing over again and that went on for quite a long time, until he must have got tired of it, because in the end he put down the receiver and lay back on his bed. He was roaring with laughter.

'The lousy old bitch,' he said, and he laughed some more.

Stuffy said, 'Was she angry?'

'Angry,' said Stag. 'Was she angry? You should have heard her. Wanted to know the colonel's regiment and God knows what else and said he'd have to pay. She said you boys think you can fool around with me but you can't.'

'Hooray,' said Stuffy. 'The filthy old whore.'

'Now what are we going to do?' said the Stag. 'It's six o'clock already.'

'Let's go out and do a little drinking in some of those Gyppi places.'

'Fine. We'll do a Gyppi pub crawl.'

They had one more drink, then they went out. They went to a place called the Excelsior, then they went to a place called the Sphinx, then to a small place called by an Egyptian name, and by ten o'clock they were sitting happily in a place which hadn't got a name at all, drinking beer and watching a kind of stage show. At the Sphinx they had picked up a pilot from 33 Squadron, who said that his name was William. He was about the same age as Stuffy, but his face was younger, for he had not been flying so long. It was especially around his mouth that he was younger. He had a round schoolboy face and a small turned-up nose and his skin was brown from the desert.

The three of them sat happily in the place without a name drinking beer, because beer was the only thing that they served there. It was a long wooden room with an unpolished wooden sawdust floor and wooden tables and chairs. At the far end there was a raised wooden stage where there was a show going on. The room was full of

Egyptians, sitting drinking black coffee with the red tarbooshes on their heads. There were two fat girls on the stage dressed in shiny silver pants and silver brassières. One was waggling her bottom in time to the music. The other was waggling her bosom in time to the music. The bosom waggler was the more skilful. She could waggle one bosom without waggling the other and sometimes she would waggle her bottom as well. The Egyptians were spellbound and kept giving her a big hand. The more they clapped the more she waggled and the more she waggled the faster the music played, and the faster the music played, the faster she waggled, faster and faster and faster, never losing the tempo, never losing the fixed brassy smile that was upon her face, and the Egyptians clapped more and more and louder and louder as the speed increased. Everyone was very happy.

When it was over William said, 'Why do they always have those dreary fat women? Why don't they have beautiful women?'

The Stag said, 'The Gyppies like them fat. They like them like that.'

'Impossible,' said Stuffy.

'It's true,' Stag said. 'It's an old business. It comes from the days when there used to be lots of famines here, and all the poor people were thin and all the rich people and the aristocracy were well fed and fat. If you got someone fat you couldn't go wrong; she was bound to be high class.'

'Bullshit,' said Stuffy.

William said, 'Well, we'll soon find out. I'm going to ask

those Gyppies.' He jerked his thumb towards two middle-aged Egyptians who were sitting at the next table, only four feet away.

'No,' said Stag. 'No, William. We don't want them over here.'

'Yes,' said Stuffy.

'Yes,' said William. 'We've got to find out why the Gyppies like fat women.'

He was not drunk. None of them was drunk, but they were happy with a fair amount of beer and whisky, and William was the happiest. His brown schoolboy face was radiant with happiness, his turned-up nose seemed to have turned up a little more and he was probably relaxing for the first time in many weeks. He got up, took three paces over to the table of the Egyptians and stood in front of them, smiling.

'Gentlemen,' he said, 'my friends and I would be honoured if you would join us at our table.'

The Egyptians had dark greasy skin and podgy faces. They were wearing the red hats and one of them had a gold tooth. At first, when William addressed them, they looked a little alarmed. Then they caught on, looked at each other, grinned and nodded.

'Pleess,' said one.

'Pleess,' said the other, and they got up, shook hands with William and followed him over to where the Stag and Stuffy were sitting.

William said, 'Meet my friends. This is the Stag. This is Stuffy. I am William.'

The Stag and Stuffy stood up, they all shook hands, the

Egyptians said 'Pleess' once more and then everyone sat down.

The Stag knew that their religion forbade them to drink. 'Have a coffee,' he said.

The one with the gold tooth grinned broadly, raised his hands, palms upward and hunched his shoulders a little. 'For me,' he said, 'I am accustomed. But for my frient,' and he spread out his hands towards the other, 'for my frient – I cannot speak.'

The Stag looked at the friend. 'Coffee?' he asked.

'Pleess,' he answered. 'I am accustomed.'

'Good,' said Stag. 'Two coffees.'

He called a waiter. 'Two coffees,' he said. 'And, wait a minute. Stuffy, William, more beer?'

'For me,' Stuffy said, 'I am accustomed. But for my friend,' and he turned towards William, 'for my friend – I cannot speak.'

William said, 'Please. I am accustomed.' None of them smiled.

The Stag said, 'Good. Waiter, two coffees and three beers.' The waiter fetched the order and the Stag paid. The Stag lifted his glass towards the Egyptians and said, 'Bung ho.'

'Bung ho,' said Stuffy.

'Bung ho,' said William.

The Egyptians seemed to understand and they lifted their coffee cups. 'Pleess,' said the one. 'Thank you,' said the other. They drank.

The Stag put down his glass and said, 'It is an honour to be in your country.'

'You like?'

'Yes,' said the Stag. 'Very fine.'

The music had started again and the two fat women in silver tights were doing an encore. The encore was a knockout. It was surely the most remarkable exhibition of muscle control that has ever been witnessed; for although the bottom-waggler was still just waggling her bottom, the bosom-waggler was standing like an oak tree in the centre of the stage with her arms above her head. Her left bosom she was rotating in a clockwise direction and her right bosom in an anti-clockwise direction. At the same time she was waggling her bottom and it was all in time to the music. Gradually the music increased its speed, and as it got faster, the rotating and the waggling got faster and some of the Egyptians were so spellbound by the contra-rotating bosoms of the woman that they were unconsciously following the movements of the bosoms with their hands, holding their hands up in front of them and describing circles in the air. Everyone stamped their feet and screamed with delight and the two women on the stage continued to smile their fixed brassy smiles.

Then it was over. The applause gradually died down.

'Remarkable,' said the Stag.

'You like?'

'Please, it was remarkable.'

'Those girls,' said the one with the gold tooth, 'very special.'

William couldn't wait any longer. He leaned across the table and said, 'Might I ask you a question?'

'Pleess,' said Golden Tooth. 'Pleess.'

'Well,' said William, 'how do you like your women? Like this – slim?' and he demonstrated with his hands. 'Or like this – fat?'

The gold tooth shone brightly behind a big grin. 'For me, I like like this, fat,' and a pair of podgy hands drew a big circle in the air.

'And your friend?' said William.

'For my frient,' he answered, 'I cannot speak.'

'Pleess,' said the friend. 'Like this.' He grinned and drew a fat girl in the air with his hands.

Stuffy said, 'Why do you like them fat?'

Golden Tooth thought for a moment, then he said, 'You like them slim, eh?'

'Please,' said Stuffy. 'I like them slim.'

'Why you like them slim? You tell me.'

Stuffy rubbed the back of his neck with the palm of his hand. 'William,' he said, 'why do we like them slim?'

'For me,' said William, 'I am accustomed.'

'So am I,' Stuffy said. 'But why?'

William considered. 'I don't know,' he said. 'I don't know why we like them slim.'

'Ha,' said Golden Tooth. 'You don't know.' He leaned over the table towards William and said triumphantly, 'And me, I do not know either.'

But that wasn't good enough for William. 'The Stag,' he said, 'says that all rich people in Egypt used to be fat and all poor people were thin.'

'No,' said Golden Tooth, 'No no no. Look those girls up there. Very fat; very poor. Look Queen of Egypt, Queen Farida. Very thin; very rich. Quite wrong.'

'Yes, but what about years ago?' said William.

'What is this, years ago?'

William said, 'Oh all right. Let's leave it.'

The Egyptians drank their coffee and made noises like the last bit of water running out of the bath tub. When they had finished, they got up to go.

'Going?' said the Stag.

'Pleess,' said Golden Tooth.

William said, 'Thank you.' Stuffy said, 'Pleess.' The other Egyptian said, 'Pleess,' and the Stag said, 'Thank you.' They all shook hands and the Egyptians departed.

'Ropey types,' said William.

'Very,' said Stuffy. 'Very ropey types.'

The three of them sat on drinking happily until midnight, when the waiter came up and told them that the place was closing and that there were no more drinks. They were still not really drunk because they had been taking it slowly, but they were feeling healthy.

'He says we've got to go.'

'All right. Where shall we go? Where shall we go, Stag?'

'I don't know. Where do you want to go?'

'Let's go to another place like this,' said William. 'This is a fine place.'

There was a pause. Stuffy was stroking the back of his neck with his hand. 'Stag,' he said slowly, 'I know where I want to go. I want to go to Madame Rosette's and I want to rescue all the girls there.'

'Who's Madame Rosette?' William said.

'She's a great woman,' said the Stag.

'She's a filthy old whore,' said Stuffy.

'She's a lousy old bitch,' said the Stag.

'All right,' said William. 'Let's go. But who is she?'

They told him who she was. They told him about their telephone calls and about Colonel Higgins, and William said, 'Come on, let's go. Let's go and rescue all the girls.'

They got up and left. When they went outside, they remembered that they were in a rather remote part of the town.

'We'll have to walk a bit,' said Stag. 'No gharries here.'

It was a dark starry night with no moon. The street was narrow and blacked-out. It smelled strongly with the smell of Cairo. It was quiet as they walked along, and now and again they passed a man or sometimes two men standing back in the shadow of a house, leaning against the wall of the house, smoking.

'I say,' said William, 'ropey, what?'

'Very,' said Stuffy. 'Very bad types.'

They walked on, the three of them walking abreast; square short ginger-haired Stag, tall dark Stuffy and tall young William who went barehead because he had lost his cap. They headed roughly towards the centre of town where they knew that they would find a gharri to take them on to Rosette.

Stuffy said, 'Oh, won't the girls be pleased when we rescue them?'

'Jesus,' said the Stag, 'it ought to be a party.'

'Does she actually keep them locked up?' William said.

'Well, no,' said Stag. 'Not exactly. But if we rescue them now, they won't have to work any more tonight anyway. You see, the girls she has at her place are nothing but ordinary shop girls who still work during the day in the shops. They have all of them made some mistake or other which Rosette either engineered or found out about, and now she has put the screws on them; she makes them come along in the evening. But they hate her and they do not depend on her for a living. They would kick her in the teeth if they got the chance.'

Stuffy said, 'We'll give them the chance.'

They crossed over a street. William said, 'How many girls will there be there, Stag?'

'I don't know. I suppose there might be thirty.'

'Good God,' said William. 'This *will* be a party. Does she really treat them very badly?'

The Stag said, 'Thirty-three Squadron told me that she pays them nothing, about twenty akkers a night. She charges the customers a hundred or two hundred akkers each. Every girl earns for Rosette between five hundred and a thousand akkers every night.'

'Good God,' said William. 'A thousand piastres a night and thirty girls. She must be a millionaire.'

'She is. Someone calculated that not even counting her outside business, she makes the equivalent of about fifteen hundred pounds a week. That's, let me see, that's between five and six thousand pounds a month. Sixty thousand pounds a year.'

Stuffy came out of his dream. 'Jesus,' he said, 'Jesus Christ. The filthy old whore.'

'The lousy old bitch,' said William.

They were coming into a more civilized section of the town, but still there were no gharries.

The Stag said, 'Did you hear about Mary's House?'

'What's Mary's House?' said William.

'It's a place in Alexandria. Mary is the Rosette of Alex.'

'Lousy old bitch,' said William.

'No,' Stag said. 'They say she's a good woman. But any-way, Mary's House was hit by a bomb last week. The Navy was in port at the time and the place was full of sailors, nautic types.'

'Killed?'

'Lots of them killed. And d'you know what happened? They posted them as killed in action.'

'The admiral is a gentleman,' said Stuffy.

'Magnificent,' said William.

Then they saw a gharri and hailed it.

Stuffy said, 'We don't know the address.'

'He'll know it,' said Stag. 'Madame Rosette,' he said to the driver.

The driver grinned and nodded. Then William said, 'I'm going to drive. Give me the reins, driver, and sit up here beside me and tell me where to go.'

The driver protested vigorously, but when William gave him ten piastres, he gave him the reins. William sat high up on the driver's seat with the driver beside him. The Stag and Stuffy got in the back of the carriage.

'Take off,' said Stuffy. William took off. The horses began to gallop.

'No good,' shrieked the driver. 'No good. Stop.'

'Which way Rosette?' shouted William.

'Stop,' shrieked the driver.

William was happy. 'Rosette,' he shouted. 'Which way?'

The driver made a decision. He decided that the only way to stop this madman was to get him to his destination. 'This way,' he shrieked. 'Left.' William pulled hard on the left rein and the horses swerved round the corner. The gharri took it on one wheel.

'Too much bank,' shouted Stuffy from the back seat.

'Which way now?' shouted William.

'Left,' shrieked the driver. They took the next street to the left, then they took one to the right, two more to the left, then one to the right again and suddenly the driver yelled, 'Here pleess, here Rosette. Stop.'

William pulled hard on the reins and gradually the horses raised their heads with the pulling and slowed down to a trot.

'Where?' said William.

'Here,' said the driver. 'Pleess.' He pointed to a house twenty yards ahead. William brought the horses to a stop right in front of it.

'Nice work, William,' said Stuffy.

'Jesus,' said the Stag. 'That was quick.'

'Marvellous,' said William. 'Wasn't it?' He was very happy.

The driver was sweating through his shirt and he was too frightened to be angry.

William said, 'How much?'

'Pleess, twenty piastres.'

William gave him forty and said, 'Thank you very much. Fine horses.' The little man took the money, jumped up on to the gharri and drove off. He was in a hurry to get away.

They were in another of those narrow, dark streets, but the houses, what they could see of them, looked huge and prosperous. The one which the driver had said was Rosette's was wide and thick and three storeys high, built of grey concrete, and it had a large thick front door which stood wide open. As they went in, the Stag said, 'Now leave this to me. I've got a plan.'

Inside there was a cold grey dusty stone hall, lit by a bare electric light bulb in the ceiling, and there was a man standing in the hall. He was a mountain of a man, a huge Egyptian with a flat face and two cauliflower ears. In his wrestling days he had probably been billed as Abdul the Killer or The Poisonous Pasha, but now he wore a dirty white cotton suit.

The Stag said, 'Good evening. Is Madame Rosette here?'

Abdul looked hard at the three pilots, hesitated, then said, 'Madame Rosette top floor.'

'Thank you,' said Stag. 'Thank you very much.' Stuffy noticed that the Stag was being polite. There was always trouble for somebody when he was like that. Back in the squadron, when he was leading a flight, when they sighted the enemy and when there was going to be a battle, the Stag never gave an order without saying 'Please' and he never received a message without saying 'Thank you'. He was saying 'Thank you' now to Abdul.

They went up the bare stone steps, which had iron railings. They went past the first landing and the second landing, and the place was as bare as a cave. At the top of the third flight of steps, there was no landing; it was walled

27

off, and the stairs ran up to a door. The Stag pressed the bell. They waited a while, then a little panel in the door slid back and a pair of small black eyes peeked through. A woman's voice said, 'What you boys want?' Both the Stag and Stuffy recognized the voice from the telephone. The Stag said, 'We would like to see Madame Rosette.' He pronounced the Madame in the French way because he was being polite.

'You officers? Only officers here,' said the voice. She had a voice like a broken board.

'Yes,' said Stag. 'We are officers.'

'You don't look like officers. What kind of officers?'

'RAF.'

There was a pause. The Stag knew that she was considering. She had probably had trouble with pilots before, and he hoped only that she would not see William and the light that was dancing in his eyes; for William was still feeling the way he had felt when he drove the gharri. Suddenly the panel closed and the door opened.

'All right, come in,' she said. She was too greedy, this woman, even to pick her customers carefully.

They went in and there she was. Short, fat, greasy, with wisps of untidy black hair straggling over her forehead; a large, mud-coloured face, a large wide nose and a small fish mouth, with just the trace of a black moustache above the mouth. She had on a loose black satin dress.

'Come into the office, boys,' she said, and started to waddle down the passage to the left. It was a long wide passage, about fifty yards long and four or five yards wide. It ran through the middle of the house, parallel with the street, and as you came in from the stairs, you had to turn left along it. All the way down there were doors, about eight or ten of them on each side. If you turned right as you came in from the stairs, you ran into the end of the passage, but there was one door there too, and as the three of them walked in, they heard a babble of female voices from behind that door. The Stag noted that it was the girls' dressing-room.

'This way, boys,' said Rosette. She turned left and slopped down the passage, away from the door with the voices. The three followed her, Stag first, then Stuffy, then William, down the passage, which had a red carpet on the floor and huge pink lampshades hanging from the ceiling. They got about halfway down the passage when there was a yell from the dressing-room behind them. Rosette stopped and looked around.

'You go on, boys,' she said, 'into the office, last door on the left. I won't be a minute.' She turned and went back towards the dressing-room door. They didn't go on. They stood and watched her, and just as she got to the door, it opened and a girl rushed out. From where they stood, they could see that her fair hair was all over her face and that she had on an untidy-looking green evening dress. She saw Rosette in front of her and she stopped. They heard Rosette say something, something angry and quick-spoken, and they heard the girl shout something back at her. They saw Rosette raise her right arm and they saw her hit the girl smack on the side of the face with the palm of her hand. They saw her draw back her hand and hit her again in the same place. She hit her hard. The girl put her hands up to her face and began to cry. Rosette opened the door of the dressing-room and pushed her back inside.

'Jesus,' said the Stag. 'She's tough.' William said, 'So am I.' Stuffy didn't say anything.

Rosette came back to them and said, 'Come along, boys. Just a bit of trouble, that's all.' She led them to the end of the passage and in through the last door on the left. This was the office. It was a medium-sized room with two red plush sofas, two or three red plush armchairs and a thick red carpet on the floor. In one corner was a small desk, and Rosette sat herself behind it, facing the room.

'Sit down, boys,' she said.

The Stag took an armchair, Stuffy and William sat on a sofa.

'Well,' she said, and her voice became sharp and urgent. 'Let's do business.'

The Stag leaned forward in his chair. His short ginger hair looked somehow wrong against the bright red plush. 'Madame Rosette,' he said, 'it is a great pleasure to meet you. We have heard so much about you.' Stuffy looked at the Stag. He was being polite again. Rosette looked at him too, and her little black eyes were suspicious. 'Believe me,' the Stag went on, 'we've really been looking forward to this for quite a time now.'

His voice was so pleasant and he was so polite that Rosette took it.

'That's nice of you boys,' she said. 'You'll always have a good time here. I see to that. Now – business.'

William couldn't wait any longer. He said slowly, 'The Stag says that you're a great woman.'

'Thanks, boys.'

Stuffy said, 'The Stag says that you're a filthy old whore.'

William said quickly, 'The Stag says that you're a lousy old bitch.'

'And I know what I'm talking about,' said the Stag.

Rosette jumped to her feet. 'What's this?' she shrieked, and her face was no longer the colour of mud; it was the colour of red clay. The men did not move. They did not smile or laugh; they sat quite still, leaning forward a little in their seats, watching her.

Rosette had had trouble before, plenty of it, and she knew how to deal with it. But this was different. They didn't seem drunk, it wasn't about money and it wasn't about one of her girls. It was about herself and she didn't like it.

'Get out,' she yelled. 'Get out unless you want trouble.' But they did not move.

For a moment she paused, then she stepped quickly from behind her desk and made for the door. But the Stag was there first and when she went for him, Stuffy and William each caught one of her arms from behind.

'We'll lock her in,' said the Stag. 'Let's get out.'

Then she really started yelling and the words which she used cannot be written down on paper, for they were terrible words. They poured out of her small fish mouth in one long unbroken high-pitched stream, and little bits of spit and saliva came out with them. Stuffy and William pulled her back by the arms towards one of the big chairs and she fought and yelled like a large fat pig being dragged to the slaughter. They got her in front of the chair and gave her a quick push so that she fell backwards into it. Stuffy nipped across to her desk, bent down quickly and jerked the telephone cord from its connection. The Stag had the door open and all three of them were out of the room before Rosette had time to get up. The Stag had taken the key from the inside of the door, and now he locked it. The three of them stood outside in the passage.

'Jesus,' said the Stag. 'What a woman!'

'Mad as hell,' William said. 'Listen to her.'

They stood outside in the passage and they listened. They heard her yelling, then she began banging on the door, but she went on yelling and her voice was not the voice of a woman, it was the voice of an enraged but articulate bull.

The Stag said, 'Now quick. The girls. Follow me. And from now on you've got to act serious. You've got to act serious as hell.'

He ran down the passage towards the dressing-room, followed by Stuffy and William. Outside the door he stopped, the other two stopped and they could still hear Rosette yelling from her office. The Stag said, 'Now don't say anything. Just act serious as hell,' and he opened the door and went in.

There were about a dozen girls in the room. They all looked up. They stopped talking and looked up at the Stag, who was standing in the doorway. The Stag clicked his heels and said, 'This is the Military Police. *Les Gendarmes Militaires.*'

He said it in a stern voice and with a straight face and he was standing there in the doorway at attention with his cap on his head. Stuffy and William stood behind him.

'This is the Military Police,' he said again, and he produced his identification card and held it up between two fingers.

The girls didn't move or say anything. They stayed still in the middle of what they were doing and they were like a tableau because they stayed still. One had been pulling on a stocking and she stayed like that, sitting on a chair with her leg out straight and the stocking up to her knee with her hands on the stocking. One had been doing her hair in front of a mirror and when she looked round she kept her hands up to her hair. One was standing up and had been applying lipstick and she raised her eyes to the Stag but still held the lipstick to her mouth. Several were just sitting around on plain wooden chairs, doing nothing, and they raised their heads and turned them to the door, but they went on sitting. Most of them were in some sort of shiny evening dress, one or two were half clothed, but most of them were in shiny green or shiny blue or shiny red or shiny gold, and when they turned to look at the Stag, they were so still that they were like a tableau.

The Stag paused. Then he said, 'I am to state on behalf of the authorities that they are sorry to disturb you. My apologies, Mesd'moiselles. But it is necessary that you come with us for purposes of registration, et cetera. Afterwards you will be allowed to go. It is a mere formality. But now you must come, please. I have conversed with Madame.'

The Stag stopped speaking, but still the girls did not move.

'Please,' said the Stag, 'get your coats. We are the military.' He stepped aside and held open the door. Suddenly the tableau dissolved, the girls got up, puzzled and murmuring, and two or three of them moved towards the door. The others followed. The ones that were half clothed quickly slipped into dresses, patted their hair with their hands and came too. None of them had coats.

'Count them,' said the Stag to Stuffy as they filed out of the door. Stuffy counted them aloud and there were fourteen.

'Fourteen, sir,' said Stuffy, who was trying to talk like a sergeant-major.

The Stag said, 'Correct,' and he turned to the girls who were crowded in the passage. 'Now, Mesd'moiselles, I have the list of your names from Madame, so please do not try to run away. And do not worry. This is merely a formality of the military.'

William was out in the passage opening the door which led to the stairs, and he went out first. The girls followed and the Stag and Stuffy brought up the rear. The girls were quiet and puzzled and worried and a little frightened and they didn't talk, none of them talked except for a tall one with black hair who said, '*Mon Dieu*, a formality of the military. *Mon Dieu, mon Dieu*, what next?' But that was all and they went on down. In the hall they met the Egyptian who had a flat face and two cauliflower ears. For a moment it looked as though there would be trouble. But the Stag waved his identification card in his face and said, 'The

Military Police,' and the man was so surprised that he did nothing and let them pass.

And so they came out into the street and the Stag said, 'It is necessary to walk a little way, but only a very little way,' and they turned right and walked along the sidewalk with the Stag leading, Stuffy at the rear and William walking out on the road, guarding the flank. There was some moon now. One could see quite well and William tried to keep in step with Stag and Stuffy tried to keep in step with William, and they swung their arms and held their heads up high and looked very military, and the whole thing was a sight to behold. Fourteen girls in shiny evening dresses, fourteen girls in the moonlight in shiny green, shiny blue, shiny red, shiny black and shiny gold, marching along the street with the Stag in front, William alongside and Stuffy at the rear. It was a sight to behold.

The girls had started chattering. The Stag could hear them, although he didn't look around. He marched on at the head of the column and when they came to the crossroads he turned right. The others followed and they had walked fifty yards down the block when they came to an Egyptian café. The Stag saw it and he saw the lights burning behind the blackout curtains. He turned around and shouted, 'Halt!' The girls stopped, but they went on chattering and anyone could see now that there was mutiny in the ranks. You can't make fourteen girls in high heels and shiny evening dresses march all over town with you at night, not for long anyway, not for long, even if it is a formality of the military. The Stag knew it and now he was speaking.

'Mesd'moiselles,' he said, 'listen to me.' But there was mutiny in the ranks and they went on talking and the tall one with dark hair was saying, '*Mon Dieu*, what is this? What in hell's name sort of a thing is this, oh *mon Dieu*?'

'Quiet,' said the Stag. 'Quiet!', and the second time he shouted it as a command. The talking stopped.

'Mesd'moiselles,' he said, and now he became polite. He talked to them in his best way and when the Stag was polite there wasn't anyone who didn't take it. It was an extraordinary thing because he could make a kind of smile with his voice without smiling with his lips. His voice smiled while his face remained serious. It was a most forcible thing because it gave people the impression that he was being serious about being nice.

'Mesd'moiselles,' he said, and his voice was smiling. 'With the military there always has to be formality. It is something unavoidable. It is something that I regret exceedingly. But there can be chivalry also. And you must know that with the RAF there is great chivalry. So now it will be a pleasure if you will all come in here and take with us a glass of beer. It is the chivalry of the military.' He stepped forward, opened the door of the café and said, 'Oh for God's sake, let's have a drink. Who wants a drink?'

Suddenly the girls saw it all. They saw the whole thing as it was, all of them at once. It took them by surprise. For a second they considered. Then they looked at one another, then they looked at the Stag, then they looked around at Stuffy and at William, and when they looked at those two they caught their eyes and the laughter that was in them. All at once the girls began to laugh and William laughed and Stuffy laughed and they moved forward and poured into the café.

The tall one with dark hair took the Stag by the arm and said, '*Mon Dieu*, Military Police, *mon Dieu*, oh *mon Dieu*,' and she threw her head back and laughed and the Stag laughed with her. William said, 'It is the chivalry of the military,' and they moved into the café.

The place was rather like the one that they had been in before, wooden and sawdusty, and there were a few coffee-drinking Egyptians sitting around with the red tarbooshes on their heads. William and Stuffy pushed three round tables together and fetched chairs. The girls sat down. The Egyptians at the other tables put down their coffee cups, turned around in their chairs and gaped. They gaped like so many fat muddy fish, and some of them shifted their chairs round facing the party so that they could get a better view, and they went on gaping.

A waiter came up and the Stag said, 'Seventeen beers. Bring us seventeen beers.' The waiter said, 'Pleess,' and went away.

As they sat waiting for the drinks the girls looked at the three pilots and the pilots looked at the girls. William said, 'It is the chivalry of the military,' and the tall dark girl said, '*Mon Dieu*, you are crazy people, oh *mon Dieu*.'

The waiter brought the beer. William raised his glass and said, 'To the chivalry of the military.' The dark girl said, 'Oh *mon Dieu*.' Stuffy didn't say anything. He was busy looking around at the girls, sizing them up, trying to decide now which one he liked best so that he could go to work at once. The Stag was smiling and the girls were sitting there in their shiny evening dresses, shiny red, shiny gold, shiny blue, shiny green, shiny black and shiny silver, and once again it was almost a tableau, certainly it was a picture, and the girls were sitting there sipping their beer, seeming quite happy, not seeming suspicious any more because to them the whole thing now appeared exactly as it was and they understood.

'Jesus,' said the Stag. He put down his glass and looked around him. 'Oh Jesus, there's enough here for the whole squadron. How I wish the whole squadron was here!' He took another drink, stopped in the middle of it and put down his glass quickly. 'I know what,' he said. 'Waiter, oh waiter.'

'Pleess.'

'Get me a big piece of paper and a pencil.'

'Pleess.' The waiter went away and came back with a sheet of paper. He took a pencil from behind his ear and handed it to the Stag. The Stag banged the table for silence.

'Mesd'moiselles,' he said, 'for the last time there is a formality. It is the last of all the formalities.'

'Of the military,' said William.

'Oh *mon Dieu*,' said the dark girl.

'It is nothing,' the Stag said. 'You are required to write your name and your telephone number on this piece of paper. It is for my friends in the squadron. It is so that they can be as happy as I am now, but without the same trouble beforehand.' The Stag's voice was smiling again. One could see that the girls liked his voice. 'You would be very kind if you would do that,' he went on, 'for they too would like to meet you. It would be a pleasure.'

'Wonderful,' said William.

'Crazy,' said the dark girl, but she wrote her name and number on the paper and passed it on. The Stag ordered another round of beer. The girls certainly looked funny sitting there in their dresses, but they were writing their names down on the paper. They looked happy and William particularly looked happy, but Stuffy looked serious because the problem of choosing was a weighty one and it was heavy on his mind. They were good-looking girls, young and good-looking, all different, completely different from each other, because they were Greek and Syrian and French and Italian and light Egyptian and Yugoslav and many other things, but they were good-looking, all of them were good-looking and handsome.

The piece of paper had come back to the Stag now and they had written on it; fourteen strangely written names and fourteen telephone numbers. The Stag looked at it slowly. 'This will go on the squadron notice-board,' he said, 'and I will be regarded as a great benefactor.'

William said, 'It should go to Headquarters. It should be mimeographed and circulated to all squadrons. It would be good for morale.'

'Oh *mon Dieu*,' said the dark girl. 'You are crazy.'

Slowly Stuffy got to his feet, picked up his chair, carried it round to the other side of the table and pushed it between two of the girls. All he said was, 'Excuse me. Do you mind if I sit here?' At last he had made up his mind, and now he turned towards the one on his right and quietly went to work. She was very pretty; very dark and very pretty and she had plenty of shape. Stuffy began to talk to her, completely oblivious to the rest of the company, turning towards her and leaning his head on his hand. Watching him, it was not so difficult to understand why he was the greatest pilot in the squadron. He was a young concentrator, this Stuffy; an intense athletic concentrator who moved towards what he wanted in a dead-straight line. He took hold of winding roads and carefully he made them straight, then he moved over them with great speed and nothing stopped him. He was like that, and now he was talking to the pretty girl but no one could hear what he was saying.

Meanwhile the Stag was thinking. He was thinking about the next move, and when everyone was getting towards the end of their third beer, he banged the table again for silence.

'Mesd'moiselles,' he said, 'it will be a pleasure for us to escort you home. I will take five of you' – he had worked it all out – 'Stuffy will take five, and Jamface will take four. We will take three gharries and I will take five of you in mine and I will drop you home one at a time.'

William said, 'It is the chivalry of the military.'

'Stuffy,' said the Stag. 'Stuffy, is that all right? You take five. It's up to you whom you drop off last.'

Stuffy looked around. 'Yes,' he said. 'Oh yes. That suits me.'

'William, you take four. Drop them home one by one; you understand.'

'Perfectly,' said William. 'Oh perfectly.'

They all got up and moved towards the door. The tall one with dark hair took the Stag's arm and said, 'You take me?'

'Yes,' he answered. 'I take you.'

'You drop me off last?'

'Yes. I drop you off last.'

'Oh *mon Dieu*,' she said. 'That will be fine.'

Outside they got three gharries and they split up into parties. Stuffy was moving quickly. He got his girls into the carriage quickly, climbed in after them and the Stag saw the gharri drive off down the street. Then he saw William's gharri move off, but it seemed to start away with a sudden jerk, with the horses breaking into a gallop at once. The Stag looked again and he saw William perched high up on the driver's seat with the reins in his hands.

The Stag said, 'Let's go,' and his five girls got into their gharri. It was a squash, but everyone got in. The Stag sat back in his seat and then he felt an arm pushing up and under and linking with his. It was the tall one with dark hair. He turned and looked at her.

'Hello,' he said. 'Hello, you.'

'Ah,' she whispered. 'You are such goddam crazy people.' And the Stag felt a warmness inside him and he began to hum a little tune as the gharri rattled on through the dark streets.

Neck

First published in *Someone Like You* (1953)

When, about eight years ago, old Sir William Turton died and his son Basil inherited *The Turton Press* (as well as the title), I can remember how they started laying bets around Fleet Street as to just how long it would be before some nice young woman managed to persuade the little fellow that she must look after him. That is to say, him and his money.

The new Sir Basil Turton was maybe forty years old at the time, a bachelor, a man of mild and simple character who up to then had shown no interest in anything at all except his collection of modern paintings and sculpture. No woman had disturbed him; no scandal or gossip had ever touched his name. But now that he had become the proprietor of quite a large newspaper and magazine empire, it was necessary for him to emerge from the calm of his father's country house and come up to London.

Naturally, the vultures started gathering at once, and I believe that not only Fleet Street but very nearly the whole of the city was looking on eagerly as they scrambled for the body. It was slow motion, of course, deliberate and deadly slow motion, and therefore not so much like vultures as a bunch of agile crabs clawing for a piece of horsemeat under water.

But to everyone's surprise the little chap proved to be

remarkably elusive, and the chase dragged on right through the spring and early summer of that year. I did not know Sir Basil personally, nor did I have any reason to feel friendly towards him, but I couldn't help taking the side of my own sex and found myself cheering loudly every time he managed to get himself off the hook.

Then, round about the beginning of August, apparently at some secret female signal, the girls declared a sort of truce among themselves while they went abroad, and rested, and regrouped, and made fresh plans for the winter kill. This was a mistake because precisely at that moment a dazzling creature called Natalia something or other, whom nobody had heard of before, swept in from the Continent, took Sir Basil firmly by the wrist and led him off in a kind of swoon to the Registry Office at Caxton Hall, where she married him before anyone else, least of all the bridegroom, realized what was happening.

You can imagine that the London ladies were indignant, and naturally they started disseminating a vast amount of fruity gossip about the new Lady Turton ('That dirty poacher,' they called her). But we don't have to go into that. In fact, for the purposes of this story we can skip the next six years, which brings us right up to the present, to an occasion exactly one week ago today when I myself had the pleasure of meeting her ladyship for the first time. By now, as you must have guessed, she was not only running the whole of *The Turton Press*, but as a result had become a considerable political force in the country. I realize that other women have done this sort of thing before, but what made her particular case unusual was the fact that she was a foreigner and that nobody seemed to know precisely what country she came from – Yugoslavia, Bulgaria or Russia.

So last Thursday I went to this small dinner party at a friend's in London, and while we were standing around in the drawing-room before the meal, sipping good Martinis and talking about the atom bomb and Mr Bevan, the maid popped her head in to announce the last guest.

'Lady Turton,' she said.

Nobody stopped talking; we were too well-mannered for that. No heads were turned. Only our eyes swung round to the door, waiting for the entrance.

She came in fast – tall and slim in a red-gold dress with sparkles on it – the mouth smiling, the hand outstretched towards her hostess, and my heavens, I must say she was a beauty.

'Mildred, good evening!'

'My dear Lady Turton! How nice!'

I believe we *did* stop talking then, and we turned and stared and stood waiting quite meekly to be introduced, just like she might have been the Queen or a famous film star. But she was better looking than either of those. The hair was black, and to go with it she had one of those pale, oval, innocent fifteenth-century Flemish faces, almost exactly a Madonna by Memling or Van Eyck. At least that was the first impression. Later, when my turn came to shake hands, I got a closer look and saw that except for the outline and colouring it wasn't really a Madonna at all – far, far from it.

The nostrils for example were very odd, somehow

more open, more flaring, than any I had seen before, and excessively arched. This gave the whole nose a kind of open, snorting look that had something of the wild animal about it – the mustang.

And the eyes, when I saw them close, were not wide and round the way the Madonna painters used to make them, but long and half closed, half smiling, half sullen, and slightly vulgar, so that in one way and another they gave her a most delicately dissipated air. What's more, they didn't look at you directly. They came to you slowly from over on one side with a curious sliding motion that made me nervous. I tried to see their colour, thought it was pale grey, but couldn't be sure.

Then she was led away across the room to meet other people. I stood watching her. She was clearly conscious of her success and of the way these Londoners were deferring to her. 'Here am I,' she seemed to be saying, 'and I only came over a few years ago, but already I am richer and more powerful than any of you.' There was a little prance of triumph in her walk.

A few minutes later we went in to dinner, and to my surprise I found myself seated on her ladyship's right. I presumed that our hostess had done this as a kindness to me, thinking I might pick up some material for the special column I write each day in the evening paper. I settled myself down, ready for an interesting meal. But the famous lady took no notice of me at all; she spent her time talking to the man on her left, the host. Until at last, just as I was finishing my ice-cream, she suddenly turned, reached over, picked up my place card and read the name.

Then, with that queer sliding motion of the eyes, she looked into my face. I smiled and made a little bow. She didn't smile back, but started shooting questions at me, rather personal questions – job, age, family, things like that – in a peculiar lapping voice, and I found myself answering as best I could.

During this inquisition it came out among other things that I was a lover of painting and sculpture.

'Then you should come down to the country some time and see my husband's collection.' She said it casually, merely as a form of conversation, but you must realize that in my job I cannot afford to lose an opportunity like this.

'How kind of you, Lady Turton. But I'd simply love to. When shall I come?'

Her head went up and she hesitated, frowned, shrugged her shoulders, and then said, 'Oh, I don't care. Any time.'

'How about this next week-end? Would that be all right?'

The slow narrow eyes rested a moment on mine, then travelled away. 'I suppose so, if you wish. I don't care.'

And that was how on the following Saturday afternoon I came to be driving down to Wooton with my suitcase in the back of the car. You may think that perhaps I forced the invitation a bit, but I couldn't have got it any other way. And apart from the professional aspect, I personally wanted very much to see the house. As you know, Wooton is one of the truly great stone houses of the Early English Renaissance. Like its sisters, Longleat, Wollaton and Montacute, it was built in the latter half of the sixteenth century, when for the first time a great man's house could be designed as a comfortable dwelling, not as a castle, and when a new group of architects such as John Thorpe and the Smithsons were starting to do marvellous things all over the country. It lies south of Oxford, near a small town called Princes Risborough – not a long trip from London – and as I swung in through the main gates the sky was closing overhead and the early winter evening was beginning.

I went slowly up the long drive, trying to see as much of the grounds as possible, especially the famous topiary which I had heard such a lot about. And I must say it was an impressive sight. On all sides there were massive yew trees, trimmed and clipped into many different comical shapes – hens, pigeons, bottles, boots, armchairs, castles, egg-cups, lanterns, old women with flaring petticoats, tall pillars, some crowned with a ball, others with big rounded roofs and stemless mushroom finials – and in the half-darkness the greens had turned to black so that each figure, each tree, took on a dark, smooth, sculptural quality. At one point I saw a lawn covered with gigantic chessmen, each a live yew tree, marvellously fashioned. I stopped the car, got out and walked among them, and they were twice as tall as me. What's more, the set was complete, kings, queens, bishops, knights, rooks and pawns standing in position as for the start of a game.

Around the next bend I saw the great grey house itself, and in front of it the large entrance forecourt enclosed by a high balustraded wall with small pillared pavilions at its outer angles. The piers of the balustrades were surmounted by stone obelisks – the Italian influence on the Tudor mind – and a flight of steps at least a hundred feet wide led up to the house.

As I drove into the forecourt I noticed with rather a shock that the fountain basin in the middle supported a large statue by Epstein. A lovely thing, mind you, but surely not quite in sympathy with its surroundings. Then, looking back as I climbed the stairway to the front door, I saw that on all the little lawns and terraces round about there were other modern statues and many kinds of curious sculpture. In the distance, I thought I recognized Gaudier Brzeska, Brancusi, Saint-Gaudens, Henry Moore and Epstein again.

The door was opened by a young footman who led me up to a bedroom on the first floor. Her ladyship, he explained, was resting, so were the other guests, but they would all be down in the main drawing-room in an hour or so, dressed for dinner.

Now in my job it is necessary to do a lot of week-ending. I suppose I spend around fifty Saturdays and Sundays a year in other people's houses, and as a result I have become fairly sensitive to unfamiliar atmosphere. I can tell good or bad almost by sniffing with my nose the moment I get in the front door; and this one I was in now I did not like. The place smelled wrong. There was the faint, desiccated whiff of something troublesome in the air; I was conscious of it even as I lay steaming luxuriously in my great marble bath; and I couldn't help hoping that no unpleasant things were going to happen before Monday came.

The first of them – though more of a surprise than an

unpleasantness – occurred ten minutes later. I was sitting on the bed putting on my socks when softly the door opened, and an ancient lop-sided gnome in black tails slid into the room. He was the butler, he explained, and his name was Jelks, and he did so hope I was comfortable and had everything I wanted.

I told him I was and had.

He said he would do all he could to make my week-end agreeable. I thanked him and waited for him to go. He hesitated, and then, in a voice dripping with unction, he begged permission to mention a rather delicate matter. I told him to go ahead.

To be quite frank, he said, it was about tipping. The whole business of tipping made him acutely miserable.

Oh? And why was that?

Well, if I really wanted to know, he didn't like the idea that his guests felt under an obligation to tip him when they left the house – as indeed they did. It was an undignified proceeding both for the tipper and the tipped. Moreover, he was well aware of the anguish that was often created in the minds of guests such as myself, if I would pardon the liberty, who might feel compelled by convention to give more than they could really afford.

He paused, and two small crafty eyes watched my face for a sign. I murmured that he needn't worry himself about such things so far as I was concerned.

On the contrary, he said, he hoped sincerely that I would agree from the beginning to give him no tip at all.

'Well,' I said. 'Let's not fuss about it now, and when the time comes we'll see how we feel.'

'No, sir!' he cried. 'Please, I really must insist.'

So I agreed.

He thanked me, and shuffled a step or two closer. Then, laying his head on one side and clasping his hands before him like a priest, he gave a tiny apologetic shrug of the shoulders. The small sharp eyes were still watching me, and I waited, one sock on, the other in my hands, trying to guess what was coming next.

All that he would ask, he said softly, so softly now that his voice was like music heard faintly in the street outside a great concert hall, all that he would ask was that instead of a tip I should give him thirty-three and a third per cent of my winnings at cards over the week-end. If I lost, there would be nothing to pay.

It was all so soft and smooth and sudden that I was not even surprised.

'Do they play a lot of cards, Jelks?'

'Yes, sir, a great deal.'

'Isn't thirty-three and a third a bit steep?'

'I don't think so, sir.'

'I'll give you ten per cent.'

'No, sir, I couldn't do that.' He was now examining the fingernails of his left hand, and patiently frowning.

'Then we'll make it fifteen. All right?'

'Thirty-three and a third, sir. It's very reasonable. After all, sir, seeing that I don't even know if you are a good player, what I'm actually doing, not meaning to be personal, is backing a horse and I've never even seen it run.'

No doubt you think that I should never have started bargaining with the butler in the first place, and perhaps you are right. But being a liberal-minded person, I always try my best to be affable with the lower classes. Apart from that, the more I thought about it, the more I had to admit to myself that it was an offer no sportsman had the right to reject.

'All right then, Jelks. As you wish.'

'Thank you, sir.' He moved towards the door, walking slowly sideways like a crab; but once more he hesitated, a hand on the knob. 'If I may give you a little advice, sir – may I?'

'Yes?'

'It's simply that her ladyship tends to overbid her hand.'

Now this *was* going too far. I was so startled I dropped my sock. After all, it's one thing to have a harmless little sporting arrangement with the butler about tipping, but when he begins conniving with you to take money away from the hostess then it's time to call a halt.

'All right, Jelks. Now that'll do.'

'No offence, sir, I hope. All I mean is you're bound to be playing against her ladyship. She always partners Major Haddock.'

'Major Haddock? You mean Major Jack Haddock?'

'Yes, sir.'

I noticed there was the trace of a sneer around the corners of Jelks's nose when he spoke about this man. And it was worse with Lady Turton. Each time he said 'her ladyship' he spoke the words with the outsides of his lips as though he were nibbling a lemon, and there was a subtle, mocking inflexion in his voice.

'You'll excuse me now, sir. *Her ladyship* will be down at

seven o'clock. So will *Major Haddock* and the others.' He slipped out of the door, leaving behind him a certain dampness in the room and a faint smell of embrocation.

Shortly after seven, I found my way to the main drawing-room, and Lady Turton, as beautiful as ever, got up to greet me.

'I wasn't even sure you were coming,' she said in that peculiar lilting voice. 'What's your name again?'

'I'm afraid I took you at your word, Lady Turton. I hope it's all right.'

'Why not?' she said. 'There're forty-seven bedrooms in the house. This is my husband.'

A small man came around the back of her and said, 'You know, I'm so glad you were able to come.' He had a lovely warm smile and when he took my hand I felt instantly a touch of friendship in his fingers.

'And Carmen La Rosa,' Lady Turton said.

This was a powerfully built woman who looked as though she might have something to do with horses. She nodded at me, and although my hand was already halfway out she didn't give me hers, thus forcing me to convert the movement into a noseblow.

'You have a cold?' she said. 'I'm sorry.'

I did not like Miss Carmen La Rosa.

'And this is Jack Haddock.'

I knew this man slightly. He was a director of companies (whatever that may mean), and a well-known member of society. I had used his name a few times in my column, but I had never liked him, and this I think was mainly because I have a deep suspicion of all people who carry their military titles back with them into private life – especially majors and colonels. Standing there in his dinner-jacket with his full-blooded animal face and black eyebrows and large white teeth, he looked so handsome there was almost something indecent about it. He had a way of raising his upper lip when he smiled, baring the teeth, and he was smiling now as he gave me a hairy brown hand.

'I hope you're going to say some nice things about us in your column.'

'He better had,' Lady Turton said, 'or I'll say some nasty ones about him on my front page.'

I laughed, but the three of them, Lady Turton, Major Haddock and Carmen La Rosa, had already turned away and were settling themselves back on the sofa. Jelks gave me a drink, and Sir Basil drew me gently aside for a quiet chat at the other end of the room. Every now and again Lady Turton would call her husband to fetch her something – another Martini, a cigarette, an ashtray, a handkerchief – and he, half rising from his chair, would be forestalled by the watchful Jelks, who fetched it for him.

Clearly, Jelks loved his master; and just as clearly he hated the wife. Each time he did something for her he made a little sneer with his nose and drew his lips together so they puckered like a turkey's bottom.

At dinner, our hostess sat her two friends, Haddock and La Rosa, on either side of her. This unconventional arrangement left Sir Basil and me at the other end of the table, where we were able to continue our pleasant talk about painting and sculpture. Of course it was obvious to me by now that the major was infatuated with her ladyship. And again, although I hate to say it, it seemed as though the La Rosa woman was hunting the same bird.

All this foolishness appeared to delight the hostess. But it did not delight her husband. I could see that he was conscious of the little scene all the time we were talking; and often his mind would wander from our subject and he would stop short in mid-sentence, his eyes travelling down to the other end of the table to settle pathetically for a moment on that lovely head with the black hair and the curiously flaring nostrils. He must have noticed then how exhilarated she was, how the hand that gestured as she spoke rested every now and again on the major's arm, and how the other woman, the one who perhaps had something to do with horses, kept saying, 'Nata-*li*-a! Now Nata-*li*-a, listen to me!'

'Tomorrow,' I said, 'you must take me round and show me the sculptures you've put up in the garden.'

'Of course,' he said, 'with pleasure.' He glanced again at the wife, and his eyes had a sort of supplicating look that was piteous beyond words. He was so mild and passive a man in every way that even now I could see there was no anger in him, no danger, no chance of an explosion.

After dinner I was ordered straight to the card table to partner Miss Carmen La Rosa against Major Haddock and Lady Turton. Sir Basil sat quietly on the sofa with a book.

There was nothing unusual about the game itself; it was routine and rather dull. But Jelks was a nuisance. All evening he prowled around us, emptying ashtrays and asking about drinks and peering at our hands. He was obviously short-sighted and I doubt whether he saw much of what was going on because, as you may or may not know, here in England no butler has ever been permitted to wear spectacles – nor, for that matter, a moustache. This is the golden, unbreakable rule, and a very sensible one it is too, although I'm not quite sure what lies behind it. I presume that a moustache would make him look too much like a gentleman, and spectacles too much like an American, and where would we be then I should like to know? In any event, Jelks was a nuisance all evening; and so was Lady Turton, who was constantly being called to the phone on newspaper business.

At eleven o'clock she looked up from her cards and said, 'Basil, it's time you went to bed.'

'Yes, my dear, perhaps it is.' He closed the book, got up, and stood for a minute watching the play. 'Are you having a good game?' he asked.

The others didn't answer him, so I said, 'It's a nice game.'

'I'm so glad. And Jelks will look after you and get anything you want.'

'Jelks can go to bed too,' the wife said.

I could hear Major Haddock breathing through his nose beside me, and the soft drop of the cards one by one on to the table, and then the sound of Jelks's feet shuffling over the carpet towards us.

'You wouldn't prefer me to stay, m'lady?'

'No. Go to bed. You too, Basil.'

'Yes, my dear. Good night. Good night all.'

Jelks opened the door for him, and he went slowly out, followed by the butler.

As soon as the next rubber was over, I said that I too wanted to go to bed.

'All right,' Lady Turton said. 'Good night.'

I went up to my room, locked the door, took a pill and went to sleep.

The next morning, Sunday, I got up and dressed around ten o'clock and went down to the breakfast-room. Sir Basil was there before me, and Jelks was serving him with grilled kidneys and bacon and fried tomatoes. He was delighted to see me and suggested that as soon as we had finished eating we should take a long walk around the grounds. I told him nothing would give me more pleasure.

Half an hour later we started out, and you've no idea what a relief it was to get away from that house and into the open air. It was one of those warm shining days that come occasionally in mid-winter after a night of heavy rain, with a bright surprising sun and no breath of wind. Bare trees seemed beautiful in the sunlight, water still dripping from the branches, and wet places all around were sparkling with diamonds. The sky had small faint clouds.

'*What* a lovely day!'

'Yes – isn't it a lovely day!'

We spoke hardly another word during the walk; it wasn't necessary. But he took me everywhere and I saw it all – the huge chessmen and all the rest of the topiary. The

elaborate garden houses, the pools, the fountains, the children's maze whose hedges were hornbeam and lime so
that it was only good in summer when the leaves were out,
and the parterres, the rockeries, the greenhouses with
their vines and nectarine trees. And of course, the sculpture. Most of the contemporary European sculptors were
there, in bronze, granite, limestone and wood; and
although it was a pleasure to see them warming and glowing in the sun, to me they still looked a trifle out of place
in these vast formal surroundings.

'Shall we rest here now a little while?' Sir Basil said after
we had walked for more than an hour. So we sat down on
a white bench beside a water-lily pond full of carp and
goldfish, and lit cigarettes. We were some way from the
house, on a piece of ground that was raised above its surroundings, and from where we sat the gardens were spread
out below us like a drawing in one of those old books on
garden architecture, with the hedges and lawns and terraces and fountains making a pretty pattern of squares
and rings.

'My father bought this place just before I was born,' Sir
Basil said. 'I've lived here ever since, and I know every
inch of it. Each day I grow to love it more.'

'It must be wonderful in summer.'

'Oh, but it is. You should come down and see it in May
and June. Will you promise to do that?'

'Of course,' I said. 'I'd love to come,' and as I spoke I
was watching the figure of a woman dressed in red moving among the flowerbeds in the far distance. I saw her
cross over a wide expanse of lawn, and there was a lilt in

her walk, a little shadow attending her, and when she was over the lawn, she turned left and went along one side of a high wall of clipped yew until she came to another smaller lawn that was circular and had in its centre a piece of sculpture.

'This garden is younger than the house,' Sir Basil said. 'It was laid out early in the eighteenth century by a Frenchman called Beaumont, the same fellow who did Levens, in Westmorland. For at least a year he had two hundred and fifty men working on it.'

The woman in the red dress had been joined now by a man, and they were standing face to face, about a yard apart, in the very centre of the whole garden panorama, on this little circular patch of lawn, apparently conversing. The man had some small black object in his hand.

'If you're interested, I'll show you the bills that Beaumont put in to the old Duke while he was making it.'

'I'd like very much to see them. They must be fascinating.'

'He paid his labourers a shilling a day and they worked ten hours.'

In the clear sunlight it was not difficult to follow the movements and gestures of the two figures on the lawn. They had turned now towards the piece of sculpture, and were pointing at it in a sort of mocking way, apparently laughing and making jokes about its shape. I recognized it as being one of the Henry Moores, done in wood, a thin smooth object of singular beauty that had two or three holes in it and a number of strange limbs protruding.

'When Beaumont planted the yew trees for the chessmen and the other things, he knew they wouldn't amount to much for at least a hundred years. We don't seem to possess that sort of patience in our planning these days, do we? What do you think?'

'No,' I said. 'We don't.'

The black object in the man's hand turned out to be a camera, and now he had stepped back and was taking pictures of the woman beside the Henry Moore. She was striking a number of different poses, all of them, so far as I could see, ludicrous and meant to be amusing. Once she put her arms around one of the protruding wooden limbs and hugged it, and another time she climbed up and sat side-saddle on the thing, holding imaginary reins in her hands. A great wall of yew hid these two people from the house, and indeed from all the rest of the garden except the little hill on which we sat. They had every right to believe that they were not overlooked, and even if they had happened to glance our way – which was into the sun – I doubt whether they would have noticed the two small motionless figures sitting on the bench beside the pond.

'You know, I love these yews,' Sir Basil said. 'The colour of them is so wonderful in a garden because it rests the eye. And in the summer it breaks up the areas of brilliance into little patches and makes them more comfortable to admire. Have you noticed the different shades of green on the planes and facets of each clipped tree?'

'It's lovely, isn't it?'

The man now seemed to be explaining something to the woman, and pointing at the Henry Moore, and I could tell by the way they threw back their heads that they were laughing again. The man continued to point, and then the woman walked around the back of the wood carving, bent down and poked her head through one of its holes. The thing was about the size, shall I say, of a small horse, but thinner than that, and from where I sat I could see both sides of it – to the left, the woman's body, to the right, her head protruding through. It was very much like one of those jokes at the seaside where you put your head through a hole in a board and get photographed as a fat lady. The man was photographing her now.

'There's another thing about yews,' Sir Basil said. 'In the early summer when the young shoots come out . . .' At that moment he paused and sat up straighter and leaned slightly forward, and I could sense his whole body suddenly stiffening.

'Yes,' I said, 'when the young shoots come out?'

The man had taken the photograph, but the woman still had her head through the hole, and now I saw him put both hands (as well as the camera) behind his back and advance towards her. Then he bent forward so his face was close to hers, touching it, and he held it there while he gave her, I suppose, a few kisses or something like that. In the stillness that followed, I fancied I heard a faint faraway tinkle of female laughter coming to us through the sunlight across the garden.

'Shall we go back to the house?' I asked.

'Back to the house?'

'Yes, shall we go back and have a drink before lunch?'

'A drink? Yes, we'll have a drink.' But he didn't move. He sat very still, gone far away from me now, staring intently at the two figures. I also was staring at them. I couldn't take my eyes away; I *had* to look. It was like seeing a dangerous little ballet in miniature from a great distance, and you knew the dancers and the music but not the end of the story, nor the choreography, nor what they were going to do next, and you were fascinated, and you *had* to look.

'Gaudier Brzeska,' I said. 'How great do you think he might've become if he hadn't died so young?'

'Who?'

'Gaudier Brzeska.'

'Yes,' he said. 'Of course.'

I noticed now that something queer was happening. The woman still had her head through the hole, but she was beginning to wriggle her body from side to side in a slow unusual manner, and the man was standing motionless, a pace or so away, watching her. He seemed suddenly uneasy the way he stood there, and I could tell by the drop of the head and by the stiff intent set of the body that there was no laughter in him any more. For a while he remained still, then I saw him place his camera on the ground and go forward to the woman, taking her head in his hands; and all at once it was more like a puppet show than a ballet, with tiny wooden figures performing tiny jerky movements, crazy and unreal, on a faraway sunlit stage.

We sat quietly together on the white bench, and we watched while the tiny puppet man began to manipulate the woman's head with his hands. He was doing it gently, there was no doubt about that, slowly and gently, stepping back every now and then to think about it some more, and several times crouching down to survey the situation from another angle. Whenever he left her alone the woman would again start to wriggle her body, and the peculiar way she did it reminded me of a dog that feels a collar round its neck for the first time.

'She's stuck,' Sir Basil said.

And now the man was walking to the other side of the carving, the side where the woman's body was, and he put out his hands and began trying to do something with her neck. Then, as though suddenly exasperated, he gave the neck two or three quick jerky pulls, and this time the sound of the woman's voice, raised high in anger, or pain, or both, came back to us small and clear through the sunlight.

Out of the corner of one eye I could see Sir Basil nodding his head quietly up and down. 'I got my fist caught in a jar of boiled sweets once,' he said, 'and I couldn't get it out.'

The man had retreated a few yards, and was standing with hands on hips, head up, looking furious and sullen. The woman, from her uncomfortable position, appeared to be talking to him, or rather shouting at him, and although the body itself was pretty firmly fixed and could only wriggle, the legs were free and did a good deal of moving and stamping.

'I broke the jar with a hammer and told my mother I'd knocked it off the shelf by mistake.' He seemed calmer now, not tense at all, although his voice was curiously flat. 'I suppose we'd better go down and see if we can help.'

'Perhaps we should.'

But still he didn't move. He took out a cigarette and lit it, putting the used match carefully back in the box.

'I'm sorry,' he said. 'Will you have one?'

'Thanks, I think I will.' He made a little ceremony of giving me the cigarette and lighting it for me, and again he put the used match back in the box. Then we got up and walked slowly down the grass slope.

We came upon them silently, through an archway in the yew hedge, and it was naturally quite a surprise.

'What's the matter here?' Sir Basil asked. He spoke softly, with a dangerous softness that I'm sure his wife had never heard before.

'She's gone and put her head through the hole and now she can't get it out,' Major Haddock said. 'Just for a lark, you know.'

'For a what?'

'Basil!' Lady Turton shouted. 'Don't be such a damn fool! Do something, can't you!' She may not have been able to move much, but she could still talk.

'Pretty obvious we're going to have to break up this lump of wood,' the major said. There was a small smudge of red on his grey moustache, and this, like the single extra touch of colour that ruins a perfect painting, managed somehow to destroy all his manly looks. It made him comic.

'You mean break the Henry Moore?'

'My dear sir, there's no other way of setting the lady free. God knows how she managed to squeeze it in, but I know for a fact that she can't pull it out. It's the ears get in the way.'

'Oh dear,' Sir Basil said. 'What a terrible pity. My beautiful Henry Moore.'

At this stage Lady Turton began abusing her husband

in a most unpleasant manner, and there's no knowing how long it would have gone on had not Jelks suddenly appeared out of the shadows. He came sidling silently on to the lawn and stationed himself at a respectful distance from Sir Basil, as though awaiting instructions. His black clothes looked perfectly ridiculous in the morning sunlight, and with his ancient pink-white face and white hands he was like some small crabby animal that has lived all its life in a hole under the ground.

'Is there anything I can do, Sir Basil?' He kept his voice level, but I didn't think his face was quite straight. When he looked at Lady Turton there was a little exulting glimmer in his eyes.

'Yes, Jelks, there is. Go back and get me a saw or something so I can cut out a section of this wood.'

'Shall I call one of the men, Sir Basil? William is a good carpenter.'

'No, I'll do it myself. Just get the tools – and hurry.'

While they were waiting for Jelks, I strolled away because I didn't want to hear any more of the things that Lady Turton was saying to her husband. But I was back in time to see the butler returning, followed now by the other woman, Carmen La Rosa, who made a rush for the hostess.

'Nata-*li*-a! My dear Nata-*li*-a! What *have* they done to you?'

'Oh shut up,' the hostess said. 'And get out of the way, will you?'

Sir Basil took up a position close to his lady's head, waiting for Jelks. Jelks advanced slowly, carrying a saw in one hand, an axe in the other, and he stopped maybe a yard away. He then held out both implements in front of him so his master could choose, and there was a brief moment – no more than two or three seconds – of silence, and of waiting, and it just happened that I was watching Jelks at this time. I saw the hand that was carrying the axe come forward an extra fraction of an inch towards Sir Basil. It was so slight a movement it was barely noticeable – a tiny pushing forward of the hand, slow and secret, a little offer, a little coaxing offer that was accompanied perhaps by an infinitesimal lift of the eyebrows.

I'm not sure whether Sir Basil saw it, but he hesitated, and again the hand that held the axe came edging forward, and it was almost exactly like that card trick where the man says, 'Take one, whichever one you want,' and you always get the one he means you to have. Sir Basil got the axe. I saw him reach out in a dreamy sort of way, accepting it from Jelks, and then, the instant he felt the handle in his grasp he seemed to realize what was required of him and he sprang to life.

For me, after that, it was like the awful moment when you see a child running out into the road and a car is coming and all you can do is shut your eyes tight and wait until the noise tells you it has happened. The moment of waiting becomes a long lucid period of time with yellow and red spots dancing on a black field, and even if you open your eyes again and find that nobody has been killed or hurt, it makes no difference because so far as you and your stomach were concerned you saw it all.

I saw this one all right, every detail of it, and I didn't

open my eyes again until I heard Sir Basil's voice, even softer than usual, calling in gentle protest to the butler.

'Jelks,' he was saying, and I looked and saw him standing there as calm as you please, still holding the axe. Lady Turton's head was there too, still sticking through the hole, but her face had turned a terrible ashy grey, and the mouth was opening and shutting and making a kind of gurgling sound.

'Look here, Jelks,' Sir Basil was saying. 'What on earth are you thinking about? This thing's much too dangerous. Give me the saw.' And as he exchanged implements I noticed for the first time two little warm roses of colour appearing on his cheeks, and above them, all around the corners of his eyes, the twinkling tiny wrinkles of a smile.

Georgy Porgy

First published in *Kiss Kiss* (1960)

Without in any way wishing to blow my own trumpet, I think that I can claim to being in most respects a moderately well-matured and rounded individual. I have travelled a good deal. I am adequately read. I speak Greek and Latin. I dabble in science. I can tolerate a mildly liberal attitude in the politics of others. I have compiled a volume of notes upon the evolution of the madrigal in the fifteenth century. I have witnessed the death of a large number of persons in their beds; and in addition, I have influenced, at least I hope I have, the lives of quite a few others by the spoken word delivered from the pulpit.

Yet in spite of all this, I must confess that I have never in my life – well, how shall I put it? – I have never really had anything much to do with women.

To be perfectly honest, up until three weeks ago I had never so much as laid a finger on one of them except perhaps to help her over a stile or something like that when the occasion demanded. And even then I always tried to ensure that I touched only the shoulder or the waist or some other place where the skin was covered, because the one thing I never could stand was actual contact between my skin and theirs. Skin touching skin, my skin, that is, touching the skin of a female, whether it were leg, neck, face, hand or merely finger, was so repugnant to me that

I invariably greeted a lady with my hands clasped firmly behind my back to avoid the inevitable handshake.

I could go further than that and say that any sort of physical contact with them, even when the skin wasn't bare, would disturb me considerably. If a woman stood close to me in a queue so that our bodies touched, or if she squeezed in beside me on a bus seat, hip to hip and thigh to thigh, my cheeks would begin burning like mad and little prickles of sweat would start coming out all over the crown of my head.

This condition is all very well in a schoolboy who has just reached the age of puberty. With him it is simply Dame Nature's way of putting on the brakes and holding the lad back until he is old enough to behave himself like a gentleman. I approve of that.

But there was no reason on God's earth why I, at the ripe old age of thirty-one, should continue to suffer a similar embarrassment. I was well trained to resist temptation, and I was certainly not given to vulgar passions.

Had I been even the slightest bit ashamed of my own personal appearance, then that might possibly have explained the whole thing. But I was not. On the contrary, and though I say it myself, the fates had been rather kind to me in that regard. I stood exactly five and a half feet tall in my stockinged feet, and my shoulders, though they sloped downwards a little from the neck, were nicely in balance with my small neat frame. (Personally, I've always thought that a little slope on the shoulder lends a subtle and faintly aesthetic air to a man who is not overly tall, don't you agree?) My features were regular, my teeth were in excellent condition (protruding only a smallish amount from the upper jaw), and my hair, which was an unusually brilliant ginger-red, grew thickly all over my scalp. Good heavens above, I had seen men who were perfect shrimps in comparison with me displaying an astonishing aplomb in their dealings with the fairer sex. And oh, how I envied them! How I longed to do likewise – to be able to share in a few of those pleasant little rituals of contact that I observed continually taking place between men and women – the touching of hands, the peck on the cheek, the linking of arms, the pressure of knee against knee or foot against foot under the dining-table, and most of all, the full-blown violent embrace that comes when two of them join together on the floor – for a dance.

But such things were not for me. Alas, I had to spend my time avoiding them instead. And this, my friends, was easier said than done, even for a humble curate in a small country region far from the fleshpots of the metropolis.

My flock, you understand, contained an inordinate number of ladies. There were scores of them in the parish, and the unfortunate thing about it was that at least sixty per cent of them were spinsters, completely untamed by the benevolent influence of holy matrimony.

I tell you I was jumpy as a squirrel.

One would have thought that with all the careful training my mother had given me as a child, I should have been capable of taking this sort of thing well in my stride; and no doubt I would have done if only she had lived long enough to complete my education. But alas, she was killed when I was still quite young.

She was a wonderful woman, my mother. She used to wear huge bracelets on her wrists, five or six of them at a time, with all sorts of things hanging from them and tinkling against each other as she moved. It didn't matter where she was, you could always find her by listening for the noise of those bracelets. It was better than a cowbell. And in the evenings she used to sit on the sofa in her black trousers with her feet tucked up underneath her, smoking endless cigarettes from a long black holder. And I'd be crouching on the floor, watching her.

'You want to taste my martini, George?' she used to ask.

'Now stop it, Clare,' my father would say. 'If you're not careful you'll stunt the boy's growth.'

'Go on,' she said. 'Don't be frightened of it. Drink it.'

I always did everything my mother told me.

'That's enough,' my father said. 'He only has to know what it tastes like.'

'Please don't interfere, Boris. This is *very* important.'

My mother had a theory that nothing in the world should be kept secret from a child. Show him everything. Make him *experience* it.

'I'm not going to have any boy of mine going around whispering dirty secrets with other children and having to guess about this thing and that simply because no one will tell him.'

Tell him everything. Make him listen.

'Come over here, George, and I'll tell you what there is to know about God.'

She never read stories to me at night before I went to

70

bed; she just 'told' me things instead. And every evening it was something different.

'Come over here, George, because now I'm going to tell you about Mohammed.'

She would be sitting on the sofa in her black trousers with her legs crossed and her feet tucked up underneath her, and she'd beckon to me in a queer languorous manner with the hand that held the long black cigarette-holder, and the bangles would start jingling all the way up her arm.

'If you must have a religion I suppose Mohammedanism is as good as any of them. It's all based on keeping healthy. You have lots of wives, and you mustn't ever smoke or drink.'

'Why mustn't you smoke or drink, Mummy?'

'Because if you've got lots of wives you have to keep healthy and virile.'

'What is virile?'

'I'll go into that tomorrow, my pet. Let's deal with one subject at a time. Another thing about the Mohammedan is that he never never gets constipated.'

'Now, Clare,' my father would say, looking up from his book. 'Stick to the facts.'

'My dear Boris, you don't know anything about it. Now if only *you* would try bending forward and touching the ground with your forehead morning, noon and night every day, facing Mecca, you might have a bit less trouble in that direction yourself.'

I used to love listening to her, even though I could only understand about half of what she was saying. She really was telling me secrets, and there wasn't anything more exciting than that.

'Come over here, George, and I'll tell you precisely how your father makes his money.'

'Now, Clare, that's quite enough.'

'Nonsense, darling. Why make a *secret* out of it with the child? He'll only imagine something much much worse.'

I was exactly ten years old when she started giving me detailed lectures on the subject of sex. This was the biggest secret of them all, and therefore the most enthralling.

'Come over here, George, because now I'm going to tell you how you came into this world, right from the very beginning.'

I saw my father glance up quietly, and open his mouth wide the way he did when he was going to say something vital, but my mother was already fixing him with those brilliant shining eyes of hers, and he went slowly back to his book without uttering a sound.

'Your poor father is embarrassed,' she said, and she gave me her private smile, the one that she gave to nobody else, only to me – the one-sided smile where just one corner of her mouth lifted slowly upwards until it made a lovely long wrinkle that stretched right up to the eye itself, and became a sort of wink-smile instead.

'Embarrassment, my pet, is the one thing that I want you never to feel. And don't think for a moment that your father is embarrassed only because of *you*.'

My father started wriggling about in his chair.

'My God, he's even embarrassed about things like that when he's alone with me, his own wife.'

'About things like what?' I asked.

At that point my father got up and quietly left the room.

I think it must have been about a week after this that my mother was killed. It may possibly have been a little later, ten days or a fortnight, I can't be sure. All I know is that we were getting near the end of this particular series of 'talks' when it happened; and because I myself was personally involved in the brief chain of events that led up to her death, I can still remember every single detail of that curious night just as clearly as if it were yesterday. I can switch it on in my memory any time I like and run it through in front of my eyes exactly as though it were the reel of a cinema film; and it never varies. It always ends at precisely the same place, no more and no less, and it always begins in the same peculiarly sudden way, with the screen in darkness, and my mother's voice somewhere above me, calling my name:

'George! Wake up, George, wake up!'

And then there is a bright electric light dazzling in my eyes, and right from the very centre of it, but far away, the voice is still calling to me:

'George, wake up and get out of bed and put your dressing-gown on! Quickly! You're coming downstairs. There's something I want you to see. Come on, child, come on! Hurry up! And put your slippers on. We're going outside.'

'Outside?'

'Don't argue with me, George. Just do as you're told.' I am so sleepy I can hardly see to walk, but my mother takes me firmly by the hand and leads me downstairs and out through the front door into the night where the cold air is like a sponge of water in my face, and I open my eyes wide and see the lawn all sparkling with frost and the cedar tree with its tremendous arms standing black against a thin small moon. And overhead a great mass of stars is wheeling up into the sky.

We hurry across the lawn, my mother and I, her bracelets all jingling like mad and me having to trot to keep up with her. Each step I take I can feel the crisp frosty grass crunching softly underfoot.

'Josephine has just started having her babies,' my mother says. 'It's a perfect opportunity. You shall watch the whole process.'

There is a light burning in the garage when we get there, and we go inside. My father isn't there, nor is the car, and the place seems huge and bare, and the concrete floor is freezing cold through the soles of my bedroom slippers. Josephine is reclining on a heap of straw inside the low wire cage in one corner of the room – a large blue rabbit with small pink eyes that watch us suspiciously as we go towards her. The husband, whose name is Napoleon, is now in a separate cage in the opposite corner, and I notice that he is standing up on his hind legs scratching impatiently at the netting.

'Look!' my mother cries. 'She's just having the first one! It's almost out!'

We both creep closer to Josephine, and I squat down beside the cage with my face right up against the wire. I am fascinated. Here is one rabbit coming out of another. It is magical and rather splendid. It is also very quick.

'Look how it comes out all neatly wrapped up in its own little cellophane bag!' my mother is saying.

'And just look how she's taking care of it now! The poor darling doesn't have a face-flannel, and even if she did she couldn't hold it in her paws, so she's washing it with her tongue instead.'

The mother rabbit rolls her small pink eyes anxiously in our direction, and then I see her shifting position in the straw so that her body is between us and the young one.

'Come round the other side,' my mother says. 'The silly thing has moved. I do believe she's trying to hide her baby from us.'

We go round the other side of the cage. The rabbit follows us with her eyes. A couple of yards away the buck is prancing madly up and down, clawing at the wire.

'Why is Napoleon so excited?' I ask.

'I don't know, dear. Don't you bother about him. Watch Josephine. I expect she'll be having another one soon. Look how carefully she's washing that little baby! She's treating it just like a human mother treats hers! Isn't it funny to think that I did almost exactly the same sort of thing to you once?'

The big blue doe is still watching us, and now, again, she pushes the baby away with her nose and rolls slowly over to face the other way. Then she goes on with her licking and cleaning.

'Isn't it wonderful how a mother knows instinctively just what she has to do?' my mother says. 'Now you just imagine, my pet, that that baby is *you*, and Josephine is *me* – wait a minute, come back over here again so you can get a better look.'

We creep back round the cage to keep the baby in view.

'See how she's fondling it and kissing it all over! There! She's *really* kissing it now, isn't she! Exactly like me and you!'

I peer closer. It seems a queer way of kissing to me.

'Look!' I scream. 'She's eating it!'

And sure enough, the head of the baby rabbit is now disappearing swiftly into the mother's mouth.

'Mummy! Quick!'

But almost before the sound of my scream has died away, the whole of that tiny pink body has vanished down the mother's throat.

I swing quickly round, and the next thing I know I'm looking straight into my own mother's face, not six inches above me, and no doubt she is trying to say something or it may be that she is too astonished to say anything, but all I see is the mouth, the huge red mouth opening wider and wider and wider until it is just a great big round gaping hole with a black black centre, and I scream again, and this time I can't stop. Then suddenly out come her hands, and I can feel her skin touching mine, the long cold fingers closing tightly over my fists, and I jump back and jerk myself free and rush blindly out into the night. I run down the drive and through the front gates, screaming all the way, and then, above the noise of my own voice I can hear the jingle of bracelets coming up behind me in the dark, getting louder and louder as she keeps gaining on me all the way down the long hill to the bottom of the lane and over the bridge on to the main road where the cars are streaming by at sixty miles an hour with head-lights blazing.

Then somewhere behind me I hear a screech of tyres skidding on the road surface, and then there is silence, and I notice suddenly that the bracelets aren't jingling behind me any more.

Poor mother.

If only she could have lived a little longer.

I admit that she gave me a nasty fright with those rabbits, but it wasn't her fault, and anyway queer things like that were always happening between her and me. I had come to regard them as a sort of toughening process that did me more good than harm. But if only she could have lived long enough to complete my education, I'm sure I should never have had all that trouble I was telling you about a few minutes ago.

I want to get on with that now. I didn't mean to begin talking about my mother. She doesn't have anything to do with what I originally started out to say. I won't mention her again.

I was telling you about the spinsters in my parish. It's an ugly word, isn't it – spinster? It conjures up the vision either of a stringy old hen with a puckered mouth or of a huge ribald monster shouting around the house in riding-breeches. But these were not like that at all. They were a clean, healthy, well-built group of females, the majority of them highly bred and surprisingly wealthy, and I feel sure that the average unmarried man would have been gratified to have them around.

In the beginning, when I first came to the vicarage, I didn't have too bad a time. I enjoyed a measure of protection, of course, by reason of my calling and my cloth. In addition, I myself adopted a cool dignified attitude that was calculated to discourage familiarity. For a few months, therefore, I was able to move freely among my parishioners, and no one took the liberty of linking her arm in mine at a charity bazaar, or of touching my fingers with hers as she passed me the cruet at suppertime. I was very happy. I was feeling better than I had in years. Even that little nervous habit I had of flicking my earlobe with my forefinger when I talked began to disappear.

This was what I call my first period, and it extended over approximately six months. Then came trouble.

I suppose I should have known that a healthy male like myself couldn't hope to evade embroilment indefinitely simply by keeping a fair distance between himself and the ladies. It just doesn't work. If anything it has the opposite effect.

I would see them eyeing me covertly across the room at a whist drive, whispering to one another, nodding, running their tongues over their lips, sucking at their cigarettes, plotting the best approach, but always whispering, and sometimes I overheard snatches of their talk – 'What a shy person . . . he's just a trifle nervous, isn't he . . . he's much too tense . . . he needs companionship . . . he wants loosening up . . . we must teach him how to relax.' And then slowly, as the weeks went by, they began to stalk me. I knew they were doing it. I could feel it happening although at first they did nothing definite to give themselves away.

That was my second period. It lasted for the best part of a year and was very trying indeed. But it was paradise compared with the third and final phase.

For now, instead of sniping at me sporadically from far away, the attackers suddenly came charging out of the wood with bayonets fixed. It was terrible, frightening. Nothing is more calculated to unnerve a man than the swift unexpected assault. Yet I am not a coward. I will stand my ground against any single individual of my own size under any circumstances. But this onslaught, I am now convinced, was conducted by vast numbers operating as one skilfully co-ordinated unit.

The first offender was Miss Elphinstone, a large woman with moles. I had dropped in on her during the afternoon to solicit a contribution towards a new set of bellows for the organ, and after some pleasant conversation in the library she had graciously handed me a cheque for two guineas. I told her not to bother to see me to the door and I went out into the hall to get my hat. I was about to reach for it when all at once – she must have come tiptoeing up behind me – all at once I felt a bare arm sliding through mine, and one second later her fingers were entwined in my own, and she was squeezing my hand hard, in out, in out, as though it were the bulb of a throat-spray.

'Are you really so Very Reverend as you're always pretending to be?' she whispered.

Well!

All I can tell you is that when that arm of hers came sliding in under mine, it felt exactly as though a cobra was coiling itself round my wrist. I leaped away, pulled open the front door, and fled down the drive without looking back.

The very next day we held a jumble sale in the village

hall (again to raise money for the new bellows), and towards the end of it I was standing in a corner quietly drinking a cup of tea and keeping an eye on the villagers crowding round the stalls when all of a sudden I heard a voice beside me saying, 'Dear me, what a hungry look you have in those eyes of yours.' The next instant a long curvaceous body was leaning up against mine and a hand with red fingernails was trying to push a thick slice of coconut cake into my mouth.

'Miss Prattley,' I cried. 'Please!'

But she'd got me up against the wall, and with a teacup in one hand and a saucer in the other I was powerless to resist. I felt the sweat breaking out all over me and if my mouth hadn't quickly become full of the cake she was pushing into it, I honestly believe I would have started to scream.

A nasty incident, that one; but there was worse to come.

The next day it was Miss Unwin. Now Miss Unwin happened to be a close friend of Miss Elphinstone's *and* of Miss Prattley's, and this of course should have been enough to make me very cautious. Yet who would have thought that she of all people, Miss Unwin, that quiet gentle little mouse who only a few weeks before had presented me with a new hassock exquisitely worked in needlepoint with her own hands, who would have thought that *she* would ever have taken a liberty with anyone? So when she asked me to accompany her down to the crypt to show her the Saxon murals, it never entered my head that there was devilry afoot. But there was.

I don't propose to describe this encounter; it was too

painful. And the ones which followed were no less savage. Nearly every day from then on, some new outrageous incident would take place. I became a nervous wreck. At times I hardly knew what I was doing. I started reading the burial service at young Gladys Pitcher's wedding. I dropped Mrs Harris's new baby into the font during the christening and gave it a nasty ducking. An uncomfortable rash that I hadn't had in over two years reappeared on the side of my neck, and that annoying business with my ear-lobe came back worse than ever before. Even my hair began coming out in my comb. The faster I retreated, the faster they came after me. Women are like that. Nothing stimulates them quite so much as a display of modesty or shyness in a man. And they become doubly persistent if underneath it all they happen to detect – and here I have a most difficult confession to make – if they happen to detect, as they did in me, a little secret gleam of longing shining in the backs of the eyes.

You see, actually I was mad about women.

Yes, I know. You will find this hard to believe after all that I have said, but it was perfectly true. You must understand that it was only when they touched me with their fingers or pushed up against me with their bodies that I became alarmed. Providing they remained at a safe distance, I could watch them for hours on end with the same peculiar fascination that you yourself might experience in watching a creature you couldn't bear to touch – an octopus, for example, or a long poisonous snake. I loved the smooth white look of a bare arm emerging from a sleeve, curiously naked like a peeled banana. I could get enormously excited just from watching a girl walk across the room in a tight dress; and I particularly enjoyed the back view of a pair of legs when the feet were in rather high heels – the wonderful braced-up look behind the knees, with the legs themselves very taut as though they were made of strong elastic stretched out almost to breaking-point, but not quite. Sometimes, in Lady Birdwell's drawing-room, sitting near the window on a summer's afternoon, I would glance over the rim of my teacup towards the swimming-pool and become agitated beyond measure by the sight of a little patch of sunburned stomach bulging between the top and bottom of a two-piece bathing-suit.

There is nothing wrong in having thoughts like these. All men harbour them from time to time. But they did give me a terrible sense of guilt. Is it me, I kept asking myself, who is unwittingly responsible for the shameless way in which these ladies are now behaving? Is it the gleam in my eye (which I cannot control) that is constantly rousing their passions and egging them on? Am I unconsciously giving them what is sometimes known as the come-hither signal every time I glance their way? Am I?

Or is this brutal conduct of theirs inherent in the very nature of the female?

I had a pretty fair idea of the answer to this question, but that was not good enough for me. I happen to possess a conscience that can never be consoled by guesswork; it has to have proof. I simply had to find out who was really the guilty party in this case – me or them – and with this object in view, I now decided to perform a simple experiment of my own invention, using Snelling's rats.

A year or so previously I had had some trouble with an objectionable choirboy named Billy Snelling. On three consecutive Sundays this youth had brought a pair of white rats into church and had let them loose on the floor during my sermon. In the end I had confiscated the animals and carried them home and placed them in a box in the shed at the bottom of the vicarage garden. Purely for humane reasons I had then proceeded to feed them, and as a result, but without any further encouragement from me, the creatures began to multiply very rapidly. The two became five, and the five became twelve.

It was at this point that I decided to use them for research purposes. There were exactly equal numbers of males and females, six of each, so that conditions were ideal.

I first isolated the sexes, putting them into two separate cages, and I left them like that for three whole weeks. Now a rat is a very lascivious animal, and any zoologist will tell you that for them this is an inordinately long period of separation. At a guess I would say that one week of enforced celibacy for a rat is equal to approximately one year of the same treatment for someone like Miss Elphinstone or Miss Prattley; so you can see that I was doing a pretty fair job in reproducing actual conditions.

When the three weeks were up, I took a large box that was divided across the centre by a little fence, and I placed the females on one side and the males on the other. The fence consisted of nothing more than three single strands of naked wire, one inch apart, but there was a powerful electric current running through the wires.

To add a touch of reality to the proceedings, I gave

each female a name. The largest one, who also had the longest whiskers, was Miss Elphinstone. The one with a short thick tail was Miss Prattley. The smallest of them all was Miss Unwin, and so on. The males, all six of them, were *ME*.

I now pulled up a chair and sat back to watch the result.

All rats are suspicious by nature, and when I first put the two sexes together in the box with only the wire between them, neither side made a move. The males stared hard at the females through the fence. The females stared back, waiting for the males to come forward. I could see that both sides were tense with yearning. Whiskers quivered and noses twitched and occasionally a long tail would flick sharply against the wall of the box.

After a while, the first male detached himself from his group and advanced gingerly towards the fence, his belly close to the ground. He touched a wire and was immediately electrocuted. The remaining eleven rats froze, motionless.

There followed a period of nine and a half minutes during which neither side moved; but I noticed that while all the males were now staring at the dead body of their colleague, the females had eyes only for the males.

Then suddenly Miss Prattley with the short tail could stand it no longer. She came bounding forward, hit the wire, and dropped dead.

The males pressed their bodies closer to the ground and gazed thoughtfully at the two corpses by the fence. The females also seemed to be quite shaken, and there was another wait, with neither side moving.

Now it was Miss Unwin who began to show signs of impatience. She snorted audibly and twitched a pink mobile nose-end from side to side, then suddenly she started jerking her body quickly up and down as though she were doing push-ups. She glanced round at her remaining four companions, raised her tail high in the air as much as to say 'Here I go, girls,' and with that she advanced briskly to the wire, pushed her head through it, and was killed.

Sixteen minutes later, Miss Foster made her first move. Miss Foster was a woman in the village who bred cats, and recently she had had the effrontery to put up a large sign outside her house in the High Street, saying FOSTER'S CATTERY. Through long association with the creatures she herself seemed to have acquired all their most noxious characteristics, and whenever she came near me in a room I could detect, even through the smoke of her Russian cigarette, a faint but pungent aroma of cat. She had never struck me as having much control over her baser instincts, and it was with some satisfaction, therefore, that I watched her now as she foolishly took her own life in a last desperate plunge towards the masculine sex.

A Miss Montgomery-Smith came next, a small determined woman who had once tried to make me believe that she had been engaged to a bishop. She died trying to creep on her belly under the lowest wire, and I must say I thought this a very fair reflection upon the way in which she lived her life.

And still the five remaining males stayed motionless, waiting.

The fifth female to go was Miss Plumley. She was a devious one who was continually slipping little messages addressed to me into the collection bag. Only the Sunday before, I had been in the vestry counting the money after morning service and had come across one of them tucked inside a folded ten-shilling note. 'Your poor throat sounded hoarse today during the sermon,' it said. 'Let me bring you a bottle of my own cherry pectoral to soothe it down. Most affectionately, Eunice Plumley.'

Miss Plumley ambled slowly up to the wire, sniffed the centre strand with the tip of her nose, came a fraction too close, and received two hundred and forty volts of alternating current through her body.

The five males stayed where they were, watching the slaughter.

And now only Miss Elphinstone remained on the feminine side.

For a full half-hour neither she nor any of the others made a move. Finally one of the males stirred himself slightly, took a step forward, hesitated, thought better of it, and slowly sank back into a crouch on the floor.

This must have frustrated Miss Elphinstone beyond measure, for suddenly, with eyes blazing, she rushed forward and took a flying leap at the wire. It was a spectacular jump and she nearly cleared it; but one of her hind legs grazed the top strand, and thus she also perished with the rest of her sex.

I cannot tell you how much good it did me to watch this simple and, though I say it myself, this rather ingenious experiment. In one stroke I had laid open the incredibly lascivious, stop-at-nothing nature of the female. My own sex was vindicated; my own conscience was cleared. In a trice, all those awkward little flashes of guilt from which I had continually been suffering flew out the window. I felt suddenly very strong and serene in the knowledge of my own innocence.

For a few moments I toyed with the absurd idea of electrifying the black iron railings that ran round the vicarage garden; or perhaps just the gate would be enough. Then I would sit back comfortably in a chair in the library and watch through the window as the real Misses Elphinstone and Prattley and Unwin came forward one after the other and paid the final penalty for pestering an innocent male.

Such foolish thoughts!

What I must actually do now, I told myself, was to weave round me a sort of invisible electric fence constructed entirely out of my own personal moral fibre. Behind this I would sit in perfect safety while the enemy, one after another, flung themselves against the wire.

I would begin by cultivating a brusque manner. I would speak crisply to all women, and refrain from smiling at them. I would no longer step back a pace when one of them advanced upon me. I would stand my ground and glare at her, and if she said something that I considered suggestive, I would make a sharp retort.

It was in this mood that I set off the very next day to attend Lady Birdwell's tennis party.

I was not a player myself, but her ladyship had graciously invited me to drop in and mingle with the guests when play was over at six o'clock. I believe she thought that it lent a certain tone to a gathering to have a clergyman present, and she was probably hoping to persuade me to repeat the performance I gave the last time I was there, when I sat at the piano for a full hour and a quarter after supper and entertained the guests with a detailed description of the evolution of the madrigal through the centuries.

I arrived at the gates on my cycle promptly at six o'clock and pedalled up the long drive towards the house. This was the first week of June, and the rhododendrons were massed in great banks of pink and purple all the way along on either side. I was feeling unusually blithe and dauntless. The previous day's experiment with the rats had made it impossible now for anyone to take me by surprise. I knew exactly what to expect and I was armed accordingly. All round me the little fence was up.

'Ah, good evening, Vicar,' Lady Birdwell cried, advancing upon me with both arms outstretched.

I stood my ground and looked her straight in the eye. 'How's Birdwell?' I said. 'Still up in the city?'

I doubt whether she had ever before in her life heard Lord Birdwell referred to thus by someone who had never even met him. It stopped her dead in her tracks. She looked at me queerly and didn't seem to know how to answer.

'I'll take a seat if I may,' I said, and walked past her towards the terrace where a group of nine or ten guests were settled comfortably in cane chairs, sipping their drinks. They were mostly women, the usual crowd, all of them dressed in white tennis clothes, and as I strode in among them, my own sober black suiting seemed to give me, I thought, just the right amount of separateness for the occasion.

The ladies greeted me with smiles. I nodded to them and sat down in a vacant chair, but I didn't smile back.

'I think perhaps I'd better finish my story another time,' Miss Elphinstone was saying. 'I don't believe the vicar would approve.' She giggled and gave me an arch look. I knew she was waiting for me to come out with my usual little nervous laugh and to say my usual little sentence about how broad-minded I was; but I did nothing of the sort. I simply raised one side of my upper lip until it shaped itself into a tiny curl of contempt (I had practised in the mirror that morning), and then I said sharply, in a loud voice, 'Mens sana in corpore sano.'

'What's that?' she cried. 'Come again, Vicar.'

'A clean mind in a healthy body,' I answered. 'It's a family motto.'

There was an odd kind of silence for quite a long time after this. I could see the women exchanging glances with one another, frowning, shaking their heads.

'The vicar's in the dumps,' Miss Foster announced. She was the one who bred cats. 'I think the vicar needs a drink.'

'Thank you,' I said, 'but I never imbibe. You know that.'

'Then do let me fetch you a nice cooling glass of fruit cup?'

This last sentence came softly and rather suddenly from someone just behind me, to my right, and there was a note of such genuine concern in the speaker's voice that I turned around.

I saw a lady of singular beauty whom I had met only once before, about a month ago. Her name was Miss Roach, and I remembered that she had struck me then as being a person far out of the usual run. I had been particularly impressed by her gentle and reticent nature; and the fact that I had felt comfortable in her presence proved beyond doubt that she was not the sort of person who would try to impinge herself upon me in any way.

'I'm sure you must be tired after cycling all that distance,' she was saying now.

I swivelled right round in my chair and looked at her carefully. She was certainly a striking person – unusually muscular for a woman, with broad shoulders and powerful arms and a huge calf bulging on each leg. The flush of the afternoon's exertions was still upon her, and her face glowed with a healthy red sheen.

'Thank you so much, Miss Roach,' I said, 'but I never touch alcohol in any form. Maybe a small glass of lemon squash . . .'

'The fruit cup is only made of fruit, Padre.'

How I loved a person who called me 'Padre'. The word has a military ring about it that conjures up visions of stern discipline and officer rank.

'Fruit cup?' Miss Elphinstone said. 'It's harmless.'

'My dear man, it's nothing but vitamin C,' Miss Foster said.

'Much better for you than fizzy lemonade,' Lady Birdwell said. 'Carbon dioxide attacks the lining of the stomach.'

'I'll get you some,' Miss Roach said, smiling at me pleasantly. It was a good open smile, and there wasn't a trace of guile or mischief from one corner of the mouth to the other.

She stood up and walked over to the drink table. I saw her slicing an orange, then an apple, then a cucumber, then a grape, and dropping the pieces into a glass. Then she poured in a large quantity of liquid from a bottle whose label I couldn't quite read without my spectacles, but I fancied that I saw the name JIM on it, or TIM, or PIM, or some such word.

'I hope there's enough left,' Lady Birdwell called out. 'Those greedy children of mine do love it so.'

'Plenty,' Miss Roach answered, and she brought the drink to me and set it on the table.

Even without tasting it I could easily understand why children adored it. The liquid itself was dark amber-red and there were great hunks of fruit floating around among the ice cubes; and on top of it all, Miss Roach had placed a sprig of mint. I guessed that the mint had been put there specially for me, to take some of the sweetness away and to lend a touch of grown-upness to a concoction that was otherwise so obviously for youngsters.

'Too sticky for you, Padre?'

'It's delectable,' I said, sipping it. 'Quite perfect.'

It seemed a pity to gulp it down quickly after all the trouble Miss Roach had taken to make it, but it was so refreshing I couldn't resist.

'Do let me make you another?'

I liked the way she waited until I had set the glass on the table, instead of trying to take it out of my hand.

'I wouldn't eat the mint if I were you,' Miss Elphin-stone said.

'I'd better get another bottle from the house,' Lady Birdwell called out. 'You're going to need it, Mildred.'

'Do that,' Miss Roach replied. 'I drink gallons of the stuff myself,' she went on, speaking to me. 'And I don't think you'd say that I'm exactly what you might call emaciated.'

'No indeed,' I answered fervently. I was watching her again as she mixed me another brew, noticing how the muscles rippled under the skin of the arm that raised the bottle. Her neck also was uncommonly fine when seen from behind; not thin and stringy like the necks of a lot of these so-called modern beauties, but thick and strong with a slight ridge running down either side where the sinews bulged. It wasn't easy to guess the age of a person like this, but I doubted whether she could have been more than forty-eight or -nine.

I had just finished my second big glass of fruit cup when I began to experience a most peculiar sensation. I seemed to be floating up out of my chair, and hundreds of little warm waves came washing in under me, lifting me higher and higher. I felt as buoyant as a bubble, and every-thing around me seemed to be bobbing up and down and swirling gently from side to side. It was all very pleasant, and I was overcome by an almost irresistible desire to break into song.

'Feeling happy?' Miss Roach's voice sounded miles and miles away, and when I turned to look at her, I was aston-ished to see how near to me she really was. She, also, was bobbing up and down.

'Terrific,' I answered. 'I'm feeling absolutely terrific.'

Her face was large and pink, and it was so close to me now that I could see the pale carpet of fuzz covering both her cheeks, and the way the sunlight caught each tiny separate hair and made it shine like gold. All of a sudden I found myself wanting to put out a hand and stroke those cheeks of hers with my fingers. To tell the truth, I wouldn't have objected in the least if she had tried to do the same to me.

'Listen,' she said softly. 'How about the two of us taking a little stroll down the garden to see the lupins?'

'Fine,' I answered. 'Lovely. Anything you say.'

There is a small Georgian summer-house alongside the croquet lawn in Lady Birdwell's garden, and the very next thing I knew, I was sitting inside it on a kind of chaise longue and Miss Roach was beside me. I was still bobbing up and down, and so was she, and so, for that matter, was the summer-house, but I was feeling wonderful. I asked Miss Roach if she would like me to give her a song.

'Not now,' she said, encircling me with her arms and squeezing my chest against hers so hard that it hurt.

'Don't,' I said, melting.

'That's better,' she kept saying. 'That's much better, isn't it?'

Had Miss Roach or any other female tried to do this sort of thing to me an hour before, I don't quite know what would have happened. I think I would probably have fainted. I might even have died. But here I was now, the same old me, actually relishing the contact of those enormous bare arms against my body! Also – and this was the most amazing thing of all – I was beginning to feel the urge to reciprocate.

I took the lobe of her left ear between my thumb and forefinger, and tugged it playfully.

'Naughty boy,' she said.

I tugged harder and squeezed it a bit at the same time. This roused her to such a pitch that she began to grunt and snort like a hog. Her breathing became loud and stertorous.

'Kiss me,' she ordered.

'What?' I said.

'Come on, kiss me.'

At that moment, I saw her mouth. I saw this great mouth of hers coming slowly down on top of me, starting to open, and coming closer and closer, and opening wider and wider; and suddenly my whole stomach began to roll right over inside me and I went stiff with terror.

'No!' I shrieked. 'Don't!'

I can only tell you that I had never in all my life seen anything more terrifying than that mouth. I simply could not *stand* it coming at me like that. Had it been a red-hot iron someone was pushing into my face I wouldn't have been nearly so petrified, I swear I wouldn't. The strong arms were around me, pinning me down so that I couldn't move, and the mouth kept getting larger and larger, and then all at once it was right on top of me, huge and wet and cavernous, and the next second – I was inside it.

I was right inside this enormous mouth, lying on my stomach along the length of the tongue, with my feet somewhere around the back of the throat; and I knew instinctively that unless I got myself out again at once I was going to be swallowed alive – just like that baby rabbit. I could feel my legs being drawn down the throat by some kind of suction, and quickly I threw up my arms and grabbed hold of the lower front teeth and held on for dear life. My head was near the mouth-entrance, and I could actually look right out between the lips and see a little patch of the world outside – sunlight shining on the polished wooden floor of the summer-house, and on the floor itself a gigantic foot in a white tennis shoe.

I had a good grip with my fingers on the edge of the teeth, and in spite of the suction, I was managing to haul myself up slowly towards the daylight when suddenly the upper teeth came down on my knuckles and started chopping away at them so fiercely I had to let go. I went sliding back down the throat, feet first, clutching madly at this and that as I went, but everything was so smooth and slippery I couldn't get a grip. I glimpsed a bright flash of gold on the left as I slid past the last of the molars, and then three inches farther on I saw what must have been the uvula above me, dangling like a thick red stalactite from the roof of the throat. I grabbed at it with both hands but the thing slithered through my fingers and I went on down.

I remember screaming for help, but I could barely hear the sound of my own voice above the noise of the wind that was caused by the throat-owner's breathing. There seemed to be a gale blowing all the time, a queer erratic gale that blew alternately very cold (as the air came in) and very hot (as it went out again).

I managed to get my elbows hooked over a sharp fleshy

ridge – I presume the epiglottis – and for a brief moment I hung there, defying the suction and scrabbling with my feet to find a foothold on the wall of the larynx; but the throat gave a huge heaving swallow that jerked me away, and down I went again.

From then on, there was nothing else for me to catch hold of, and down and down I went until soon my legs were dangling below me in the upper reaches of the stomach, and I could feel the slow powerful pulsing of peristalsis dragging away at my ankles, pulling me down and down and down . . .

Far above me, outside in the open air, I could hear the distant babble of women's voices:

'It's not true . . .'

'But my dear Mildred, how awful . . .'

'The man must be mad . . .'

'Your poor mouth, just look at it . . .'

'A sex maniac . . .'

'A sadist . . .'

'Someone ought to write to the bishop . . .'

And then Miss Roach's voice, louder than the others, swearing and screeching like a parakeet:

'He's damn lucky I didn't kill him, the little bastard! . . . I said to him, listen, I said, if ever I happen to want any of my teeth extracted, I'll go to a dentist, not to a goddam vicar . . . It isn't as though I'd given him any encouragement either! . . .'

'Where is he now, Mildred?'

'God knows. In the bloody summer-house, I suppose.'

'Hey girls, let's go and root him out!'

Oh dear, oh dear. Looking back on it all now, some three weeks later, I don't know how I ever came through the nightmare of that awful afternoon without taking leave of my senses.

A gang of witches like that is a very dangerous thing to fool around with, and had they managed to catch me in the summer-house right then and there when their blood was up, they would likely as not have torn me limb from limb on the spot.

Either that, or I should have been frog-marched down to the police station with Lady Birdwell and Miss Roach leading the procession through the main street of the village.

But of course they didn't catch me.

They didn't catch me then, and they haven't caught me yet, and if my luck continues to hold, I think I've got a fair chance of evading them altogether – or anyway for a few months, until they forget about the whole affair.

As you might guess, I am having to keep entirely to myself and to take no part in public affairs or social life. I find that writing is a most salutary occupation at a time like this, and I spend many hours each day playing with sentences. I regard each sentence as a little wheel, and my ambition lately has been to gather several hundred of them together at once and to fit them all end to end, with the cogs interlocking, like gears, but each wheel a different size, each turning at a different speed. Now and again I try to put a really big one right next to a very small one in such a way that the big one, turning slowly, will make the small one spin so fast that it hums. Very tricky, that.

I also sing madrigals in the evenings, but I miss my own harpsichord terribly.

All the same, this isn't such a bad place, and I have made myself as comfortable as I possibly can. It is a small chamber situated in what is almost certainly the primary section of the duodenal loop, just before it begins to run vertically downwards in front of the right kidney. The floor is quite level – indeed it was the first level place I came to during that horrible descent down Miss Roach's throat – and that's the only reason I managed to stop at all. Above me, I can see a pulpy sort of opening that I take to be the pylorus, where the stomach enters the small intestine (I can still remember some of those diagrams my mother used to show me), and below me, there is a funny little hole in the wall where the pancreatic duct enters the lower section of the duodenum.

It is all a trifle bizarre for a man of conservative tastes like myself. Personally I prefer oak furniture and parquet flooring. But there is anyway one thing here that pleases me greatly, and that is the walls. They are lovely and soft, like a sort of padding, and the advantage of this is that I can bounce up against them as much as I wish without hurting myself.

There are several other people about, which is rather surprising, but thank God they are every one of them males. For some reason or other, they all wear white coats, and they bustle around pretending to be very busy and important. In actual fact, they are an uncommonly ignorant bunch of fellows. They don't even seem to realize where they *are*. I try to tell them, but they refuse to listen.

Sometimes I get so angry and frustrated with them that I lose my temper and start to shout; and then a sly mistrustful look comes over their faces and they begin backing slowly away, and saying, 'Now then. Take it easy. Take it easy, Vicar, there's a good boy. Take it easy.'

What sort of talk is that?

But there is one oldish man – he comes in to see me every morning after breakfast – who appears to live slightly closer to reality than the others. He is civil and dignified, and I imagine he is lonely because he likes nothing better than to sit quietly in my room and listen to me talk. The only trouble is that whenever we get on to the subject of our whereabouts, he starts telling me that he's going to help me to escape. He said it again this morning, and we had quite an argument about it.

'But can't you see,' I said patiently, 'I don't *want* to escape.'

'My dear Vicar, why ever not?'

'I keep telling you – because they're all searching for me outside.'

'Who?'

'Miss Elphinstone and Miss Roach and Miss Prattley and all the rest of them.'

'What nonsense.'

'Oh yes they are! And I imagine they're after *you* as well, but you won't admit it.'

'No, my friend, they are not after me.'

'Then may I ask precisely what you are doing down here?'

A bit of a stumper for him, that one. I could see he didn't know how to answer it.

'I'll bet you were fooling around with Miss Roach and got yourself swallowed up just the same as I did. I'll bet that's exactly what happened, only you're ashamed to admit it.'

He looked suddenly so wan and defeated when I said this that I felt sorry for him.

'Would you like me to sing you a song?' I asked.

But he got up without answering and went quietly out into the corridor.

'Cheer up,' I called after him. 'Don't be depressed. There is always some balm in Gilead.'

The Visitor

First published in *Playboy* (May 1965)

Not long ago, a large wooden case was deposited at the
door of my house by the railway delivery service. It was
an unusually strong and well-constructed object, and
made of some kind of dark red hardwood, not unlike
mahogany. I lifted it with great difficulty on to a table in
the garden, and examined it carefully. The stencilling on
one side said that it had been shipped from Haifa by the
m/v *Waverley Star*, but I could find no sender's name or
address. I tried to think of somebody living in Haifa or
thereabouts who might be wanting to send me a magnificent present. I could think of no one. I walked slowly to
the toolshed, still pondering the matter deeply, and
returned with a hammer and screwdriver. Then I began
gently to prise open the top of the case.

Behold, it was filled with books! Extraordinary books!
One by one, I lifted them all out (not yet looking inside
any of them) and stacked them in three tall piles on the
table. There were twenty-eight volumes altogether, and
very beautiful they were indeed. Each of them was identi-
cally and superbly bound in rich green morocco, with the
initials O.H.C. and a Roman numeral (I to XXVIII) tooled
in gold upon the spine.

I took up the nearest volume, number XVI, and opened
it. The unlined white pages were filled with a neat small

handwriting in black ink. On the title page was written '1934'. Nothing else. I took up another volume, number XXI. It contained more manuscript in the same handwriting, but on the title page it said '1939'. I put it down and pulled out Vol. 1, hoping to find a preface of some kind there, or perhaps the author's name. Instead, I found an envelope inside the cover. The envelope was addressed to me. I took out the letter it contained and glanced quickly at the signature. 'Oswald Hendryks Cornelius', it said.

It was Uncle Oswald!

No member of the family had heard from Uncle Oswald for over thirty years. The letter was dated 10 March 1964, and until its arrival, we could only assume that he still existed. Nothing was really known about him except that he lived in France, that he travelled a great deal, that he was a wealthy bachelor with unsavoury but glamorous habits who steadfastly refused to have anything to do with his own relatives. The rest was all rumour and hearsay, but the rumours were so splendid and the hearsay so exotic that Oswald had long since become a shining hero and a legend to us all.

'My dear boy,' the letter began

I believe that you and your three sisters are my closest surviving blood relations. You are therefore my rightful heirs, and because I have made no will, all that I leave behind me when I die will be yours. Alas, I have nothing to leave. I used to have quite a lot, and the fact that I have recently disposed of it all in my own way is none of your business. As consolation, though, I am sending you my private diaries. These, I think, ought to remain in the family. They cover all the best years of my life, and it will do you no harm to read them. But if you show them around or lend them out to strangers, you do so at your own great peril. If you publish them, then that, I should imagine, would be the end of both you and your publisher simultaneously. For you must understand that thousands of the heroines whom I mention in the diaries are still only half dead, and if you were foolish enough to splash their lily-white reputations with scarlet print, they would have your head on a salver in two seconds flat, and probably roast it in the oven for good measure. So you'd better be careful. I only met you once. That was years ago, in 1921, when your family was living in that large ugly house in South Wales. I was your big uncle and you were a very small boy, about five years old. I don't suppose you remember the young Norwegian nursemaid you had then. A remarkably clean, well-built girl she was, and exquisitely shaped even in her uniform with its ridiculous starchy white shield concealing her lovely bosom. The afternoon I was there, she was taking you for a walk in the woods to pick bluebells, and I asked if I might come along. And when we got well into the middle of the woods, I told you I'd give you a bar of chocolate if you could find your own way home. And you did (see Vol. III). You were a sensible child. Farewell – Oswald Hendryks Cornelius.

The sudden arrival of the diaries caused much excitement in the family, and there was a rush to read them. We were not disappointed. It was astonishing stuff – hiliarious, witty, exciting, and often quite touching as well. The man's vitality was unbelievable. He was always on the move, from city to city, from country to country, from woman to woman, and in between the women, he would be searching for spiders in Kashmir or tracking down a blue porcelain vase in Nanking. But the women always came first. Wherever he went, he left an endless trail of females in his wake, females ruffled and ravished beyond words, but purring like cats.

Twenty-eight volumes with exactly three hundred pages to each volume take a deal of reading, and there are precious few writers who could hold an audience over a distance like that. But Oswald did it. The narrative never seemed to lose its flavour, the pace seldom slackened, and almost without exception, every single entry, whether it was long or short, and whatever the subject, became a marvellous little individual story that was complete in itself. And at the end of it all, when the last page of the last volume had been read, one was left with the rather breathless feeling that this might just possibly be one of the major autobiographical works of our time.

If it were regarded solely as a chronicle of a man's amorous adventures, then without a doubt there was nothing to touch it. Casanova's *Memoirs* read like a parish magazine in comparison, and the famous lover himself, beside Oswald, appears positively undersexed.

There was social dynamite on every page; Oswald was right about that. But he was surely wrong in thinking that the explosions would all come from the women. What about their husbands, the humiliated cock-sparrows, the cuckolds? The cuckold, when aroused, is a very fierce bird indeed, and there would be thousands upon thousands of them rising up out of the bushes if *The Cornelius Diaries*, unabridged, saw the light of day while they were still alive. Publication, therefore, was right out of the question.

A pity, this. Such a pity, in fact, that I thought something ought to be done about it. So I sat down and reread the diaries from beginning to end in the hope that I might discover at least one complete passage which could be printed and published without involving both the publisher and myself in serious litigation. To my joy, I found no less than six. I showed them to a lawyer. He said he thought they *might* be 'safe', but he wouldn't guarantee it. One of them – 'The Sinai Desert Episode' – seemed 'safer' than the other five, he added.

So I have decided to start with that one and to offer it for publication right away, at the end of this short preface. If it is accepted and all goes well, then perhaps I shall release one or two more.

The Sinai entry is from the last volume of all, Vol. XXVIII, and is dated 24 August 1946. In point of fact, it is the *very last entry* of the last volume of all, the last thing Oswald ever wrote, and we have no record of where he went or what he did after that date. One can only guess. You shall have the entry verbatim in a moment, but first of all, and so that you may more easily understand some of the things Oswald says and does in his story, let me try to tell you a little about the man himself. Out of the mass of confession and opinion contained in those twenty-eight volumes, there emerges a fairly clear picture of his character.

At the time of the Sinai episode, Oswald Hendryks Cornelius was fifty-one years old, and he had, of course, never been married. 'I am afraid,' he was in the habit of saying, 'that I have been blessed, or should I call it burdened, with an uncommonly fastidious nature.'

In some ways, this was true, but in others, and especially in so far as marriage was concerned, the statement was the exact opposite of the truth.

The real reason Oswald had refused to get married was simply that he had never in his life been able to confine his attentions to one particular woman for longer than the time it took to conquer her. When that was done, he lost interest and looked around for another victim.

A normal man would hardly consider this a valid reason for remaining single, but Oswald was not a normal man. He was not even a normally polygamous man. He was, to be honest, such a wanton and incorrigible philanderer that no bride on earth would have put up with him for more than a few days, let alone for the duration of a honeymoon – although heaven knows there were enough who would have been willing to give it a try.

He was a tall, narrow person with a fragile and faintly aesthetic air. His voice was soft, his manner was courteous, and at first sight he seemed more like a gentleman-in-waiting to the Queen than a celebrated rapscallion. He never discussed his amorous affairs with other men, and a stranger, though he might sit and talk with him all evening, would be unable to observe the slightest sign of deceit in Oswald's clear blue eyes. He was, in fact, precisely the sort of man that an anxious father would be likely to choose to escort his daughter safely home.

But sit Oswald beside a *woman*, a woman who interested him, and instantaneously his eyes would change, and as he looked at her, a small dangerous spark would begin dancing slowly in the very centre of each pupil; and then he would set about her with his conversation, talking to her rapidly and cleverly and almost certainly more wittily than anyone else had ever done before. This was a gift he had, a most singular talent, and when he put his mind to it, he could make his words coil themselves round and round the listener until they held her in some sort of a mild hypnotic spell.

But it wasn't only his fine talk and the look in his eyes that fascinated the women. It was also his nose. (In Vol. xiv, Oswald includes, with obvious relish, a note written to him by a certain lady in which she describes such things as this in great detail.) It appears that when Oswald was aroused, something odd would begin to happen around the edges of his nostrils, a tightening of the rims, a visible flaring which enlarged the nostril holes and revealed whole areas of the bright red skin inside. This created a queer, wild, animalistic impression, and although it may not sound particularly attractive when described on paper, its effect upon the ladies was electric.

Almost without exception, women were drawn towards Oswald. In the first place, he was a man who refused to be owned at any price, and this automatically made him desirable. Add to this the unusual combination of a first-rate intellect, an abundance of charm and a reputation for excessive promiscuity, and you have a potent recipe.

Then again, and forgetting for a moment the disreputable and licentious angle, it should be noted that there were a number of other surprising facets to Oswald's character that in themselves made him a rather intriguing person. There was, for example, very little that he did not know about nineteenth-century Italian opera, and he had written a curious little manual upon the three composers Donizetti, Verdi and Ponchielli. In it, he listed by name all the important mistresses that these men had had during their lives, and he went on to examine, in a most serious vein, the relationship between creative passion and carnal passion, and the influence of the one upon the other, particularly as it affected the works of these composers.

Chinese porcelain was another of Oswald's interests, and he was acknowledged as something of an international authority in this field. The blue vases of the Tchin-Hoa period were his special love, and he had a small but exquisite collection of these pieces.

He also collected spiders and walking-sticks.

His collection of spiders, or more accurately, his collection of Arachnida, because it included scorpions and pedipalps, was possibly as comprehensive as any outside a museum, and his knowledge of the hundreds of genera and species was impressive. He maintained, incidentally (and probably correctly), that spiders' silk was superior in quality to the ordinary stuff spun by silkworms, and he never wore a tie that was made of any other material. He possessed about forty of these ties altogether, and in order to acquire them in the first place, and in order also to be able to add two new ties a year to his wardrobe, he had to keep thousands and thousands of *Arana* and *Epeira diademata* (the common English garden spiders) in an old conservatory in the garden of his country house outside Paris, where they bred and multiplied at approximately the same rate as they ate one another. From them, he collected the raw thread himself – no one else would enter that ghastly glasshouse – and sent it to Avignon, where it was reeled and thrown and scoured and dyed and made into cloth. From Avignon, the cloth was delivered directly to Sulka, who were enchanted by the whole business, and only too glad to fashion ties out of such a rare and wonderful material.

'But you can't *really* like spiders?' the women visitors would say to Oswald as he displayed his collection.

'Oh, but I adore them,' he would answer. 'Especially the females. They remind me so much of certain human females that I know. They remind me of my very favourite human females.'

'What nonsense, darling.'

'Nonsense? I think not.'

'It's rather insulting.'

'On the contrary, my dear, it is the greatest compliment I could pay. Did you not know, for instance, that the female spider is so savage in her love-making that the male is very lucky indeed if he escapes with his life at the end of it all. Only if he is exceedingly agile and marvellously ingenious will he get away in one piece.'

'Now, *Oswald*!'

'And the crab spider, my beloved, the teeny-weeny little crab spider is so dangerously passionate that her lover has to tie her down with intricate loops and knots of his own thread before he dares to embrace her . . .'

'Oh, *stop* it, Oswald, this *minute!*' the women would cry, their eyes shining.

Oswald's collection of walking-sticks was something else again. Every one of them had belonged either to a distinguished or a disgusting person, and he kept them all in his Paris apartment, where they were displayed in two long racks standing against the walls of the passage (or should one call it the highway?) which led from the living-room to the bedroom. Each stick had its own little ivory label above it, saying Sibelius, Milton, King Farouk, Dickens, Robespierre, Puccini, Oscar Wilde, Franklin Roosevelt, Goebbels, Queen Victoria, Toulouse-Lautrec, Hindenburg, Tolstoy, Laval, Sarah Bernhardt, Goethe, Voroshiloff, Cézanne, Tojo . . . There must have been over a hundred of them in all, some very beautiful, some very plain, some with gold or silver tops, and some with curly handles.

'Take down the Tolstoy,' Oswald would say to a pretty visitor. 'Go on, take it down . . . that's right . . . and now . . . now rub your own palm gently over the knob that has been worn to a shine by the great man himself. Is it not rather wonderful, the mere contact of your skin with that spot?'

'It is, rather, isn't it.'

'And now take the Goebbels and do the same thing. Do it properly, though. Allow your palm to fold tightly over the handle . . . good . . . and now . . . now lean your weight on it, lean hard, exactly as the little deformed doctor used to do . . . there . . . that's it . . . now stay like that for a minute or so and then tell me if you do not feel a thin finger of ice creeping all the way up your arm and into your chest.'

'It's terrifying!'

'Of course it is. Some people pass out completely. They keel right over.'

Nobody ever found it dull to be in Oswald's company, and perhaps that, more than anything else, was the reason for his success.

We come now to the Sinai episode. Oswald, during that month, had been amusing himself by motoring at a fairly leisurely pace down from Khartoum to Cairo. His car was a superlative prewar Lagonda which had been carefully stored in Switzerland during the war years, and as you can imagine, it was fitted with every kind of gadget under the sun. On the day before Sinai (23 August 1946), he was in Cairo, staying at Shepheard's Hotel, and that evening, after a series of impudent manoeuvres, he had succeeded in getting hold of a Moorish lady of supposedly aristocratic descent, called Isabella. Isabella happened to be the jealously guarded mistress of none other than a certain notorious and dyspeptic Royal Personage (there was still a monarchy in Egypt then). This was a typically Oswaldian move.

But there was more to come. At midnight, he drove the lady out to Giza and persuaded her to climb with him in the moonlight right to the very top of the great pyramid of Cheops.

'. . . There can be no safer place,' he wrote in the diary,

> nor a more romantic one, than the apex of a pyramid on a warm night when the moon is full. The passions are stirred not only by the magnificent view but also by that curious sensation of power that surges within the body whenever one surveys the world from a great height. And as for safety – this pyramid is exactly 481 feet high, which is 115 feet higher than the dome of St Paul's Cathedral, and from the summit one can observe all the approaches with the greatest of ease. No other boudoir on earth can offer this facility. None has so many emergency exits, either, so that if some sinister figure should happen to come clambering up in pursuit on one side of the pyramid, one has only to slip calmly and quietly down the other . . .

As it happened, Oswald had a very narrow squeak indeed that night. Somehow, the palace must have got word of the little affair, for Oswald, from his lofty moon-lit pinnacle, suddenly observed *three* sinister figures, not one, closing in on three different sides, and starting to climb. But luckily for him, there is a fourth side to the great pyramid of Cheops, and by the time those Arab thugs had reached the top, the two lovers were already at the bottom and getting into the car.

The entry for 24 August takes up the story at exactly this point. It is reproduced here word for word and comma for comma as Oswald wrote it. Nothing has been altered or added or taken away:

24 August 1946

'He'll chop off Isabella's head if he catch her now,' Isabella said.

'Rubbish,' I answered, but I reckoned she was probably right.

'He'll chop off Oswald's head, too,' she said.

'Not mine, dear lady. I shall be a long way away from here when daylight comes. I'm heading straight up the Nile for Luxor immediately.'

We were driving quickly away from the pyramids now. It was about two thirty a.m.

'To Luxor?' she said.

'Yes.'

'And Isabella is going with you.'

'No,' I said.

'Yes,' she said.

'It is against my principles to travel with a lady,' I said.

I could see some lights ahead of us. They came from the Mena House Hotel, a place where tourists stay out in the desert, not far from the pyramids. I drove fairly close to the hotel and stopped the car.

'I'm going to drop you here,' I said. 'We had a fine time.'

'So you won't take Isabella to Luxor?'

'I'm afraid not,' I said. 'Come on, hop it.'

She started to get out of the car, then she paused with one foot on the road, and suddenly she swung round and poured out upon me a torrent of language so filthy yet so fluent that I had heard nothing like it from the lips of a lady since . . . well, since 1931, in Marrakesh, when the greedy old Duchess of Glasgow put her hand into a chocolate box and got nipped by a scorpion I happened to have placed there for safe-keeping (Vol. XIII, 5 June 1931).

'You are disgusting,' I said.

Isabella leaped out and slammed the door so hard the whole car jumped on its wheels. I drove off very fast. Thank heaven I was rid of her. I cannot abide bad manners in a pretty girl.

As I drove, I kept one eye on the mirror, but as yet no car seemed to be following me. When I came to the outskirts of Cairo, I began threading my way through the side roads, avoiding the centre of the city. I was not particularly worried. The royal watch-dogs were unlikely to carry the matter much further. All the same, it would have been foolhardy to go back to Shepheard's at this point. It wasn't necessary anyway, because all my baggage, except for a small valise, was with me in the car. I never leave suitcases behind me in my room when I go out of an evening in a foreign city. I like to be mobile.

I had no intention, of course, of going to Luxor. I wanted now to get away from Egypt altogether. I didn't like the country at all. Come to think of it, I never had. The place made me feel uncomfortable in my skin. It was the dirtiness of it all, I think, and the putrid smells. But then let us face it, it really is a rather squalid country; and I have a powerful suspicion, though I hate to say it, that the Egyptians wash themselves less thoroughly than any other peoples in the world – with the possible exception of the Mongolians. Certainly they do not wash their crockery to my taste. There was, believe it or not, a long, crusted, coffee-coloured lipmark stamped upon the rim of the cup they placed before me at breakfast yesterday. Ugh! It was repulsive! I kept staring at it and wondering whose slobbery lower lip had done the deed.

I was driving now through the narrow dirty streets of the eastern suburbs of Cairo. I knew precisely where I was going. I had made up my mind about that before I was even halfway down the pyramid with Isabella. I was going to Jerusalem. It was no distance to speak of, and it was a city that I always enjoyed. Furthermore, it was the quickest way out of Egypt. I would proceed as follows:

1. Cairo to Ismailia. About three hours driving. Sing an opera on the way, as usual. Arrive Ismailia 6–7 a.m. Take a room and have a two-hour sleep. Then shower, shave and breakfast.

2. At 10 a.m., cross over the Suez Canal by the Ismailia bridge and take the desert road across Sinai to the Palestine border. Make a search for scorpions en route in the Sinai Desert. Time, about four hours, arriving Palestine border 2 p.m.

3. From there, continue straight on to Jerusalem via Beersheba, reaching the King David Hotel in time for cocktails and dinner.

It was several years since I had travelled that particular road, but I remembered that the Sinai Desert was an outstanding place for scorpions. I badly wanted another female opisthophthalmus, a large one. My present specimen had the fifth segment of its tail missing, and I was ashamed of it.

It didn't take me long to find the main road to Ismailia, and as soon as I was on it, I settled the Lagonda down to a steady sixty-five miles an hour. The road was narrow, but it had a smooth surface, and there was no traffic. The Delta country lay bleak and dismal around me in the moonlight, the flat treeless fields, the ditches running between, and the black soil everywhere. It was inexpressibly dreary.

But it didn't worry *me*. I was no part of it. I was completely isolated in my own luxurious little shell, as snug as a hermit crab and travelling a lot faster. Oh, how I do love to be on the move, winging away to new people and new places and leaving the old ones far behind! Nothing in the world exhilarates me more than that. And how I despise the average citizen, who settles himself down upon one tiny spot of land with one asinine woman, to breed and stew and rot in that condition unto his life's end. And always with the same woman! I simply cannot *believe* that any man in his senses would put up with just one female day after day and year after year. Some of them, of course, don't. But millions pretend they do.

I myself have never, absolutely never permitted an intimate relationship to last for more than twelve hours. That is the furthest limit. Even eight hours is stretching it a bit, to my mind. Look what happened, for example, with Isabella. While we were upon the summit of the pyramid, she was a lady of scintillating parts, as pliant and playful as a puppy, and had I left her there to the mercy of those three Arab thugs, and skipped down on my own, all would have been well. But I foolishly stuck by her and helped her to descend, and as a result, the lovely lady turned into a vulgar screeching trollop, disgusting to behold.

What a world we live in! One gets no thanks these days for being chivalrous.

The Lagonda moved on smoothly through the night. Now for an opera. Which one should it be this time? I was in the mood for a Verdi. What about *Aida*? Of course! It must be *Aida* – the Egyptian opera! Most appropriate.

I began to sing. I was in exceptionally good voice tonight. I let myself go. It was delightful; and as I drove through the small town of Bilbeis, I was Aida herself, singing '*Numei pieta*', the beautiful concluding passage of the first scene.

Half an hour later, at Zagazig, I was Amonasro begging the King of Egypt to save the Ethiopian captives with '*Ma tu, re, tu signore possente*'.

Passing through El Abbasa, I was Rhadames, rendering '*Fuggiam gli adori nospiti*', and now I opened all the windows of the car so that this incomparable love song might reach the ears of the fellaheen snoring in their hovels along the roadside, and perhaps mingle with their dreams.

As I pulled into Ismailia, it was six o'clock in the morning and the sun was already climbing high in a milky-blue heaven, but I myself was in the terrible sealed-up dungeon with Aida, singing, '*O terra, addio; addio valle di pianti!*'

How swiftly the journey had gone. I drove to an hotel. The staff was just beginning to stir. I stirred them up some more and got the best room available. The sheets and blanket on the bed looked as though they had been slept in by twenty-five unwashed Egyptians on twenty-five consecutive nights, and I tore them off with my own hands (which I scrubbed immediately afterward with antiseptic soap) and replaced them with my personal bedding. Then I set my alarm and slept soundly for two hours.

For breakfast I ordered a poached egg on a piece of toast. When the dish arrived – and I tell you, it makes my stomach curdle just to write about it – there was a *gleaming, curly, jet-black hair*, three inches long, lying diagonally across the yolk of my poached egg. It was too much. I leaped up from the table and rushed out of the dining-room. '*Addio!*' I cried, flinging some money at the cashier as I went by, '*Addio valle di pianti!*' And with that I shook the filthy dust of the hotel from my feet.

Now for the Sinai Desert. What a welcome change that would be. A real desert is one of the least contaminated places on earth, and Sinai was no exception. The road across it was a narrow strip of black tarmac about a hundred and forty miles long, with only a single filling-station and a group of huts at the halfway mark, at a place called B'ir Rawd Salim. Otherwise there was nothing but pure uninhabited desert all the way. It would be very hot at this time of year, and it was essential to carry drinking water in case of a breakdown. I therefore pulled up outside a kind of general store in the main street of Ismailia to get my emergency canister refilled.

I went in and spoke to the proprietor. The man had a nasty case of trachoma. The granulation on the under surfaces of his eyelids was so acute that the lids themselves were raised right up off the eyeballs – a beastly sight. I asked him if he would sell me a gallon of *boiled* water. He thought I was mad, and madder still when I insisted on following him back into his grimy kitchen to make sure that he did things properly. He filled a kettle with tap-water and placed it on a paraffin stove. The stove had a tiny little smoky yellow flame. The proprietor seemed very proud of the stove and of its performance. He stood admiring it, his head on one side. Then he suggested that I might prefer to go back and wait in the shop. He would bring me the water, he said, when it was ready. I refused to leave. I stood there watching the kettle like a lion, waiting for the water to boil; and while I was doing this, the break-fast scene suddenly started coming back to me in all its horror – the egg, the yolk and the hair. Whose hair was it that had lain embedded in the slimy yolk of my egg at breakfast? Undoubtedly it was the cook's hair. And when, pray, had the cook last washed his head? He had probably never washed his head. Very well, then. He was almost certainly verminous. But that in itself would not cause a hair to fall out. What *did* cause the cook's hair, then, to fall out on to my poached egg this morning as he transferred the egg from the pan to the plate? There is a reason for all things, and in this case the reason was obvious. The cook's scalp was infested with purulent seborrhoeic impetigo. And the hair itself, the long black hair that I might so easily have swallowed had I been less alert, was therefore swarm-ing with millions and millions of living pathogenic cocci whose exact scientific name I have, happily, forgotten.

Can I, you ask, be absolutely sure that the cook had purulent seborrhoeic impetigo? Not absolutely sure – no. But if he hadn't, then he certainly had ringworm instead.

And what did that mean? I knew only too well what it meant. It meant that ten million microsporons had been clinging and clustering round that awful hair, waiting to go into my mouth.

I began to feel sick.

'The water boils,' the shopkeeper said triumphantly.

'Let it boil,' I told him. 'Give it eight minutes more. What is it you want me to get – typhus?'

Personally, I never drink plain water by itself if I can help it, however pure it may be. Plain water has no flavour at all. I take it, of course, as tea or as coffee, but even then I try to arrange for bottled Vichy or Malvern to be used in the preparation. I avoid tap-water. Tap-water is diabolical stuff. Often it is nothing more nor less than reclaimed sewage.

'Soon this water will be boiled away in steam,' the proprietor said, grinning at me with green teeth.

I lifted the kettle myself and poured the contents into my canister.

Back in the shop, I bought six oranges, a small watermelon and a slab of well-wrapped English chocolate. Then I returned to the Lagonda. Now at last I was away.

A few minutes later, I had crossed the sliding bridge that went over the Suez Canal just above Lake Timsah, and ahead of me lay the flat blazing desert and the little tarmac road stretching out before me like a black ribbon all the way to the horizon. I settled the Lagonda down to the usual steady sixty-five miles an hour, and I opened the windows wide. The air that came in was like the breath of an oven. The time was almost noon, and the sun was throwing its heat directly on to the roof of the car. My thermometer inside registered 103°. But as you know, a touch of warmth never bothers me so long as I am sitting still and am wearing suitable clothes – in this case a pair of cream-coloured linen slacks, a white Aertex shirt and a spider's-silk tie of the loveliest rich moss-green. I felt perfectly comfortable and at peace with the world.

For a minute or two I played with the idea of performing another opera en route – I was in the mood for *La Gioconda* – but after singing a few bars of the opening chorus, I began to perspire slightly; so I rang down the curtain, and lit a cigarette instead.

I was now driving through some of the finest scorpion country in the world, and I was eager to stop and make a search before I reached the halfway filling-station at B'ir Rawd Salim. I had so far met not a single vehicle nor seen a living creature since leaving Ismailia an hour before. This pleased me. Sinai was authentic desert. I pulled up on the side of the road and switched off the engine. I was thirsty, so I ate an orange. Then I put my white topee on my head, and eased myself slowly out of the car, out of my comfortable hermit-crab shell and into the sunlight. For a full minute I stood motionless in the middle of the road, blinking at the brilliance of the surroundings.

There was a blazing sun, a vast hot sky and beneath it all on every side a great pale sea of yellow sand that was not quite of this world. There were mountains now in the distance on the south side of the road, bare, pale, tanagra-coloured mountains faintly glazed with blue and purple, that rose up suddenly out of the desert and faded away in a haze of heat against the sky. The stillness was over-powering. There was no sound at all, no voice of bird or insect anywhere, and it gave me a queer godlike feeling to be standing there alone in the middle of such a splendid, hot, inhuman landscape – as though I were on another planet altogether, on Jupiter or Mars, or in some place more distant and desolate still, where never would the grass grow nor the clouds turn red.

I went to the boot of the car and took out my killing-box, my net and my trowel. Then I stepped off the road into the soft burning sand. I walked slowly for about a hundred yards into the desert, my eyes searching the ground. I was not looking for scorpions but the lairs of scorpions. The scorpion is a cryptozoic and nocturnal creature that hides all through the day either under a stone or in a burrow, according to its type. Only after the sun has gone down does it come out to hunt for food.

The one I wanted, opisthophthalmus, was a burrower, so I wasted no time turning over stones. I searched only for burrows. After ten or fifteen minutes, I had found none; but already the heat was getting to be too much for me, and I decided reluctantly to return to the car. I walked back very slowly, still watching the ground, and I had reached the road and was in the act of stepping on to it when all at once, in the sand, not more than twelve inches from the edge of the tarmac, I caught sight of a scor-pion's burrow.

I put the killing-box and the net on the ground beside me. Then, with my little trowel, I began very cautiously to scrape away the sand all round the hole. This was an operation that never failed to excite me. It was like a treasure hunt – a treasure hunt with just the right amount of danger accompanying it to stir the blood. I could feel my heart beating away in my chest as I probed deeper and deeper into the sand.

And suddenly . . . there she was!

Oh, my heavens, what a whopper! A gigantic female scorpion, not opisthophthalmus, as I saw immediately, but pandinus, the other large African burrower. And clinging to her back – this was too good to be true! – swarming all over her, were one, two, three, four, five . . . a total of fourteen tiny babies! The mother was six inches long at least! Her children were the size of small revolver bullets. She had seen me now, the first human she had ever seen in her life, and her pincers were wide open, her tail was curled high over her back like a question mark, ready to strike. I took up the net, and slid it swiftly underneath her, and scooped her up. She twisted and squirmed, striking wildly in all directions with the end of her tail. I saw a single drop of venom fall through the mesh on to the sand. Quickly, I transferred her, together with all the offspring, to the killing-box, and closed the lid. Then I fetched the ether from the car, and poured it through the little gauze hole in the top of the box until the pad inside was well soaked.

How splendid she would look in my collection! The babies would, of course, fall away from her as they died, but I would stick them on again with glue in more or less their correct positions; and then I would be the proud possessor of a huge female pandinus with her own fourteen offspring on her back! I was extremely pleased.

I lifted the killing-box (I could feel her thrashing about furiously inside) and placed it in the boot, together with the net and trowel. Then I returned to my seat in the car, lit a cigarette, and drove on.

The more contented I am, the slower I drive. I drove quite slowly now, and it must have taken me nearly an hour more to reach B'ir Rawd Salim, the halfway station. It was a most unenticing place. On the left, there was a single gasoline pump and a wooden shack. On the right, there were three more shacks, each about the size of a potting-shed. The rest was desert. There was not a soul in sight. The time was twenty minutes before two in the afternoon, and the temperature inside the car was 106°.

What with the nonsense of getting the water boiled before leaving Ismailia, I had forgotten completely to fill up with gasoline before leaving, and my gauge was now registering slightly less than two gallons. I'd cut it rather fine – but no matter. I pulled in alongside the pump, and waited. Nobody appeared. I pressed the horn button, and the four tuned horns on the Lagonda shouted their wonderful *'Son gia mille e tre!'* across the desert. Nobody appeared. I pressed again.

Son gia mille e tre

sang the horns. Mozart's phrase sounded magnificent in these surroundings. But still nobody appeared. The inhabitants of B'ir Rawd Salim didn't give a damn, it seemed, about my friend Don Giovanni and the one thousand and three women he had deflowered in Spain.

At last, after I had played the horns no less than six times, the door of the hut behind the gasoline pump opened and a tallish man emerged and stood on the threshold, doing up his buttons with both hands. He took his time over this, and not until he had finished did he glance up at the Lagonda. I looked back at him through my open window. I saw him take the first step in my direction . . . he took it very, very slowly . . . Then he took a second step . . .

My God! I thought at once. The spirochetes have got him!

He had the slow, wobbly walk, the loose-limbed, high-stepping gait of a man with locomotor ataxia. With each step he took, the front foot was raised high in the air before him and brought down violently to the ground, as though he were stamping on a dangerous insect.

I thought: I had better get out of here. I had better start the motor and get the hell out of here before he reaches me. But I knew I couldn't. I *had* to have the gasoline. I sat in the car staring at the awful creature as he came stamping laboriously over the sand. He must have had the revolting disease for years and years, otherwise it wouldn't have developed into ataxia. *Tabes dorsalis*, they call it in professional circles, and pathologically this means that the victim is suffering from degeneration of the posterior columns of the spinal cord. But ah my foes and oh my friends, it is really a lot worse than that; it is a slow and merciless consuming of the actual nerve fibres of the body by syphilitic toxins.

The man – the Arab, I shall call him – came right up to the door of my side of the car and peered in through the open window. I leaned away from him, praying that he would come not an inch closer. Without a doubt, he was one of the most blighted humans I had ever seen. His face had the eroded, eaten-away look of an old wood-carving when the worm has been at it, and the sight of it made me wonder how many other diseases the man was suffering from, besides syphilis.

'Salaam,' he mumbled.

'Fill up the tank,' I told him.

He didn't move. He was inspecting the interior of the Lagonda with great interest. A terrible feculent odour came wafting in from his direction.

'Come along!' I said sharply. 'I want some gasoline!'

He looked at me and grinned. It was more of a leer than a grin, an insolent mocking leer that seemed to be saying, 'I am the king of the gasoline pump at B'ir Rawd Salim! Touch me if you dare!' A fly had settled in the corner of one of his eyes. He made no attempt to brush it away.

'You want gasoline?' he said, taunting me.

I was about to swear at him, but I checked myself just in time, and answered politely, 'Yes please, I would be very grateful.'

He watched me slyly for a few moments to be sure I wasn't mocking him, then he nodded as though satisfied now with my behaviour. He turned away and started slowly towards the rear of the car. I reached into the door-pocket for my bottle of Glenmorangie. I poured myself a stiff one, and sat sipping it. The man's face had been within a yard of my own; his foetid breath had come pouring into the car . . . and who knows how many billions of airborne viruses might not have come pouring in with it? On such an occasion it is a fine thing to sterilize the mouth and throat with a drop of Highland whisky. The whisky is also a solace. I emptied the glass, and poured myself another. Soon I began to feel less alarmed. I noticed the watermelon lying on the seat beside me. I decided that a slice of it at this moment would be refreshing. I took my knife from its case and cut out a thick section. Then, with the point of the knife, I carefully picked out all the black seeds, using the rest of the melon as a receptacle.

I sat drinking the whisky and eating the melon. Both were delicious.

'Gasoline is done,' the dreadful Arab said, appearing at the window. 'I check water now, and oil.'

I would have preferred him to keep his hands off the Lagonda altogether, but rather than risk an argument, I said nothing. He went clumping off towards the front of the car, and his walk reminded me of a drunken Hitler Stormtrooper doing the goosestep in very slow motion.

Tabes dorsalis, as I live and breathe.

The only other disease to induce that queer high-stepping gait is chronic beriberi. Well – he probably had that one, too. I cut myself another slice of watermelon, and concentrated for a minute or so on taking out the seeds with the knife. When I looked up again, I saw that the Arab had raised the bonnet of the car on the right-hand side, and was bending over the engine. His head and shoulders were out of sight, and so were his hands and arms. What on earth was the man doing? The oil dipstick was on the other side. I rapped on the windshield. He seemed not to hear me. I put my head out of the window and shouted, 'Hey! Come out of there!'

Slowly, he straightened up, and as he drew his right arm out of the bowels of the engine, I saw that he was holding in his fingers something that was long and black and curly and very thin.

'Good God!' I thought. 'He's found a snake in there!'

He came round to the window, grinning at me and holding the object out for me to see; and only then, as I got a closer look, did I realize that it was not a snake at all – *it was the fan-belt of my Lagonda!*

All the awful implications of suddenly being stranded in this outlandish place with this disgusting man came flooding over me as I sat there staring dumbly at my broken fan-belt.

'You can see,' the Arab was saying, 'it was hanging on by a single thread. A good thing I noticed it.'

I took it from him and examined it closely. 'You cut it!' I cried.

'Cut it?' he answered softly. 'Why should I cut it?'

To be perfectly honest, it was impossible for me to judge whether he had or had not cut it. If he had, then he had also taken the trouble to fray the severed ends with some instrument to make it look like an ordinary break. Even so, my guess was that he *had* cut it, and if I was right then the implications were more sinister than ever.

'I suppose you know I can't go on without a fan-belt?' I said.

He grinned again with that awful mutilated mouth, showing ulcerated gums. 'If you go now,' he said, 'you will boil over in three minutes.'

'So what do you suggest?'

'I shall get you another fan-belt.'

'You will?'

'Of course. There is a telephone here, and if you will pay for the call, I will telephone to Ismailia. And if they haven't got one in Ismailia, I will telephone to Cairo. There is no problem.'

'No problem!' I shouted, getting out of the car. 'And when, pray, do you think the fan-belt is going to arrive in this ghastly place?'

'There is a mail-truck comes through every morning about ten o'clock. You would have it tomorrow.'

The man had all the answers. He never even had to think before replying.

This bastard, I thought, *has cut fan-belts before.*

I was very alert now, and watching him closely.

'They will not have a fan-belt for a machine of this make in Ismailia,' I said. 'It would have to come from the agents in Cairo. I will telephone them myself.' The fact that there was a telephone gave me some comfort. The telephone poles had followed the road all the way across the desert, and I could see the two wires leading into the hut from the nearest pole. 'I will ask the agents in Cairo to set out immediately for this place in a special vehicle,' I said.

The Arab looked along the road towards Cairo, some two hundred miles away. 'Who is going to drive six hours here and six hours back to bring a fan-belt?' he said. 'The mail will be just as quick.'

'Show me the telephone,' I said, starting towards the hut. Then a nasty thought struck me, and I stopped.

How could I possibly use this man's contaminated instrument? The earpiece would have to be pressed against my ear, and the mouthpiece would almost certainly touch my mouth; and I didn't give a damn what the doctors said about the impossibility of catching syphilis from remote contact. A syphilitic mouthpiece was a syphilitic mouthpiece, and you wouldn't catch *me* putting it anywhere near *my* lips, thank you very much. I wouldn't even enter his hut.

I stood there in the sizzling heat of the afternoon and looked at the Arab with his ghastly diseased face, and the Arab looked back at me, as cool and unruffled as you please.

'You want the telephone?' he asked.

'No,' I said. 'Can you read English?'

'Oh, yes.'

'Very well. I shall write down for you the name of the agents and the name of this car, and also my own name. They know me there. You will then tell them what is wanted. And listen . . . tell them to dispatch a special car immediately at my expense. I will pay them well. And if they won't do that, tell them they *have* to get the fan-belt to Ismailia in time to catch the mail-truck. You understand?'

'There is no problem,' the Arab said.

So I wrote down what was necessary on a piece of paper and gave it to him. He walked away with that slow, stamping tread towards the hut, and disappeared inside. I closed the bonnet of the car. Then I went back and sat in the driver's seat to think things out.

I poured myself another whisky, and lit a cigarette. There must be *some* traffic on this road. Somebody would surely come along before nightfall. But would that help me? No, it wouldn't – unless I were prepared to hitch a ride and leave the Lagonda and all my baggage behind to the tender mercies of the Arab. Was I prepared to do that? I didn't know. Probably yes. But if I were forced to stay the night, I would lock myself in the car and try to keep awake as much as possible. On no account would I enter the shack where that creature lived. Nor would I touch his food. I had whisky and water, and I had half a watermelon and a slab of chocolate. That was ample.

The heat was pretty bad. The thermometer in the car was still around 104°. It was hotter outside in the sun. I was perspiring freely. My God, what a place to get stranded in! And what a companion!

After about fifteen minutes, the Arab came out of the hut. I watched him all the way to the car.

'I talked to garage in Cairo,' he said, pushing his face through the window. 'Fan-belt will arrive tomorrow by mail-truck. Everything arranged.'

'Did you ask them about sending it at once?'

'They said impossible,' he answered.

'You're sure you asked them?'

He inclined his head to one side and gave me that sly insolent grin. I turned away and waited for him to go. He stayed where he was. 'We have house for visitors,' he said. 'You can sleep there very nice. My wife will make food, but you will have to pay.'

'Who else is here besides you and your wife?'

'Another man,' he said. He waved an arm in the direction of the three shacks across the road, and I turned and saw a man standing in the doorway of the middle shack, a short wide man who was dressed in dirty khaki slacks and shirt. He was standing absolutely motionless in the shadow of the doorway, his arms dangling at his sides. He was looking at me.

'Who is he?' I said.

'Saleh.'

'What does he do?'

'He helps.'

'I will sleep in the car,' I said. 'And it will not be necessary for your wife to prepare food. I have my own.' The Arab shrugged and turned away and started back towards the shack where the telephone was. I stayed in the car. What else could I do? It was just after two thirty. In three or four hours' time it would start to get a little cooler. Then I could take a stroll and maybe hunt up a few scorpions. Meanwhile, I had to make the best of things as they were. I reached into the back of the car where I kept my box of books and, without looking, I took out the first one I touched. The box contained thirty or forty of the best books in the world, and all of them could be reread a hundred times and would improve with each reading.

It was immaterial which one I got. It turned out to be *The Natural History of Selborne*. I opened it at random . . .

. . . We had in this village more than twenty years ago an idiot boy, whom I well remember, who, from a child, showed a strong propensity to bees; they were his food, his amusement, his sole object. And as people of this cast have seldom more than one point of view, so this lad exerted all his few faculties on this one pursuit. In winter he dozed away his time, within his father's house, by the fireside, in a kind of torpid state, seldom departing from the chimney-corner; but in the summer he was all alert, and in quest of his game in the fields, and on sunny banks. Honey-bees, bumble-bees, wasps, were his prey wherever he found them; he had no apprehensions from their stings, but would seize them *nudis manibus*, and at once disarm them of their weapons, and suck their bodies for the sake of their honey-bags. Sometimes he would fill his bosom, between his shirt and his skin, with a number of these captives, and sometimes confine them to bottles. He was a very *merops apiaster*, or bee-bird, and very injurious to men that kept bees; for he would slide into their bee-gardens, and, sitting down before the stools, would rap with his fingers on the hives, and so take the bees as they came out. He has been known to overturn hives for the sake of honey, of which he is passionately fond. Where metheglin was making, he would linger around the tubs and vessels, begging a draught of what he called bee-wine. As he ran about, he used to make a humming noise with his lips, resembling the buzzing of bees . . .

I glanced up from the book and looked around me. The motionless man across the road had disappeared. There was nobody in sight. The silence was eerie, and the stillness, the utter stillness and desolation of the place was profoundly oppressive. I knew I was being watched. I knew that every little move I made, every sip of whisky and every puff of a cigarette, was being carefully noticed. I detest violence and I never carry a weapon. But I could have done with one now. For a while, I toyed with the idea of starting the motor and driving on down the road until the engine boiled over. But how far would I get? Not very far in this heat and without a fan. One mile, perhaps, or two at the most . . .

No — to hell with it. I would stay where I was and read my book.

It must have been about an hour later that I noticed a small dark speck moving towards me along the road in the far distance, coming from the Jerusalem direction. I laid aside my book without taking my eyes away from the speck. I watched it growing bigger and bigger. It was travelling at a great speed, at a really amazing speed. I got out of the Lagonda and hurried to the side of the road and stood there, ready to signal the driver to stop.

Closer and closer it came, and when it was about a quarter of a mile away, it began to slow down. Suddenly, I noticed the shape of its radiator. It was a *Rolls-Royce*! I raised an arm and kept it raised, and the big green car with a man at the wheel pulled in off the road and stopped beside my Lagonda.

I felt absurdly elated. Had it been a Ford or a Morris,

I would have been pleased enough, but I would not have been elated. The fact that it was a Rolls – a Bentley would have done equally well, or an Isotta, or another Lagonda – was a virtual guarantee that I would receive all the assistance I required; for whether you know it or not, there is a powerful brotherhood existing among people who own very costly automobiles. They respect one another automatically, and the reason they respect one another is simply that wealth respects wealth. In point of fact, there is nobody in the world that a very wealthy person respects more than another very wealthy person, and because of this, they naturally seek each other out wherever they go. Recognition signals of many kinds are used among them. With the female, the wearing of massive jewels is perhaps the most common; but the costly automobile is also much favoured, and is used by both sexes. It is a travelling placard, a public declaration of affluence, and as such, it is also a card of membership to that excellent unofficial society, the Very-Wealthy-People's Union. I am a member myself of long standing, and am delighted to be one. When I meet another member, as I was about to do now, I feel an immediate rapport. I respect him. We speak the same language. He is one of *us*. I had good reason, therefore, to be elated.

The driver of the Rolls climbed out and came towards me. He was a small dark man with olive skin, and he wore an immaculate white linen suit. Probably a Syrian, I thought. Just possibly a Greek. In the heat of the day he looked as cool as could be.

'Good afternoon,' he said. 'Are you having trouble?'

I greeted him, and then, bit by bit, I told him everything that had happened.

'My dear fellow,' he said in perfect English, 'but my *dear
fellow*, how very distressing. What rotten luck. This is no
place to get stranded in.'

'It isn't, is it?'

'And you say that a new fan-belt has definitely been
ordered?'

'Yes,' I answered, 'if I can rely upon the proprietor of
this establishment.'

The Arab, who had emerged from his shack almost
before the Rolls had come to a stop, now joined us, and
the stranger proceeded to question him swiftly in Arabic
about the steps he had taken on my behalf. It seemed to
me that the two knew each other pretty well, and it was
clear that the Arab was in great awe of the new arrival.
He was practically crawling along the ground in his
presence.

'Well – that seems to be all right,' the stranger said at
last, turning to me. 'But quite obviously you won't be able
to move on from here until tomorrow morning. Where
were you headed for?'

'Jerusalem,' I said. 'And I don't relish the idea of spend-
ing the night in this infernal spot.'

'I should say not, my dear man. That would be most
uncomfortable.' He smiled at me, showing exceptionally
white teeth. Then he took out a cigarette case, and offered
me a cigarette. The case was gold, and on the outside of it
there was a thin line of green jade inlaid diagonally from

corner to corner. It was a beautiful thing. I accepted the cigarette. He lit it for me, then lit his own.

The stranger took a long pull at his cigarette, inhaling deeply. Then he tilted back his head and blew the smoke up into the sun. 'We shall both get heat-stroke if we stand around here much longer,' he said. 'Will you permit me to make a suggestion?'

'But of course.'

'I do hope you won't consider it presumptuous, coming from a complete stranger . . .'

'Please . . .'

'You can't possibly remain here, so I suggest you come back and stay the night in my house.'

There! The Rolls-Royce was smiling at the Lagonda – smiling at it as it would never have smiled at a Ford or a Morris!

'You mean in Ismailia?' I said.

'No, no,' he answered, laughing. 'I live just around the corner, just over there.' He waved a hand in the direction he had come from.

'But surely you were going to Ismailia? I wouldn't want you to change your plans on my behalf.'

'I wasn't going to Ismailia at all,' he said. 'I was coming down here to collect the mail. My house – and this may surprise you – is quite close to where we are standing. You see that mountain? That's Maghara. I'm immediately behind it.'

I looked at the mountain. It lay about ten miles to the north, a yellow rocky lump, perhaps two thousand feet high. 'Do you really mean that you have a house in the middle of all this . . . this wasteland?' I asked.

'You don't believe me?' he said, smiling.

'Of course I believe you,' I answered. 'Nothing surprises me any more. Except, perhaps,' and here I smiled back at him, 'except when I meet a stranger in the middle of the desert, and he treats me like a brother. I am overwhelmed by your offer.'

'Nonsense, my dear fellow. My motives are entirely self-ish. Civilized company is not easy to come by in these parts. I am quite thrilled at the thought of having a guest for dinner. Permit me to introduce myself – Abdul Aziz.' He made a quick little bow.

'Oswald Cornelius,' I said. 'It is a great pleasure.' We shook hands.

'I live partly in Beirut,' he said.

'I live in Paris.'

'Charming. And now – shall we go? Are you ready?'

'But my car,' I said. 'Can I leave it here safely?'

'Have no fear about that. Omar is a friend of mine. He's not much to look at, poor chap, but he won't let you down if you're with me. And the other one, Saleh, is a good mechanic. He'll fit your new fan-belt when it arrives tomorrow. I'll tell him now.'

Saleh, the man from across the road, had walked over while we were talking. Mr Aziz gave him his instructions. He then spoke to both men about guarding the Lagonda. He was brief and incisive. Omar and Saleh stood bowing and scraping. I went across to the Lagonda to get a suit-case. I needed a change of clothes badly.

'Oh, by the way,' Mr Aziz called over to me, 'I usually put on a black tie for dinner.'

'Of course,' I murmured, quickly pushing back my first choice of suitcase and taking another.

'I do it for the ladies mostly. They seem to like dressing themselves up for dinner.'

I turned sharply and looked at him, but he was already getting into his car.

'Ready?' he said.

I took the suitcase and placed it in the back of the Rolls. Then I climbed into the front seat beside him, and we drove off.

During the drive, we talked casually about this and that. He told me that his business was in carpets. He had offices in Beirut and Damascus. His forefathers, he said, had been in the trade for hundreds of years.

I mentioned that I had a seventeenth-century Damascus carpet on the floor of my bedroom in Paris.

'You don't mean it!' he cried, nearly swerving off the road with excitement. 'Is it silk and wool, with the warp made entirely of silk? And has it got a ground of gold and silver threads?'

'Yes,' I said. 'Exactly.'

'But my dear fellow! You mustn't put a thing like that on the floor!'

'It is touched only by bare feet,' I said.

That pleased him. It seemed that he loved carpets almost as much as I loved the blue vases of Tchin-Hoa.

Soon we turned left off the tarred road on to a hard stony track and headed straight over the desert towards the mountain. 'This is my private driveway,' Mr Aziz said. 'It is five miles long.'

'You are even on the telephone,' I said, noticing the poles that branched off the main road to follow his private drive.

And then suddenly a queer thought struck me.

That Arab at the filling-station . . . he also was on the telephone . . .

Might not this, then, explain the fortuitous arrival of Mr Aziz?

Was it possible that my lonely host had devised a clever method of shanghai-ing travellers off the road in order to provide himself with what he called 'civilized company' for dinner? Had he, in fact, given the Arab standing instructions to immobilize the cars of all likely-looking persons one after the other as they came along? 'Just cut the fan-belt, Omar. Then phone me up quick. But make sure it's a decent-looking fellow with a good car. Then I'll pop along and see if I think he's worth inviting to the house . . .'

It was ridiculous, of course.

'I think,' my companion was saying, 'that you are wondering why in the world I should choose to have a house out here in a place like this.'

'Well, yes. I am a bit.'

'Everyone does,' he said.

'*Everyone*,' I said.

'Yes,' he said.

Well, well, I thought – everyone.

'I live here,' he said, 'because I have a peculiar affinity

with the desert. I am drawn to it the same way as a sailor is drawn to the sea. Does that seem so very strange to you?'

'No,' I answered, 'it doesn't seem strange at all.'

He paused and took a pull at his cigarette. Then he said, 'That is one reason. But there is another. Are you a family man, Mr Cornelius?'

'Unfortunately not,' I answered cautiously.

'I am,' he said. 'I have a wife and a daughter. Both of them, in my eyes at any rate, are very beautiful. My daughter is just eighteen. She has been to an excellent boarding-school in England, and she is now ...' he shrugged ... 'she is now just sitting around and waiting until she is old enough to get married. But this waiting period – what does one do with a beautiful young girl during that time? I can't let her loose. She is far too desirable for that. When I take her to Beirut, I see the men hanging around her like wolves waiting to pounce. It drives me nearly out of my mind. I know all about men, Mr Cornelius. I know how they behave. It is true, of course, that I am not the only father who has had this problem. But the others seem somehow able to face it and accept it. They let their daughters go. They just turn them out of the house and look the other way. I cannot do that. I simply *cannot bring* myself to do it! I refuse to allow her to be mauled by every Achmed, Ali and Hamil that comes along. And that, you see, is the other reason why I live in the desert – to protect my lovely child for a few more years from the wild beasts. Did you say that you had no family at all, Mr Cornelius?'

'I'm afraid that's true.'

'Oh.' He seemed disappointed. 'You mean you've never been married?'

'Well . . . no,' I said. 'No, I haven't.' I waited for the next inevitable question. It came about a minute later.

'Have you never *wanted* to get married and have children?'

They all asked that one. It was simply another way of saying, 'Are you, in that case, homosexual?'

'Once,' I said. 'Just once.'

'What happened?'

'There was only one person ever in my life, Mr Aziz . . . and after she went . . .' I sighed.

'You mean she died?'

I nodded, too choked up to answer.

'My dear fellow,' he said. 'Oh, I am so sorry. Forgive me for intruding.'

We drove on for a while in silence.

'It's amazing,' I murmured, 'how one loses all interest in matters of the flesh after a thing like that. I suppose it's the shock. One never gets over it.'

He nodded sympathetically, swallowing it all.

'So now I just travel around trying to forget. I've been doing it for years . . .'

We had reached the foot of Mount Maghara now and were following the track as it curved round the mountain towards the side that was invisible from the road – the north side. 'As soon as we round the next bend you'll see the house,' Mr Aziz said.

We rounded the bend . . . and there it was! I blinked

and stared, and I tell you that for the first few seconds I literally could not believe my eyes. I saw before me a white castle – I mean it – a *tall, white castle* with turrets and towers and little spires all over it, standing like a fairy-tale in the middle of a small splash of green vegetation on the lower slope of the blazing-hot, bare, yellow mountain! It was fantastic! It was straight out of Hans Christian Andersen or Grimm. I had seen plenty of romantic-looking Rhine and Loire valley castles in my time, but never before had I seen anything with such a slender, graceful, fairy-tale quality as this! The greenery, as I observed when we drew closer, was a pretty garden of lawns and date-palms, and there was a high white wall going all the way round to keep out the desert.

'Do you approve?' my host asked, smiling.

'It's fabulous!' I said. 'It's like all the fairy-tale castles in the world made into one.'

'That's exactly what it is!' he cried. 'It's a fairy-tale castle! I built it especially for my daughter, my beautiful Princess.'

And the beautiful Princess is imprisoned within its walls by her strict and jealous father, King Abdul Aziz, who refuses to allow her the pleasures of masculine company. But watch out, for here comes Prince Oswald Cornelius to the rescue! Unbeknownst to the King, he is going to ravish the beautiful Princess, and make her very happy.

'You have to admit it's different,' Mr Aziz said.

'It is that.'

'It is also nice and private. I sleep very peacefully here. So does the Princess. No unpleasant young men are likely to come climbing in through *those* windows during the night.'

'Quite so,' I said.

'It used to be a small oasis,' he went on. 'I bought it from the government. We have ample water for the house, the swimming-pool and three acres of garden.'

We drove through the main gates, and I must say it was wonderful to come suddenly into a miniature paradise of green lawns and flowerbeds and palm trees. Everything was in perfect order, and water-sprinklers were playing on the lawns. When we stopped at the front door of the house, two servants in spotless gallabiyahs and scarlet tarbooshes ran out immediately, one to each side of the car, to open the doors for us.

Two servants? But would both of them have come out like that unless they'd been expecting *two* people? I doubted it. More and more, it began to look as though my odd little theory about being shanghaied as a dinner guest was turning out to be correct. It was all very amusing.

My host ushered me in through the front door, and at once I got that lovely shivery feeling that comes over the skin as one walks suddenly out of intense heat into an air-conditioned room. I was standing in the hall. The floor was of green marble. On my right, there was a wide archway leading to a large room, and I received a fleeting impression of cool white walls, fine pictures and superlative Louis XV furniture. What a place to find oneself in, in the middle of the Sinai Desert!

And now a woman was coming slowly down the stairs. My host had turned away to speak to the servants, and he didn't see her at once, so when she reached the bottom step, the woman paused, and she laid her naked arm like a white anaconda along the rail of the banister, and there she stood, looking at me as though she were Queen Semiramis on the steps of Babylon, and I was a candidate who might or might not be to her taste. Her hair was jet-black, and she had a figure that made me wet my lips.

When Mr Aziz turned and saw her, he said, 'Oh darling, there you are. I've brought you a guest. His car broke down at the filling-station – such rotten luck – so I asked him to come back and stay the night. Mr Cornelius . . . my wife.'

'How very nice,' she said quietly, coming forward.

I took her hand and raised it to my lips. 'I am overcome by your kindness, madame,' I murmured. There was, upon that hand of hers, a diabolical perfume. It was almost exclusively animal. The subtle, sexy secretions of the sperm-whale, the male musk-deer and the beaver were all there, pungent and obscene beyond words; they dominated the blend completely, and only faint traces of the clean vegetable oils – lemon, cajuput and zeroli – were allowed to come through. It was superb! And another thing I noticed in the flash of that first moment was this: when I took her hand, she did not, as other women do, let it lie limply across my palm like a fillet of raw fish. Instead, she placed her thumb *underneath* my hand, with the fingers on top; and thus she was able to – and I swear she did – exert a gentle but suggestive pressure upon my hand as I administered the conventional kiss.

'Where is Diana?' asked Mr Aziz.

'She's out by the pool,' the woman said. And turning to me, 'Would *you* like a swim, Mr Cornelius? You must be roasted after hanging around that awful filling-station.'

She had huge velvet eyes, so dark they were almost black, and when she smiled at me, the end of her nose moved upwards, distending the nostrils.

There and then, Prince Oswald Cornelius decided that he cared not one whit about the beautiful Princess who was held captive in the castle by the jealous King. He would ravish the Queen instead.

'Well . . .' I said.

'I'm going to have one,' Mr Aziz said.

'Let's all have one,' his wife said. 'We'll lend you a pair of trunks.'

I asked if I might go up to my room first and get out a clean shirt and clean slacks to put on after the swim, and my hostess said, 'Yes, of course,' and told one of the servants to show me the way. He took me up two flights of stairs, and we entered a large white bedroom which had in it an exceptionally large double-bed. There was a well-equipped bathroom leading off to one side, with a pale-blue bathtub and a bidet to match. Everywhere, things were scrupulously clean and very much to my liking. While the servant was unpacking my case, I went over to the window and looked out, and I saw the great blazing desert sweeping in like a yellow sea all the way from the horizon until it met the white garden wall just below me, and there, within the wall, I could see the swimming-pool, and beside the pool there was a girl lying on her back in the shade of a big pink parasol. The girl was wearing a white swimming-costume, and she was reading a book. She had long slim legs and black hair. She was the Princess.

What a set-up, I thought. The white castle, the comfort, the cleanliness, the air-conditioning, the two dazzlingly beautiful females, the watchdog husband, and a whole evening to work in! The situation was so perfectly designed for my entertainment that it would have been impossible to improve upon it. The problems that lay ahead appealed to me very much. A simple straightforward seduction did not amuse me any more. There was no artistry in that sort of thing; and I can assure you that had I been able, by waving a magic wand, to make Mr Abdul Aziz, the jealous watchdog, disappear for the night, I would not have done so. I wanted no pyrrhic victories.

When I left the room, the servant accompanied me. We descended the first flight of stairs, and then, on the landing of the floor below my own, I paused and said casually, 'Does the whole family sleep on this floor?'

'Oh, yes,' the servant said. 'That is the master's room there' – indicating a door – 'and next to it is Mrs Aziz. Miss Diana is opposite.'

Three separate rooms. All very close together. Virtually impregnable. I tucked the information away in my mind and went on down to the pool. My host and hostess were there before me.

'This is my daughter, Diana,' my host said.

The girl in the white swimming-suit stood up and I kissed her hand. 'Hello, Mr Cornelius,' she said.

She was using the same heavy animal perfume as her mother – ambergris, musk and castor! What a smell it had – bitchy, brazen and marvellous! I sniffed at it like a dog. She was, I thought, even more beautiful than the parent, if that were possible. She had the same large velvety eyes, the same black hair, and the same shape of face; but

LUST

her legs were unquestionably longer, and there was something about her body that gave it a slight edge over the
older woman's: it was more sinuous, more snaky and
almost certain to be a good deal more flexible. But the
older woman, who was probably thirty-seven and looked
no more than twenty-five, had a spark in her eye that her
daughter could not possibly match.

*Eeny, meeny, miny, mo – just a little while ago, Prince Oswald
had sworn that he would ravish the Queen alone, and to hell with the
Princess. But now that he had seen the Princess in the flesh, he did
not know which one to prefer. Both of them, in their different ways,
held forth a promise of innumerable delights, the one innocent and
eager, the other expert and voracious. The truth of the matter was
that he would like to have them both – the Princess as an hors
d'œuvre, and the Queen as the main dish.*

'Help yourself to a pair of trunks in the changing-
room, Mr Cornelius,' Mrs Aziz was saying, so I went into
the hut and changed, and when I came out again the three
of them were already splashing about in the water. I dived
in and joined them. The water was so cold it made me
gasp.

'I thought that would surprise you,' Mr Aziz said, laughing. 'It's cooled. I keep it at sixty-five degrees. It's more
refreshing in this climate.'

Later, when the sun began dropping lower in the sky,
we all sat around in our wet swimming-clothes while a
servant brought us pale, ice-cold martinis, and it was at
this point that I began, very slowly, very cautiously, to
seduce the two ladies in my own particular fashion. Normally, when I am given a free hand, this is not especially

difficult for me to do. The curious little talent that I happen to possess – the ability to hypnotize a woman with words – very seldom lets me down. It is not, of course, done only with words. The words themselves, the innocuous, superficial words, are spoken only by the mouth, whereas the real message, the improper and exciting promise, comes from all the limbs and organs of the body, and is transmitted through the eyes. More than that I cannot honestly tell you about how it is done. The point is that it works. It works like cantharides. I believe that I could sit down opposite the Pope's wife, if he had one, and within fifteen minutes, were I to try hard enough, she would be leaning towards me over the table with her lips apart and her eyes glazed with desire. It is a minor talent, not a great one, but I am none the less thankful to have had it bestowed upon me, and I have done my best at all times to see that it has not been wasted.

So the four of us, the two wondrous women, the little man and myself, sat close together in a semicircle beside the swimming-pool, lounging in deck-chairs and sipping our drinks and feeling the warm six o'clock sunshine upon our skin. I was in good form. I made them laugh a great deal. The story about the greedy old Duchess of Glasgow putting her hand in the chocolate box and getting nipped by one of my scorpions had the daughter falling out of her chair with mirth; and when I described in detail the interior of my spider breeding-house in the garden outside Paris, both ladies began wriggling with revulsion and pleasure.

It was at this stage that I noticed the eyes of Mr Abdul

Aziz resting upon me in a good-humoured, twinkling kind of way. 'Well, well,' the eyes seemed to be saying, 'we are glad to see that you are not quite so disinterested in women as you led us to believe in the car . . . Or is it, perhaps, that these congenial surroundings are helping you to forget that great sorrow of yours at last . . .' Mr Aziz smiled at me, showing his pure white teeth. It was a friendly smile. I gave him a friendly smile back. What a friendly little fellow he was. He was genuinely delighted to see me paying so much attention to the ladies. So far, then, so good.

I shall skip very quickly over the next few hours, for it was not until after midnight that anything really tremendous happened to me. A few brief notes will suffice to cover the intervening period:

At seven o'clock, we all left the swimming-pool and returned to the house to dress for dinner.

At eight o'clock, we assembled in the big living-room to drink another cocktail. The two ladies were both superbly turned out, and sparkling with jewels. Both of them wore low-cut, sleeveless evening-dresses which had come, without any doubt at all, from some great fashion house in Paris. My hostess was in black, her daughter in pale blue, and the scent of that intoxicating perfume was everywhere about them. What a pair they were! The older woman had that slight forward hunch to her shoulders which one sees only in the most passionate and practised of females; for in the same way as a horsey woman will become bandy-legged from sitting constantly upon a horse, so a woman of great passion will develop a curious roundness of the shoulders from continually embracing men. It is an occupational deformity, and the noblest of them all.

The daughter was not yet old enough to have acquired this singular badge of honour, but with her it was enough for me simply to stand back and observe the shape of her body and to notice the splendid sliding motion of her thighs underneath the tight silk dress as she wandered about the room. She had a line of tiny soft golden hairs growing all the way up the exposed length of her spine, and when I stood behind her it was difficult to resist the temptation of running my knuckles up and down those lovely vertebrae.

At eight thirty, we moved into the dining-room. The dinner that followed was a really magnificent affair, but I shall waste no time here describing food or wine. Throughout the meal I continued to play most delicately and insidiously upon the sensibilities of the women, employing every skill that I possessed; and by the time the dessert arrived, they were melting before my eyes like butter in the sun.

After dinner we returned to the living-room for coffee and brandy, and then, at my host's suggestion, we played a couple of rubbers of bridge.

By the end of the evening, I knew for certain that I had done my work well. The old magic had not let me down. Either of the two ladies, should circumstances permit, was mine for the asking. I was not deluding myself over this. It was a straightforward, obvious fact. It stood out a mile. The face of my hostess was bright with excitement, and whenever she looked at me across the card table, those huge dark velvety eyes would grow bigger and bigger, and the nostrils would dilate, and the mouth would open slightly to reveal the tip of a moist pink tongue squeezing through between the teeth. It was a marvellously lascivious gesture, and more than once it caused me to trump my own trick. The daughter was less daring but equally direct. Each time her eyes met mine, and that was often enough, she would raise her brows just the tiniest fraction of a centimetre, as though asking a question; then she would make a quick sly little smile, supplying the answer.

'I think it's time we all went to bed,' Mr Aziz said, examining his watch. 'It's after eleven. Come along, my dears.'

Then a queer thing happened. At once, without a second's hesitation and without another glance in my direction, both ladies rose and made for the door! It was astonishing. It left me stunned. I didn't know what to make of it. It was the quickest thing I'd ever seen. And yet it wasn't as though Mr Aziz had spoken angrily. His voice, to me at any rate, had sounded as pleasant as ever. But now he was already turning out the lights, indicating clearly that he wished me also to retire. What a blow! I had expected at least to receive a whisper from either the wife or the daughter before we separated for the night, just a quick three or four words telling me where to go and when; but instead, I was left standing like a fool beside the card table while the two ladies glided out of the room.

My host and I followed them up the stairs. On the landing of the first floor, the mother and daughter stood side by side, waiting for me.

'Goodnight, Mr Cornelius,' my hostess said.

'Goodnight, Mr Cornelius,' the daughter said.

'Goodnight, my dear fellow,' Mr Aziz said. 'I do hope you have everything you want.'

They turned away, and there was nothing for me to do but continue slowly, reluctantly, up the second flight of stairs to my own room. I entered it and closed the door. The heavy brocade curtains had already been drawn by one of the servants, but I parted them and leaned out of the window to take a look at the night. The air was still and warm, and a brilliant moon was shining over the desert. Below me, the swimming-pool in the moonlight looked something like an enormous glass mirror lying flat on the lawn, and beside it I could see the four deck-chairs we had been sitting in earlier.

Well, well, I thought. What happens now?

One thing I knew I must not do in this house was to venture out of my room and go prowling around the corridors. That would be suicide. I had learned many years ago that there are three breeds of husband with whom one must never take unnecessary risks – the Bulgarian, the Greek and the Syrian. None of them, for some reason, resents you flirting quite openly with his wife, but he will kill you at once if he catches you getting into her bed. Mr Aziz was a Syrian. A degree of prudence was therefore essential, and if any move were going to be made now, it must be made not by me but by one of the two women, for only she (or they) would know precisely what was safe and what was dangerous. Yet I had to admit that after witnessing the way in which my host had called them both to heel four minutes ago, there was very little hope of further action in the near future. The trouble was, though, that I had gotten myself so infernally steamed up.

I undressed and took a long cold shower. That helped. Then, because I have never been able to sleep in the moonlight, I made sure that the curtains were tightly drawn together. I got into bed, and for the next hour or so I lay reading some more of Gilbert White's *Natural History of Selborne*. That also helped, and at last, somewhere between midnight and one a.m., there came a time when I was able to switch out the light and prepare myself for sleep without altogether too many regrets.

I was just beginning to doze off when I heard some tiny sounds. I recognized them at once. They were sounds that I had heard many times before in my life, and yet they were still, for me, the most thrilling and evocative in the whole world. They consisted of a series of little soft metallic noises, of metal grating gently against metal, and they were made, they were always made by somebody who was very slowly, very cautiously, turning the handle of one's door from the outside. Instantly, I became wide awake. But I did not move. I simply opened my eyes and stared in the direction of the door; and I can remember wishing at that moment for a gap in the curtain, for just a small thin shaft of moonlight to come in from outside so that I could at least catch a glimpse of the shadow of the lovely form that was about to enter. But the room was as dark as a dungeon.

I did not hear the door open. No hinge squeaked. But suddenly a little gust of air swept through the room and rustled the curtains and a moment later I heard the soft thud of wood against wood as the door was carefully closed again. Then came the click of the latch as the handle was released.

Next, I heard feet tiptoeing towards me over the carpet.

For one horrible second, it occurred to me that this might just possibly be Mr Abdul Aziz creeping in upon me with a long knife in his hand, but then all at once a warm extensile body was bending over mine, and a woman's voice was whispering in my ear, '*Don't make a sound!*'

'My dearest beloved,' I said, wondering which one of them it was, 'I knew you'd . . .' Instantly her hand came over my mouth.

'*Please!*' she whispered. '*Not another word!*'

I didn't argue. My lips had many better things to do than that. So had hers.

Here I must pause. This is not like me at all – I know that. But just for once, I wish to be excused a detailed description of the great scene that followed. I have my own reasons for this and I beg you to respect them. In any case, it will do you no harm to exercise your own imagination for a change, and if you wish, I will stimulate it a little by saying simply and truthfully that of the many thousands and thousands of women I have known in my time, none has transported me to greater extremes of ecstasy than this lady of the Sinai Desert. Her dexterity was amazing. Her passion was intense. Her range was unbelievable. At every turn, she was ready with some new and intricate manoeuvre. And to cap it all, she possessed the subtlest and most recondite style I have ever encountered. She was a great artist. She was a genius.

All this, you will probably say, indicated clearly that my visitor must have been the older woman. You would be wrong. It indicated nothing. True genius is a gift of birth. It has very little to do with age; and I can assure you I had no way of knowing for certain which of them it was in the darkness of that room. I wouldn't have bet a penny on it either way. At one moment, after some particularly boisterous cadenza, I would be convinced it was the wife. *It must be the wife!* Then suddenly the whole tempo would begin to change, and the melody would become so childlike and innocent that I found myself swearing it was the daughter. *It must be the daughter!*

Maddening it was not to know the true answer. It tantalized me. It also humbled me, for, after all, a connoisseur, a supreme connoisseur, should always be able to guess the vintage without seeing the label on the bottle. But this one really had me beat. At one point, I reached for cigarettes, intending to solve the mystery in the flare of a match, but her hand was on me in a flash, and cigarettes and matches both were snatched away and flung across the room. More than once, I began to whisper the question itself into her ear, but I never got three words out before the hand shot up again and smacked itself over my mouth. Rather violently, too.

Very well, I thought. Let it be for now. Tomorrow morning, downstairs in the daylight, I shall know by the glow on the face, by the way the eyes look back into mine, and by a hundred other little tell-tale signs. I shall also know by the marks that my teeth have made on the left side of the neck, above the dress line. A rather wily move, that one, I thought, and so perfectly timed – my vicious bite was administered during the height of her passion – that she never for one moment realized the significance of the act.

It was altogether a most memorable night, and at least four hours must have gone by before she gave me a final fierce embrace, and slipped out of the room as quickly as she had come in.

The next morning I did not awaken until after ten o'clock. I got out of bed and drew open the curtains. It was another brilliant, hot, desert day. I took a leisurely bath, then dressed myself as carefully as ever. I felt relaxed and chipper. It made me very happy to think that I could still summon a woman to my room with my eyes alone, even in middle-age. And what a woman! It would be fascinating to find out which one of them she was. I would soon know.

I made my way slowly down the two flights of stairs.

'Good morning, my dear fellow, good morning!' Mr Aziz said, rising from a small desk he had been writing at in the living-room. 'Did you have a good night?'

'Excellent, thank you,' I answered, trying not to sound smug.

He came and stood close to me, smiling with his very white teeth. His shrewd little eyes rested on my face and moved over it slowly, as though searching for something.

'I have good news for you,' he said. 'They called up from B'ir Rawd Salim five minutes ago and said your new fan-belt had arrived by the mail-truck. Saleh is fitting it on now. It'll be ready in an hour. So when you've had some breakfast, I'll drive you over and you can be on your way.'

I told him how grateful I was.

'We'll be sorry to see you go,' he said. 'It's been an immense pleasure for all of us having you drop in like this, an immense pleasure.'

I had my breakfast alone in the dining-room. Afterwards, I returned to the living-room to smoke a cigarette while my host continued writing at his desk.

'Do forgive me,' he said. 'I just have a couple of things to finish here. I won't be long. I've arranged for your case to be packed and put in the car, so you have nothing to worry about. Sit down and enjoy your cigarette. The ladies ought to be down any minute now.'

The wife arrived first. She came sailing into the room looking more than ever like the dazzling Queen Semiramis of the Nile, and the first thing I noticed about her was the pale-green chiffon scarf knotted casually round her neck! Casually but carefully! So carefully that no part of the skin of the neck was visible. The woman went straight over to her husband and kissed him on the cheek. 'Good morning, my darling,' she said.

You cunning beautiful bitch, I thought.

'Good *morning*, Mr Cornelius,' she said gaily, coming over to sit in the chair opposite mine. 'Did you have a good night? I do hope you had everything you wanted.'

Never in my life have I seen such a sparkle in a woman's eyes as I saw in hers that morning, nor such a glow of pleasure in a woman's face.

'I had a very good night indeed, thank *you*,' I answered, showing her that I knew.

She smiled and lit a cigarette. I glanced over at Mr Aziz,

who was still writing away busily at the desk with his back to us. He wasn't paying the slightest attention to his wife or to me. He was, I thought, exactly like all the other poor cuckolds that I had ever created. Not one of them would believe that it could happen to him, not right under his own nose.

'Good morning, everybody!' cried the daughter, sweeping into the room. 'Good morning, Daddy! Good morning, Mummy!' She gave them each a kiss. 'Good morning, Mr Cornelius!' She was wearing a pair of pink slacks and a rust-coloured blouse, and I'll be damned if she didn't also have a scarf tied carelessly but carefully round her neck! A chiffon scarf!

'Did you have a decent night?' she asked, perching herself like a young bride on the arm of my chair, arranging herself in such a way that one of her thighs rested against my forearm. I leaned back and looked at her closely. She looked back at me and winked. She actually winked! Her face was glowing and sparkling every bit as much as her mother's, and if anything, she seemed even more pleased with herself than the older woman.

I felt pretty confused. Only one of them had a bite mark to conceal, yet both of them had covered their necks with scarves. I conceded that this might be a coincidence, but on the face of it, it looked much more like a conspiracy to me. It looked as though they were both working closely together to keep me from discovering the truth. But what an extraordinarily screwy business! And what was the purpose of it all? And in what other peculiar ways, might I ask, did they plot and plan together among themselves? Had they drawn lots or something the night before? Or did they simply take it in turns with visitors? I *must* come back again, I told myself, for another visit as soon as possible just to see what happens the next time. In fact, I might motor down specially from Jerusalem in a day or two. It would be easy, I reckoned, to get myself invited again.

'Are you ready, Mr Cornelius?' Mr Aziz said, rising from his desk.

'Quite ready,' I answered.

The ladies, sleek and smiling, led the way outside to where the big green Rolls-Royce was waiting. I kissed their hands and murmured a million thanks to each of them. Then I got into the front seat beside my host, and we drove off. The mother and daughter waved. I lowered my window and waved back. Then we were out of the garden and into the desert, following the stony yellow track as it skirted the base of Mount Maghara, with the telegraph poles marching along beside us.

During the journey, my host and I conversed pleasantly about this and that. I was at pains to be as agreeable as possible because my one object now was to get myself invited to stay at the house again. If I didn't succeed in getting *him* to ask *me*, then I should have to ask *him*. I would do it at the last moment. 'Good-bye, my dear friend,' I would say, gripping him warmly by the throat. 'May I have the pleasure of dropping in to see you again if I happen to be passing this way?' And of course he would say yes.

'Did you think I exaggerated when I told you my daughter was beautiful?' he asked me.

'You understated it,' I said. 'She's a raving beauty. I do congratulate you. But your wife is no less lovely. In fact, between the two of them they almost swept me off my feet,' I added, laughing.

'I noticed that,' he said, laughing with me. 'They're a couple of very naughty girls. They do so love to flirt with other men. But why should I mind? There's no harm in flirting.'

'None whatsoever,' I said.

'I think it's gay and fun.'

'It's charming,' I said.

In less than half an hour we had reached the main Ismailia–Jerusalem road. Mr Aziz turned the Rolls on to the black tarmac strip and headed for the filling-station at seventy miles an hour. In a few minutes we would be there. So now I tried moving a little closer to the subject of another visit, fishing gently for an invitation. 'I can't get over your house,' I said. 'I think it's simply wonderful.'

'It is nice, isn't it?'

'I suppose you're bound to get pretty lonely out there, on and off, just the three of you together?'

'It's no worse than anywhere else,' he said. 'People get lonely wherever they are. A desert, or a city – it doesn't make much difference, really. But we do have visitors, you know. You'd be surprised at the number of people who drop in from time to time. Like you, for instance. It was a great pleasure having you with us, my dear fellow.'

'I shall never forget it,' I said. 'It is a rare thing to find kindness and hospitality of that order nowadays.'

I waited for him to tell me that I must come again, but he didn't. A little silence sprang up between us, a slightly uneasy little silence. To bridge it, I said, 'I think yours is the most thoughtful paternal gesture I've ever heard of in my life.'

'Mine?'

'Yes. Building a house right out there in the back of beyond and living in it just for your daughter's sake, to protect her. I think it's remarkable.'

I saw him smile, but he kept his eyes on the road and said nothing. The filling-station and the group of huts were now in sight about a mile ahead of us. The sun was high and it was getting hot inside the car.

'Not many fathers would put themselves out to that extent,' I went on.

Again he smiled, but somewhat bashfully this time, I thought. And then he said, 'I don't deserve *quite* as much credit as you like to give me, really I don't. To be absolutely honest with you, that pretty daughter of mine isn't the only reason for my living in such splendid isolation.'

'I know that.'

'You do?'

'You told me. You said the other reason was the desert. You loved it, you said, as a sailor loves the sea.'

'So I did. And it's quite true. But there's still a third reason.'

'Oh, and what is that?'

He didn't answer me. He sat quite still with his hands on the wheel and his eyes fixed on the road ahead.

'I'm sorry,' I said. 'I shouldn't have asked the question. It's none of my business.'

'No, no, that's quite all right,' he said. 'Don't apologize.'

I stared out of the window at the desert. 'I think it's hotter than yesterday,' I said. 'It must be well over a hundred already.'

'Yes.'

I saw him shifting a little in his seat, as though trying to get comfortable, and then he said, 'I don't really see why I shouldn't tell you the truth about that house. You don't strike me as being a gossip.'

'Certainly not,' I said.

We were close to the filling-station now, and he had slowed the car down almost to walking-speed to give himself time to say what he had to say. I could see the two Arabs standing beside my Lagonda, watching us.

'That daughter,' he said at length, 'the one you met – she isn't the only daughter I have.'

'Oh, really?'

'I've got another who is five years older than she.'

'And just as beautiful, no doubt,' I said. 'Where does she live? In Beirut?'

'No, she's in the house.'

'In which house? Not the one we've just left?'

'Yes.'

'But I never saw her!'

'Well,' he said, turning suddenly to watch my face, 'maybe not.'

'But why?'

'She has leprosy.'

I jumped.

'Yes, I know,' he said, 'it's a terrible thing. She has the worst kind, too, poor girl. It's called anaesthetic leprosy. It is highly resistant, and almost impossible to cure. If only it were the nodular variety, it would be much easier. But it isn't, and there you are. So when a visitor comes to the house, she keeps to her own apartment, on the third floor . . .'

The car must have pulled into the filling-station about then because the next thing I can remember was seeing Mr Abdul Aziz sitting there looking at me with those small clever black eyes of his, and he was saying, 'But my dear fellow, you mustn't alarm yourself like this. Calm yourself down, Mr Cornelius, calm yourself down! There's absolutely nothing in the world for you to worry about. It is not a very contagious disease. You have to have the most *intimate* contact with the person in order to catch it . . .'

I got out of the car very slowly and stood in the sunshine. The Arab with the diseased face was grinning at me and saying, 'Fan-belt all fixed now. Everything fine.' I reached into my pocket for cigarettes, but my hand was shaking so violently I dropped the packet on the ground. I bent down and retrieved it. Then I got a cigarette out and managed to light it. When I looked up again, I saw the green Rolls-Royce already half a mile down the road, and going away fast.

The Last Act

First published in *Playboy* (January 1966)

Anna was in the kitchen washing a head of Boston lettuce for the family supper when the doorbell rang. The bell itself was on the wall directly above the sink, and it never failed to make her jump if it rang when she happened to be near. For this reason, neither her husband nor any of the children ever used it. It seemed to ring extra loud this time, and Anna jumped extra high.

When she opened the door, two policemen were standing outside. They looked at her out of pale waxen faces, and she looked back at them, waiting for them to say something.

She kept looking at them, but they didn't speak or move. They stood so still and so rigid that they were like two wax figures somebody had put on her doorstep as a joke. Each of them was holding his helmet in front of him in his two hands.

'What is it?' Anna asked.

They were both young, and they were wearing leather gauntlets up to their elbows. She could see their enormous motor-cycles propped up along the edge of the sidewalk behind them, and dead leaves were falling around the motor-cycles and blowing along the sidewalk and the whole of the street was brilliant in the yellow light of a clear, gusty September evening. The taller of the two policemen shifted uneasily on his feet. Then he said quietly, 'Are you Mrs Cooper, ma'am?'

'Yes, I am.'

The other said, 'Mrs Edmund J. Cooper?'

'Yes.' And then slowly it began to dawn upon her that these men, neither of whom seemed anxious to explain his presence, would not be behaving as they were unless they had some distasteful duty to perform.

'Mrs Cooper,' she heard one of them saying, and from the way he said it, as gently and softly as if he were comforting a sick child, she knew at once that he was going to tell her something terrible. A great wave of panic came over her, and she said, 'What happened?'

'We have to inform you, Mrs Cooper . . .'

The policeman paused, and the woman, watching him, felt as though her whole body were shrinking and shrinking and shrinking inside its skin.

'. . . that your husband was involved in an accident on the Hudson River Parkway at approximately five forty-five this evening, and died in the ambulance . . .'

The policeman who was speaking produced the crocodile wallet she had given Ed on their twentieth wedding anniversary, two years back, and as she reached out to take it, she found herself wondering whether it might not still be warm from having been close to her husband's chest only a short while ago.

'If there's anything we can do,' the policeman was saying, 'like calling up somebody to come over . . . some friend or relative maybe . . .'

Anna heard his voice drifting away, then fading out

altogether, and it must have been about then that she began to scream. Soon she became hysterical, and the two policemen had their hands full trying to control her until the doctor arrived some forty minutes later and injected something into her arm.

She was no better, though, when she woke up the following morning. Neither her doctor nor her children were able to reason with her in any way at all, and had she not been kept under almost constant sedation for the next few days, she would undoubtedly have taken her own life. In the brief lucid periods between drug-takings, she acted as though she were demented, calling out her husband's name and telling him that she was coming to join him as soon as she possibly could. It was terrible to listen to her. But in defence of her behaviour, it should be said at once that this was no ordinary husband she had lost.

Anna Greenwood had married Ed Cooper when they were both eighteen, and over the time they were together, they grew to be closer and more dependent upon each other than it is possible to describe in words. Every year that went by, their love became more intense and overwhelming, and towards the end, it had reached such a ridiculous peak that it was almost impossible for them to endure the daily separation caused by Ed's departure for the office in the mornings. When he returned at night he would rush through the house to seek her out, and she, who had heard the noise of the front door slamming, would drop everything and rush simultaneously in his direction, meeting him head on, recklessly, at full speed, perhaps halfway up the stairs, or on the landing, or between the kitchen and the hall; and as they came together, he would take her in his arms and hug her and kiss her for minutes on end as though she were yesterday's bride. It was wonderful. It was so utterly unbelievably wonderful that one is very nearly able to understand why she should have had no desire and no heart to continue living in a world where her husband did not exist any more.

Her three children, Angela (twenty), Mary (nineteen) and Billy (seventeen and a half), stayed around her constantly right from the start of the catastrophe. They adored their mother, and they certainly had no intention of letting her commit suicide if they could help it. They worked hard and with loving desperation to convince her that life could still be worth living, and it was due entirely to them that she managed in the end to come out of the nightmare and climb back slowly into the ordinary world.

Four months after the disaster, she was pronounced 'moderately safe' by the doctors, and she was able to return, albeit rather listlessly, to the old routine of running the house and doing the shopping and cooking the meals for her grown-up children.

But then what happened?

Before the snows of that winter had melted away, Angela married a young man from Rhode Island and went off to live in the suburbs of Providence.

A few months later, Mary married a fair-haired giant from a town called Slayton, in Minnesota, and away she flew for ever and ever and ever. And although Anna's heart was now beginning to break all over again into tiny pieces, she was proud to think that neither of the two girls had the slightest inkling of what was happening to her. ('Oh, Mummy, isn't it wonderful!' 'Yes, my darling, I think it's the most beautiful wedding there's ever been! I'm even more excited than you are!' etc. etc.)

And then, to put the lid on everything, her beloved Billy, who had just turned eighteen, went off to begin his first year at Yale.

So all at once, Anna found herself living in a completely empty house.

It is an awful feeling, after twenty-three years of boisterous, busy, magical family life, to come down alone to breakfast in the mornings, to sit there in silence with a cup of coffee and a piece of toast, and to wonder what you are going to do with the day that lies ahead. The room you are sitting in, which has heard so much laughter, and seen so many birthdays, so many Christmas trees, so many presents being opened, is quiet now and feels curiously cold. The air is heated and the temperature itself is normal, but the place still makes you shiver. The clock has stopped because you were never the one who wound it in the first place. A chair stands crooked on its legs, and you sit staring at it, wondering why you hadn't noticed it before. And when you glance up again, you have a sudden panicky feeling that all the four walls of the room have begun creeping in upon you very very slowly when you weren't looking.

In the beginning, she would carry her coffee cup over to the telephone and start calling up friends. But all her friends had husbands and children, and although they were always as nice and warm and cheerful as they could possibly be, they simply could not spare the time to sit and chat with a desolate lady from across the way first thing in the morning. So then she started calling up her married daughters instead.

They, also, were sweet and kind to her at all times, but Anna detected, very soon, a subtle change in their attitudes towards her. She was no longer number one in their lives. They had husbands now, and were concentrating everything upon them. Gently but firmly, they were moving their mother into the background. It was quite a shock. But she knew they were right. They were absolutely right. She was no longer entitled to impinge upon their lives or to make them feel guilty for neglecting her.

She saw Dr Jacobs regularly, but he wasn't really any help. He tried to get her to talk and she did her best, and sometimes he made little speeches to her full of oblique remarks about sex and sublimation. Anna never properly understood what he was driving at, but the burden of his song appeared to be that she should get herself another man.

She took to wandering around the house and fingering things that used to belong to Ed. She would pick up one of his shoes and put her hand into it and feel the little dents that the ball of his foot and his toes had made upon the sole. She found a sock with a hole in it, and the pleasure it gave her to darn that sock was indescribable. Occasionally, she took out a shirt, a tie and a suit, and laid them on the bed, all ready for him to wear, and once, one rainy Sunday morning, she made an Irish stew . . .

It was hopeless to go on.

So how many pills would she need to make absolutely sure of it this time? She went upstairs to her secret store and counted them. There were only nine. Was that enough? She doubted that it was. Oh, hell. The one thing she was not prepared to face all over again was failure – the rush to the hospital, the stomach-pump, the seventh floor of the Payne Whitney Pavilion, the psychiatrists, the humiliation, the misery of it all . . .

In that case, it would have to be the razor-blade. But the trouble with the razor-blade was that it had to be done properly. Many people failed miserably when they tried to use the razor-blade on the wrist. In fact, nearly all of them failed. They didn't cut deep enough. There was a big artery down there somewhere that simply had to be reached. Veins were no good. Veins made plenty of mess, but they never quite managed to do the trick. Then again, the razor-blade was not an easy thing to hold, not if one had to make a firm incision, pressing it right home all the way, deep deep down. But *she* wouldn't fail. The ones who failed were the ones who actually *wanted* to fail. She wanted to succeed.

She went to the cupboard in the bathroom, searching for blades. There weren't any. Ed's razor was still there, and so was hers. But there was no blade in either of them, and no little packet lying alongside. That was understandable. Such things had been removed from the house on an earlier occasion. But there was no problem. Anyone could buy a packet of razor-blades.

She returned to the kitchen and took the calendar down

from the wall. She chose 23 September, which was Ed's birthday, and wrote r-b (for razor-blades) against the date. She did this on 9 September, which gave her exactly two weeks' grace to put her affairs in order. There was much to be done – old bills to be paid, a new will to be written, the house to be tidied up, Billy's college fees to be taken care of for the next four years, letters to the children, to her own parents, to Ed's mother, and so on and so forth.

Yet, busy as she was, she found that those two weeks, those fourteen long days, were going far too slowly for her liking. She wanted to use the blade, and eagerly every morning she counted the days that were left. She was like a child counting the days before Christmas. For wherever it was that Ed Cooper had gone when he died, even if it were only to the grave, she was impatient to join him.

It was in the middle of this two-week period that her friend Elizabeth Paoletti came calling on her at eight thirty one morning. Anna was making coffee in the kitchen at the time, and she jumped when the bell rang and jumped again when it gave a second long blast.

Liz came sweeping in through the front door, talking non-stop as usual. 'Anna, my darling woman, I need your help! Everyone's down with flu at the office. You've *got* to come! Don't argue with me! I know you can type and I know you haven't got a damn thing in the world to do all day except mope. Just grab your hat and purse and let's get going. Hurry up, girl, hurry up! I'm late as it is!'

Anna said, 'Go away, Liz. Leave me alone.'

'The cab is waiting,' Liz said.

'Please,' Anna said, 'don't try to bully me now. I'm not coming.'

'You are coming,' Liz said. 'Pull yourself together. Your days of glorious martyrdom are over.'

Anna continued to resist, but Liz wore her down, and in the end she agreed to go along just for a few hours.

Elizabeth Paoletti was in charge of an adoption society, one of the best in the city. Nine of the staff were down with flu. Only two were left, excluding herself. 'You don't know a thing about the work,' she said in the cab, 'but you're just going to have to help us all you can . . .'

The office was bedlam. The telephones alone nearly drove Anna mad. She kept running from one cubicle to the next, taking messages that she did not understand. And there were girls in the waiting-room, young girls with ashen stony faces, and it became part of her duty to type their answers on an official form.

'The father's name?'

'Don't know.'

'You've no idea?'

'What's the father's name got to do with it?'

'My dear, if the father is known, then his consent has to be obtained as well as yours before the child can be offered for adoption.'

'You're quite sure about that?'

'Jesus, I told you, didn't I?'

At lunchtime, somebody brought her a sandwich, but there was no time to eat it. At nine o'clock that night, exhausted and famished and considerably shaken by some of the knowledge she had acquired, Anna staggered home, took a stiff drink, fried up some eggs and bacon, and went to bed.

'I'll call for you at eight o'clock tomorrow morning,' Liz had said. 'And for God's sake be ready.' Anna was ready. And from then on she was hooked.

It was as simple as that.

All she'd needed right from the beginning was a good hard job of work to do, and plenty of problems to solve – other people's problems instead of her own.

The work was arduous and often quite shattering emotionally, but Anna was absorbed by every moment of it, and within about – we are skipping right forward now – within about a year and a half, she began to feel moderately happy once again. She was finding it more and more difficult to picture her husband vividly, to see him precisely as he was when he ran up the stairs to meet her, or when he sat across from her at supper in the evenings. The exact sound of his voice was becoming less easy to recall, and even the face itself, unless she glanced at a photograph, was no longer sharply etched in the memory. She still thought about him constantly, but she discovered that she could do so now without bursting into tears, and when she looked back on the way she had behaved a while ago, she felt slightly embarrassed. She started taking a mild interest in her clothes and in her hair, she returned to using lipstick and to shaving the hair from her legs. She enjoyed her food, and when people smiled at her, she smiled right back at them and meant it. In other words, she was back in the swim once again. She was pleased to be alive.

It was at this point that Anna had to go down to Dallas on office business.

Liz's office did not normally operate beyond state lines, but in this instance, a couple who had adopted a baby through the agency had subsequently moved away from New York and gone to live in Texas. Now, five months after the move, the wife had written to say that she no longer wanted to keep the child. Her husband, she announced, had died of a heart attack soon after they'd arrived in Texas. She herself had remarried almost at once, and her new husband 'found it impossible to adjust to an adopted baby . . .'

Now this was a serious situation, and quite apart from the welfare of the child itself, there were all manner of legal obligations involved.

Anna flew down to Dallas in a plane that left New York very early, and she arrived before breakfast. After checking in at her hotel, she spent the next eight hours with the persons concerned in the affair, and by the time she had done all that could be done that day, it was around four thirty in the afternoon and she was utterly exhausted. She took a cab back to the hotel, and went up to her room. She called Liz on the phone to report the situation, then she undressed and soaked herself for a long time in a warm bath. Afterwards, she wrapped up in a towel and lay on the bed, smoking a cigarette.

Her efforts on behalf of the child had so far come to nothing. There had been two lawyers there who had treated her with absolute contempt. How she hated them. She detested their arrogance and their softly spoken hints that nothing she might do would make the slightest difference to their client. One of them kept his feet up on the table all the way through the discussion, and both of them had rolls of fat on their bellies, and the fat spilled out into their shirts like liquid and hung in huge folds over their belted trouser-tops.

Anna had visited Texas many times before in her life, but until now she had never gone there alone. Her visits had always been with Ed, keeping him company on business trips; and during those trips, he and she had often spoken about the Texans in general and about how difficult it was to like them. One could ignore their coarseness and their vulgarity. It wasn't that. But there was, it seemed, a quality of ruthlessness still surviving among these people, something quite brutal, harsh, inexorable, that it was impossible to forgive. They had no bowels of compassion, no pity, no tenderness. The only so-called virtue they possessed – and this they paraded ostentatiously and endlessly to strangers – was a kind of professional benevolence. It was plastered all over them. Their voices, their smiles, were rich and syrupy with it. But it left Anna cold. It left her quite, quite cold inside.

'Why do they love acting so tough?' she used to ask.

'Because they're children,' Ed would answer. 'They're dangerous children who go about trying to imitate their grandfathers. Their grandfathers *were* pioneers. These people aren't.'

It seemed that they lived, these present-day Texans, by a sort of egotistic will, push and be pushed. Everybody was pushing. Everybody was being pushed. And it was all very fine for a stranger in their midst to step aside and announce firmly, 'I will *not* push, and I will *not* be pushed.' That was impossible. It was especially impossible in Dallas. Of all the cities in the state, Dallas was the one that had always disturbed Anna the most. It was such a godless city, she thought, such a rapacious, gripped, iron, godless city. It was a place that had run amok with its money, and no amount of gloss and phony culture and syrupy talk could hide the fact that the great golden fruit was rotten inside.

Anna lay on the bed with her bath towel around her. She was alone in Dallas this time. There was no Ed with her now to envelop her in his incredible strength and love; and perhaps it was because of this that she began, all of a sudden, to feel slightly uneasy. She lit a second cigarette and waited for the uneasiness to pass. It didn't pass; it got worse. A hard little knot of fear was gathering itself in the top of her stomach, and there it stayed, growing bigger every minute. It was an unpleasant feeling, the kind one might experience if one were alone in the house at night and heard, or thought one heard, a footstep in the next room.

In this place there were a million footsteps, and she could hear them all.

She got off the bed and went over to the window, still wrapped in her towel. Her room was on the twenty-second floor, and the window was open. The great city lay pale and milky-yellow in the evening sunshine. The street below was solid with automobiles. The sidewalk was filled with people. Everybody was hustling home from work, pushing and being pushed. She felt the need of a friend. She wanted very badly to have someone to talk to at this moment. She would have liked a house to go to, a house with a family – a wife and husband and children and rooms full of toys, and the husband and wife would fling their arms around her at the front door and cry out, 'Anna! How marvellous to see you! How long can you stay? A week, a month, a year?'

All of a sudden, as so often happens in situations like this, her memory went *click*, and she said aloud, 'Conrad Kreuger! Good heavens above! *He* lives in Dallas . . . at least he used to . . .'

She hadn't seen Conrad since they were classmates in high school, in New York. They were both about seventeen then, and Conrad had been her beau, her love, her everything. For over a year they had gone around together, and each of them had sworn eternal loyalty to the other, with marriage in the near future. Then suddenly Ed Cooper had flashed into her life, and that, of course, had been the end of the romance with Conrad. But Conrad did not seem to have taken the break too badly. It certainly couldn't have *shattered* him, because not more than a month or two later he had started going strong with another girl in the class . . .

Now what was *her* name?

A big handsome bosomy girl she was, with flaming red hair and a peculiar name, a very old-fashioned name. What was it? Arabella? No, not Arabella. Ara-something, though. Araminty? Yes! Araminty it was! And what is more, within a year or so, Conrad Kreuger had married

Araminty and had carried her back with him to Dallas, the place of his birth.

Anna went over to the bedside table and picked up the telephone directory.

Kreuger, Conrad P., MD.

That was Conrad all right. He had always said he was going to be a doctor. The book gave an office number and a residence number.

Should she phone him?

Why not?

She glanced at her watch. It was five twenty. She lifted the receiver and gave the number of his office.

'Doctor Kreuger's surgery,' a girl's voice answered.

'Hello,' Anna said. 'Is Doctor Kreuger there?'

'The doctor is busy right now. May I ask who's calling?'

'Will you please tell him that Anna Greenwood telephoned him.'

'Who?'

'Anna Greenwood.'

'Yes, Miss Greenwood. Did you wish for an appointment?'

'No, thank you.'

'Is there something I can do for you?'

Anna gave the name of her hotel, and asked her to pass it on to Dr Kreuger.

'I'll be very glad to,' the secretary said. 'Good-bye, Miss Greenwood.'

'Good-bye,' Anna said. She wondered whether Dr Conrad P. Kreuger would remember her name after all these years. She believed he would. She lay back again on the bed and began trying to recall what Conrad himself used to look like. Extraordinarily handsome, that he was. Tall ... lean ... big-shouldered ... with almost pure-black hair ... and a marvellous face ... a strong carved face like one of those Greek heroes, Perseus or Ulysses. Above all, though, he had been a very gentle boy, a serious, decent, quiet, gentle boy. He had never kissed her much – only when he said good-bye in the evenings. And he'd never gone in for necking, as all the others had. When he took her home from the movies on Saturday nights, he used to park his old Buick outside her house and sit there in the car beside her, just talking and talking about the future, his future and hers, and how he was going to go back to Dallas to become a famous doctor. His refusal to indulge in necking and all the nonsense that went with it had impressed her no end. He respects me, she used to say. He loves me. And she was probably right. In any event, he had been a nice man, a nice good man. And had it not been for the fact that Ed Cooper was a super-nice, super-good man, she was sure she would have married Conrad Kreuger.

The telephone rang. Anna lifted the receiver. 'Yes,' she said. 'Hello.'

'Anna Greenwood?'

'Conrad Kreuger!'

'My dear Anna! What a fantastic surprise. Good gracious me. After all these years.'

'It's a long time, isn't it.'

'It's a lifetime. Your voice sounds just the same.'

'So does yours.'

'What brings you to our fair city? Are you staying long?'

'No, I have to go back tomorrow. I hope you didn't mind my calling you.'

'Hell, no, Anna. I'm delighted. Are you all right?'

'Yes, I'm fine. I'm fine now. I had a bad time of it for a bit after Ed died . . .'

'What!'

'He was killed in an automobile two and a half years ago.'

'Oh gee, Anna, I *am* sorry. How terrible. I . . . I don't know what to say . . .'

'Don't say anything.'

'You're okay now?'

'I'm fine. Working like a slave.'

'That's the girl . . .'

'How's . . . how's Araminty?'

'Oh, she's fine.'

'Any children?'

'One,' he said. 'A boy. How about you?'

'I have three, two girls and a boy.'

'Well, well, what d'you know! Now listen, Anna . . .'

'I'm listening.'

'Why don't I run over to the hotel and buy you a drink? I'd like to do that. I'll bet you haven't changed one iota.'

'I look old, Conrad.'

'You're lying.'

'I feel old, too.'

'You want a good doctor?'

'Yes. I mean no. Of course I don't. I don't want any more doctors. All I need is . . . well . . .'

'Yes?'

'This place worries me, Conrad. I guess I need a friend. That's all I need.'

'You've got one. I have just one more patient to see, and then I'm free. I'll meet you down in the bar, the something room, I've forgotten what it's called, at six, in about half an hour. Will that suit you?'

'Yes,' she said. 'Of course. And . . . thank you, Conrad.' She replaced the receiver, then got up from the bed, and began to dress.

She felt mildly flustered. Not since Ed's death had she been out and had a drink alone with a man. Dr Jacobs would be pleased when she told him about it on her return. He wouldn't congratulate her madly, but he would certainly be pleased. He'd say it was a step in the right direction, a beginning. She still went to him regularly, and now that she had gotten so much better, his oblique references had become far less oblique and he had more than once told her that her depressions and suicidal tendencies would never completely disappear until she had actually and physically 'replaced' Ed with another man.

'But it is impossible to replace a person one has loved to distraction,' Anna had said to him the last time he had brought up the subject. 'Heavens above, doctor, when Mrs Crummlin-Brown's parakeet died last month, her *parakeet*, mind you, not her husband, she was so shook up about it, she swore she'd never have another bird again!'

'Mrs Cooper,' Dr Jacobs had said, 'one doesn't normally have sexual intercourse with a parakeet.'

'Well . . . no . . .'

'That's why it doesn't have to be replaced. But when a husband dies, and the surviving wife is still an active and a healthy woman, she will invariably get a replacement within three years if she possibly can. And vice versa.'

Sex. It was about the only thing that sort of doctor ever thought about. He had sex on the brain.

By the time Anna had dressed and taken the elevator downstairs, it was ten minutes after six. The moment she walked into the bar, a man stood up from one of the tables. It was Conrad. He must have been watching the door. He came across the floor to meet her. He was smiling nervously. Anna was smiling, too. One always does.

'Well, well,' he said. 'Well well well,' and she, expecting the usual peck on the cheek, inclined her face upwards towards his own, still smiling. But she had forgotten how formal Conrad was. He simply took her hand in his and shook it – once. 'This *is* a surprise,' he said. 'Come and sit down.'

The room was the same as any other hotel drinking-room. It was lit by dim lights, and filled with many small tables. There was a saucer of peanuts on each table, and there were leather bench-seats all around the walls. The waiters were rigged out in white jackets and maroon pants. Conrad led her to a corner table, and they sat down facing each other. A waiter was standing over them at once.

'What will you have?' Conrad asked.

'Could I have a martini?'

'Of course. Vodka?'

'No, gin, please.'

'One gin martini,' he said to the waiter. 'No. Make it

two. I've never been much of a drinker, Anna, as you probably remember, but I think this calls for a celebration.'

The waiter went away. Conrad leaned back in his chair and studied her carefully. 'You look pretty good,' he said.

'You look pretty good yourself, Conrad,' she told him. And so he did. It was astonishing how little he had aged in twenty-five years. He was just as lean and handsome as he'd ever been – in fact, more so. His black hair was still black, his eye was clear, and he looked altogether like a man who was no more than thirty years old.

'You *are* older than me, aren't you?' he said.

'What sort of a question is that?' she said, laughing. 'Yes, Conrad, I am exactly one year older than you. I'm forty-two.'

'I thought you were.' He was still studying her with the utmost care, his eyes travelling all over her face and neck and shoulders. Anna felt herself blushing.

'Are you an enormously successful doctor?' she asked. 'Are you the best in town?'

He cocked his head over to one side, right over, so that the ear almost touched the top of the shoulder. It was a mannerism that Anna had always liked. 'Successful?' he said. 'Any doctor can be successful these days in a big city – financially, I mean. But whether or not I am absolutely first rate at my job is another matter. I only hope and pray that I am.'

The drinks arrived and Conrad raised his glass and said, 'Welcome to Dallas, Anna. I'm so pleased you called me up. It's good to see you again.'

'It's good to see you, too, Conrad,' she said, speaking the truth.

He looked at her glass. She had taken a huge first gulp, and the glass was now half empty. 'You prefer gin to vodka?' he asked.

'I do,' she said, 'yes.'

'You ought to change over.'

'Why?'

'Gin is not good for females.'

'It's not?'

'It's very bad for them.'

'I'm sure it's just as bad for males,' she said.

'Actually, no. It isn't nearly so bad for males as it is for females.'

'Why is it bad for females?'

'It just is,' he said. 'It's the way they're built. What kind of work are you engaged in, Anna? And what brought you all the way down to Dallas? Tell me about you.'

'Why is gin bad for females?' she said, smiling at him.

He smiled back at her and shook his head, but he didn't answer.

'Go on,' she said.

'No, let's drop it.'

'You can't leave me up in the air like this,' she said. 'It's not fair.'

After a pause, he said, 'Well, if you really want to know, gin contains a certain amount of the oil which is squeezed out of juniper berries. They use it for flavouring.'

'What does it do?'

'Plenty.'

'Yes, but what?'

'Horrible things.'

'Conrad, don't be shy. I'm a big girl now.'

He was still the same old Conrad, she thought, still as diffident, as scrupulous, as shy as ever. For that she liked him. 'If this drink is really doing horrible things to me,' she said, 'then it is unkind of you not to tell me what those things are.'

Gently, he pinched the lobe of his left ear with the thumb and forefinger of his right hand. Then he said, 'Well, the truth of the matter is, Anna, oil of juniper has a direct inflammatory effect upon the uterus.'

'Now come on!'

'I'm not joking.'

'Mother's ruin,' Anna said. 'It's an old wives' tale.'

'I'm afraid not.'

'But you're talking about women who are pregnant.'

'I'm talking about all women, Anna.' He had stopped smiling now, and he was speaking quite seriously. He seemed to be concerned about her welfare.

'What do you specialize in?' she asked him. 'What kind of medicine? You haven't told me that.'

'Gynaecology and obstetrics.'

'Ah-ha!'

'Have you been drinking gin for many years?' he asked.

'Oh, about twenty,' Anna said.

'Heavily?'

'For heaven's sake, Conrad, stop worrying about my insides. I'd like another martini, please.'

'Of course.'

He called the waiter and said, 'One vodka martini.'

'No,' Anna said, 'gin.'

He sighed and shook his head and said, 'Nobody listens to her doctor these days.'

'You're not my doctor.'

'No,' he said. 'I'm your friend.'

'Let's talk about your wife,' Anna said. 'Is she still as beautiful as ever?'

He waited a few moments, then he said, 'Actually, we're divorced.'

'Oh, no!'

'Our marriage lasted for the grand total of two years. It was hard work to keep it going even that long.'

For some reason, Anna was profoundly shocked. 'But she was such a beautiful girl,' she said. 'What happened?'

'Everything happened, everything you could possibly think of that was bad.'

'And the child?'

'She got him. They always do.' He sounded very bitter. 'She took him back to New York. He comes to see me once a year, in the summer. He's twenty years old now. He's at Princeton.'

'Is he a fine boy?'

'He's a wonderful boy,' Conrad said. 'But I hardly know him. It isn't much fun.'

'And you never married again?'

'No, never. But that's enough about me. Let's talk about you.'

Slowly, gently, he began to draw her out on the subject of her health and the bad times she had gone through after Ed's death. She found she didn't mind talking to him about it, and she told him more or less the whole story.

'But what makes your doctor think you're not completely cured?' he said. 'You don't look very suicidal to me.'

'I don't think I am. Except that sometimes, not often, mind you, but just occasionally, when I get depressed, I have the feeling that it wouldn't take such a hell of a big push to send me over the edge.'

'In what way?'

'I kind of start edging towards the bathroom cupboard.'

'What do you have in the bathroom cupboard?'

'Nothing very much. Just the ordinary equipment a girl has for shaving her legs.'

'I see.' Conrad studied her face for a few moments, then he said, 'Is that how you were feeling just now when you called me?'

'Not quite. But I'd been thinking about Ed. And that's always a bit dangerous.'

'I'm glad you called.'

'So am I,' she said.

Anna was getting to the end of her second martini. Conrad changed the subject and began talking about his practice. She was watching him rather than listening to him. He was so damned handsome it was impossible not to watch him. She put a cigarette between her lips, then offered the pack to Conrad.

'No thanks,' he said. 'I don't.' He picked up a book of matches from the table and gave her a light, then he blew out the match and said, 'Are those cigarettes mentholated?'

'Yes, they are.'

She took a deep drag, and blew the smoke slowly up into the air. 'Now go ahead and tell me that they're going to shrivel up my entire reproductive system,' she said.

He laughed and shook his head.

'Then why did you ask?'

'Just curious, that's all.'

'You're lying. I can tell it from your face. You were about to give me the figures for the incidence of lung cancer in heavy smokers.'

'Lung cancer has nothing to do with menthol, Anna,' he said, and he smiled and took a tiny sip of his original martini, which he had so far hardly touched. He set the glass back carefully on the table. 'You still haven't told me what work you are doing,' he went on, 'or why you came to Dallas.'

'Tell me about menthol first. If it's even half as bad as the juice of the juniper berry, I think I ought to know about it quick.'

He laughed and shook his head.

'Please!'

'No, ma'am.'

'Conrad, you simply cannot start things up like this and then drop them. It's the second time in five minutes.'

'I don't want to be a medical bore,' he said.

'You're not being a bore. These things are fascinating. Come on! Tell! Don't be mean.'

It was pleasant to be sitting there feeling moderately high on two big martinis, and making easy talk with this graceful man, this quiet, comfortable, graceful person. He was not being coy. Far from it. He was simply being his normal scrupulous self.

189

'Is it something shocking?' she asked.

'No. You couldn't call it that.'

'Then go ahead.'

He picked up the packet of cigarettes still lying in front of her, and studied the label. 'The point is this,' he said. 'If you inhale menthol, you absorb it into the bloodstream. And that isn't good, Anna. It does things to you. It has certain very definite effects upon the central nervous system. Doctors still prescribe it occasionally.'

'I know that,' she said. 'Nose-drops and inhalations.'

'That's one of its minor uses. Do you know the other?'

'You rub it on the chest when you have a cold.'

'You can if you like, but it wouldn't help.'

'You put it in ointment and it heals cracked lips.'

'That's camphor.'

'So it is.'

He waited for her to have another guess.

'Go ahead and tell me,' she said.

'It may surprise you a bit.'

'I'm ready to be surprised.'

'Menthol,' Conrad said, 'is a well-known anti-aphrodisiac.'

'A what?'

'It suppresses sexual desire.'

'Conrad, you're making these things up.'

'I swear to you I'm not.'

'Who uses it?'

'Very few people nowadays. It has too strong a flavour. Saltpetre is much better.'

'Ah yes. I know about saltpetre.'

'What do you know about saltpetre?'

'They give it to prisoners,' Anna said. 'They sprinkle it on their cornflakes every morning to keep them quiet.'

'They also use it in cigarettes,' Conrad said.

'You mean prisoners' cigarettes?'

'I mean *all* cigarettes.'

'That's nonsense.'

'Is it?'

'Of course it is.'

'Why do you say that?'

'Nobody would stand for it,' she said.

'They stand for cancer.'

'That's quite different, Conrad. How do you know they put saltpetre in cigarettes?'

'Have you never wondered,' he said, 'what makes a cigarette go on burning when you lay it in the ashtray? Tobacco doesn't burn of its own accord. Any pipe smoker will tell you that.'

'They use special chemicals,' she said.

'Exactly; they use saltpetre.'

'Does saltpetre burn?'

'Sure it burns. It used to be one of the prime ingredients of old-fashioned gunpowder. Fuses, too. It makes very good fuses. That cigarette of yours is a first-rate slow-burning fuse, is it not?'

Anna looked at her cigarette. Though she hadn't drawn on it for a couple of minutes, it was still smouldering away and the smoke was curling upwards from the tip in a slim blue-grey spiral.

'So this has menthol in it *and* saltpetre?' she said.

'Absolutely.'

'And they're *both* anti-aphrodisiacs?'

'Yes. You're getting a double dose.'

'It's ridiculous, Conrad. It's too little to make any difference.'

He smiled but didn't answer this.

'There's not enough there to inhibit a cockroach,' she said.

'That's what you think, Anna. How many do you smoke a day?'

'About thirty.'

'Well,' he said, 'I guess it's none of my business.' He paused, and then he added, 'But you and I would be a lot better off today if it was.'

'Was what?'

'My business.'

'Conrad, what *do* you mean?'

'I'm simply saying that if you, once upon a time, hadn't suddenly decided to drop me, none of this misery would have happened to either of us. We'd still be happily married to each other.'

His face had suddenly taken on a queer sharp look.

'Drop you?'

'It was quite a shock, Anna.'

'Oh dear,' she said, 'but everybody drops everybody else at that age, don't they?'

'I wouldn't know,' Conrad said.

'You're not cross with me still, are you, for doing that?'

'Cross!' he said. 'Good God, Anna! Cross is what children get when they lose a toy! I lost a wife!'

She stared at him, speechless.

'Tell me,' he went on, 'didn't you have any idea how I felt at the time?'

'But, Conrad, we were so *young*.'

'It destroyed me, Anna. It just about destroyed me.'

'But how . . .'

'How what?'

'How, if it meant so much, could you turn right around and get engaged to somebody else a few weeks later?'

'Have you never heard of the rebound?' he asked.

She nodded, gazing at him in dismay.

'I was wildly in love with you, Anna.'

She didn't answer.

'I'm sorry,' he said. 'That was a silly outburst. Please forgive me.'

There was a long silence.

Conrad was leaning back in his chair, studying her from a distance. She took another cigarette from the pack, and lit it. Then she blew out the match and placed it carefully in the ashtray. When she glanced up again, he was still watching her. There was an intent, far look in his eyes.

'What are you thinking about?' she asked.

He didn't answer.

'Conrad,' she said, 'do you still hate me for doing what I did?'

'Hate you?'

'Yes, hate me. I have a queer feeling that you do. I'm sure you do, even after all these years.'

'Anna,' he said.

'Yes, Conrad?'

He hitched his chair closer to the table, and leaned forward. 'Did it ever cross your mind . . .'

He stopped.

She waited.

He was looking so intensely earnest all of a sudden that she leaned forward herself.

'Did what cross my mind?' she asked.

'The fact that you and I . . . that both of us . . . have a bit of unfinished business.'

She stared at him.

He looked back at her, his eyes as bright as two stars. 'Don't be shocked,' he said, 'please.'

'Shocked?'

'You look as though I'd just asked you to jump out of the window with me.'

The room was full of people now, and it was very noisy. It was like being at a cocktail party. You had to shout to be heard.

Conrad's eyes waited on her, impatient, eager.

'I'd like another martini,' she said.

'Must you?'

'Yes,' she said, 'I must.'

In her whole life, she had been made love to by only one man – her husband, Ed.

And it had always been wonderful.

Three thousand times?

She thought more. Probably a good deal more. Who counts?

Assuming, though, for the sake of argument, that the

exact figure (for there has to be an exact figure) was three thousand, six hundred and eighty . . .

. . . and knowing that every single time it happened it was an act of pure, passionate, authentic love-making between the same man and the same woman . . .

. . . then how in heaven's name could an entirely new man, an unloved stranger, hope to come in suddenly on the three thousand, six hundred and eighty-*first* time and be even halfway acceptable?

He'd be a trespasser.

All the memories would come rushing back. She would be lying there suffocated by memories.

She had raised this very point with Dr Jacobs during one of her sessions a few months back, and old Jacobs had said, 'There will be no nonsense about memories, my dear Mrs Cooper. I wish you would forget that. Only the present will exist.'

'But how do I get there?' she had said. 'How can I summon up enough nerve suddenly to go upstairs to a bedroom and take off my clothes in front of a new man, a stranger, in cold blood? . . .'

'Cold blood!' he had cried. 'Good God, woman, it'll be boiling hot!' And later he had said, 'Do at any rate try to believe me, Mrs Cooper, when I tell you that any woman who has been deprived of sexual congress after more than twenty years of practice – of uncommonly frequent practice in your case, if I understand you correctly – any woman in those circumstances is going to suffer continually from severe psychological disturbances until the routine is re-established. You are feeling a lot better, I know that, but it is my duty to inform you that you are by no means back to normal . . .'

To Conrad, Anna said, 'This isn't by any chance a therapeutic suggestion, is it?'

'A *what*?'

'A therapeutic suggestion.'

'What in the world do you mean?'

'It sounds exactly like a plot hatched up by my Dr Jacobs.'

'Look,' he said, and now he leaned right across the table and touched her left hand with the tip of one finger. 'When I knew you before, I was too damn young and nervous to make that sort of a proposition, much as I wanted to. I didn't think there was any particular hurry then, anyway. I figured we had a whole lifetime before us. I wasn't to know you were going to drop me.'

Her martini arrived. Anna picked it up and began to drink it fast. She knew exactly what it was going to do to her. It was going to make her float. A third martini always did that. Give her a third martini and within seconds her body would become completely weightless and she would go floating around the room like a wisp of hydrogen gas.

She sat there holding the glass with both hands as though it were a sacrament. She took another gulp. There was not much of it left now. Over the rim of her glass she could see Conrad watching her with disapproval as she drank. She smiled at him radiantly.

'You're not against the use of anaesthetics when you operate, are you?' she asked.

'Please, Anna, don't talk like that.'

'I am beginning to float,' she said.

'So I see,' he answered. 'Why don't you stop there?'

'What did you say?'

'I said, why don't you stop?'

'Do you want me to tell you why?'

'No,' he said. He made a little forward movement with his hands as though he were going to take her glass away from her, so she quickly put it to her lips and tipped it high, holding it there for a few seconds to allow the last drop to run out. When she looked at Conrad again, he was placing a ten-dollar bill on the waiter's tray, and the waiter was saying, 'Thank *you*, sir. Thank you indeed,' and the next thing she knew she was floating out of the room and across the lobby of the hotel with Conrad's hand cupped lightly under one of her elbows, steering her towards the elevators. They floated up to the twenty-second floor, and then along the corridor to the door of her bedroom. She fished the key out of her purse and unlocked the door and floated inside. Conrad followed, closing the door behind him. Then very suddenly, he grabbed hold of her and folded her up in his enormous arms and started kissing her with great gusto.

She let him do it.

He kissed her all over her mouth and cheeks and neck, taking deep breaths in between the kisses. She kept her eyes open, watching him in a queer detached sort of way, and the view she got reminded her vaguely of the blurry close-up view of a dentist's face when he is working on an upper back tooth.

Then all of a sudden, Conrad put his tongue into one of her ears. The effect of this upon her was electric. It was as though a live two-hundred-volt plug had been pushed into an empty socket, and all the lights came on and the bones began to melt and the hot molten sap went running down into her limbs and she exploded into a frenzy. It was the kind of marvellous, wanton, reckless, flaming frenzy that Ed used to provoke in her so very often in the olden days by just a touch of the hand here and there. She flung her arms around Conrad's neck and started kissing him back with far more gusto than he had ever kissed her, and although he looked at first as though he thought she were going to swallow him alive, he soon recovered his balance.

Anna hadn't the faintest idea how long they stood there embracing and kissing with such violence, but it must have been for quite a while. She felt such happiness, such . . . such *confidence* again at last, such sudden overwhelming confidence in herself that she wanted to tear off her clothes and do a wild dance for Conrad in the middle of the room. But she did no such foolish thing. Instead, she simply floated away to the edge of the bed and sat down to catch her breath. Conrad quickly sat down beside her. She leaned her head against his chest and sat there glowing all over while he gently stroked her hair. Then she undid one button of his shirt and slid her hand inside and laid it against his chest. Through the ribs, she could feel the beating of his heart.

'What do I see here?' Conrad said.

'What do you see where, my darling?'

'On your scalp. You want to watch this, Anna.'

'You watch it for me, dearest.'

'Seriously,' he said, 'you know what this looks like? It looks like a tiny touch of androgenic alopecia.'

'Good.'

'No, it is not good. It's actually an inflammation of the hair follicles, and it causes baldness. It's quite common on women in their later years.'

'Oh, shut up, Conrad,' she said, kissing him on the side of the neck. 'I have the most gorgeous hair.'

She sat up and pulled off his jacket. Then she undid his tie and threw it across the room.

'There's a little hook on the back of my dress,' she said. 'Undo it, please.'

Conrad unhooked the hook, then unzipped the zipper and helped her to get out of the dress. She had on a rather nice pale-blue slip. Conrad was wearing an ordinary white shirt, as doctors do, but it was now open at the neck, and this suited him. His neck had a little ridge of sinewy muscle running up vertically on either side, and when he turned his head the muscle moved under the skin. It was the most beautiful neck Anna had ever seen.

'Let's do this very very slowly,' she said. 'Let's drive ourselves crazy with anticipation.'

His eyes rested a moment on her face, then travelled away, all the way down the length of her body, and she saw him smile.

'Shall we be very stylish and dissipated, Conrad, and order a bottle of champagne? I can ask room service to bring it up, and you can hide in the bathroom when they come in.'

'No,' he said. 'You've had enough to drink already. Stand up, please.'

The tone of his voice caused her to stand up at once.

'Come here,' he said.

She went close to him. He was still sitting on the bed, and now, without getting up, he reached forward and began to take off the rest of her clothes. He did this slowly and deliberately. His face had become suddenly rather pale.

'Oh, darling,' she said, 'how marvellous! You've got that famous thing! A real thick clump of hair growing out of each of your ears! You know what that means, don't you? It's *the* absolutely positive sign of enormous virility!' She bent down and kissed him on the ear. He went on taking off her clothes – the bra, the shoes, the girdle, the pants, and finally the stockings, all of which he dropped in a heap on the floor. The moment he had peeled off her last stocking and dropped it, he turned away. He turned right away from her as though she didn't exist, and now he began to undress himself.

It was rather odd to be standing so close to him in nothing but her own skin and him not even giving her a second look. But perhaps men did these things. Ed might have been an exception. How could *she* know? Conrad took off his white shirt first, and after folding it very carefully, he stood up and carried it to a chair and laid it on one of the arms. He did the same with his undershirt. Then he sat down again on the edge of the bed and started removing his shoes. Anna remained quite still, watching him. His sudden change of mood, his silence, his curious intensity, were making her a bit afraid. But they were also exciting her. There was a stealth, almost a menace in his movements, as though he were some splendid animal treading softly towards the kill. A leopard.

She became hypnotized watching him. She was watching his fingers, the surgeon's fingers, as they untied and loosened the laces of the left shoe, easing it off the foot, and placing it neatly half under the bed. The right shoe came next. Then the left sock and the right sock, both of them being folded together and laid with the utmost precision across the toes of the shoes. Finally the fingers moved up to the top of the trousers, where they undid one button and then began to manipulate the zipper. The trousers, when taken off, were folded along the creases, then carried over to the chair. The underpants followed.

Conrad, now naked, walked slowly back to the edge of the bed, and sat. Then at last, he turned his head and noticed her. She stood waiting ... and trembling. He looked her slowly up and down. Then abruptly, he shot out a hand and took her by the wrist, and with a sharp pull he had her sprawled across the bed.

The relief was enormous. Anna flung her arms around him and held on to him tightly, oh so tightly, for fear that he might go away. She was in mortal fear that he might go away and not come back. And there they lay, she holding on to him as though he were the only thing left in the world to hold on to, and he, strangely quiet, watchful, intent, slowly disentangling himself and beginning to touch her now in a number of different places with those fingers of his, those expert surgeon's fingers. And once again she flew into a frenzy.

The things he did to her during the next few moments were terrible and exquisite. He was, she knew, merely getting her ready, preparing her, or as they say in the hospital, prepping her for the operation itself, but oh God, she had never known or experienced anything even remotely like this. And it was all exceedingly quick, for in what seemed to her no more than a few seconds, she had reached that excruciating point of no return where the whole room becomes compressed into a single tiny blinding speck of light that is going to explode and tear one to pieces at the slightest extra touch. At this stage, in a swift rapacious parabola, Conrad swung his body on top of her for the final act.

And now Anna felt her passion being drawn out of her as if a long live nerve were being drawn slowly out of her body, a long live thread of electric fire, and she cried out to Conrad to go on and on and on, and as she did so, in the middle of it all, somewhere above her, she heard another voice, and this other voice grew louder and louder, more and more insistent, demanding to be heard:

'I said are you *wearing* something?' the voice wanted to know.

'Oh darling, what is it?'

'I keep asking you, are you *wearing* something?'

'Who, me?'

'There's an obstruction here. You must be wearing a diaphragm or some other appliance.'

'Of course not, darling. Everything's wonderful. Oh, do be quiet.'

'Everything is *not* wonderful, Anna.'

Like a picture on a screen, the room swam back into focus. In the foreground was Conrad's face. It was suspended above her, on naked shoulders. The eyes were looking directly into hers. The mouth was still talking.

'If you're going to use a device, then for heaven's sake learn to introduce it in the proper manner. There is nothing so aggravating as careless positioning. The diaphragm has to be placed right back against the cervix.'

'But I'm not wearing anything!'

'You're not? Well, there's still an obstruction.'

Not only the room but the whole world as well seemed slowly to be sliding away from under her now.

'I feel sick,' she said.

'You what?'

'I feel sick.'

'Don't be childish, Anna.'

'Conrad, I'd like you to go, please. Go now.'

'What on earth are you talking about?'

'Go away from me, Conrad!'

'That's ridiculous, Anna. Okay, I'm sorry I spoke. Forget it.'

'*Go away!*' she cried. '*Go away! Go away! Go away!*'

She tried to push him away from her, but he was huge and strong and he had her pinned.

'Calm yourself,' he said. 'Relax. You can't suddenly change your mind like this, in the middle of everything. And for heaven's sake, don't start weeping.'

'Leave me alone, Conrad, I beg you.'

He seemed to be gripping her with everything he had, arms and elbows, hands and fingers, thighs and knees, ankles and feet. He was like a toad the way he gripped her. He was exactly like an enormous clinging toad, gripping and grasping and refusing to let go. She had seen a toad once doing precisely this. It was copulating with a frog on a stone beside a stream, and there it sat, motionless, repulsive, with an evil yellow gleam in its eye, gripping the frog with its two powerful front paws and refusing to let go . . .

'Now stop struggling, Anna. You're acting like a hysterical child. For God's sake, woman, what's eating you?'

'You're hurting me!' she cried.

'*Hurting* you?'

'It's hurting me terribly!'

She told him this only to get him away.

'You know why it's hurting?' he said.

'Conrad! Please!'

'Now wait a minute, Anna. Allow me to explain . . .'

'No!' she cried. 'I've had enough explaining!'

'My dear woman . . .'

'No!' She was struggling desperately to free herself, but he still had her pinned.

'The reason it hurts,' he went on, 'is that you are not manufacturing any fluid. The mucosa is virtually dry . . .'

'Stop!'

'The actual name is senile atrophic vaginitis. It comes with age, Anna. That's why it's called *senile* vaginitis. There's not much one can do . . .'

At that point, she started to scream. The screams were not very loud, but they were screams nevertheless, terrible, agonized stricken screams, and after listening to them for a few seconds, Conrad, in a single graceful movement, suddenly rolled away from her and pushed her to one side with both hands. He pushed her with such force that she fell on to the floor.

She climbed slowly to her feet, and as she staggered into the bathroom, she was crying 'Ed! . . . Ed! . . . Ed! . . .' in a queer supplicating voice. The door shut.

Conrad lay very still listening to the sounds that came from behind the door. At first, he heard only the sobbing of the woman, but a few seconds later, above the sobbing, he heard the sharp metallic click of a cupboard being opened. Instantly, he sat up and vaulted off the bed and began to dress himself with great speed. His clothes, so neatly folded, lay ready at hand, and it took him no more than a couple of minutes to put them on. When that was done, he crossed to the mirror and wiped the lipstick off his face with a handkerchief. He took a comb from his pocket and ran it through his fine black hair. He walked once round the bed to see if he had forgotten anything, and then, carefully, like a man who is tiptoeing from a room where a child is sleeping, he moved out into the corridor, closing the door softly behind him.

The Great Switcheroo

First published in *Playboy* (April 1974)

There were about forty people at Jerry and Samantha's cocktail party that evening. It was the usual crowd, the usual discomfort, the usual appalling noise. People had to stand very close to one another and shout to make themselves heard. Many were grinning, showing capped white teeth. Most of them had a cigarette in the left hand, a drink in the right.

I moved away from my wife Mary and her group. I headed for the small bar in the far corner, and when I got there, I sat down on a bar-stool and faced the room. I did this so that I could look at the women. I settled back with my shoulders against the bar-rail, sipping my Scotch and examining the women one by one over the rim of my glass.

I was studying not their figures but their faces, and what interested me there was not so much the face itself but the big red mouth in the middle of it all. And even then, it wasn't the whole mouth but only the lower lip. The lower lip, I had recently decided, was the great revealer. It gave away more than the eyes. The eyes hid their secrets. The lower lip hid very little. Take, for example, the lower lip of Jacinth Winkleman, who was standing nearest to me. Notice the wrinkles on that lip, how some were parallel and some radiated outwards. No two people had the same pattern of lip-wrinkles, and come to think of it, you could catch a criminal that way if you had his lip-print on file and he had taken a drink at the scene of the crime. The lower lip is what you suck and nibble when you're ruffled, and Martha Sullivan was doing that right now as she watched from a distance her fatuous husband slobbering over Judy Martinson. You lick it when lecherous. I could see Ginny Lomax licking hers with the tip of her tongue as she stood beside Ted Dorling and gazed up into his face. It was a deliberate lick, the tongue coming out slowly and making a slow wet wipe along the entire length of the lower lip. I saw Ted Dorling looking at Ginny's tongue, which was what she wanted him to do.

It really does seem to be a fact, I told myself, as my eyes wandered from lower lip to lower lip across the room, that all the less attractive traits of the human animal, arrogance, rapacity, gluttony, lasciviousness and the rest of them, are clearly signalled in that little carapace of scarlet skin. But you have to know the code. The protuberant or bulging lower lip is supposed to signify sensuality. But this is only half true in men and wholly untrue in women. In women, it is the thin line you should look for, the narrow blade with the sharply delineated bottom edge. And in the nymphomaniac there is a tiny just visible crest of skin at the top centre of the lower lip.

Samantha, my hostess, had that.

Where was she now, Samantha?

Ah, there she was, taking an empty glass out of a guest's hand. Now she was heading my way to refill it.

'Hello, Vic,' she said. 'You all alone?'

She's a nympho-bird all right, I told myself. But a very rare example of the species, because she is entirely and utterly monogamous. She is a married monogamous nympho-bird who stays for ever in her own nest.

She is also the fruitiest female I have ever set eyes upon in my whole life.

'Let me help you,' I said, standing up and taking the glass from her hand. 'What's wanted in here?'

'Vodka on the rocks,' she said. 'Thanks, Vic.' She laid a lovely long white arm upon the top of the bar and she leaned forward so that her bosom rested on the bar-rail, squashing upwards. 'Oops,' I said, pouring vodka outside the glass.

Samantha looked at me with huge brown eyes, but said nothing.

'I'll wipe it up,' I said.

She took the refilled glass from me and walked away. I watched her go. She was wearing black pants. They were so tight around the buttocks that the smallest mole or pimple would have shown through the cloth. But Samantha Rainbow had not a blemish on her bottom. I caught myself licking my own lower lip. That's right, I thought. I want her. I lust after that woman. But it's too risky to try. It would be suicide to make a pass at a girl like that. First of all, she lives next door, which is too close. Secondly, as I have already said, she is monogamous. Thirdly, she is thick as a thief with Mary, my own wife. They exchange dark female secrets. Fourthly, her husband Jerry is my very old and good friend, and not even I, Victor Hammond, though I am churning with lust, would dream of trying to seduce the wife of a man who is my very old and trusty friend.

Unless . . .

It was at this point, as I sat on the bar-stool letching over Samantha Rainbow, that an interesting idea began to filter quietly into the centre of my brain. I remained still, allowing the idea to expand. I watched Samantha across the room, and began fitting her into the framework of the idea. Oh, Samantha, my gorgeous and juicy little jewel, I shall have you yet.

But could anybody seriously hope to get away with a crazy lark like that?

No, not in a million nights.

One couldn't even *try* it unless Jerry agreed. So why think about it?

Samantha was standing about six yards away, talking to Gilbert Mackesy. The fingers of her right hand were curled around a tall glass. The fingers were long and almost certainly dexterous.

Assuming, just for the fun of it, that Jerry did agree, then even so, there would still be gigantic snags along the way. There was, for example, the little matter of physical characteristics. I had seen Jerry many times at the club having a shower after tennis, but right now I couldn't for the life of me recall the necessary details. It wasn't the sort of thing one noticed very much. Usually, one didn't even look.

Anyway, it would be madness to put the suggestion to Jerry point-blank. I didn't know him *that* well. He might be horrified. He might even turn nasty. There could be an ugly scene. I must test him out, therefore, in some subtle fashion.

'You know something,' I said to Jerry about an hour later when we were sitting together on the sofa having a last drink. The guests were drifting away and Samantha was by the door saying goodbye to them. My own wife Mary was out on the terrace talking to Bob Swain. I could see through the open french windows. 'You know something funny?' I said to Jerry as we sat together on the sofa.

'What's funny?' Jerry asked me.

'A fellow I had lunch with today told me a fantastic story. Quite unbelievable.'

'What story?' Jerry said. The whisky had begun to make him sleepy.

'This man, the one I had lunch with, had a terrific letch after the wife of his friend who lived nearby. And his friend had an equally big letch after the wife of the man I had lunch with. Do you see what I mean?'

'You mean two fellers who lived close to each other both fancied each other's wives.'

'Precisely,' I said.

'Then there was no problem,' Jerry said.

'There was a very big problem,' I said. 'The wives were both very faithful and honourable women.'

'Samantha's the same,' Jerry said. 'She wouldn't look at another man.'

'Nor would Mary,' I said. 'She's a fine girl.'

Jerry emptied his glass and set it down carefully on the sofa-table. 'So what happened in your story?' he said. 'It sounds dirty.'

'What happened,' I said, 'was that these two randy sods cooked up a plan which made it possible for each of them to ravish the other's wife without the wives ever knowing it. If you can believe such a thing.'

'With chloroform?' Jerry said.

'Not at all. They were fully conscious.'

'Impossible,' Jerry said. 'Someone's been pulling your leg.'

'I don't think so,' I said. 'From the way this man told it to me, with all the little details and everything, I don't think he was making it up. In fact, I'm sure he wasn't. And listen, they didn't do it just once, either. They've been doing it every two or three weeks for months!'

'And the wives don't know?'

'They haven't a clue.'

'I've got to hear this,' Jerry said. 'Let's get another drink first.'

We crossed to the bar and refilled our glasses, then returned to the sofa.

'You must remember,' I said, 'that there had to be a tremendous lot of preparation and rehearsal beforehand. And many intimate details had to be exchanged to give the plan a chance of working. But the essential part of the scheme was simple:

'They fixed a night, call it Saturday. On that night the husbands and wives were to go up to bed as usual, at say eleven or eleven thirty.

'From then on, normal routine would be preserved. A little reading, perhaps, a little talking, then out with the lights.

'After lights out, the husbands would at once roll over

and pretend to go to sleep. This was to discourage their wives from getting fresh, which at this stage must on no account be permitted. So the wives went to sleep. But the husbands stayed awake. So far so good.

'Then at precisely one a.m., by which time the wives would be in a good deep sleep, each husband would slip quietly out of bed, put on a pair of bedroom slippers and creep downstairs in his pyjamas. He would open the front door and go out into the night, taking care not to close the door behind him.

'They lived,' I went on, 'more or less across the street from one another. It was a quiet suburban neighbourhood and there was seldom anyone about at that hour. So these two furtive pyjama-clad figures would pass each other as they crossed the street, each one heading for another house, another bed, another woman.'

Jerry was listening to me carefully. His eyes were a little glazed from drink, but he was listening to every word.

'The next part,' I said, 'had been prepared very thoroughly by both men. Each knew the inside of his friend's house almost as well as he knew his own. He knew how to find his way in the dark both downstairs and up without knocking over the furniture. He knew his way to the stairs and exactly how many steps there were to the top and which of them creaked and which didn't. He knew on which side of the bed the woman upstairs was sleeping.

'Each took off his slippers and left them in the hall, then up the stairs he crept in his bare feet and pyjamas. This part of it, according to my friend, was rather exciting. He was in a dark silent house that wasn't his own, and on his way to the main bedroom he had to pass no less than three children's bedrooms where the doors were always left slightly open.'

'Children!' Jerry cried. 'My God, what if one of them had woken up and said, "Daddy, is that you?"'

'That was all taken care of,' I said. 'Emergency procedure would then come into effect immediately. Also if the wife, just as he was creeping into her room, woke up and said, "Darling, what's wrong? Why are you wandering about?"; then again, emergency procedure.'

'What emergency procedure?' Jerry said.

'Simple,' I answered. 'The man would immediately dash downstairs and out the front door and across to his own house and ring the bell. This was a signal for the other character, no matter what he was doing at the time, also to rush downstairs at full speed and open the door and let the other fellow in while he went out. This would get them both back quickly to their proper houses.'

'With egg all over their faces,' Jerry said.

'Not at all,' I said.

'That doorbell would have woken the whole house,' Jerry said.

'Of course,' I said. 'And the husband, returning upstairs in his pyjamas, would merely say, "I went to see who the hell was ringing the bell at this ungodly hour. Couldn't find anyone. It must have been a drunk."'

'What about the other guy?' Jerry asked. 'How does he explain why he rushed downstairs when his wife or child spoke to him?'

'He would say, "I heard someone prowling about

outside, so I rushed down to get him, but he escaped."
"Did you actually see him?" his wife would ask anxiously.
"Of course I saw him," the husband would answer. "He
ran off down the street. He was too damn fast for me."
Whereupon the husband would be warmly congratulated
for his bravery.'

'Okay,' Jerry said. 'That's the easy part. Everything so
far is just a matter of good planning and good timing. But
what happens when these two horny characters actually
climb into bed with each other's wives?'

'They go right to it,' I said.

'The wives are sleeping,' Jerry said.

'I know,' I said. 'So they proceed immediately with some
very gentle but very skilful love-play, and by the time these
dames are fully awake, they're as randy as rattlesnakes.'

'No talking, I presume,' Jerry said.

'Not a word.'

'Okay, so the wives are awake,' Jerry said. 'And their
hands get to work. So just for a start, what about the simple question of body size? What about the difference
between the new man and the husband? What about tall-
ness and shortness and fatness and thinness? You're not
telling me these men were physically identical?'

'Not identical, obviously,' I said. 'But they were more or
less similar in build and height. That was essential. They
were both clean-shaven and had roughly the same amount
of hair on their heads. That sort of similarity is common-
place. Look at you and me, for instance. We're roughly the
same height and build, aren't we?'

'Are we?' Jerry said.

'How tall are you?' I said.

'Six foot exactly.'

'I'm five eleven,' I said. 'One inch difference. What do you weigh?'

'One hundred and eighty-seven.'

'I'm a hundred and eighty-four,' I said. 'What's three pounds among friends?'

There was a pause. Jerry was looking out through the french windows on to the terrace where my wife, Mary, was standing. Mary was still talking to Bob Swain and the evening sun was shining in her hair. She was a dark pretty girl with a bosom. I watched Jerry. I saw his tongue come out and go sliding along the surface of his lower lip.

'I guess you're right,' Jerry said, still looking at Mary. 'I guess we are about the same size, you and me.' When he turned back and faced me again, there was a little red rose high up on each cheek. 'Go on about these two men,' he said. 'What about some of the other differences?'

'You mean faces?' I said. 'No one's going to see faces in the dark.'

'I'm not talking about faces,' Jerry said.

'What are you talking about, then?'

'I'm talking about their cocks,' Jerry said. 'That's what it's all about, isn't it? And you're not going to tell me . . .'

'Oh yes, I am,' I said. 'Just so long as both men were either circumcised or uncircumcised, then there was really no problem.'

'Are you seriously suggesting that all men have the same size in cocks?' Jerry said. 'Because they don't.'

'I know they don't,' I said.

'Some are enormous,' Jerry said. 'And some are titchy.'

'There are always exceptions,' I told him. 'But you'd be surprised at the number of men whose measurements are virtually the same, give or take a centimetre. According to my friend, ninety per cent are normal. Only ten per cent are notably large or small.'

'I don't believe that,' Jerry said.

'Check on it sometime,' I said. 'Ask some well-travelled girl.'

Jerry took a long slow sip of his whisky, and his eyes over the top of his glass were looking again at Mary on the terrace. 'What about the rest of it?' he said.

'No problem,' I said.

'No problem, my arse,' he said. 'Shall I tell you why this is a phony story?'

'Go ahead.'

'Everybody knows that a wife and husband who have been married for some years develop a kind of routine. It's inevitable. My God, a new operator would be spotted instantly. You know damn well he would. You can't suddenly wade in with a totally different style and expect the woman not to notice it, and I don't care how randy she was. She'd smell a rat in the first minute!'

'A routine can be duplicated,' I said. 'Just so long as every detail of that routine is described beforehand.'

'A bit personal, that,' Jerry said.

'The whole thing's personal,' I said. 'So each man tells his story. He tells precisely what he usually does. He tells everything. The lot. The works. The whole routine from beginning to end.'

'Jesus,' Jerry said.

'Each of these men,' I said, 'had to learn a new part. He had, in effect, to become an actor. He was impersonating another character.'

'Not so easy, that,' Jerry said.

'No problem at all, according to my friend. The only thing one had to watch out for was not to get carried away and start improvising. One had to follow the stage directions very carefully and stick to them.'

Jerry took another pull at his drink. He also took another look at Mary on the terrace. Then he leaned back against the sofa, glass in hand.

'These two characters,' he said. 'You mean they actually pulled it off?'

'I'm damn sure they did,' I said. 'They're still doing it. About once every three weeks.'

'Fantastic story,' Jerry said. 'And a damn crazy dangerous thing to do. Just imagine the sort of hell that would break loose if you were caught. Instant divorce. Two divorces, in fact. One on each side of the street. Not worth it.'

'Takes a lot of guts,' I said.

'The party's breaking up,' Jerry said. 'They're all going home with their goddamn wives.'

I didn't say any more after that. We sat there for a couple of minutes sipping our drinks while the guests began drifting towards the hall.

'Did he say it was fun, this friend of yours?' Jerry asked suddenly.

'He said it was a gas,' I answered. 'He said all the normal

pleasures got intensified one hundred per cent because of the risk. He swore it was the greatest way of doing it in the world, impersonating the husband and the wife not knowing it.'

At that point, Mary came in through the french windows with Bob Swain. She had an empty glass in one hand and a flame-coloured azalea in the other. She had picked the azalea on the terrace.

'I've been watching you,' she said, pointing the flower at me like a pistol. 'You've hardly stopped talking for the last ten minutes. What's he been telling you, Jerry?'

'A dirty story,' Jerry said, grinning.

'He does that when he drinks,' Mary said.

'Good story,' Jerry said. 'But totally impossible. Get him to tell it to you sometime.'

'I don't like dirty stories,' Mary said. 'Come along, Vic. It's time we went.'

'Don't go yet,' Jerry said, fixing his eyes upon her splendid bosom. 'Have another drink.'

'No thanks,' she said. 'The children'll be screaming for their supper. I've had a lovely time.'

'Aren't you going to kiss me good night?' Jerry said, getting up from the sofa. He went for her mouth, but she turned her head quickly and he caught only the edge of her cheek.

'Go away, Jerry,' she said. 'You're drunk.'

'Not drunk,' Jerry said. 'Just lecherous.'

'Don't you get lecherous with me, my boy,' Mary said sharply. 'I hate that sort of talk.' She marched away across the room, carrying her bosom before her like a battering-ram.

'So long, Jerry,' I said. 'Fine party.'

Mary, full of dark looks, was waiting for me in the hall. Samantha was there, too, saying good-bye to the last guests – Samantha with her dexterous fingers and her smooth skin and her smooth, dangerous thighs. 'Cheer up, Vic,' she said to me, her white teeth showing. She looked like the creation, the beginning of the world, the first morning. 'Good night, Vic darling,' she said, stirring her fingers in my vitals.

I followed Mary out of the house. 'You feeling all right?' she asked.

'Yes,' I said. 'Why not?'

'The amount you drink is enough to make anyone feel ill,' she said.

There was a scrubby old hedge dividing our place from Jerry's and there was a gap in it we always used. Mary and I walked through the gap in silence. We went into the house and she cooked up a big pile of scrambled eggs and bacon, and we ate it with the children.

After the meal, I wandered outside. The summer evening was clear and cool and because I had nothing else to do I decided to mow the grass in the front garden. I got the mower out of the shed and started it up. Then I began the old routine of marching back and forth behind it. I like mowing grass. It is a soothing operation, and on our front lawn I could always look at Samantha's house going one way and think about her going the other.

I had been at it for about ten minutes when Jerry came strolling through the gap in the hedge. He was smoking a pipe and had his hands in his pockets and he stood on the edge of the grass, watching me. I pulled up in front of him, but left the motor ticking over.

'Hi, sport,' he said. 'How's everything?'

'I'm in the doghouse,' I said. 'So are you.'

'Your little wife,' he said, 'is just too goddam prim and prissy to be true.'

'Oh, I know that.'

'She rebuked me in my own house,' Jerry said.

'Not very much.'

'It was enough,' he said, smiling slightly.

'Enough for what?'

'Enough to make me want to get a little bit of my own back on her. So what would you think if I suggested you and I have a go at that thing your friend told you about at lunch?'

When he said this, I felt such a surge of excitement my stomach nearly jumped out of my mouth. I gripped the handles of the mower and started revving the engine.

'Have I said the wrong thing?' Jerry asked.

I didn't answer.

'Listen,' he said. 'If you think it's a lousy idea, let's just forget I ever mentioned it. You're not mad at me, are you?'

'I'm not mad at you, Jerry,' I said. 'It's just that it never entered my head that *we* should do it.'

'It entered mine,' he said. 'The set-up is perfect. We wouldn't even have to cross the street.' His face had gone suddenly bright and his eyes were shining like two stars. 'So what do you say, Vic?'

'I'm thinking,' I said.

'Maybe you don't fancy Samantha.'

'I don't honestly know,' I said.

'She's lots of fun,' Jerry said. 'I guarantee that.'

At this point, I saw Mary come out on to the front porch. 'There's Mary,' I said. 'She's looking for the children. We'll talk some more tomorrow.'

'Then it's a deal?'

'It could be, Jerry. But only on condition we don't rush it. I want to be dead sure everything is right before we start. Damn it all, this is a whole brand-new can of beans!'

'No, it's not!' he said. 'Your friend said it was a gas. He said it was easy.'

'Ah, yes,' I said. 'My friend. Of course. But each case is different.' I opened the throttle on the mower and went whirring away across the lawn. When I got to the far side and turned around, Jerry was already through the gap in the hedge and walking up to his front door.

The next couple of weeks was a period of high conspiracy for Jerry and me. We held secret meetings in bars and restaurants to discuss strategy, and sometimes he dropped into my office after work and we had a planning session behind the closed door. Whenever a doubtful point arose, Jerry would always say, 'How did your friend do it?' And I would play for time and say, 'I'll call him up and ask him about that one.'

After many conferences and much talk, we agreed upon the following main points:

1. That D Day should be a Saturday.
2. That on D Day evening we should take our wives out to a good dinner, the four of us together.

3. That Jerry and I should leave our houses and cross over through the gap in the hedge at precisely one a.m. Sunday morning.

4. That instead of lying in bed in the dark until one a.m. came along, we should both, as soon as our wives were asleep, go quietly downstairs to the kitchen and drink coffee.

5. That we should use the front doorbell idea if an emergency arose.

6. That the return cross-over time was fixed for two a.m.

7. That while in the wrong bed, questions (if any) from the woman must be answered by an 'Uh-uh' sounded with the lips closed tight.

8. That I myself must immediately give up cigarettes and take to a pipe so that I would 'smell' the same as Jerry.

9. That we should at once start using the same brand of hair oil and after-shave lotion.

10. That as both of us normally wore our wristwatches in bed, and they were much the same shape, it was decided not to exchange. Neither of us wore rings.

11. That each man must have something unusual about him that the woman would identify positively with her own husband. We therefore invented what became known as 'The Sticking Plaster Ploy'. It worked like this: on D Day evening, when the couples arrived back in their own homes immediately after the dinner, each husband would make a point of going to the

kitchen to cut himself a piece of cheese. At the same time, he would carefully stick a large piece of plaster over the tip of the forefinger of his right hand. Having done this, he would hold up the finger and say to his wife, 'I cut myself. It's nothing, but it was bleeding a bit.' Thus, later on, when the men have switched beds, each woman will be made very much aware of the plaster-covered finger (the man would see to that), and will associate it directly with her own husband. An important psychological ploy, this, calculated to dissipate any tiny suspicion that might enter the mind of either female.

So much for the basic plans. Next came what we referred to in our notes as 'Familiarization with the Layout'. Jerry schooled me first. He gave me three hours' training in his own house one Sunday afternoon when his wife and children were out. I had never been into their bedroom before. On the dressing table were Samantha's perfumes, her brushes, and all her other little things. A pair of her stockings was draped over the back of a chair. Her night-dress, white and blue, was hanging behind the door leading to the bathroom.

'Okay,' Jerry said. 'It'll be pitch dark when you come in. Samantha sleeps on this side, so you must tiptoe around the end of the bed and slide in on the other side, over there. I'm going to blindfold you and let you practise.'

At first, with the blindfold on, I wandered all over the room like a drunk. But after about an hour's work, I was able to negotiate the course pretty well. But before Jerry would finally pass me out, I had to go blindfold all the way from the front door through the hall, up the stairs, past the children's rooms, into Samantha's room and finish up in exactly the right place. And I had to do it silently, like a thief. All this took three hours of hard work, but I got it in the end.

The following Sunday morning when Mary had taken our children to church, I was able to give Jerry the same sort of work-out in my house. He learned the ropes faster than me, and within an hour he had passed the blindfold test without placing a foot wrong.

It was during this session that we decided to disconnect each woman's bedside lamp as we entered the bedroom. So Jerry practised finding the plug and pulling it out with his blindfold on, and the following week-end, I was able to do the same in Jerry's house.

Now came by far the most important part of our training. We called it 'Spilling the Beans', and it was here that both of us had to describe in every detail the procedure we adopted when making love to our own wives. We agreed not to worry ourselves with any exotic variations that either of us might or might not occasionally practise. We were concerned only with teaching one another the most commonly used routine, the one least likely to arouse suspicion.

The session took place in my office at six o'clock on a Wednesday evening, after the staff had gone home. At first, we were both slightly embarrassed, and neither of us wanted to begin. So I got out the bottle of whisky, and after a couple of stiff drinks, we loosened up and the teach-in started. While Jerry talked I took notes, and vice versa. At the end of it all, it turned out that the only real difference between Jerry's routine and my own was one of tempo. But what a difference it was! He took things (if what he said was to be believed) in such a leisurely fashion and he prolonged the moments to such an extravagant degree that I wondered privately to myself whether his partner did not sometimes go to sleep in the middle of it all. My job, however, was not to criticize but to copy, and I said nothing.

Jerry was not so discreet. At the end of my personal description, he had the temerity to say, 'Is that really what you do?'

'What do you mean?' I asked.

'I mean is it all over and done with as quickly as that?'

'Look,' I said. 'We aren't here to give each other lessons. We're here to learn the facts.'

'I know that,' he said. 'But I'm going to feel a bit of an ass if I copy your style exactly. My God, you go through it like an express train whizzing through a country station!'

I stared at him, mouth open.

'Don't look so surprised,' he said. 'The way you told it to me, anyone would think . . .'

'Think what?' I said.

'Oh, forget it,' he said.

'Thank you,' I said. I was furious. There are two things in this world at which I happen to know I excel. One is driving an automobile and the other is you-know-what. So to have him sit there and tell me I didn't know how to behave with my own wife was a monstrous piece of effrontery. It was he who didn't know, not me. Poor Samantha. What she must have had to put up with over the years.

'I'm sorry I spoke,' Jerry said. He poured more whisky into our glasses. 'Here's to the great switcheroo!' he said. 'When do we go?'

'Today is Wednesday,' I said. 'How about this coming Saturday?'

'Christ,' Jerry said.

'We ought to do it while everything's still fresh in our minds,' I said. 'There's an awful lot to remember.'

Jerry walked to the window and looked down at the traffic in the street below. 'Okay,' he said, turning around. 'Next Saturday it shall be!' Then we drove home in our separate cars.

'Jerry and I thought we'd take you and Samantha out to dinner Saturday night,' I said to Mary. We were in the kitchen and she was cooking hamburgers for the children.

She turned around and faced me, frying-pan in one hand, spoon in the other. Her blue eyes looked straight into mine. 'My Lord, Vic,' she said. 'How nice. But what are we celebrating?'

I looked straight back at her and said, 'I thought it would be a change to see some new faces. We're always meeting the same old bunch of people in the same old houses.'

She took a step forward and kissed me on the cheek. 'What a good man you are,' she said. 'I love you.'

'Don't forget to phone the baby-sitter.'

'No, I'll do it tonight,' she said.

Thursday and Friday passed very quickly, and suddenly it was Saturday. It was D Day. I woke up feeling madly excited. After breakfast, I couldn't sit still, so I decided to go out and wash the car. I was in the middle of this when Jerry came strolling through the gap in the hedge, pipe in mouth.

'Hi, sport,' he said. 'This is the day.'

'I know that,' I said. I also had a pipe in my mouth. I was forcing myself to smoke it, but I had trouble keeping it alight, and the smoke burned my tongue.

'How're you feeling?' Jerry asked.

'Terrific,' I said. 'How about you?'

'I'm nervous,' he said.

'Don't be nervous, Jerry.'

'This is one hell of a thing we're trying to do,' he said. 'I hope we pull it off.'

I went on polishing the windshield. I had never known Jerry to be nervous of anything before. It worried me a bit.

'I'm damn glad we're not the first people ever to try it,' he said. 'If no one had ever done it before, I don't think I'd risk it.'

'I agree,' I said.

'What stops me being too nervous,' he said, 'is the fact that your friend found it so fantastically easy.'

'My friend said it was a cinch,' I said. 'But for Chrissake, Jerry, don't be nervous when the time comes. That would be disastrous.'

'Don't worry,' he said. 'But Jesus, it's exciting, isn't it?'

'It's exciting all right,' I said.

'Listen,' he said. 'We'd better go easy on the booze tonight.'

'Good idea,' I said. 'See you at eight thirty.'

At half past eight, Samantha, Jerry, Mary and I drove in Jerry's car to Billy's Steak House. The restaurant, despite its name, was high-class and expensive, and the girls had put on long dresses for the occasion. Samantha was wearing something green that didn't start until it was halfway down her front, and I had never seen her looking lovelier. There were candles on our table. Samantha was seated opposite me and whenever she leaned forward with her face close to the flame, I could see that tiny crest of skin at the top centre of her lower lip. 'Now,' she said as she accepted a menu from the waiter, 'I wonder what I'm going to have tonight.'

Ho-ho-ho, I thought, that's a good question.

Everything went fine in the restaurant and the girls enjoyed themselves. When we arrived back at Jerry's house, it was eleven forty-five, and Samantha said, 'Come in and have a nightcap.'

'Thanks,' I said, 'but it's a bit late. And the baby-sitter has to be driven home.' So Mary and I walked across to our house, and *now*, I told myself as I entered the front door, *from now on* the countdown begins. I must keep a clear head and forget nothing.

While Mary was paying the baby-sitter, I went to the fridge and found a piece of Canadian cheddar. I took a knife from the drawer and a strip of plaster from the cupboard. I stuck the plaster around the tip of the forefinger of my right hand and waited for Mary to turn around.

'I cut myself,' I said, holding up the finger for her to see. 'It's nothing, but it was bleeding a bit.'

'I'd have thought you'd had enough to eat for the evening,' was all she said. But the plaster registered on her mind and my first little job had been done.

I drove the baby-sitter home and by the time I got back up to the bedroom it was round about midnight and Mary was already half asleep with her light out. I switched out the light on my side of the bed and went into the bathroom to undress. I pottered about in there for ten minutes or so and when I came out, Mary, as I had hoped, was well and truly sleeping. There seemed no point in getting into bed beside her. So I simply pulled back the covers a bit on my side to make it easier for Jerry, then with my slippers on, I went downstairs to the kitchen and switched on the electric kettle. It was now twelve seventeen. Forty-three minutes to go.

At twelve thirty-five, I went upstairs to check on Mary and the kids. Everyone was sound asleep.

At twelve fifty-five, five minutes before zero hour, I went up again for a final check. I went right up close to Mary's bed and whispered her name. There was no answer. Good. *That's it! Let's go!*

I put a brown raincoat over my pyjamas. I switched off the kitchen light so that the whole house was in darkness. I put the front door lock on the latch. And then, feeling an enormous sense of exhilaration, I stepped silently out into the night.

There were no lamps on our street to lighten the darkness. There was no moon or even a star to be seen. It was a black black night, but the air was warm and there was a little breeze blowing from somewhere.

I headed for the gap in the hedge. When I got very close, I was able to make out the hedge itself and find the gap. I stopped there, waiting. Then I heard Jerry's footsteps coming towards me.

'Hi, sport,' he whispered. 'Everything okay?'

'All ready for you,' I whispered back.

He moved on. I heard his slippered feet padding softly over the grass as he went towards my house. I went towards his.

I opened Jerry's front door. It was even darker inside than out. I closed the door carefully. I took off my raincoat and hung it on the doorknob. I removed my slippers and placed them against the wall by the door. I literally could not see my hands before my face. Everything had to be done by touch.

My goodness, I was glad Jerry had made me practise blindfold for so long. It wasn't my feet that guided me now but my fingers. The fingers of one hand or another were never for a moment out of contact with something, a wall, the banister, a piece of furniture, a window-curtain. And I knew or thought I knew exactly where I was all the time. But it was an awesome eerie feeling trespassing on tiptoe through someone else's house in the middle of the night. As I fingered my way up the stairs, I found myself thinking of the burglars who had broken into our front room last winter and stolen the television set. When the police came next morning, I pointed out to them an enormous turd lying in the snow outside the garage. 'They nearly always do that,' one of the cops told me. 'They can't help it. They're scared.'

I reached the top of the stairs. I crossed the landing with my right fingertips touching the wall all the time. I started down the corridor, but paused when my hand found the door of the first children's room. The door was slightly open. I listened. I could hear young Robert Rainbow, aged eight, breathing evenly inside. I moved on. I found the door to the second children's bedroom. This one belonged to Billy, aged six and Amanda, three. I stood listening. All was well.

The main bedroom was at the end of the corridor, about four yards on. I reached the door. Jerry had left it open, as planned. I went in. I stood absolutely still just inside the door, listening for any sign that Samantha might be awake. All was quiet. I felt my way around the wall until I reached Samantha's side of the bed. Immediately, I knelt on the floor and found the plug connecting her bedside lamp. I drew it from its socket and laid it on the carpet. Good. Much safer now. I stood up. I couldn't see Samantha, and at first I couldn't hear anything either. I bent low over the bed. Ah yes, I could hear her breathing. Suddenly I caught a whiff of the heavy musky perfume she had been using that evening, and I felt the blood rushing to my groin. Quickly I tiptoed around the big bed, keeping two fingers in gentle contact with the edge of the bed the whole way.

All I had to do now was get in. I did so, but as I put my

weight upon the mattress, the creaking of the springs underneath sounded as though someone was firing a rifle in the room. I lay motionless, holding my breath. I could hear my heart thumping away like an engine in my throat. Samantha was facing away from me. She didn't move. I pulled the covers up over my chest and turned towards her. A female glow came out of her to me. Here we go, then! *Now!*

I slid a hand over and touched her body. Her nightdress was warm and silky. I rested the hand gently on her hips. Still she didn't move. I waited a minute or so, then I allowed the hand that lay upon the hip to steal onwards and go exploring. Slowly, deliberately, and very accurately, my fingers began the process of setting her on fire.

She stirred. She turned on to her back. Then she murmured sleepily, 'Oh, dear . . . Oh, my goodness me . . . Good heavens, darling!'

I, of course, said nothing. I just kept on with the job.

A couple of minutes went by.

She was lying quite still.

Another minute passed. Then another. She didn't move a muscle.

I began to wonder how much longer it would be before she caught alight.

I persevered.

But why the silence? Why this absolute and total immobility, this frozen posture?

Suddenly it came to me. I had forgotten completely about Jerry! I was so hotted up, I had forgotten all about his own personal routine! I was doing it my way, not his! His way was far more complex than mine. It was ridiculously elaborate. It was quite unnecessary. But it was what she was used to. And now she was noticing the difference and trying to figure out what on earth was going on.

But it was too late to change direction now. I must keep going.

I kept going. The woman beside me was like a coiled spring lying there. I could feel the tension under her skin. I began to sweat.

Suddenly, she uttered a queer little groan.

More ghastly thoughts rushed through my mind. Could she be ill? Was she having a heart attack? Ought I to get the hell out quick?

She groaned again, louder this time. Then all at once, she cried out, 'Yes-yes-yes-yes-yes!' and like a bomb whose slow fuse had finally reached the dynamite, she exploded into life. She grabbed me in her arms and went for me with such incredible ferocity, I felt I was being set upon by a tiger.

Or should I say tigress?

I never dreamed a woman could do the things Samantha did to me then. She was a whirlwind, a dazzling frenzied whirlwind that tore me up by the roots and spun me around and carried me high into the heavens, to places I did not know existed.

I myself did not contribute. How could I? I was helpless. I was the palm tree spinning in the heavens, the lamb in the claws of the tiger. It was as much as I could do to keep breathing.

Thrilling it was, all the same, to surrender to the hands of a violent woman, and for the next ten, twenty, thirty minutes – how would I know? – the storm raged on. But

I have no intention here of regaling the reader with bizarre details. I do not approve of washing juicy linen in public. I am sorry, but there it is. I only hope that my reticence will not create too strong a sense of anticlimax. Certainly, there was nothing anti about my own climax, and in the final searing paroxysm I gave a shout which should have awakened the entire neighbourhood. Then I collapsed. I crumpled up like a drained wineskin.

Samantha, as though she had done no more than drink a glass of water, simply turned away from me and went right back to sleep.

Phew!

I lay still, recuperating slowly.

I had been right, you see, about that little thing on her lower lip, had I not?

Come to think of it, I had been right about more or less everything that had to do with this incredible escapade. What a triumph! I felt wonderfully relaxed and well-spent.

I wondered what time it was. My watch was not a luminous one. I'd better go. I crept out of bed. I felt my way, a trifle less cautiously this time, around the bed, out of the bedroom, along the corridor, down the stairs and into the hall of the house. I found my raincoat and slippers. I put them on. I had a lighter in the pocket of my raincoat. I used it and read the time. It was eight minutes before two. Later than I thought, I opened the front door and stepped out into the black night.

My thoughts now began to concentrate upon Jerry. Was he all right? Had he gotten away with it? I moved through the darkness towards the gap in the hedge.

'Hi, sport,' a voice whispered beside me.

'Jerry!'

'Everything okay?' Jerry asked.

'Fantastic,' I said. 'Amazing. What about you?'

'Same with me,' he said. I caught the flash of his white teeth grinning at me in the dark. 'We made it, Vic!' he whispered, touching my arm. 'You were right! It worked! It was sensational!'

'See you tomorrow,' I whispered. 'Go home.'

We moved apart. I went through the hedge and entered my house. Three minutes later, I was safely back in my own bed, and my own wife was sleeping soundly alongside me.

The next morning was Sunday. I was up at eight thirty and went downstairs in pyjamas and dressing-gown, as I always do on a Sunday, to make breakfast for the family. I had left Mary sleeping. The two boys, Victor, aged nine, and Wally, seven, were already down.

'Hi, Daddy,' Wally said.

'I've got a great new breakfast,' I announced.

'What?' both boys said together. They had been into town and fetched the Sunday paper and were now reading the comics.

'We make some buttered toast and we spread orange marmalade on it,' I said. 'Then we put strips of crisp bacon on top of the marmalade.'

'*Bacon!*' Victor said. 'With *orange marmalade!*'

'I know. But you wait till you try it. It's wonderful.'

I dished out the grapefruit juice and drank two glasses of it myself. I set another on the table for Mary when she came down. I switched on the electric kettle, put the bread in the toaster, and started to fry the bacon. At this point, Mary came into the kitchen. She had a flimsy peach-coloured chiffon thing over her nightdress.

'Good morning,' I said, watching her over my shoulder as I manipulated the frying-pan.

She did not answer. She went to her chair at the kitchen table and sat down. She started to sip her juice. She looked neither at me nor at the boys. I went on frying the bacon.

'Hi, Mummy,' Wally said.

She didn't answer this either.

The smell of the bacon fat was beginning to turn my stomach.

'I'd like some coffee,' Mary said, not looking around. Her voice was very odd.

'Coming right up,' I said. I pushed the frying-pan away from the heat and quickly made a cup of black instant coffee. I placed it before her.

'Boys,' she said, addressing the children, 'would you please do your reading in the other room till breakfast is ready.'

'Us?' Victor said. 'Why?'

'Because I say so.'

'Are we doing something wrong?' Wally asked.

'No, honey, you're not. I just want to be left alone for a moment with Daddy.'

I felt myself shrink inside my skin. I wanted to run. I wanted to rush out the front door and go running down the street and hide.

'Get yourself a coffee, Vic,' she said, 'and sit down.'

Her voice was quite flat. There was no anger in it. There was just nothing. And she still wouldn't look at me. The boys went out, taking the comic section with them.

'Shut the door,' Mary said to them.

I put a spoonful of powdered coffee into my cup and poured boiling water over it. I added milk and sugar. The silence was shattering. I crossed over and sat down in my chair opposite her. It might just as well have been an electric chair, the way I was feeling.

'Listen, Vic,' she said, looking into her coffee cup. 'I want to get this said before I lose my nerve and then I won't be able to say it.'

'For heaven's sake, what's all the drama about?' I asked. 'Has something happened?'

'Yes, Vic, it has.'

'What?'

Her face was pale and still and distant, unconscious of the kitchen around her.

'Come on, then, out with it,' I said bravely.

'You're not going to like this very much,' she said, and her big blue haunted-looking eyes rested a moment on my face, then travelled away.

'What am I not going to like very much?' I said. The sheer terror of it all was beginning to stir my bowels. I felt the same way as those burglars the cops had told me about.

'You know I hate talking about love-making and all that sort of thing,' she said. 'I've never once talked to you about it all the time we've been married.'

'That's true,' I said.

She took a sip of her coffee, but she wasn't tasting it. 'The point is this,' she said. 'I've never liked it. If you really want to know, I've hated it.'

'Hated what?' I asked.

'Sex,' she said. 'Doing it.'

'Good Lord!' I said.

'It's never given me even the slightest little bit of pleasure.'

This was shattering enough in itself, but the real cruncher was still to come, I felt sure of that.

'I'm sorry if that surprises you,' she added.

I couldn't think of anything to say, so I kept quiet.

Her eyes rose again from the coffee cup and looked into mine, watchful, as if calculating something, then fell again. 'I wasn't ever going to tell you,' she said. 'And I never would have if it hadn't been for last night.'

I said very slowly, 'What about last night?'

'Last night,' she said, 'I suddenly found out what the whole crazy thing is all about.'

'You did?'

She looked full at me now, and her face was as open as a flower. 'Yes,' she said. 'I surely did.'

I didn't move.

'Oh darling!' she cried, jumping up and rushing over and giving me an enormous kiss. 'Thank you so much for last night! You were marvellous! And I was marvellous! We were both marvellous! Don't look so embarrassed, my darling! You ought to be proud of yourself! You were fantastic! I love you! I do! I do!'

I just sat there.

She leaned close to me and put an arm around my shoulders. 'And now,' she said softly, 'now that you have . . . I don't quite know how to say this . . . now that you have sort of discovered what it is I *need*, everything is going to be so marvellous from now on!'

I still sat there. She went slowly back to her chair. A big tear was running down one of her cheeks. I couldn't think why.

'I was right to tell you, wasn't I?' she said, smiling through her tears.

'Yes,' I said. 'Oh, yes.' I stood up and went over to the cooker so that I wouldn't be facing her. Through the kitchen window, I caught sight of Jerry crossing his garden with the Sunday paper under his arm. There was a lilt in his walk, a little prance of triumph in each pace he took, and when he reached the steps of his front porch, he ran up them two at a time.

Bitch

First published in *Playboy* (July 1974)

I have so far released for publication only one episode from Uncle Oswald's diaries. It concerned, as some of you may remember, a carnal encounter between my uncle and a Syrian female leper in the Sinai Desert. Six years have gone by since its publication and nobody has yet come forward to make trouble. I am therefore encouraged to release a second episode from these curious pages. My lawyer has advised against it. He points out that some of the people concerned are still living and are easily recognizable. He says I will be sued mercilessly. Well, let them sue. I am proud of my uncle. He knew how life should be lived. In a preface to the first episode I said that Casanova's *Memoirs* read like a parish magazine beside Uncle Oswald's diaries, and that the great lover himself, when compared with my uncle, appears positively undersexed. I stand by that, and given time I shall prove it to the world. Here then is a little episode from Volume XXIII, precisely as Uncle Oswald wrote it:

Paris
Wednesday

Breakfast at ten. I tried the honey. It was delivered yesterday in an early Sèvres sucrier which had that lovely canary-coloured ground known as *jonquille*. 'From Suzie,' the note said, 'and thank you.' It is nice to be appreciated. And the honey was interesting. Suzie Jolibois had, among other things, a small farm south of Casablanca, and was fond of bees. Her hives were set in the midst of a planta- tion of *Cannabis indica*, and the bees drew their nectar exclusively from this source. They lived, those bees, in a state of perpetual euphoria and were disinclined to work. The honey was therefore very scarce. I spread a third piece of toast. The stuff was almost black. It had a pun- gent aroma. The telephone rang. I put the receiver to my ear and waited. I never speak first when called. After all, I'm not phoning them. They're phoning me.

'Oswald! Are you there?'

I knew the voice. 'Yes, Henri,' I said. 'Good morning.'

'Listen!' he said, speaking fast and sounding excited. 'I think I've got it! I'm almost certain I've got it! Forgive me if I'm out of breath, but I've just had a rather fantastic experience. It's all right now. Everything's fine. Will you come over?'

'Yes,' I said. 'I'll come over.' I replaced the receiver and poured myself another cup of coffee. Had Henri really done it at last? If he had, then I wanted to be around to share the fun.

I must pause here to tell you how I met Henri Biotte. Some three years ago I drove down to Provence to spend a summer weekend with a lady who was interesting to me simply because she possessed an extraordinarily powerful muscle in a region where other women have no muscles at all. An hour after my arrival, I was strolling alone on the lawn beside the river when a small dark man approached me. He had black hairs on the backs of his hands and he made me a little bow and said, 'Henri Biotte, a fellow guest.'

'Oswald Cornelius,' I said.

Henri Biotte was as hairy as a goat. His chin and cheeks were covered with bristly black hair and thick tufts of it were sprouting from his nostrils. 'May I join you?' he said, falling into step beside me and starting immediately to talk. And what a talker he was! How Gallic, how excitable. He walked with a mad little hop, and his fingers flew as if he wanted to scatter them to the four winds of heaven, and his words went off like firecrackers, with terrific speed. He was a Belgian chemist, he said, working in Paris. He was an olfactory chemist. He had devoted his life to the study of olfaction.

'You mean smell?' I said.

'Yes, yes!' he cried. 'Exactly! I am an expert on smells. I know more about smells than anyone else in the world!'

'Good smells or bad?' I asked, trying to slow him down.

'Good smells, lovely smells, glorious smells!' he said. 'I make them! I can make any smell you want!'

He went on to tell me he was the chief perfume blender to one of the great couturiers in the city. And his nose, he said, placing a hairy finger on the tip of his hairy proboscis, probably looked just like any other nose, did it not? I wanted to tell him it had more hairs sprouting from the noseholes than wheat from the prairies and why didn't he get his barber to snip them out, but instead I confessed politely that I could see nothing unusual about it.

'Quite so,' he said. 'But in actual fact it is a smelling

organ of phenomenal sensitivity. With two sniffs it can detect the presence of a single drop of macrocylic musk in a gallon of geranium oil.'

'Extraordinary,' I said.

'On the Champs Elysées,' he went on, 'which is a wide thoroughfare, my nose can identify the precise perfume being used by a woman walking on the other side of the street.'

'With the traffic in between?'

'With heavy traffic in between,' he said.

He went on to name two of the most famous perfumes in the world, both of them made by the fashion house he worked for. 'Those are my personal creations,' he said modestly. 'I blended them myself. They have made a fortune for the celebrated old bitch who runs the business.'

'But not for you?'

'Me! I am but a poor miserable employee on a salary,' he said, spreading his palms and hunching his shoulders so high they touched his earlobes. 'One day, though, I shall break away and pursue my dream.'

'You have a dream?'

'I have a glorious, tremendous, exciting dream, my dear sir!'

'Then why don't you pursue it?'

'Because first I must find a man farsighted enough and wealthy enough to back me.'

Ah-ha, I thought, so that's what it's all about. 'With a reputation like yours, that shouldn't be too difficult,' I said.

'The sort of rich man I seek is hard to find,' he said.

'He must be a sporty gambler with a very keen appetite for the bizarre.'

That's me, you clever little bugger, I thought. 'What is this dream you wish to pursue?' I asked him. 'Is it making perfumes?'

'My dear fellow!' he cried. 'Anyone can make *perfumes!* I'm talking about *the* perfume! The *only* one that counts!'

'Which would that be?'

'Why, the *dangerous* one, of course! And when I have made it, I shall rule the world!'

'Good for you,' I said.

'I am not joking, Monsieur Cornelius. Would you permit me to explain what I am driving at?'

'Go ahead.'

'Forgive me if I sit down,' he said, moving towards a bench. 'I had a heart attack last April and I have to be careful.'

'I'm sorry to hear that.'

'Oh, don't be sorry. All will be well so long as I don't overdo things.'

It was a lovely afternoon and the bench was on the lawn near the riverbank and we sat down on it. Beside us, the river flowed slow and smooth and deep, and there were little clouds of water-flies hovering over the surface. Across the river there were willows along the bank and beyond the willows an emerald-green meadow, yellow with buttercups, and a single cow grazing. The cow was brown and white.

'I will tell you what kind of perfume I wish to make,' he

said. 'But it is essential I explain a few other things to you on the way or you will not fully understand. So please bear with me a while.' One hand lay limp upon his lap, the hairy part upwards. It looked like a black rat. He was stroking it gently with the fingers of the other hand.

'Let us consider first,' he said, 'the phenomenon that occurs when a dog meets a bitch in heat. The dog's sexual drive is tremendous. All self-control disappears. He has only one thought in his head, which is to fornicate on the spot, and unless he is prevented by force, he will do so. But do you know what it is that causes this tremendous sex-drive in a dog?'

'Smell,' I said.

'Precisely, Monsieur Cornelius. Odorous molecules of a special conformation enter the dog's nostrils and stimulate his olfactory nerve-endings. This causes urgent signals to be sent to the olfactory bulb and thence to the higher brain centres. It is *all* done by smell. If you sever a dog's olfactory nerve, he will lose interest in sex. This is also true of many other mammals, but it is not true of man. Smell has nothing to do with the sexual appetite of the human male. He is stimulated in this respect by sight, by tactility and by his lively imagination. Never by smell.'

'What about perfume?' I said.

'It's all rubbish!' he answered. 'All those expensive scents in small bottles, the ones I make, they have no aphrodisiac effect at all upon a man. Perfume was never intended for that purpose. In the old days, women used it to conceal the fact that they stank. Today, when they no longer stink, they use it purely for narcissistic reasons.

They enjoy putting it on and smelling their own good smells. Men hardly notice the stuff. I promise you that.'

'I do,' I said.

'Does it stir you physically?'

'No, not physically. Aesthetically, yes.'

'You enjoy the smell. So do I. But there are plenty of other smells I enjoy more – the bouquet of a good Lafite, the scent of a fresh Comice pear, or the smell of the air blowing in from the sea on the Brittany coast.'

A trout jumped high in midstream and the sunlight flashed on its body. 'You must forget,' said Monsieur Biotte, 'all the nonsense about musk and ambergris and the testicular secretions of the civet cat. We make our perfumes from chemicals these days. If I want a musky odour I will use ethylene sebacate. Phenylacetic acid will give me civet and benzaldehyde will provide the smell of almonds. No sir, I am no longer interested in mixing up chemicals to make pretty smells.'

For some minutes his nose had been running slightly, wetting the black hairs in his nostrils. He noticed it and produced a handkerchief and gave it a blow and a wipe. 'What I intend to do,' he said, 'is to produce a perfume which will have the same electrifying effect upon a man as the scent of a bitch in heat has upon a dog! One whiff and that'll be it! The man will lose all control. He'll rip off his pants and ravish the lady on the spot!'

'We could have some fun with that,' I said.

'We could rule the world!' he cried.

'Yes, but you told me just now that smell has nothing to do with the sexual appetite of the human male.'

'It doesn't,' he said. 'But it used to. I have evidence that in the period of the post-glacial drift, when primitive man was far more closely related to the ape than he is now, he still retained the ape-like characteristic of jumping on any right-smelling female he ran across. And later, in the Palaeolithic and Neolithic periods, he continued to become sexually animated by smell, but to a lesser and lesser degree. By the time the higher civilizations had come along in Egypt and China around 10,000 BC, evolution had played its part and had completely suppressed man's ability to be stimulated sexually by smell. Am I boring you?'

'Not at all. But tell me, does that mean an actual physical change has taken place in man's smelling apparatus?'

'Absolutely not,' he said, 'otherwise there'd be nothing we could do about it. The little mechanism that enabled our ancestors to smell these subtle odours is still there. I happen to know it is. Listen, you've seen how some people can make their ears move a tiny bit?'

'I can do it myself,' I said, doing it.

'You see,' he said, 'the ear-moving muscle is still there. It's a leftover from the time when man used to be able to cock his ears forwards for better hearing, like a dog. He lost that ability over a hundred thousand years ago, but the muscle remains. And the same applies to our smelling apparatus. The mechanism for smelling those secret smells is still there, but we have lost the ability to use it.'

'How can you be so certain it's still there?' I asked.

'Do you know how our smelling system works?' he said.

'Not really.'

'Then I shall tell you, otherwise I cannot answer your question. Attend closely, please. Air is sucked in through the nostrils and passes the three baffle-shaped turbinate bones in the upper part of the nose. There it gets warmer and filtered. This warm air now travels up and over two clefts that contain the smelling organs. These organs are patches of yellowish tissue, each about an inch square. In this tissue are embedded the nerve-fibres and nerve-endings of the olfactory nerve. Every nerve-ending consists of an olfactory cell bearing a cluster of tiny hair-like filaments. These filaments act as receivers. "Receptors" is a better word. And when the receptors are tickled or stimulated by odorous molecules, they send signals to the brain. If, as you come downstairs in the morning, you sniff into your nostrils the odorous molecules of frying bacon, these will stimulate your receptors, the receptors will flash a signal along the olfactory nerve to the brain, and the brain will interpret it in terms of the character and intensity of the odour. And that is when you cry out, "Ah-ha, bacon for breakfast!"'

'I never eat bacon for breakfast,' I said.

He ignored this.

'These receptors,' he went on, 'these tiny hair-like filaments are what concern us. And now you are going to ask me how on earth they can tell the difference between one odorous molecule and another, between say peppermint and camphor?'

'How can they?' I said. I was interested in this.

'Attend more closely than ever now, please,' he said.

'At the end of each receptor is an indentation, a sort of cup, except that it isn't round. This is the "receptor site". Imagine now thousands of these little hair-like filaments with tiny cups at their extremities, all waving about like the tendrils of sea anemones and waiting to catch in their cups any odorous molecules that pass by. That, you see, is what actually happens. When you sniff a certain smell, the odorous molecules of the substance which made that smell go rushing around inside your nostrils and get caught by the little cups, the receptor sites. Now the important thing to remember is this. Molecules come in all shapes and sizes. Equally, the little cups or receptor sites are also differently shaped. Thus, the molecules lodge only in the receptor sites which fit them. Pepperminty molecules go only into special pepperminty receptor sites. Camphor molecules, which have a quite different shape, will fit only into the special camphor receptor sites, and so on. It's rather like those toys for small children where they have to fit variously shaped pieces into the right holes.'

'Let me see if I understand you,' I said. 'Are you saying that my brain will know it is a pepperminty smell simply because the molecule has lodged in a pepperminty reception site?'

'Precisely.'

'But you are surely not suggesting there are differently shaped receptor sites for every smell in the world?'

'No,' he said, 'as a matter of fact, man has only seven differently shaped sites.'

'Why only seven?'

'Because our sense of smell recognizes only seven "pure primary odours". All the rest are "complex odours" made up by mixing the primaries.'

'Are you sure of that?'

'Positive. Our sense of taste has even less. It recognizes only four primaries – sweet, sour, salt and bitter! All other tastes are mixtures of these.'

'What are the seven pure primary odours?' I asked him.

'Their names are of no importance to us,' he said. 'Why confuse the issue.'

'I'd like to hear them.'

'All right,' he said. 'They are camphoraceous, pungent, musky, ethereal, floral, pepperminty and putrid. Don't look so sceptical, please. This isn't *my* discovery. Very learned scientists have worked on it for years. And their conclusions are quite accurate, *except in one respect.*'

'What's that?'

'*There is an eighth pure primary odour which they don't know about, and an eighth receptor site to receive the curiously shaped molecules of that odour!*'

'Ah-ha-ha!' I said. 'I see what you're driving at.'

'Yes,' he said, 'the eighth pure primary odour is the sexual stimulant that caused primitive man to behave like a dog thousands of years ago. It has a very peculiar molecular structure.'

'Then you know what it is?'

'Of course I know what it is.'

'And you say we still retain the receptor sites for these peculiar molecules to fit into?'

'Absolutely.'

'This mysterious smell,' I said, 'does it ever reach our own nostrils nowadays?'

'Frequently.'

'Do we smell it? I mean, are we aware of it?'

'No.'

'You mean the molecules don't get caught in the receptor sites?'

'They do, my dear fellow, they do. But nothing happens. No signal is sent off to the brain. The telephone line is out of action. It's like that ear muscle. The mechanism is still there, but we've lost the ability to use it properly.'

'And what do you propose to do about that?' I asked.

'I shall reactivate it,' he said. 'We are dealing with nerves here, not muscles. And these nerves are not dead or injured, they're merely dormant. I shall probably increase the intensity of the smell a thousandfold, and add a catalyst.'

'Go on,' I said.

'That's enough.'

'I should like to hear more,' I said.

'Forgive me for saying so, Monsieur Cornelius, but I don't think you know enough about organoleptic quality to follow me any further. The lecture is over.'

Henri Biotte sat smug and quiet on the bench beside the river stroking the back of one hand with the fingers of the other. The tufts of hair sprouting from his nostrils gave him a pixie look, but that was camouflage. He struck me rather as a dangerous and dainty little creature, someone who lurked behind stones with a sharp eye and a sting in his tail, waiting for the lone traveller to come by.

Surreptitiously I searched his face. The mouth interested me. The lips had a magenta tinge, possibly something to do with his heart trouble. The lower lip was caruncular and pendulous. It bulged out in the middle like a purse, and could easily have served as a receptacle for small coins. The skin of the lip seemed to be blown up very tight, as though by air, and it was constantly wet, not from licking but from an excess of saliva in the mouth.

And there he sat, this Monsieur Henri Biotte, smiling a wicked little smile and waiting patiently for me to react. He was a totally amoral man, that much was clear, but then so was I. He was also a wicked man, and although I cannot in all honesty claim wickedness as one of my own virtues, I find it irresistible in others. A wicked man has a lustre all his own. Then again, there was something diabolically splendid about a person who wished to set back the sex habits of civilized man half a million years.

Yes, he had me hooked. So there and then, sitting beside the river in the garden of the lady from Provence, I made an offer to Henri. I suggested he should leave his present employment forthwith and set himself up in a small laboratory. I would pay all the bills for this little venture as well as making good his salary. It would be a five-year contract, and we would go fifty-fifty on anything that came out of it.

Henri was ecstatic. 'You mean it?' he cried. 'You are serious?'

I held out my hand. He grasped it in both of his and shook it vigorously. It was like shaking hands with a yak. 'We shall control mankind!' he said. 'We'll be the gods of the earth!' He flung his arms around me and embraced me and kissed me first on one cheek, then on the other. Oh, this awful Gallic kissing. Henri's lower lip felt like the wet underbelly of a toad against my skin. 'Let's keep the celebrations until later,' I said, wiping myself dry with a linen handkerchief.

Henri Biotte made apologies and excuses to his hostess and rushed back to Paris that night. Within a week he had given up his old job and had rented three rooms to serve as a laboratory. These were on the third floor of a house on the Left Bank, on the Rue de Cassette, just off the Boulevard Raspaille. He spent a great deal of my money equipping the place with complicated apparatus, and he even installed a large cage into which he put two apes, a male and a female. He also took on an assistant, a clever and moderately presentable young lady called Jeanette. And with all that, he set to work.

You should understand that for me this little venture was of no great importance. I had plenty of other things to amuse me. I used to drop in on Henri maybe a couple of times a month to see how things were going, but otherwise I left him entirely to himself. My mind wasn't on his job. I hadn't the patience for that kind of research. And when results failed to come quickly, I began to lose all interest. Even the pair of over-sexed apes ceased to amuse me after a while.

Only once did I derive any pleasure from my visits to his laboratory. As you must know by now, I can seldom resist even a moderately presentable woman. And so, on a certain rainy Thursday afternoon, while Henri was busy applying electrodes to the olfactory organs of a frog in one room, I found myself applying something infinitely more agreeable to Jeanette in the other room. I had not, of course, expected anything out of the ordinary from this little frolic. I was acting more out of habit than anything else. But my goodness, what a surprise I got! Beneath her white overall, this rather austere research chemist turned out to be a sinewy and flexible female of immense dexterity. The experiments she performed, first with the oscillator, then with the high-speed centrifuge, were absolutely breathtaking. In fact, not since that Turkish tightrope walker in Ankara (see Vol. xxi) had I experienced anything quite like it. Which all goes to show for the thousandth time that women are as inscrutable as the ocean. You never know what you have under your keel, deep water or shallow, until you have heaved the lead.

I did not bother to visit the laboratory again after that. You know my rule. I never return to a female a second time. With me at any rate, women invariably pull out all the stops during the first encounter, and a second meeting can therefore be nothing more than the same old tune on the same old fiddle. Who wants that? Not me. So when I suddenly heard Henri's voice calling urgently to me over the telephone that morning at breakfast, I had almost forgotten his existence.

I drove through the fiendish Paris traffic to the Rue de Cassette. I parked the car and took the tiny elevator to the third floor. Henri opened the door of the laboratory. 'Don't move!' he cried. 'Stay right where you are!' He scuttled away and returned in a few seconds holding a little tray upon which lay two greasy-looking red rubber objects. 'Noseplugs,' he said. 'Put them in, please. Like me. Keep out the molecules. Go on, ram them in tight. You'll have to breathe through your mouth, but who cares?'

Each noseplug had a short length of blue string attached to its blunt lower end, presumably for pulling it back out of the nostril. I could see the two bits of blue string dangling from Henri's nostrils. I inserted my own noseplugs. Henri inspected them. He rammed them in tighter with his thumb. Then he went dancing back into the lab, waving his hairy hands and crying out, 'Come in now, my dear Oswald! Come in, come in! Forgive my excitement, but this is a great day for me!' The plugs in his nose made him speak as though he had a bad cold. He hopped over to a cupboard and reached inside. He brought out one of those small square bottles made of very thick glass that hold about an ounce of perfume. He carried it over to where I stood, cupping his hands around it as though it were a tiny bird. 'Look! Here it is! The most precious fluid in the entire world!'

This is the sort of rubbishy overstatement I dislike intensely. 'So you think you've done it?' I said.

'I know I've done it, Oswald! I am certain I've done it!'

'Tell me what happened.'

'That's not so easy,' he said. 'But I can try.'

He placed the little bottle carefully on the bench. 'I had left this particular blend, Number 1076, to distil overnight,' he went on. 'That was because only one drop of distillate is produced every half-hour. I had it dripping into a sealed beaker to prevent evaporation. All these fluids are extremely volatile. And so, soon after I arrived at eight thirty this morning, I went over to Number 1076 and lifted the seal from the beaker. I took a tiny sniff. Just one tiny sniff. Then I replaced the seal.'

'And then?'

'Oh, my God, Oswald, it was fantastic! I completely lost control of myself! I did things I would never in a million years have dreamed of doing!'

'Such as what?'

'My dear fellow, I went completely wild! I was like a wild beast, an animal! I was not human! The civilizing influences of centuries simply dropped away! I was Neolithic!'

'What did you do?'

'I can't remember the next bit very clearly. It was all so quick and violent. But I became overwhelmed by the most terrifying sensation of lust it is possible to imagine. Everything else was blotted out of my mind. All I wanted was a woman. I felt that if I didn't get hold of a woman immediately, I would explode.'

'Lucky Jeanette,' I said, glancing towards the next room. 'How is she now?'

'Jeanette left me over a year ago,' he said. 'I replaced her with a brilliant young chemist called Simone Gautier.'

'Lucky Simone, then.'

'No, no!' Henri cried. 'That was the awful thing! She hadn't arrived! Today of all days, she was late for work! I began to go mad. I dashed out into the corridor and down the stairs. I was like a dangerous animal. I was hunting for a woman, any woman, and heaven help her when I found her!'

'And who did you find?'

'Nobody, thank God. Because suddenly, I regained my senses. The effect had worn off. It was very quick, and I was standing alone on the second-floor landing. I felt cold. But I knew at once exactly what had happened. I ran back upstairs and re-entered this room with my nostrils pinched tightly between finger and thumb. I went straight to the drawer where I stored the noseplugs. Ever since I started working on this project, I have kept a supply of noseplugs ready for just such an occasion. I rammed in the plugs. Now I was safe.'

'Can't the molecules get up into the nose through the mouth?' I asked him.

'They can't reach the receptor sites,' he said. 'That's why you can't smell through your mouth. So I went over to the apparatus and switched off the heat. I then transferred the tiny quantity of precious fluid from the beaker to this very solid airtight bottle you see here. In it there are precisely eleven cubic centimetres of Number 1076.'

'Then you telephoned me.'

'Not immediately no. Because at that point, Simone arrived. She took one look at me and ran into the next room, screaming.'

'Why did she do that?'

'My God, Oswald, I was standing there stark naked and I hadn't realized it. I must have ripped off all my clothes!'

'Then what?'

'I got dressed again. After that, I went and told Simone exactly what had happened. When she heard the truth, she became as excited as me. Don't forget, we've been working on this together for over a year now.'

'Is she still here?'

'Yes. She's next door in the other lab.'

It was quite a story Henri had told me. I picked up the little square bottle and held it against the light. Through the thick glass I could see about half an inch of fluid, pale and pinkish-grey, like the juice of a ripe quince.

'Don't drop it,' Henri said. 'Better put it down.' I put it down. 'The next step,' he went on, 'will be to make an accurate test under scientific conditions. For that I shall have to spray a measured quantity on to a woman and then let a man approach her. It will be necessary for me to observe the operation at close range.'

'You are a dirty old man,' I said.

'I am an olfactory chemist,' he said primly.

'Why don't I go out into the street with my noseplugs in,' I said, 'and spray some on to the first woman who comes along. You can watch from the window here. It ought to be fun.'

'It would be fun all right,' Henri said. 'But not very scientific. I must make the tests indoors under controlled conditions.'

'And I will play the male part,' I said.

'No, Oswald.'

'What do you mean, no. I insist.'

'Now listen to me,' Henri said. 'We have not yet found out what will happen when a woman is present. This stuff is very powerful, I am certain of that. And you, my dear sir, are not exactly young. It could be extremely dangerous. It could drive you beyond the limit of your endurance.'

I was stung. 'There are no limits to my endurance,' I said.

'Rubbish,' Henri said. 'I refuse to take chances. That is why I have engaged the fittest and strongest young man I could find.'

'You mean you've already done this?'

'Certainly I have,' Henri said. 'I am excited and impatient. I want to get on. The boy will be here any minute.'

'Who is he?'

'A professional boxer.'

'Good God.'

'His name is Pierre Lacaille. I am paying him one thousand francs for the job.'

'How did you find him?'

'I know a lot more people than you think, Oswald. I am not a hermit.'

'Does the man know what he's in for?'

'I have told him that he is to participate in a scientific experiment that has to do with the psychology of sex. The less he knows the better.'

'And the woman? Who will you use there?'

'Simone, of course,' Henri said. 'She is a scientist in her own right. She will be able to observe the reactions of the male even more closely than me.'

'That she will,' I said. 'Does she realize what might happen to her?'

'Very much so. And I had one hell of a job persuading her to do it. I had to point out that she would be participating in a demonstration that will go down in history. It will be talked about for hundreds of years.'

'Nonsense,' I said.

'My dear sir, through the centuries there are certain great epic moments of scientific discovery that are never forgotten. Like the time when Dr Horace Wells of Hartford, Connecticut, had a tooth pulled out in 1844.'

'What was so historic about that?'

'Dr Wells was a dentist who had been playing about with nitrous oxide gas. One day, he got a terrible toothache. He knew the tooth would have to come out, and he called in another dentist to do the job. But first he persuaded his colleague to put a mask over his face and turn on the nitrous oxide. He became unconscious and the tooth was extracted and he woke up again as fit as a flea. Now *that*, Oswald, was the first operation ever performed in the world under general anaesthesia. It started something big. We shall do the same.'

At this point, the doorbell rang. Henri grabbed a pair of noseplugs and carried them with him to the door. And there stood Pierre, the boxer. But Henri would not allow him to enter until the plugs were rammed firmly up his nostrils. I believe the fellow came thinking he was going to act in a blue film, but the business with the plugs must have quickly disillusioned him. Pierre Lacaille was a bantamweight, small, muscular and wiry. He had a flat face and a bent nose. He was about twenty-two and not very bright.

Henri introduced me, then ushered us straight into the adjoining laboratory where Simone was working. She was standing by the lab bench in a white overall, writing something in a notebook. She looked up at us through thick glasses as we came in. The glasses had a white plastic frame.

'Simone,' Henri said, 'this is Pierre Lacaille.' Simone looked at the boxer but said nothing. Henri didn't bother to introduce me.

Simone was a slim thirtyish woman with a pleasant scrubbed face. Her hair was brushed back and plaited into a bun. This, together with the white spectacles, the white overall and the white skin of her face, gave her a quaint antiseptic air. She looked as though she had been sterilized for thirty minutes in an autoclave and should be handled with rubber gloves. She gazed at the boxer with large brown eyes.

'Let's get going,' Henri said. 'Are you ready?'

'I don't know what's going to happen,' the boxer said. 'But I'm ready.' He did a little dance on his toes.

Henri was also ready. He had obviously worked the whole thing out before I arrived. 'Simone will sit in that chair,' he said, pointing to a plain wooden chair set in the middle of the laboratory. 'And you, Pierre, will stand on the six-metre mark with your noseplugs still in.'

There were chalk lines on the floor indicating various distances from the chair, from half a metre up to six metres.

'I shall begin by spraying a small quantity of liquid on to the lady's neck,' Henri went on addressing the boxer. 'You will then remove your noseplugs and start walking slowly towards her.' To me he said, 'I wish first of all to discover the effective range, the exact distance he is from the subject when the molecules hit.'

'Does he start with his clothes on?' I asked.

'Exactly as he is now.'

'And is the lady expected to co-operate or to resist?'

'Neither. She must be a purely passive instrument in his hands.'

Simone was still looking at the boxer. I saw her slide the end of her tongue slowly over her lips.

'This perfume,' I said to Henri, 'does it have any effect upon a woman?'

'None whatsoever,' he said. 'That is why I am sending Simone out now to prepare the spray.' The girl went into the main laboratory, closing the door behind her.

'So you spray something on the girl and I walk towards her,' the boxer said. 'What happens then?'

'We shall have to wait and see,' Henri said. 'You are not worried, are you?'

'Me, worried?' the boxer said. 'About a woman?'

'Good boy,' Henri said. Henri was becoming very excited. He went hopping from one end of the room to the other, checking and rechecking the position of the chair on its chalk mark and moving all breakables such as glass beakers and bottles and test-tubes off the bench on to a high shelf. 'This isn't the ideal place,' he said, 'but we must make the best of it.' He tied a surgeon's mask over the lower part of his face, then handed one to me.

'Don't you trust the noseplugs?'

'It's just an extra precaution,' he said. 'Put it on.'

The girl returned carrying a tiny stainless-steel spray-gun.

She gave the gun to Henri. Henri took a stop-watch from his pocket. 'Get ready, please,' he said. 'You, Pierre, stand over there on the six-metre mark.' Pierre did so. The girl seated herself in the chair. It was a chair without arms. She sat very prim and upright in her spotless white overall with her hands folded on her lap, her knees together. Henri stationed himself behind the girl. I stood to one side. 'Are we ready?' Henri cried.

'Wait,' said the girl. It was the first word she had spoken. She stood up, removed her spectacles, placed them on a high shelf, then returned to her seat. She smoothed the white overall along her thighs, then clasped her hands together and laid them again on her lap.

'Are we ready now?' Henri said.

'Let her have it,' I said. 'Shoot.'

Henri aimed the little spray-gun at an area of bare skin just below Simone's ear. He pulled the trigger. The gun made a soft hiss and a fine misty spray came out of its nozzle.

'Pull your noseplugs out!' Henri called to the boxer as he skipped quickly away from the girl and took up a position next to me. The boxer caught hold of the strings dangling from his nostrils and pulled. The vaselined plugs slid out smoothly.

'Come on, come on!' Henri shouted. 'Start moving! Drop the plugs on the floor and come forwards slowly!' The boxer took a pace forwards. 'Not so fast!' Henri cried. 'Slowly does it! That's better! Keep going! Keep going! Don't stop!' He was crazy with excitement, and I must admit I was getting a bit worked up myself. I glanced at the girl. She was crouching in the chair, just a few yards away from the boxer, tense, motionless, watching his every move, and I found myself thinking about a white female rat I had once seen in a cage with a huge python. The python was going to swallow the rat and the rat knew it, and the rat was crouching very low and still, hypnotized, transfixed, utterly fascinated by the slow advancing movements of the snake.

The boxer edged forwards.

As he passed the five-metre mark, the girl unclasped her hands. She laid them palms downwards on her thighs. Then she changed her mind and placed them more or less underneath her buttocks, gripping the seat of the chair on either side, bracing herself, as it were, against the coming onslaught.

The boxer had just passed the two-metre mark when the smell hit him. He stopped dead. His eyes glazed and he swayed on his legs as though he had been tapped on the head with a mallet. I thought he was going to keel over, but he didn't. He stood there swaying gently from side to side like a drunk. Suddenly he started making noises through his nostrils, queer little snorts and grunts that reminded me of a pig sniffing around its trough. Then without any warning at all, he sprang at the girl. He ripped off her white overall, her dress and her underclothes. After that, all hell broke loose.

There is little point in describing exactly what went on during the next few minutes. You can guess most of it anyway. I do have to admit, though, that Henri had probably been right in choosing an exceptionally fit and healthy young man. I hate to say it, but I doubt my middle-aged body could have stood up to the incredibly violent gymnastics the boxer seemed driven to perform. I am not a voyeur. I hate that sort of thing. But in this case, I stood there absolutely transfixed. The sheer animal ferocity of the man was frightening. He was like a wild beast. And right in the middle of it all, Henri did an interesting thing. He produced a revolver and rushed up to the boxer and shouted, 'Get away from that girl! Leave her alone or I'll shoot you!' The boxer ignored him, so Henri fired a shot just over the top of his head and yelled, 'I mean it, Pierre! I shall kill you if you don't stop!' The boxer didn't even look up.

Henri was hopping and dancing about the room and shouting, 'It's fantastic! It's magnificent! Unbelievable! It works! It works! We've done it, my dear Oswald! We've done it!'

The action stopped as quickly as it had begun. The boxer suddenly let go of the girl, stood up, blinked a few times, and then said, 'Where the hell am I? What happened?'

Simone, who seemed to have come through it all with no bones broken, jumped up, grabbed her clothes, and ran into the next room. 'Thank you, mademoiselle,' said Henri as she flew past him.

The interesting thing was that the bemused boxer hadn't the faintest idea what he had been doing. He stood there naked and covered with sweat, gazing around the room and trying to figure out how in the world he came to be in that condition.

'What did I do?' he asked. 'Where's the girl?'

'You were terrific!' Henri shouted, throwing him a towel. 'Don't worry about a thing! The thousand francs is all yours!'

Just then the door flew open and Simone, still naked, ran back into the lab. 'Spray me again!' she cried. 'Oh, Monsieur Henri, spray me just one more time!' Her face was alight, her eyes shining brilliantly.

'The experiment is over,' Henri said. 'Go away and dress yourself.' He took her firmly by the shoulders and pushed her back into the other room. Then he locked the door.

Half an hour later, Henri and I sat celebrating our success in a small café down the street. We were drinking coffee and brandy. 'How long did it go on?' I asked.

'Six minutes and thirty-two seconds,' Henri said.

I sipped my brandy and watched the people strolling by on the sidewalk. 'What's the next move?'

'First, I must write up my notes,' Henri said. 'Then we shall talk about the future.'

'Does anyone else know the formula?'

'Nobody.'

'What about Simone?'

'She doesn't know it.'

'Have you written it down?'

'Not so anyone else could understand it. I shall do that tomorrow.'

'Do it first thing,' I said. 'I'll want a copy. What shall we call the stuff? We need a name.'

'What do you suggest?'

'*Bitch*,' I said. 'Let's call it *Bitch*.' Henri smiled and nodded his head slowly. I ordered more brandy. 'It would be great stuff for stopping a riot,' I said. 'Much better than tear-gas. Imagine the scene if you sprayed it on an angry mob.'

'Nice,' Henri said. 'Very nice.'

'Another thing we could do, we could sell it to very fat, very rich women at fantastic prices.'

'We could do that,' Henri answered.

'Do you think it would cure loss of virility in men?' I asked him.

'Of course,' Henri said. 'Impotence would go out the window.'

'What about octogenarians?'

'Them, too,' he said, 'though it would kill them at the same time.'

'And marriages on the rocks?'

'My dear fellow,' Henri said. 'The possibilities are legion.'

At that precise moment, the seed of an idea came sneaking slowly into my mind. As you know, I have a passion for politics. And my strongest passion, although I am English, is for the politics of the United States of America. I have always thought it is over there, in that mighty and mixed-up nation, that the destinies of mankind must surely lie. And right now, there was a President in office whom I could not stand. He was an evil man who pursued evil polices. Worse than that, he was a humourless and unattractive creature. So why didn't I, Oswald Cornelius, remove him from office?

The idea appealed to me.

'How much *Bitch* have you got in the lab at the moment?' I asked.

'Exactly ten cubic centimetres,' Henri said.

'And how much is one dose?'

'We used one cc for our test.'

'That's all I want,' I said. 'One cc. I'll take it home with me today. And a set of noseplugs.'

'No,' Henri said. 'Let's not play around with it at this stage. It's too dangerous.'

'It is my property,' I said. 'Half of it is mine. Don't forget our agreement.'

In the end, he had to give in. But he hated doing it. We went back to the lab, inserted our noseplugs, and Henri measured out precisely one cc of *Bitch* into a small scent bottle. He sealed the stopper with wax and gave me the bottle. 'I implore you to be discreet,' he said. 'This is probably the most important scientific discovery of the century, and it must not be treated as a joke.'

From Henri's place, I drove directly to the workshop of an old friend, Marcel Brossollet. Marcel was an inventor and manufacturer of tiny precise scientific gadgets. He did a lot of work for surgeons, devising new types of heart-valves and pacemakers and those little one-way valves that reduce intra-cranial pressure in hydrocephalics.

'I want you to make me,' I said to Marcel, 'a capsule that will hold exactly one cc of liquid. To this little capsule, there must be attached a timing device that will split the capsule and release the liquid at a predetermined moment. The entire thing must not be more than half an inch long and half an inch thick. The smaller the better. Can you manage that?'

'Very easily,' Marcel said. 'A thin plastic capsule, a tiny section of razor-blade to split the capsule, a spring to flip the razor-blade, and the usual pre-set alarm system on a very small ladies' watch. Should the capsule be fillable?'

'Yes. Make it so I myself can fill it and seal it up. Can I have it in a week?'

'Why not?' Marcel said. 'It is very simple.'

The next morning brought dismal news. That lecherous little slut Simone had apparently sprayed herself with the entire remaining stock of *Bitch*, over nine cubic centimetres of it, the moment she arrived at the lab! She had then sneaked up behind Henri, who was just settling himself at his desk to write up his notes.

I don't have to tell you what happened next. And worst of all, the silly girl had forgotten that Henri had a serious heart condition. Damn it, he wasn't even allowed to climb a flight of stairs. So when the molecules hit him the poor fellow didn't stand a chance. He was dead within a minute, killed in action as they say, and that was that.

The infernal woman might at least have waited until he had written down the formula. As it was, Henri left not a single note. I searched the lab after they had taken away his body, but I found nothing. So now more than ever, I was determined to make good use of the only remaining cubic centimetre of *Bitch* in the world.

A week later, I collected from Marcel Brossollet a beautiful little gadget. The timing device consisted of the smallest watch I had ever seen, and this, together with the capsule and all the other parts, had been secured to a tiny aluminium plate three eighths of an inch square. Marcel showed me how to fill and seal the capsule and set the timer. I thanked him and paid the bill.

As soon as possible, I travelled to New York. In Manhattan, I put up at the Plaza Hotel. I arrived there at about three in the afternoon. I took a bath, had a shave, and asked room service to send me up a bottle of Glenlivet and some ice. Feeling clean and comfortable in my dressing-gown, I poured myself a good strong drink of the delicious malt whisky, then settled down in a deep chair with the morning's *New York Times*. My suite overlooked Central Park, and through the open window I could hear the hum of traffic and the blaring of cab-drivers' horns on Central Park South. Suddenly, one of the smaller headlines on the front page of the paper caught my eye. It said, PRESIDENT ON TV TONIGHT. I read on.

> The President is expected to make an important foreign policy statement when he speaks tonight at the dinner to be given in his honour by the Daughters of the American Revolution in the ballroom of the Waldorf Astoria . . .

My God, what a piece of luck!

I had been prepared to wait in New York for many weeks before I got a chance like this. The President of the United States does not often appear with a bunch of women on television. And that was exactly how I had to have him. He was an extraordinarily slippery customer. He had fallen into many a sewer and had always come out smelling of shit. Yet he managed every time to convince the nation that the smell was coming from someone else, not him. So the way I figured it was this. A man who rapes a woman in full sight of twenty million viewers across the country would have a pretty hard time denying he ever did it.

I read on.

The President will speak for approximately twenty minutes, commencing at nine p.m. and all major TV networks will carry the speech. He will be introduced by Mrs Elvira Ponsonby, the incumbent President of the Daughters of the American Revolution. When interviewed in her suite at the Waldorf Towers, Mrs Ponsonby said . . .

It was perfect! Mrs Ponsonby would be seated on the President's right. At ten past nine precisely, with the President well into his speech and half the population of the United States watching, a little capsule nestling secretly in the region of Mrs Ponsonby's bosom would be punctured and half a centimetre of *Bitch* would come oozing out on to her gilt lamé ball-gown. The President's head would come up, he would sniff and sniff again, his eyes would bulge, his nostrils would flare, and he would start snorting like a stallion. Then suddenly he would turn and grab hold of Mrs Ponsonby. She would be flung across the dining-table and the President would leap on top of her, with the pie à la mode and strawberry shortcake flying in all directions.

I leaned back and closed my eyes, savouring the delicious scene. I saw the headlines in the papers the next morning:

PRESIDENT'S BEST PERFORMANCE TO DATE
PRESIDENTIAL SECRETS REVEALED TO NATION
PRESIDENT INAUGURATES BLUE TV

and so on.

He would be impeached the next day and I would slip quietly out of New York and head back to Paris. Come to think of it, I would be leaving tomorrow!

I checked the time. It was nearly four o'clock. I dressed myself without hurrying. I took the elevator down to the main lobby and strolled across to Madison Avenue. Somewhere around Sixty-second Street, I found a good florist's shop. There I bought a corsage of three massive orchid blooms all fastened together. The orchids were cattleyas, white and mauve splotches on them. They were particularly vulgar. So, undoubtedly, was Mrs Elvira Ponsonby. I had the shop pack them in a handsome box tied up with gold string. Then I strolled back to the Plaza, carrying the box, and went up to my suite.

I locked all doors leading to the corridor in case the maid should come in to turn back the bed. I got out the noseplugs and vaselined them carefully. I inserted them in my nostrils, ramming them home very hard. I tied a surgeon's mask over my lower face as an extra precaution, just as Henri had done. I was ready now for the next step.

With an ordinary nose-dropper, I transferred my precious cubic centimetre of *Bitch* from the scent bottle to the tiny capsule. The hand holding the dropper shook a little as I did this, but all went well. I sealed the capsule.

After that, I wound up the tiny watch and set it to the correct time. It was three minutes after five o'clock. Lastly, I set the timer to go off and break the capsule at ten minutes past nine.

The stems of the three huge orchid blooms had been tied together by the florist with a broad one-inch-wide white ribbon and it was a simple matter for me to remove the ribbon and secure my little capsule and timer to the orchid stems with cotton thread. When that was done, I wound the ribbon back around the stems and over my gadget. Then I retied the bow. It was a nice job.

Next, I telephoned the Waldorf and learned that the dinner was to begin at eight o'clock, but that the guests must be assembled in the ballroom by seven thirty before the President arrived.

At ten minutes to seven, I paid off my cab outside the Waldorf Towers entrance and walked into the building. I crossed the small lobby and placed my orchid box on the reception desk. I leaned over the desk, getting as close as possible to the clerk. 'I have to deliver this package to Mrs Elvira Ponsonby,' I whispered, using a slight American accent. 'It is a gift from the President.'

The clerk looked at me suspiciously.

'Mrs Ponsonby is introducing the President before he speaks tonight in the ballroom,' I added. 'The President wishes her to have this corsage right away.'

'Leave it here and I'll have it sent up to her suite,' the clerk said.

'No, you won't,' I told him. 'My orders are to deliver it in person. What's the number of her suite?'

The man was impressed. 'Mrs Ponsonby is in five-o-one,' he said.

I thanked him and went into the elevator. When I got out at the fifth floor and walked along the corridor, the elevator operator stayed and watched me. I rang the bell to five-o-one.

The door was opened by the most enormous female I had ever seen in my life. I have seen giant women in circuses. I have seen lady wrestlers and weight-lifters. I have seen the huge Masai women in the plains below Kilimanjaro. But never had I seen a female so tall and broad and thick as this one. Nor so thoroughly repugnant. She was groomed and dressed for the greatest occasion of her life, and in the two seconds that elapsed before either of us spoke, I was able to take most of it in – the metallic silver-blue hair with every strand glued into place, the brown pig-eyes, the long sharp nose sniffing for trouble, the curled lips, the prognathous jaw, the powder, the mascara, the scarlet lipstick and, most shattering of all, the massive shored-up bosom that projected like a balcony in front of her. It stuck out so far it was a miracle she didn't topple forwards with the weight of it all. And there she stood, this pneumatic giant, swathed from neck to ankles in the stars and stripes of the American flag.

'Mrs Elvira Ponsonby?' I murmured.

'I am Mrs Ponsonby,' she boomed. 'What do you want? I am extremely busy.'

'Mrs Ponsonby,' I said. 'The President has ordered me to deliver this to you in person.'

She melted immediately. 'The dear man!' she shouted.

'How perfectly gorgeous of him!' Two massive hands reached out to grab the box. I let her have it.

'My instructions are to make sure you open it before you go to the banquet,' I said.

'Sure I'll open it,' she said. 'Do I have to do it in front of you?'

'If you wouldn't mind.'

'Okay, come on in. But I don't have much time.'

I followed her into the living-room of the suite. 'I am to tell you,' I said, 'that it comes with all good wishes from one President to another.'

'Ha!' she roared. 'I like that! What a gorgeous man he is!' She untied the gold string of the box and lifted the lid. 'I guessed it!' she shouted. 'Orchids! How splendid! They're far grander than this poor little thing I'm wearing!'

I had been so dazzled by the galaxy of stars across her bosom that I hadn't noticed the single orchid pinned to the left-hand side.

'I must change over at once,' she said. 'The President will be expecting me to wear his gift.'

'He certainly will,' I said.

Now to give you an idea of how far her chest stuck out in front of her, I must tell you that when she reached forward to unpin the flower, she was only just able to touch it even with her arms fully extended. She fiddled around with the pin for quite a while, but she couldn't really see what she was doing and it wouldn't come undone. 'I'm terrified of tearing this gorgeous gown,' she said. 'Here, you do it.' She swung around and thrust her mammoth bust in my face. I hesitated. 'Go on!' she boomed. 'I don't have all night!' I went to it, and in the end I managed to get the pin unhooked from her dress.

'Now let's get the other one on,' she said.

I put aside the single orchid and lifted my own flowers carefully from the box.

'Have they got a pin?' she asked.

'I don't believe they have,' I said. That was something I'd forgotten.

'No matter,' she said. 'We'll use the old one.' She removed the safety pin from the first orchid, and then, before I could stop her, she seized the three orchids I was holding and jabbed the pin hard into the white ribbon around the stems. She jabbed it almost exactly into the spot where my little capsule of *Bitch* was lying hidden. The pin struck something hard and wouldn't go through. She jabbed it again. Again it struck metal. 'What the hell's under here?' she snorted.

'Let me do it!' I cried, but it was too late, because the wet stain of *Bitch* from the punctured capsule was already spreading over the white ribbon and one hundredth of a second later the smell hit me. It caught me smack under the nose and it wasn't actually like a smell at all because a smell is something intangible. You cannot feel a smell. But this stuff was palpable. It was solid. It felt as though some kind of fiery liquid were being squirted up my nostrils under high pressure. It was exceedingly uncomfortable. I could feel it pushing higher and higher, penetrating far beyond the nasal passages, forcing its way up behind the forehead and reaching for the brain. Suddenly the stars and stripes on Mrs Ponsonby's dress began to wobble and bobble about and then the whole room started wobbling and I could hear my heart thumping in my head. It felt as though I were going under an anaesthetic.

At that point, I must have blacked out completely, if only for a couple of seconds.

When I came round again, I was standing naked in a rosy room and there was a funny feeling in my groin. I looked down and saw that my beloved sexual organ was three feet long and thick to match. It was still growing. It was lengthening and swelling at a tremendous rate. At the same time, my body was shrinking. Smaller and smaller shrank my body. Bigger and bigger grew my astonishing organ, and it went on growing, by God, until it had enveloped my entire body and absorbed it within itself. I was now a gigantic perpendicular penis, seven feet tall and as handsome as they come.

I did a little dance around the room to celebrate my splendid new condition. On the way I met a maiden in a star-spangled dress. She was very big as maidens go. I drew myself up to my full height and declaimed in a loud voice:

> 'The summer's flower is to the summer sweet,
> It flourishes despite the summer's heat.
> But tell me truly, did you ever see
> A sexual organ quite so grand as me?'

The maiden leaped up and flung her arms as far around me as she could. Then cried out:

'Shall I compare thee to a summer's day?
Shall I . . . Oh dear, I know not what to say.
But all my life I've had an itch to kiss
A man who could erect himself like this.'

A moment later, the two of us were millions of miles up in outer space, flying through the universe in a shower of meteorites all red and gold. I was riding her bareback, crouching forwards and gripping her tightly between my thighs. 'Faster!' I shouted, jabbing long spurs into her flanks. 'Go faster!' Faster and still faster she flew, spurting and spinning around the rim of the sky, her mane streaming with sun, and snow waving out of her tail. The sense of power I had was overwhelming. I was unassailable, supreme. I was the Lord of the Universe, scattering the planets and catching the stars in the palm of my hand and tossing them away as though they were ping-pong balls.

Oh, ecstasy and ravishment! Oh, Jericho and Tyre and Sidon! The walls came tumbling down and the firmament disintegrated, and out of the smoke and fire of the explosion, the sitting-room in the Waldorf Towers came swimming slowly back into my consciousness like a rainy day. The place was a shambles. A tornado would have done less damage. My clothes were on the floor. I started dressing myself very quickly. I did it in about thirty seconds flat. And as I ran towards the door, I heard a voice that seemed to be coming from somewhere behind an upturned table in the far corner of the room. 'I don't know who you are, young man,' it said. 'But you've certainly done me a power of good.'

Ah, Sweet Mystery of Life

First published in *The New York Times*
(September 1974)

My cow started bulling at dawn and the noise can drive you crazy if the cowshed is right under your window. So I got dressed early and phoned Claud at the filling-station to ask if he'd give me a hand to lead her down the steep hill and across the road over to Rummins's farm to have her serviced by Rummins's famous bull.

Claud arrived five minutes later and we tied a rope around the cow's neck and set off down the lane on this cool September morning. There were high hedges on either side of the lane and the hazel bushes had clusters of big ripe nuts all over them.

'You ever seen Rummins do a mating?' Claud asked me.

I told him I had never seen anyone do an official mating between a bull and a cow.

'Rummins does it special,' Claud said. 'There's nobody in the world does a mating the way Rummins does it.'

'What's so special about it?'

'You got a treat coming to you,' Claud said.

'So has the cow,' I said.

'If the rest of the world knew about what Rummins does at a mating,' Claud said, 'he'd be world famous. It would change the whole science of dairy-farming all over the world.'

'Why doesn't he tell them then?' I asked.

'I doubt he's ever even thought about it,' Claud said. 'Rummins isn't one to bother his head about things like that. He's got the best dairy-herd for miles around and that's all he cares about. He doesn't want the newspapers swarming all over his place asking questions, which is exactly what would happen if it ever got out.'

'Why don't you tell me about it,' I said.

We walked on in silence for a while, the cow pulling ahead.

'I'm surprised Rummins said yes to lending you his bull,' Claud said. 'I've never known him do that before.'

At the bottom of the lane we crossed the Aylesbury road and climbed up the hill on the other side of the valley towards the farm. The cow knew there was a bull up there somewhere and she was pulling harder than ever on the rope. We had to trot to keep up with her.

There were no gates at the farm entrance, just a wide gap and a cobbled yard beyond. Rummins, carrying a pail of milk across the yard, saw us coming. He set the pail down slowly and came over to meet us. 'She's ready then, is she?' he said.

'Been yelling her head off,' I said.

Rummins walked around my cow, examining her carefully. He was a short man, built squat and broad like a frog. He had a wide frog-mouth and broken teeth and shifty eyes, but over the years I had grown to respect him for his wisdom and the sharpness of his mind.

'All right then,' he said. 'What is it you want, a heifer calf or a bull?'

'Can I choose?'

'Of course you can choose.'

'Then I'll have a heifer,' I said, keeping a straight face. 'We want milk not beef.'

'Hey, Bert!' Rummins called out. 'Come and give us a hand!'

Bert emerged from the cowsheds. He was Rummins's youngest son, a tall boneless boy with a runny nose and something wrong with one eye. The eye was pale and misty-grey all over, like a boiled fish-eye, and it moved quite independently from the other eye. 'Get another rope,' Rummins said.

Bert fetched a rope and looped it around my cow's neck so that she now had two ropes holding her, my own and Bert's. 'He wants a heifer,' Rummins said. 'Face her into the sun.'

'Into the sun?' I said. 'There isn't any sun.'

'There's always sun,' Rummins said. 'Them bloody clouds don't make no difference. Come on now. Get a jerk on, Bert. Bring her round. Sun's over there.'

With Bert holding one rope and Claud and me holding the other, we manoeuvred the cow round until her head was facing directly towards the place in the sky where the sun was hidden behind the clouds.

'I told you it was different,' Claud whispered. 'You're going to see something soon you've never seen in your life before.'

'Hold her steady now!' Rummins ordered. 'Don't let her jump round!' Then he hurried over to a shed in the far corner of the yard and brought out the bull. He was an enormous beast, a black-and-white Friesian, with short legs and a body like a ten-ton truck. Rummins was leading it by a chain attached to a steel ring through the bull's nose.

'Look at them bangers on him,' Claud said. 'I'll bet you've never seen a bull with bangers like that before.'

'Tremendous,' I said. They were like a couple of cantaloupe melons in a carrier bag and they were almost dragging on the ground as the bull waddled forwards.

'You better stand back and leave the rope to me,' Claud said. 'You get right out of the way.' I was happy to comply.

The bull approached my cow slowly, staring at her with dangerous white eyes. Then he started snorting and pawing the ground with one foreleg.

'Hang on tight!' Rummins shouted to Bert and Claud. They were leaning back against their respective ropes, holding them very taut and at right angles to the cow.

'Come on, boy,' Rummins whispered softly to the bull. 'Go to it, lad.'

With surprising agility the bull heaved his front part up on to my cow's back and I caught a glimpse of a long scarlet penis, as thin as a rapier and just as stiff, and then it was inside the cow and the cow staggered and the bull heaved and snorted and in thirty seconds it was all over. The bull climbed down again slowly and stood there looking somewhat pleased with himself.

'Some bulls don't know where to put it,' Rummins said. 'But mine does. Mine could thread a needle with that dick of his.'

'Wonderful,' I said. 'A bull's eye.'

'That's exactly where the word come from,' Rummins said. 'A bull's eye. Come on, lad,' he said to the bull. 'You've had your lot for today.' He led the bull back to the shed and shut him in and when he returned I thanked him, and then I asked him if he really believed that facing the cow into the sun during the mating would produce a female calf.

'Don't be so damn silly,' he said. 'Of course I believe it. Facts is facts.'

'What do you mean facts is facts?'

'I mean what I say, mister. It's a certainty. That's right, ain't it, Bert?'

Bert swivelled his misty eye around in its socket and said, 'Too bloody true it's right.'

'And if you face her away from the sun does it get you a male?'

'Every single time,' Rummins said. I smiled and he saw it. 'You don't believe me, do you?'

'Not really,' I said.

'Come with me,' he said. 'And when you see what I'm going to show you, you'll bloody well have to believe me. You two stay here and watch that cow,' he said to Claud and Bert. Then he led me into the farmhouse. The room we went into was dark and small and dirty. From a drawer in the sideboard he produced a whole stack of thin exercise books. They were the kind children use at school. 'These is calving books,' he announced. 'And in here is a record of every mating that's ever been done on this farm since I first started thirty-two years ago.'

LUST

He opened a book at random and allowed me to look. There were four columns on each page: COW'S NAME, DATE OF MATING, DATE OF BIRTH, SEX OF CALF.

I glanced down the sex column. *Heifer*, it said. *Heifer, Heifer, Heifer, Heifer, Heifer.*

'We don't want no bull calves here,' Rummins said. 'Bull calves is a dead loss on a dairy farm.'

I turned over a page. *Heifer*, it said. *Heifer, Heifer, Heifer, Heifer, Heifer.*

'Hey,' I said. 'Here's a bull calf.'

'That's quite right,' Rummins said. 'Now take a look at what I wrote opposite that one at the time of the mating.' I glanced at column two. *Cow jumped round*, it said.

'Some of them gets fractious and you can't hold 'em steady,' Rummins said. 'So they finish up facing the other way. That's the only time I ever get a bull.'

'This is fantastic,' I said, leafing through the book.

'Of course it's fantastic,' Rummins said. 'It's one of the most fantastic things in the whole world. Do you actually know what I average on this farm? I average ninety-eight per cent heifers year in year out! Check it for yourself. Go on and check it. I'm not stopping you.'

'I'd like very much to check it,' I said. 'May I sit down?'

'Help yourself,' Rummins said. 'I've got work to do.' I found a pencil and paper and I proceeded to go through each one of the thirty-two little books with great care. There was one book for each year, from 1915 to 1946. There were approximately eighty calves a year born on the farm, and my final results over the thirty-two-year period were as follows:

Heifer calves 2, 516
Bull calves 56
Total calves born, including stillborn 2, 572

I went outside to look for Rummins. Claud had disappeared. He'd probably taken my cow home. I found Rummins in the dairy pouring milk into the separator. 'Haven't you ever told anyone about this?' I asked him.

'Never have,' he said.

'Why not?'

'I reckon it ain't nobody else's business.'

'But my dear man, this could transform the entire milk industry the world over.'

'It might,' he said. 'It might easily do that. It wouldn't do the beef business no harm either if they could get bulls every time.'

'How did you hear about it in the first place?'

'My old dad told me,' Rummins said. 'When I were about eighteen, my old dad said to me, "I'll tell you a secret," he said, "that'll make you rich." And he told me this.'

'Has it made you rich?'

'I ain't done too bad for myself, have I?' he said.

'But did your father offer any sort of explanation as to why it works?' I asked.

Rummins explored the inner rim of one nostril with the end of his thumb, holding the noseflap between thumb and forefinger as he did so. 'A very clever man, my old dad was,' he said. 'Very clever indeed. Of course he told me how it works.'

'How?'

'He explained to me that a cow don't have nothing to do with deciding the sex of the calf,' Rummins said. 'All a cow's got is an egg. It's the bull decides what the sex is going to be. The sperm of the bull.'

'Go on,' I said.

'According to my old dad, a bull has two different kinds of sperm, female sperm and male sperm. You follow me so far?'

'Yes,' I said. 'Keep going.'

'So when the old bull shoots off his sperm into the cow, a sort of swimming race takes place between the male and the female sperm to see which one can reach the egg first. If the female sperm wins, you get a heifer.'

'But what's the sun got to do with it?' I asked.

'I'm coming to that,' he said, 'so listen carefully. When an animal is standing on all fours like a cow, and when you face her head into the sun, then the sperm has also got to travel directly into the sun to reach the egg. Switch the cow around and they'll be travelling away from the sun.'

'So what you're saying,' I said, 'is that the sun exerts a pull of some sort on the female sperm and makes them swim faster than the male sperm.'

'Exactly!' cried Rummins. 'That's exactly it! It exerts a pull! It drags them forwards! That's why they always win! And if you turn the cow round the other way, it's pulling them backwards and the male sperm wins instead.'

'It's an interesting theory,' I said. 'But it hardly seems likely that the sun, which is millions of miles away, could exert a pull on a bunch of spermatozoa inside a cow.'

'You're talking rubbish!' cried Rummins. 'Absolute and

utter rubbish! Don't the moon exert a pull on the bloody tides of the ocean to make 'em high and low? Of course it does! So why shouldn't the sun exert a pull on the female sperm?'

'I see your point.'

Suddenly Rummins seemed to have had enough. 'You'll have a heifer calf for sure,' he said, turning away. 'Don't you worry about that.'

'Mr Rummins,' I said.

'What?'

'Is there any reason why this shouldn't work with humans as well?'

'Of course it'll work with humans,' he said. 'Just so long as you remember everything's got to be pointed in the right direction. A cow ain't lying down you know. It's standing on all fours.'

'I see what you mean.'

'And it ain't no good doing it at night either,' he said, 'because the sun is shielded behind the earth and it can't influence anything.'

'That's true,' I said, 'but have you any sort of proof it works with humans?'

Rummins laid his head to one side and gave me another of his long sly broken-toothed grins. 'I've got four boys of my own, ain't I?' he said.

'So you have.'

'Ruddy girls ain't no use to me around here,' he said. 'Boys is what you want on a farm and I've got four of 'em, right?'

'Right,' I said, 'you're absolutely right.'

Claud's Dog

First published in *Someone Like You* (1953)

The Ratcatcher

In the afternoon the ratcatcher came to the filling-station. He came sidling up the driveway with a stealthy, soft-treading gait, making no noise at all with his feet on the gravel. He had an army knapsack slung over one shoulder and he was wearing an old-fashioned black jacket with large pockets. His brown corduroy trousers were tied around the knees with pieces of white string.

'Yes?' Claud asked, knowing very well who he was.

'Rodent operative.' His small dark eyes moved swiftly over the premises.

'The ratcatcher?'

'That's me.'

The man was lean and brown with a sharp face and two long sulphur-coloured teeth that protruded from the upper jaw, overlapping the lower lip, pressing it inward. The ears were thin and pointed and set far back on the head, near the nape of the neck. The eyes were almost black, but when they looked at you there was a flash of yellow somewhere inside them.

'You've come very quick.'

'Special orders from the health officer.'

'And now you're going to catch all the rats?'

'Yep.'

The kind of dark furtive eyes he had were those of an animal that lives its life peering out cautiously and for ever from a hole in the ground.

'How are you going to catch 'em?'

'Ah-h-h,' the ratman said darkly. 'That's all accordin' to where they is.'

'Trap 'em, I suppose.'

'Trap 'em!' he cried, disgusted. 'You won't catch many rats that way! Rats isn't rabbits, you know.'

He held his face up high, sniffing the air with a nose that twitched perceptibly from side to side.

'No,' he said, scornfully. 'Trappin's no way to catch a rat. Rats is clever, let me tell you that. If you want to catch 'em, you got to know 'em. You got to know rats on this job.'

I could see Claud staring at him with a certain fascination.

'They're more clever'n dogs, rats is.'

'Get away.'

'You know what they do? They watch you! All the time you're goin' round preparin' to catch 'em, they're sittin' quietly in dark places, watchin' you.' The man crouched, stretching his stringy neck far forward.

'So what do you do?' Claud asked, fascinated.

'Ah! That's it, you see. That's where you got to know rats.'

'How d'you catch 'em?'

'There's ways,' the ratman said, leering. 'There's various ways.'

He paused, nodding his repulsive head sagely up and

down..'It's all dependin',' he said, 'on where they is. This ain't a sewer job, is it?'

'No, it's not a sewer job.'

'Tricky things, sewer jobs. Yes,' he said, delicately sniffing the air to the left of him with his mobile nose-end, 'sewer jobs is very tricky things.'

'Not especially, I shouldn't think.'

'Oh-ho. You shouldn't, shouldn't you! Well, I'd like to see *you* do a sewer job! Just exactly how would *you* set about it, I'd like to know?'

'Nothing to it. I'd just poison 'em, that's all.'

'And where exactly would you put the poison, might I ask?'

'Down the sewer. Where the hell you think I put it!'

'There!' the ratman cried, triumphant. 'I knew it! Down the sewer! And you know what'd happen then? Get washed away, that's all. Sewer's like a river, y'know.'

'That's what *you* say,' Claud answered. 'That's only what *you* say.'

'It's facts.'

'All right, then, all right. So what would *you* do, Mr Know-all?'

'That's exactly where you got to know rats, on a sewer job.'

'Come on then, let's have it.'

'Now listen. I'll tell you.' The ratman advanced a step closer, his voice became secretive and confidential, the voice of a man divulging fabulous professional secrets. 'You works on the understandin' that a rat is a gnawin' animal, see. Rats *gnaws*. Anythin' you give 'em, don't matter what it is, anythin' new they never seen before, and what do they do? They *gnaws* it. So now! There you are! You get a sewer job on your hands. And what d'you do?'

His voice had the soft throaty sound of a croaking frog and he seemed to speak all his words with an immense wet-lipped relish, as though they tasted good on the tongue. The accent was similar to Claud's, the broad soft accent of the Buckinghamshire countryside, but his voice was more throaty, the words more fruity in his mouth.

'All you do is you go down the sewer and you take along some ordinary paper bags, just ordinary brown-paper bags, and these bags is filled with plaster of Paris powder. Nothin' else. Then you suspend the bags from the roof of the sewer so they hang down not quite touchin' the water. See? Not quite touchin', and just high enough so a rat can reach 'em.'

Claud was listening, rapt.

'There you are, y'see. Old rat comes swimmin' along the sewer and sees the bag. He stops. He takes a sniff at it and it don't smell so bad anyway. So what's he do then?'

'He *gnaws* it,' Claud cried, delighted.

'There! That's it! That's exactly it! He starts *gnawin'* away at the bag and the bag breaks and the old rat gets a mouthful of powder for his pains.'

'Well?'

'That does him.'

'What? Kills him?'

'Yep. Kills him stony!'

'Plaster of Paris ain't poisonous, you know.'

'Ah! There you are! That's exackly where you're wrong,

see. This powder swells. When you wet it, it swells. Gets into the rat's tubes and swells right up and kills him quicker'n anythin' in the world.'

'*No!*'

'That's where you got to know rats.'

The ratman's face glowed with a stealthy pride, and he rubbed his stringy fingers together, holding the hands up close to the face. Claud watched him, fascinated.

'Now – where's them rats?' The word 'rats' came out of his mouth soft and throaty, with a rich fruity relish as though he were gargling with melted butter. 'Let's take a look at them *rraats*.'

'Over there in the hayrick across the road.'

'Not in the house?' he asked, obviously disappointed.

'No. Only around the hayrick. Nowhere else.'

'I'll wager they're in the house too. Like as not gettin' in all your food in the night and spreadin' disease and sickness. You got any disease here?' he asked, looking first at me, then at Claud.

'Everyone fine here.'

'Quite sure?'

'Oh yes.'

'You never know, you see. You could be sickenin' for it weeks and weeks and not feel it. Then all of a sudden – bang! – and it's got you. That's why Dr Arbuthnot's so particular. That's why he sent me out so quick, see. To stop the spreadin' of disease.'

He had now taken upon himself the mantle of the health officer. A most important rat he was now, deeply disappointed that we were not suffering from bubonic plague.

'I feel fine,' Claud said, nervously.

The ratman searched his face again, but said nothing.

'And how are you goin' to catch 'em in the hayrick?'

The ratman grinned, a crafty toothy grin. He reached down into his knapsack and withdrew a large tin, which he held up level with his face. He peered around one side of it at Claud.

'Poison!' he whispered. But he pronounced it *pye-zn*, making it into a soft, dark, dangerous word. 'Deadly *pye-zn*, that's what this is!' He was weighing the tin up and down in his hands as he spoke. 'Enough here to kill a million men!'

'Terrifying,' Claud said.

'Exackly it! They'd put you inside for six months if they caught you with even a spoonful of this,' he said, wetting his lips with his tongue. He had a habit of craning his head forward on his neck as he spoke.

'Want to see?' he asked, taking a penny from his pocket, prising open the lid. 'There now! There it is!' He spoke fondly, almost lovingly, of the stuff, and he held it forward for Claud to look.

'Corn? Or barley, is it?'

'It's oats. Soaked in deadly *pye-zn*. You take just one of them grains in your mouth and you'd be a gonner in five minutes.'

'Honest?'

'Yep. Never out of me sight, this tin.'

He caressed it with his hands and gave it a little shake so that the oat grains rustled softly inside.

'But not today. Your rats don't get this today. They wouldn't have it anyway. That they wouldn't. There's where you got to know rats. Rats is suspicious. Terrible suspicious, rats is. So today they gets some nice clean tasty oats as'll do 'em no harm in the world. Fatten 'em, that's all it'll do. And tomorrow they gets the same again. And it'll taste so good there'll be all the rats in the districk comin' along after a couple of days.'

'Rather clever.'

'You got to be clever on this job. You got to be cleverer'n a rat and that's sayin' something.'

'You've almost got to be a rat yourself,' I said. It slipped out in error, before I had time to stop myself, and I couldn't really help it because I was looking at the man at the time. But the effect upon him was surprising.

'There!' he cried. 'Now you got it! Now you really said something! A good ratter's got to be more like a rat than anythin' else in the world! Cleverer even than a rat, and that's not an easy thing to be, let me tell you!'

'Quite sure it's not.'

'All right, then, let's go. I haven't got all day, you know. There's Lady Leonora Benson asking for me urgent up there at the manor.'

'She got rats, too?'

'Everybody's got rats,' the ratman said, and he ambled off down the driveway, across the road to the hayrick, and we watched him go. The way he walked was so like a rat it made you wonder – that slow, almost delicate ambling walk with a lot of give at the knees and no sound at all from the footsteps on the gravel. He hopped nimbly over the gate into the field, then walked quickly round the hay-rick, scattering handfuls of oats on to the ground.

The next day he returned and repeated the procedure.

The day after that he came again and this time he put down the poisoned oats. But he didn't scatter these; he placed them carefully in little piles at each corner of the rick.

'You got a dog?' he asked when he came back across the road on the third day after putting down the poison.

'Yes.'

'Now if you want to see your dog die an 'orrible twistin' death, all you got to do is let him in that gate some time.'

'We'll take care,' Claud told him. 'Don't you worry about that.'

The next day he returned once more, this time to col-lect the dead.

'You got an old sack?' he asked. 'Most likely we goin' to need a sack to put 'em in.'

He was puffed up and important now, the black eyes gleaming with pride. He was about to display the sensa-tional results of his craft to the audience.

Claud fetched a sack and the three of us walked across the road, the ratman leading. Claud and I leaned over the gate, watching. The ratman prowled around the hayrick, bending over to inspect his little piles of poison.

'Somethin' wrong here,' he muttered. His voice was soft and angry.

He ambled over to another pile and got down on his knees to examine it closely.

'Somethin' bloody wrong here.'

'What's the matter?'

He didn't answer, but it was clear that the rats hadn't touched his bait.

'These are very clever rats here,' I said.

'Exactly what I told him, Gordon. These aren't just no ordinary kind of rats you're dealing with here.'

The ratman walked over to the gate. He was very annoyed and showed it on his face and around the nose and by the way the two yellow teeth were pressing down into the skin of his lower lip. 'Don't give me that crap,' he said, looking at me. 'There's nothin' wrong with these rats except somebody's feedin' 'em. They got somethin' juicy to eat somewhere and plenty of it. There's no rats in the world'll turn down oats unless their bellies is full to burstin'.'

'They're clever,' Claud said.

The man turned away, disgusted. He knelt down again and began to scoop up the poisoned oats with a small shovel, tipping them carefully back into the tin. When he had done, all three of us walked back across the road.

The ratman stood near the petrol-pumps, a rather sorry, humble ratman now, whose face was beginning to take on a brooding aspect. He had withdrawn into himself and was brooding in silence over his failure, the eyes veiled and wicked, the little tongue darting out to one side of the two yellow teeth, keeping the lips moist. It appeared to be essential that the lips should be kept moist. He looked up at me, a quick surreptitious glance, then over at Claud. His nose-end twitched, sniffing the air. He raised himself up and down a few times on his toes, swaying gently, and in a voice soft and secretive, he said: 'Want to see somethin'?' He was obviously trying to retrieve his reputation.

'What?'

'Want to see somethin' *amazin'*?' As he said this he put his right hand into the deep poacher's pocket of his jacket and brought out a large live rat clasped tight between his fingers.

'Good God!'

'Ah! That's it, y'see!' He was crouching slightly now and craning his neck forward and leering at us and holding this enormous brown rat in his hands, one finger and thumb making a tight circle around the creature's neck, clamping its head rigid so it couldn't turn and bite.

'D'you usually carry rats around in your pockets?'

'Always got a rat or two about me somewhere.'

With that he put his free hand into the other pocket and produced a small white ferret.

'Ferret,' he said, holding it up by the neck.

The ferret seemed to know him and stayed still in his grasp.

'There's nothin'll kill a rat quicker'n a ferret. And there's nothin' a rat's more frightened of either.'

He brought his hands close together in front of him so that the ferret's nose was within six inches of the rat's face. The pink beady eyes of the ferret stared at the rat. The rat struggled, trying to edge away from the killer.

'Now,' he said. 'Watch!'

His khaki shirt was open at the neck and he lifted the rat and slipped it down inside his shirt, next to his skin. As soon as his hand was free, he unbuttoned his jacket at the front so that the audience could see the bulge the body of the rat made under his shirt. His belt prevented it from going down lower than his waist.

Then he slipped the ferret in after the rat.

Immediately there was a great commotion inside the shirt. It appeared that the rat was running around the man's body, being chased by the ferret. Six or seven times they went around, the small bulge chasing the larger one, gaining on it slightly each circuit and drawing closer and closer until at last the two bulges seemed to come together and there was a scuffle and a series of shrill shrieks.

Throughout this performance the ratman had stood absolutely still with legs apart, arms hanging loosely, the dark eyes resting on Claud's face. Now he reached one hand down into his shirt and pulled out the ferret; with the other he took out the dead rat. There were traces of blood around the white muzzle of the ferret.

'Not sure I liked that very much.'

'You never seen anythin' like it before, I'll bet you that.'

'Can't really say I have.'

'Like as not you'll get yourself a nasty little nip in the guts one of these days,' Claud told him. But he was clearly impressed, and the ratman was becoming cocky again.

'Want to see somethin' far more *amazin'n* that?' he asked. 'You want to see somethin' you'd never even *believe* unless you seen it with your own eyes?'

'Well?'

We were standing in the driveway out in front of the pumps and it was one of those pleasant warm November mornings. Two cars pulled in for petrol, one right after the other, and Claud went over and gave them what they wanted.

'You want to see?' the ratman asked.

I glanced at Claud, slightly apprehensive. 'Yes,' Claud said. 'Come on then, let's see.'

The ratman slipped the dead rat back into one pocket, the ferret into the other. Then he reached down into his knapsack and produced – if you please – a second live rat.

'Good Christ!' Claud said.

'Always got one or two rats about me somewhere,' the man announced calmly. 'You got to know rats on this job, and if you want to know 'em you got to have 'em round you. This is a sewer rat, this is. An old sewer rat, clever as buggery. See him watchin' me all the time, wonderin' what I'm goin' to do? See him?'

'Very unpleasant.'

'What are you going to do?' I asked. I had a feeling I was going to like this one even less than the last.

'Fetch me a piece of string.'

Claud fetched him a piece of string.

With his left hand, the man looped the string around one of the rat's hind legs. The rat struggled, trying to turn its head to see what was going on, but he held it tight around the neck with finger and thumb.

'Now!' he said, looking about him. 'You got a table inside?'

'We don't want the rat inside the house,' I said.

'Well – I need a table. Or somethin' flat like a table.'

'What about the bonnet of that car?' Claud said.

We walked over to the car and the man put the old sewer rat on the bonnet. He attached the string to the windshield wiper so that the rat was now tethered.

At first it crouched, unmoving and suspicious, a big-bodied grey rat with bright black eyes and a scaly tail that lay in a long curl upon the car's bonnet. It was looking away from the ratman, but watching him sideways to see what he was going to do. The man stepped back a few paces and immediately the rat relaxed. It sat up on its haunches and began to lick the grey fur on its chest. Then it scratched its muzzle with both front paws. It seemed quite unconcerned about the three men standing near by.

'Now – how about a little bet?' the ratman asked.

'We don't bet,' I said.

'Just for fun. It's more fun if you bet.'

'What d'you want to bet on?'

'I'll bet you I can kill that rat without usin' my hands. I'll put my hands in my pockets and not use 'em.'

'You'll kick it with your feet,' Claud said.

It was apparent that the ratman was out to earn some money. I looked at the rat that was going to be killed and began to feel slightly sick, not so much because it was going to be killed but because it was going to be killed in a special way, with a considerable degree of relish.

'No,' the ratman said. 'No feet.'

'Nor arms?' Claud asked.

'Nor arms. Nor legs, nor hands neither.'

'You'll sit on it.'

'No. No squashin'.'

'Let's see you do it.'

'You bet me first. Bet me a quid.'

'Don't be so bloody daft,' Claud said. 'Why should we give you a quid?'

'What'll you bet?'

'Nothin'.'

'All right. Then it's no go.'

He made as if to untie the string from the windshield wiper.

'I'll bet you a shilling,' Claud told him. The sick gastric sensation in my stomach was increasing, but there was an awful magnetism about this business and I found myself quite unable to walk away or even move.

'You too?'

'No,' I said.

'What's the matter with you?' the ratman asked.

'I just don't want to bet you, that's all.'

'So you want me to do this for a lousy shillin'?'

'I don't want you to do it.'

'Where's the money?' he said to Claud.

Claud put a shilling piece on the bonnet, near the radiator. The ratman produced two sixpences and laid them beside Claud's money. As he stretched out his hand to do this, the rat cringed, drawing its head back and flattening itself against the bonnet.

'Bet's on,' the ratman said.

Claud and I stepped back a few paces. The ratman stepped forward. He put his hands in his pockets and inclined his body from the waist so that his face was on a level with the rat, about three feet away.

His eyes caught the eyes of the rat and held them. The rat was crouching, very tense, sensing extreme danger, but not yet frightened. The way it crouched, it seemed to me it was preparing to spring forward at the man's face; but there must have been some power in the ratman's eyes that prevented it from doing this, and subdued it, and then gradually frightened it so that it began to back away, dragging its body backwards with slow crouching steps until the string tautened on its hind leg. It tried to struggle back farther against the string, jerking its leg to free it. The man leaned forward towards the rat, following it with his face, watching it all the time with his eyes, and suddenly the rat panicked and leaped sideways in the air. The string pulled it up with a jerk that must almost have dislocated its leg.

It crouched again, in the middle of the bonnet, as far away as the string would allow, and it was properly frightened now, whiskers quivering, the long grey body tense with fear.

At this point, the ratman again began to move his face closer. Very slowly he did it, so slowly there wasn't really any movement to be seen at all except that the face just happened to be a fraction closer each time you looked. He never took his eyes from the rat. The tension was considerable and I wanted suddenly to cry out and tell him to stop. I wanted him to stop because it was making me feel sick inside, but I couldn't bring myself to say the word. Something extremely unpleasant was about to happen – I was sure of that. Something sinister and cruel and ratlike, and perhaps it really would make me sick. But I had to see it now.

The ratman's face was about eighteen inches from the rat. Twelve inches. Then ten, or perhaps it was eight, and then there was not more than the length of a man's hand separating their faces. The rat was pressing its body flat against the car bonnet, tense and terrified. The ratman was also tense, but with a dangerous active tensity that was like a tight-wound spring. The shadow of a smile flickered around the skin of his mouth.

Then suddenly he struck.

He struck as a snake strikes, darting his head forward with one swift knifelike stroke that originated in the muscles of the lower body, and I had a momentary glimpse of his mouth opening very wide and two yellow teeth and the whole face contorted by the effort of mouth-opening.

More than that I did not care to see. I closed my eyes, and when I opened them again the rat was dead and the ratman was slipping the money into his pocket and spitting to clear his mouth.

'That's what they makes lickerish out of,' he said. 'Rat's blood is what the big factories and the chocolate-people use to make lickerish.'

Again the relish, the wet-lipped, lip-smacking relish as he spoke the words, the throaty richness of his voice and the thick syrupy way he pronounced the word 'lickerish'.

'No,' he said, 'there's nothin' wrong with a drop of rat's blood.'

'Don't talk so absolutely disgusting,' Claud told him.

'Ah! But that's it, you see. You eaten it many a time. Penny sticks and lickerish bootlaces is all made from rat's blood.'

'We don't want to hear about it, thank you.'

'Boiled up, it is, in great cauldrons, bubblin' and steamin' and men stirrin' it with long poles. That's one of the big secrets of the chocolate-makin' factories, and no one knows about it – no one except the ratters supplyin' the stuff.'

Suddenly he noticed that his audience was no longer with him, that our faces were hostile and sick-looking and crimson with anger and disgust. He stopped abruptly, and without another word he turned and sloped off down the driveway out on to the road, moving with the slow, that almost delicate ambling walk that was like a rat prowling, making no noise with his footsteps even on the gravel of the driveway.

Nunc Dimittis

First published in *Collier's* (4 September 1953)
as 'The Devious Bachelor'; also known as
'A Connoisseur's Revenge'

It is nearly midnight, and I can see that if I don't make a start with writing this story now, I never shall. All the evening I have been sitting here trying to force myself to begin, but the more I have thought about it, the more appalled and ashamed and distressed I have become by the whole thing.

My idea – and I believe it was a good one – was to try, by a process of confession and analysis, to discover a reason or at any rate some justification for my outrageous behaviour towards Janet de Pelagia. I wanted, essentially, to address myself to an imaginary and sympathetic listener, a kind of mythical *you*, someone gentle and understanding to whom I might tell unashamedly every detail of this unfortunate episode. I can only hope that I am not too upset to make a go of it.

If I am to be quite honest with myself, I suppose I shall have to admit that what is disturbing me most is not so much the sense of my own shame, or even the hurt that I have inflicted upon poor Janet; it is the knowledge that I have made a monstrous fool of myself and that all my friends – if I can still call them that – all those warm and lovable people who used to come so often to my house, must now be regarding me as nothing but a vicious, vengeful old man. Yes, that surely hurts. When I say to you that my friends were my whole life – everything, absolutely everything in it – then perhaps you will begin to understand.

Will you? I doubt it – unless I digress for a minute to tell you roughly the sort of person I am.

Well – let me see. Now that I come to think of it, I suppose I am, after all, a type; a rare one, mark you, but nevertheless a quite definite type – the wealthy, leisurely, middle-aged man of culture, adored (I choose the word carefully) by his many friends for his charm, his money, his air of scholarship, his generosity, and I sincerely hope for himself also. You will find him (this type) only in the big capitals – London, Paris, New York; of that I am certain. The money he has was earned by his dead father, whose memory he is inclined to despise. This is not his fault, for there is something in his make-up that compels him secretly to look down upon all people who never had the wit to learn the difference between Rockingham and Spode, Waterford and Venetian, Sheraton and Chippendale, Monet and Manet, or even Pommard and Montrachet.

He is, therefore, a connoisseur, possessing above all things an exquisite taste. His Constables, Boningtons, Lautrecs, Redons, Vuillards, Matthew Smiths are as fine as anything in the Tate; and because they are so fabulous and beautiful they create an atmosphere of suspense around him in the home, something tantalizing, breathtaking, faintly frightening – frightening to think that he has the power and the right, if he feels inclined, to slash, tear, plunge his fist through a superb Dedham Vale, a Mont

Saint-Victoire, an Arles cornfield, a Tahiti maiden, a portrait of Madame Cézanne. And from the walls on which these wonders hang there issues a little golden glow of splendour, a subtle emanation of grandeur in which he lives and moves and entertains with a sly nonchalance that is not entirely unpractised.

He is invariably a bachelor, yet he never appears to get entangled with the women who surround him, who love him so dearly. It is just possible – and this you may or may not have noticed – that there is a frustration, a discontent, a regret somewhere inside him. Even a slight aberration.

I don't think I need say any more. I have been very frank. You should know me well enough by now to judge me fairly – and dare I hope it? – to sympathize with me when you hear my story. You may even decide that much of the blame for what has happened should be placed, not upon me, but upon a lady called Gladys Ponsonby. After all, she was the one who started it. Had I not escorted Gladys Ponsonby back to her house that night nearly six months ago, and had she not spoken so freely to me about certain people, and certain things, then this tragic business could never have taken place.

It was last December, if I remember rightly, and I had been dining with the Ashendens in that lovely house of theirs that overlooks the southern fringe of Regent's Park. There were a fair number of people there, but Gladys Ponsonby was the only one beside myself who had come alone. So when it was time for us to leave, I naturally offered to see her safely back to her house. She accepted and we left together in my car; but unfortunately, when we arrived at her place she insisted that I come in and have 'one for the road', as she put it. I didn't wish to seem stuffy, so I told the chauffeur to wait and followed her in.

Gladys Ponsonby is an unusually short woman, certainly not more than four feet nine or ten, maybe even less than that – one of those tiny persons who gives me, when I am beside her, the comical, rather wobbly feeling that I am standing on a chair. She is a widow, a few years younger than me – maybe fifty-three or four, and it is possible that thirty years ago she was quite a fetching little thing. But now the face is loose and puckered with nothing distinctive about it whatsoever. The individual features, the eyes, the nose, the mouth, the chin, are buried in the folds of fat around the puckered little face and one does not notice them. Except perhaps the mouth, which reminds me – I cannot help it – of a salmon.

In the living-room, as she gave me my brandy, I noticed that her hand was a trifle unsteady. The lady is tired, I told myself, so I mustn't stay long. We sat down together on the sofa and for a while discussed the Ashendens' party and the people who were there. Finally I got up to go.

'Sit down, Lionel,' she said. 'Have another brandy.'

'No, really, I must go.'

'Sit down and don't be so stuffy. *I'm* having another one, and the least you can do is keep me company while I drink it.'

I watched her as she walked over to the sideboard, this tiny woman, faintly swaying, holding her glass out in front of her with both hands as though it were an offering; and the sight of her walking like that, so incredibly short and squat and stiff, suddenly gave me the ludicrous notion that she had no legs at all above the knees.

'Lionel, what are you chuckling about?' She half turned to look at me as she poured the drink, and some of it slopped over the side of the glass.

'Nothing, my dear. Nothing at all.'

'Well, stop it, and tell me what you think of my new portrait.' She indicated a large canvas hanging over the fireplace that I had been trying to avoid with my eye ever since I entered the room. It was a hideous thing, painted, as I well knew, by a man who was now all the rage in London, a very mediocre painter called John Royden. It was a full-length portrait of Gladys, Lady Ponsonby, painted with a certain technical cunning that made her out to be a tall and quite alluring creature.

'Charming,' I said.

'Isn't it, though! I'm so glad you like it.'

'Quite charming.'

'I think John Royden is a genius. Don't you think he's a genius, Lionel?'

'Well – that might be going a bit far.'

'You mean it's a little early to say for sure?'

'Exactly.'

'But listen, Lionel – and I think this will surprise you. John Royden is so sought after now that he won't even *consider* painting anyone for less than a thousand guineas!'

'Really?'

'Oh, yes! And everyone's queueing up, simply *queueing up* to get themselves done.'

'Most interesting.'

'Now take your Mr Cézanne or whatever his name is. I'll bet *he* never got that sort of money in *his* lifetime.'

'Never.'

'And you say *he* was a genius?'

'Sort of – yes.'

'Then so is Royden,' she said, settling herself again on the sofa. 'The money proves it.'

She sat silent for a while, sipping her brandy, and I couldn't help noticing how the unsteadiness of her hand was causing the rim of the glass to jog against her lower lip. She knew I was watching her, and without turning her head she swivelled her eyes and glanced at me cautiously out of the corners of them. 'A penny for your thoughts?'

Now, if there is one phrase in the world I cannot abide, it is this. It gives me an actual physical pain in the chest and I began to cough.

'Come on, Lionel. A penny for them.'

I shook my head, quite unable to answer. She turned away abruptly and placed the brandy glass on a small table to her left; and the manner in which she did this seemed to suggest – I don't know why – that she felt rebuffed and was now clearing the decks for action. I waited, rather uncomfortable in the silence that followed, and because I had no conversation left in me, I made a great play about smoking my cigar, studying the ash intently and blowing the smoke up slowly towards the ceiling. But she made no move. There was beginning to be something about this lady I did not much like, a mischievous brooding air that made me want to get up quickly and go away. When she looked around again, she was smiling at me slyly with those little buried eyes of hers, but the mouth – oh, just like a salmon's – was absolutely rigid.

'Lionel, I think I'll tell you a secret.'

'Really, Gladys, I simply must get home.'

'Don't be frightened, Lionel. I won't embarrass you. You look so frightened all of a sudden.'

'I'm not very good at secrets.'

'I've been thinking,' she said, 'you're such a great expert on pictures, this ought to interest you.' She sat quite still except for her fingers, which were moving all the time. She kept them perpetually twisting and twisting around each other, and they were like a bunch of small white snakes wriggling in her lap.

'Don't you want to hear my secret, Lionel?'

'It isn't that, you know. It's just that it's so awfully late . . .'

'This is probably the best-kept secret in London. A woman's secret. I suppose it's known to about – let me see – about thirty or forty women altogether. And not a single man. Except him, of course – John Royden.'

I didn't wish to encourage her, so I said nothing.

'But first of all, promise – *promise* you won't tell a soul?'

'Dear me!'

'You *promise*, Lionel?'

'Yes, Gladys, all right, I promise.'

'Good! Now listen.' She reached for the brandy glass and settled back comfortably in the far corner of the sofa. 'I suppose you know John Royden paints only women?'

'I didn't.'

'And they're always full-length portraits, either standing or sitting – like mine there. Now take a good look at it, Lionel. Do you see how beautifully the dress is painted?'

'Well . . .'

'Go over and look carefully, please.'

I got up reluctantly and went over and examined the painting. To my surprise I noticed that the paint of the dress was laid on so heavily it was actually raised out from the rest of the picture. It was a trick, quite effective in its way, but neither difficult to do nor entirely original.

'You see?' she said. 'It's thick, isn't it, where the dress is?'

'Yes.'

'But there's a bit more to it than that, you know, Lionel. I think the best way is to describe what happened the very first time I went along for a sitting.'

Oh, what a bore this woman is, I thought, and how can I get away?

'That was about a year ago, and I remember how excited I was to be going into the studio of the great painter. I dressed myself up in a wonderful new thing I'd just got from Norman Hartnell, and a special little red hat, and off I went. Mr Royden met me at the door, and of course I was fascinated by him at once. He had a small pointed beard and thrilling blue eyes, and he wore a black velvet jacket. The studio was huge, with red velvet sofas and velvet chairs – he loves velvet – and velvet curtains and even a velvet carpet on the floor. He sat me down, gave me a drink and came straight to the point. He told me about how he painted quite differently from other artists. In his opinion, he said, there was only one method of attaining perfection when painting a woman's body and I mustn't be shocked when I heard what it was.

'"I don't think I'll be shocked, Mr Royden," I told him.

'"I'm sure you won't either," he said. He had the most marvellous white teeth and they sort of shone through his beard when he smiled. "You see, it's like this," he went on. "You examine any painting you like of a woman – I don't care who it's by – and you'll see that although the dress may be well painted, there is an effect of artificiality, of flatness about the whole thing, as though the dress were draped over a log of wood. And you know why?"

'"No, Mr Royden, I don't."

'"Because the painters themselves didn't really know what was underneath!"'

Gladys Ponsonby paused to take a few more sips of brandy. 'Don't look so startled, Lionel,' she said to me. 'There's nothing wrong about this. Keep quiet and let me finish. So then Mr Royden said, "That's why I insist on painting my subjects first of all in the nude."

'"Good Heavens, Mr Royden!" I exclaimed.

'"If you object to that, I don't mind making a slight concession, Lady Ponsonby," he said. "But I prefer it the other way."

'"Really, Mr Royden, I don't know."

'"And when I've done you like that," he went on, "we'll have to wait a few weeks for the paint to dry. Then you come back and I paint on your underclothing. And when that's dry, I paint on the dress. You see, it's quite simple."'

'The man's an absolute bounder!' I cried.

'No, Lionel, no! You're quite wrong. If only you could

have heard him, so charming about it all, so genuine and sincere. Anyone could see he really *felt* what he was saying.'

'I tell you, Gladys, the man's a bounder!'

'Don't be so silly, Lionel. And anyway, let me finish. The first thing I told him was that my husband (who was alive then) would never agree.'

'"Your husband need never know," he answered. "Why trouble him? No one knows my secret except the women I've painted."

'And when I protested a bit more, I remember he said, "My dear Lady Ponsonby, there's nothing immoral about this. Art is only immoral when practised by amateurs. It's the same with medicine. You wouldn't refuse to undress before your doctor, would you?"

'I told him I would if I'd gone to him for ear-ache. That made him laugh. But he kept on at me about it and I must say he was very convincing, so after a while I gave in and that was that. So now, Lionel, my sweet, you know the secret.' She got up and went over to fetch herself some more brandy.

'Gladys, is this really true?'

'Of course it's true.'

'You mean to say that's the way he paints all his subjects?'

'Yes. And the joke is the husbands never know anything about it. All they see is a nice fully clothed portrait of their wives. Of course, there's nothing wrong with being painted in the nude; artists do it all the time. But our silly husbands have a way of objecting to that sort of thing.'

'By gad, the fellow's got a nerve!'

'I think he's a genius.'

'I'll bet he got the idea from Goya.'

'Nonsense, Lionel.'

'Of course he did. But listen, Gladys. I want you to tell me something. Did you by any chance know about this . . . this peculiar technique of Royden's before you went to him?'

When I asked the question she was in the act of pouring the brandy, and she hesitated and turned her head to look at me, a little silky smile moving the corners of her mouth, 'Damn you, Lionel,' she said. 'You're far too clever. You never let me get away with a single thing.'

'So you knew?'

'Of course. Hermione Girdlestone told me.'

'Exactly as I thought!'

'There's still nothing wrong.'

'Nothing,' I said. 'Absolutely nothing.' I could see it all quite clearly now. This Royden was indeed a bounder, practising as neat a piece of psychological trickery as ever I'd seen. The man knew only too well that there was a whole set of wealthy indolent women in the city who got up at noon and spent the rest of the day trying to relieve their boredom with bridge and canasta and shopping until the cocktail hour came along. All they craved was a little excitement, something out of the ordinary, and the more expensive the better. Why – the news of an entertainment like this would spread through their ranks like smallpox. I could just see the great plump Hermione Girdlestone leaning over the canasta table and telling them about it . . . 'But my dear, it's *simp*-ly fascinating . . . I can't *tell* you how intriguing it is . . . *much* more fun than going to your doctor . . .'

'You won't tell anyone, Lionel, will you? You promised.'

'No, of course not. But now I must go, Gladys, I really must.'

'Don't be so silly. I'm just beginning to enjoy myself. Stay till I've finished this drink, anyway.'

I sat patiently on the sofa while she went on with her interminable brandy sipping. The little buried eyes were still watching me out of their corners in that mischievous, canny way, and I had a strong feeling that the woman was now hatching out some farther unpleasantness or scandal. There was the look of serpents in those eyes and a queer curl around the mouth; and in the air – although maybe I only imagined it – the faint smell of danger.

Then suddenly, so suddenly that I jumped, she said, 'Lionel, what's this I hear about you and Janet de Pelagia?'

'Now, Gladys, please . . .'

'Lionel, you're blushing!'

'Nonsense.'

'Don't tell me the old bachelor has really taken a tumble at last?'

'Gladys, this is too absurd.' I began making movements to go, but she put a hand on my knee and stopped me.

'Don't you know by now, Lionel, that there *are* no secrets?'

'Janet is a fine girl.'

'You can hardly call her a *girl*.' Gladys Ponsonby paused, staring down into the large brandy glass that she held cupped in both hands. 'But of course, I agree with you, Lionel, she's a wonderful person in every way. Except,' and now she spoke very slowly, 'except that she *does* say some rather peculiar things occasionally.'

'What sort of things?'

'Just things, you know – things about people. About you.'

'What did she say about me?'

'Nothing at all, Lionel. It wouldn't interest you.'

'What did she say about me?'

'It's not even worth repeating, honestly it isn't. It's only that it struck me as being rather odd at the time.'

'Gladys – what did she say?' While I waited for her to answer, I could feel the sweat breaking out all over my body.

'Well now, let me see. Of course, she was only joking or I couldn't dream of telling you, but I suppose she *did* say how it was all a wee bit of a bore.'

'What was?'

'Sort of going out to dinner with you nearly every night – that kind of thing.'

'She said it was a bore?'

'Yes.' Gladys Ponsonby drained the brandy glass with one last big gulp, and sat up straight. 'If you really want to know, she said it was a crashing bore. And then . . .'

'What did she say then?'

'Now look, Lionel – there's no need to get excited. I'm only telling you this for your own good.'

'Then please hurry up and tell it.'

'It's just that I happened to be playing canasta with Janet this afternoon and I asked her if she was free to dine with me tomorrow. She said no, she wasn't.'

'Go on.'

'Well – actually what she said was "I'm dining with that crashing old bore Lionel Lampson."'

'Janet said that?'

'Yes, Lionel dear.'

'What else?'

'Now, that's enough. I don't think I should tell the rest.'

'Finish it, please!'

'Why, Lionel, don't keep shouting at me like that. Of course I'll tell you if you insist. As a matter of fact, I wouldn't consider myself a true friend if I didn't. Don't you think it's the sign of true friendship when two people like us . . .'

'Gladys! *Please* hurry.'

'Good heavens, you must give me time to *think*. Let me see now – so far as I can remember, what she *actually* said was this . . .' – and Gladys Ponsonby, sitting upright on the sofa with her feet not quite touching the floor, her eyes away from me now, looking at the wall, began cleverly to mimic the deep tone of that voice I knew so well – '"Such a bore, my dear, because with Lionel one can *always* tell exactly what will happen *right* from beginning to end. For dinner we'll go to the Savoy Grill – it's *always* the Savoy Grill – and for two hours I'll have to listen to the pompous old . . . I mean I'll have to listen to him droning away about pictures and porcelain – *always* pictures and porcelain. Then in the taxi going home he'll reach out for my hand, and he'll lean closer, and I'll get a whiff of stale cigar smoke and brandy, and he'll start burbling about how he wished – oh, how he wished he was just twenty years younger. And I will say, 'Could you open a window, do you mind?' And when we arrive at my house I'll tell him to keep the taxi, but he'll pretend he hasn't heard and pay it off quickly. And then at the front door, while I fish for my key, he'll stand beside me with a sort of silly spaniel look in his eyes, and I'll slowly put the key in the lock, and slowly turn it, and then – very quickly, before he has time to move – I'll say good night and skip inside and shut the door behind me . . ." Why, Lionel! What's the matter, dear? You look positively ill . . .'

At that point, mercifully, I must have swooned clear away. I can remember practically nothing of the rest of that terrible night except for a vague and disturbing suspicion that when I regained consciousness I broke down completely and permitted Gladys Ponsonby to comfort me in a variety of different ways. Later, I believe I walked out of the house and was driven home, but I remained more or less unconscious of everything about me until I woke up in my bed the next morning.

I awoke feeling weak and shaken. I lay still with my eyes closed, trying to piece together the events of the night before – Gladys Ponsonby's living-room, Gladys on the sofa sipping brandy, the little puckered face, the mouth that was like a salmon's mouth, the things she had said . . . What was it she had said? Ah, yes. About me. My God, yes! About Janet and me! Those outrageous, unbelievable remarks! Could Janet really have made them? Could she?

I can remember with what terrifying swiftness my hatred of Janet de Pelagia now began to grow. It all happened in a few minutes – a sudden, violent welling up of a hatred that filled me till I thought I was going to burst. I tried to dismiss it, but it was on me like a fever, and in no time at all I was hunting around, as would some filthy gangster, for a method of revenge.

A curious way to behave, you may say, for a man such as me; to which I would answer – no, not really, if you consider the circumstances. To my mind, this was the sort of thing that could drive a man to murder. As a matter of fact, had it not been for a small sadistic streak that caused me to seek a more subtle and painful punishment for my victim, I might well have become a murderer myself. But mere killing, I decided, was too good for this woman, and far too crude for my taste. So I began looking for a superior alternative.

I am not normally a scheming person; I consider it an odious business and have had no practice in it whatsoever. But fury and hate can concentrate a man's mind to an astonishing degree, and in no time at all a plot was forming and unfolding in my head – a plot so superior and exciting that I began to be quite carried away at the idea of it. By the time I had filled in the details and overcome one or two minor objections, my brooding vengeful mood had changed to one of extreme elation, and I remember how I started bouncing up and down absurdly on my bed and clapping my hands. The next thing I knew I had the telephone directory on my lap and was searching eagerly for a name. I found it, picked up the phone and dialled the number.

'Hello,' I said. 'Mr Royden? Mr John Royden?'

'Speaking.'

Well – it wasn't difficult to persuade the man to call around and see me for a moment. I had never met him, but of course he knew my name, both as an important collector of paintings and as a person of some consequence in society. I was a big fish for him to catch.

'Let me see now, Mr Lampson,' he said, 'I think I ought to be free in about a couple of hours. Will that be all right?'

I told him it would be fine, gave my address and rang off.

I jumped out of bed. It was really remarkable how exhilarated I felt all of a sudden. One moment I had been in an agony of despair, contemplating murder and suicide and I don't know what, the next, I was whistling an aria from Puccini in my bath. Every now and again I caught myself rubbing my hands together in a devilish fashion, and once, during my exercises, when I overbalanced doing a double knee-bend, I sat on the floor and giggled like a schoolboy.

At the appointed time Mr John Royden was shown into my library and I got up to meet him. He was a small neat man with a slightly ginger goatee beard. He wore a black velvet jacket, a rust-brown tie, a red pullover and black suède shoes. I shook his small neat hand.

'Good of you to come along so quickly, Mr Royden.'

'Not at all, sir.' The man's lips – like the lips of nearly all bearded men – looked wet and naked, a trifle indecent, shining pink in among all that hair. After telling him again how much I admired his work, I got straight down to business.

'Mr Royden,' I said. 'I have a rather unusual request to make of you, something quite personal in its way.'

'Yes, Mr Lampson?' He was sitting in the chair opposite me and he cocked his head over to one side, quick and
perky like a bird.

'Of course, I know I can trust you to be discreet about
anything I say.'

'Absolutely, Mr Lampson.'

'All right. Now my proposition is this: there is a certain
lady in town here whose portrait I would like you to paint.
I very much want to possess a fine painting of her. But
there are certain complications. For example, I have my
own reasons for not wishing her to know that it is I who
am commissioning the portrait.'

'You mean . . .'

'Exactly, Mr Royden. That is exactly what I mean. As a
man of the world I'm sure you will understand.'

He smiled, a crooked little smile that only just came
through his beard, and he nodded his head knowingly up
and down.

'Is it not possible,' I said, 'that a man might be – how
shall I put it? – extremely fond of a lady and at the same
time have his own good reasons for not wishing her to
know about it yet?'

'More than possible, Mr Lampson.'

'Sometimes a man has to stalk his quarry with great
caution, waiting patiently for the right moment to reveal
himself.'

'Precisely, Mr Lampson.'

'There are better ways of catching a bird than by chasing it through the woods.'

'Yes, indeed, Mr Lampson.'

'Putting salt on its tail, for instance.'

'Ha-ha!'

'All right, Mr Royden. I think you understand. Now – do you happen by any chance to know a lady called Janet de Pelagia?'

'Janet de Pelagia? Let me see now – yes. At least, what I mean is, I've heard of her. I couldn't exactly say I know her.'

'That's a pity. It makes it a little more difficult. Do you think you could get to meet her – perhaps at a cocktail party or something like that?'

'Shouldn't be too tricky, Mr Lampson.'

'Good, because what I suggest is this: that you go up to her and tell her she's the sort of model you've been searching for for years – just the right face, the right figure, the right coloured eyes. You know the sort of thing. Then ask her if she'd mind sitting for you free of charge. Say you'd like to do a picture of her for next year's Academy. I feel sure she'd be delighted to help you, and honoured too, if I may say so. Then you will paint her and exhibit the picture and deliver it to me after the show is over. No one but you need know that I have bought it.'

The small round eyes of Mr John Royden were watching me shrewdly, I thought, and the head was again cocked over to one side. He was sitting on the edge of his chair, and in this position, with the pullover making a flash of red down his front, he reminded me of a robin on a twig listening for a suspicious noise.

'There's really nothing wrong about it at all,' I said. 'Just call it – if you like – a harmless little conspiracy being perpetrated by a . . . well . . . by a rather romantic old man.'

'I know, Mr Lampson, I know . . .' He still seemed to be hesitating, so I said quickly, 'I'll be glad to pay you double your usual fee.'

That did it. The man actually licked his lips. 'Well, Mr Lampson, I must say this sort of thing's not really in my line, you know. But all the same, it'd be a very heartless man who refused such a – shall I say, such a romantic assignment?'

'I should like a full-length portrait, Mr Royden, please. A large canvas – let me see – about twice the size of that Manet on the wall there.'

'About sixty by thirty-six?'

'Yes. And I should like her to be standing. That to my mind is her most graceful attitude.'

'I quite understand, Mr Lampson. And it'll be a pleasure to paint such a lovely lady.'

I expect it will, I told myself. The way you go about it, my boy, I'm quite sure it will. But I said, 'All right, Mr Royden, then I'll leave it all to you. And don't forget, please – this is a little secret between ourselves.'

When he had gone I forced myself to sit still and take twenty-five deep breaths. Nothing else would have restrained me from jumping up and shouting for joy like an idiot. I have never in my life felt so exhilarated. My plan was working! The most difficult part was already accomplished. There would be a wait now, a long wait. The way this man painted, it would take him several months to finish the picture. Well, I would just have to be patient, that's all.

I now decided, on the spur of the moment, that it would be best if I were to go abroad in the interim; and the very next morning, after sending a message to Janet (with whom, you will remember, I was due to dine that night) telling her I had been called away, I left for Italy.

There, as always, I had a delightful time, marred only by a constant nervous excitement caused by the thought of returning to the scene of action.

I eventually arrived back, four months later, in July, on the day after the opening of the Royal Academy, and I found to my relief that everything had gone according to plan during my absence. The picture of Janet de Pelagia had been painted and hung in the Exhibition, and it was already the subject of much favourable comment both by the critics and the public. I myself refrained from going to see it, but Royden told me on the telephone that there had been several inquiries by persons who wished to buy it, all of whom had been informed that it was not for sale. When the show was over, Royden delivered the picture to my house and received his money.

I immediately had it carried up to my workroom, and with mounting excitement I began to examine it closely. The man had painted her standing up in a black evening dress and there was a red plush sofa in the background. Her left hand was resting on the back of a heavy chair, also of red plush, and there was a huge crystal chandelier hanging from the ceiling.

My God, I thought, what a hideous thing! The portrait

itself wasn't so bad. He had caught the woman's expression – the forward drop of the head, the wide blue eyes, the large, ugly-beautiful mouth with the trace of a smile in one corner. He had flattered her, of course. There wasn't a wrinkle on her face or the slightest suggestion of fat under her chin. I bent forward to examine the painting of the dress. Yes – here the paint was thicker, much thicker. At this point, unable to wait another moment, I threw off my coat and prepared to go to work.

I should mention here that I am myself an expert cleaner and restorer of paintings. The cleaning, particularly, is a comparatively simple process, provided one has patience and a gentle touch, and those professionals who make such a secret of their trade and charge such shocking prices get no business from me. Where my own pictures are concerned I always do the job myself.

I poured out the turpentine and added a few drops of alcohol. I dipped a small wad of cotton-wool in the mixture, squeezed it out, and then gently, with a circular motion, I began to work upon the black paint of the dress. I could only hope that Royden had allowed each layer to dry thoroughly before applying the next, otherwise the two would merge and the process I had in mind would be impossible. Soon I would know. I was working on one square inch of black dress somewhere around the lady's stomach and I took plenty of time, cautiously testing and teasing the paint, adding a drop or two more alcohol to my mixture, testing again, adding another drop until finally it was just strong enough to loosen the pigment.

For perhaps a whole hour I worked away on this little

square of black, proceeding more and more gently as I came closer to the layer below. Then, a tiny pink spot appeared, and gradually it spread and spread until the whole of my square inch was a clear shining patch of pink. Quickly I neutralized with pure turps.

So far so good. I knew now that the black paint could be removed without disturbing what was underneath. So long as I was patient and industrious I would easily be able to take it all off. Also, I had discovered the right mixture to use and just how hard I could safely rub, so things should go much quicker now.

I must say it was rather an amusing business. I worked first from the middle of her body downward, and as the lower half of her dress came away bit by bit on to my little wads of cotton, a queer pink undergarment began to reveal itself. I didn't for the life of me know what the thing was called, but it was a formidable apparatus constructed of what appeared to be a strong thick elastic material, and its purpose was apparently to contain and to compress the woman's bulging figure into a neat streamlined shape, giving a quite false impression of slimness. As I travelled lower and lower down, I came upon a striking arrangement of suspenders, also pink, which were attached to this elastic armour and hung downwards four or five inches to grip the tops of the stockings.

Quite fantastic the whole thing seemed to me as I stepped back a pace to survey it. It gave me a strong sense of having somehow been cheated; for had I not, during all these past months, been admiring the sylph-like figure of this lady? She was a faker. No question about it. But do many other females practise this sort of deception, I wondered. I knew, of course, that in the days of stays and corsets it was usual for ladies to strap themselves up; yet for some reason I was under the impression that nowadays all they had to do was diet.

When the whole of the lower half of the dress had come away, I immediately turned my attention to the upper portion, working my way slowly upward from the lady's middle. Here, around the midriff, there was an area of naked flesh; then higher up upon the bosom itself and actually containing it, I came upon a contrivance made of some heavy black material edged with frilly lace. This, I knew very well, was the brassière – another formidable appliance upheld by an arrangement of black straps as skilfully and scientifically rigged as the supporting cables of a suspension bridge.

Dear me, I thought. One lives and learns.

But now at last the job was finished, and I stepped back again to take a final look at the picture. It was truly an astonishing sight! This woman, Janet de Pelagia, almost life size, standing there in her underwear – in a sort of drawing-room, I suppose it was – with a great chandelier above her head and a red plush chair by her side; and she herself – this was the most disturbing part of all – looking so completely unconcerned, with the wide placid blue eyes, the faintly smiling, ugly-beautiful mouth. Also I noticed, with something of a shock, that she was exceedingly bow-legged, like a jockey. I tell you frankly, the whole thing embarrassed me. I felt as though I had no right to be in the room, certainly no right to stare. So after a while I went out and shut the door behind me. It seemed like the only decent thing to do.

Now, for the next and final step! And do not imagine simply because I have not mentioned it lately that my thirst for revenge had in any way diminished during the last few months. On the contrary, it had if anything increased; and with the last act about to be performed, I can tell you I found it hard to contain myself. That night, for example, I didn't even go to bed.

You see, I couldn't wait to get the invitations out. I sat up all night preparing them and addressing the envelopes. There were twenty-two of them in all, and I wanted each to be a personal note. 'I'm having a little dinner on Friday night, the twenty-second, at eight. I do hope you can come along . . . I'm so looking forward to seeing you again . . .'

The first, the most carefully phrased, was to Janet de Pelagia. In it I regretted not having seen her for so long . . . I had been abroad . . . It was time we got together again, etc., etc. The next was to Gladys Ponsonby. Then one to Lady Hermione Girdlestone, another to Princess Bicheno, Mrs Cudbird, Sir Hubert Kaul, Mrs Galbally, Peter Euan-Thomas, James Pisker, Sir Eustace Piegrome, Peter van Santen, Elizabeth Moynihan, Lord Mulherrin, Bertram Sturt, Philip Cornelius, Jack Hill, Lady Akeman, Mrs Icely, Humphrey King-Howard, Johnny O'Coffey, Mrs Uvary and the Dowager Countess of Waxworth.

It was a carefully selected list, containing as it did the most distinguished men, the most brilliant and influential women in the top crust of our society.

I was well aware that a dinner at my house was regarded

as quite an occasion; everybody liked to come. And now, as I watched the point of my pen moving swiftly over the paper, I could almost see the ladies in their pleasure picking up their bedside telephones the morning the invitations arrived, shrill voices calling to shriller voices over the wires . . . 'Lionel's giving a party . . . he's asked you too? My dear, how nice . . . his food is always *so* good . . . and *such* a lovely man, isn't he though, yes . . .'

Is that really what they would say? It suddenly occurred to me that it might not be like that at all. More like this perhaps: 'I agree, my dear, yes, not a bad old man . . . but a bit of a bore, don't you think? . . . What did you say? . . . dull? But desperately, my dear. You've hit the nail right on the head . . . did you ever hear what Janet de Pelagia once said about him? . . . Ah yes, I thought you'd heard that one . . . screamingly funny, don't you think? . . . poor Janet . . . how she stood it as long as she did I don't know . . .'

Anyway, I got the invitations off, and within a couple of days everybody with the exception of Mrs Cudburd and Sir Hubert Kaul, who were away, had accepted with pleasure.

At eight thirty on the evening of the twenty-second, my large drawing-room was filled with people. They stood about the room, admiring the pictures, drinking their Martinis, talking with loud voices. The women smelled strongly of scent, the men were pink-faced and carefully buttoned up in their dinner-jackets. Janet de Pelagia was wearing the same black dress she had used for the portrait, and every time I caught sight of her, a kind of huge bubble-vision – as in those absurd cartoons – would float up above my head, and in it I would see Janet in her under-clothes, the black brassière, the pink elastic belt, the suspenders, the jockey's legs.

I moved from group to group, chatting amiably with them all, listening to their talk. Behind me I could hear Mrs Galbally telling Sir Eustace Piegrome and James Pisker how the man at the next table to hers at Claridges the night before had had red lipstick on his white moustache. 'Simply *plastered* with it,' she kept on saying, 'and the old boy was ninety if he was a day . . .' On the other side, Lady Girdlestone was telling somebody where one could get truffles cooked in brandy, and I could see Mrs Icely whispering something to Lord Mulherrin while his Lordship kept shaking his head slowly from side to side like an old and dispirited metronome.

Dinner was announced, and we all moved out.

'My goodness!' they cried as they entered the dining-room. 'How dark and sinister!'

'I can hardly see a thing!'

'What divine little candles!'

'But Lionel, how romantic!'

There were six very thin candles set about two feet apart from each other down the centre of the long table. Their small flames made a little glow of light around the table itself, but left the rest of the room in darkness. It was an amusing arrangement and apart from the fact that it suited my purpose well, it made a pleasant change. The guests soon settled themselves in their right places and the meal began.

They all seemed to enjoy the candlelight and things went famously, though for some reason the darkness caused them to speak much louder than usual. Janet de Pelagia's voice struck me as being particularly strident. She was sitting next to Lord Mulherrin, and I could hear her telling him about the boring time she had had at Cap Ferrat the week before. 'Nothing but Frenchmen,' she kept saying. 'Nothing but Frenchmen in the whole place . . .'

For my part, I was watching the candles. They were so thin that I knew it would not be long before they burned down to their bases. Also I was mighty nervous – I will admit that – but at the same time intensely exhilarated, almost to the point of drunkenness. Every time I heard Janet's voice or caught sight of her face shadowed in the light of the candles, a little ball of excitement exploded inside me and I felt the fire of it running under my skin.

They were eating their strawberries when at last I decided the time had come. I took a deep breath and in a loud voice I said, 'I'm afraid we'll have to have the lights on now. The candles are nearly finished. Mary,' I called. 'Oh, Mary, switch on the lights, will you please?'

There was a moment of silence after my announcement. I heard the maid walking over to the door, then the gentle click of the switch and the room was flooded with a blaze of light. They all screwed up their eyes, opened them again, gazed about them.

At that point I got up from my chair and slid quietly from the room, but as I went I saw a sight that I shall never forget as long as I live. It was Janet, with both hands in mid-air, stopped, frozen rigid, caught in the act of gesticulating towards someone across the table. Her mouth had dropped open two inches and she wore the surprised, not-quite-understanding look of a person who precisely one second before has been shot dead, right through the heart.

In the hall outside I paused and listened to the beginning of the uproar, the shrill cries of the ladies and the outraged unbelieving exclamations of the men; and soon there was a great hum of noise with everybody talking or shouting at the same time. Then – and this was the sweetest moment of all – I heard Lord Mulherrin's voice, roaring above the rest, 'Here! Someone! Hurry! Give her some water quick!'

Out in the street the chauffeur helped me into my car, and soon we were away from London and bowling merrily along the Great North Road towards this, my other house, which is only ninety-five miles from Town anyway.

The next two days I spent in gloating. I mooned around in a dream of ecstasy, half drowned in my own complacency and filled with a sense of pleasure so great that it constantly gave me pins and needles all along the lower parts of my legs. It wasn't until this morning when Gladys Ponsonby called me on the phone that I suddenly came to my senses and realized I was not a hero at all but an outcast. She informed me – with what I thought was just a trace of relish – that everybody was up in arms, that all of them, all my old and loving friends, were saying the most terrible things about me and had sworn never never to speak to me again. Except her, she kept saying. Everybody except her. And didn't I think it would be rather cosy, she asked, if she were to come down and stay with me a few days to cheer me up?

I'm afraid I was too upset by that time even to answer her politely. I put the phone down and went away to weep.

Then at noon today came the final crushing blow. The post arrived, and with it – I can hardly bring myself to write about it, I am so ashamed – came a letter, the sweetest, most tender little note imaginable from none other than Janet de Pelagia herself. She forgave me completely, she wrote, for everything I had done. She knew it was only a joke and I must not listen to the horrid things other people were saying about me. She loved me as she always had and always would to her dying day.

Oh, what a cad, what a brute I felt when I read this! The more so when I found that she had actually sent me by the same post a small present as an added sign of her affection – a half-pound jar of my favourite food of all, fresh caviare.

I can never under any circumstances resist good caviare. It is perhaps my greatest weakness. So although I naturally had no appetite whatsoever for food at dinnertime this evening, I must confess I took a few spoonfuls of the stuff in an effort to console myself in my misery. It is even possible that I took a shade too much, because I haven't been feeling any too chipper this last hour or so. Perhaps I ought to go up right away and get myself some bicarbonate of soda. I can easily come back and finish this later, when I'm in better trim.

You know – now I come to think of it, I really do feel rather ill all of a sudden.

ROALD DAHL

Roald Dahl was a spy, ace fighter-pilot, chocolate historian and medical inventor. He was also the author of Charlie and the Chocolate Factory, Matilda, The BFG and many more brilliant stories. He remains the World's No.1 storyteller.

CHARMING BAKER

Born in Hampshire 1964, Charming Baker spent much of his early life travelling around the world following his father, a commando in the British Army. At the age of twelve, he and his family finally settled in Ripon, North Yorkshire. Baker left school at sixteen and worked various manual jobs. In 1985, having gone back to college, he was accepted onto a course at the prestigious Central Saint Martin's, where he later returned as a lecturer. After graduating, Baker worked for many years as a commercial artist as well as developing his personal work.

Solo exhibitions include the Truman Brewery, London, 2007, Redchurch Street Gallery, London, 2009, New York Studio Gallery, NYC, 2010, Mercer Street, London, 2011 and Milk Studios, LA, 2013. Baker has also exhibited with the Fine Art Society, collaborated with Sir Paul Smith for a sculpture entitled 'Triumph in the Face of Absurdity', which was displayed at the Victoria and Albert Museum, and continues to be committed to creating work to raise money for many charities. He has recently been commissioned to be a presenter on *The Art Show*. His work is in many international collections.

Although Baker has produced sculptural pieces in a wide and varied choice of materials, as well as many large-scale and detailed drawings, he remains primarily a painter with an interest in narrative and an understanding of the tradition of painting. Known to purposefully damage his work by drilling, cutting and even shooting it, Baker intentionally puts in to question the preciousness of art and the definition of its beauty, adding to the emotive charge of the work he produces. Indeed Edward Lucie-Smith has described Baker's paintings as having, something more, a kind of romantic melancholy that is very British. And sometimes the melancholy turns out to have sharp claws. The pictures make you sit up and examine your conscience.

Charming Baker lives and works in London.

Roald Dahl
CRUELTY
Tales of Malice and Greed

CRUELTY
Tales of Malice and Greed

Even when we mean to be kind we can sometimes be cruel. We each have a streak of nastiness inside us. In these ten tales of cruelty Roald Dahl explores how and why it is we make others suffer.

Among others, you'll read the story of two young bullies and the boy they torment, the adulterous wife who uncovers her husband's secret, the man with a painting tattooed on his back whose value he doesn't appreciate and the butler and chef who run rings around their obnoxious employer.

DECEPTION
Tales of Intrigue and Lies

Why do we lie? Why do we deceive those we love most? What do we fear revealing? In these ten tales of deception Roald Dahl explores our tireless efforts to hide the truth about ourselves.

Here, among many others tales you'll read about how to get away with the perfect murder, the old man whose wagers end in a most disturbing payment, how revenge is sweeter when it is carried out by someone else and the card sharp so good at cheating he does something surprising with his life.

Roald Dahl

LUST

Tales of Craving and Desire

LUST

Tales of Craving and Desire

To what lengths would you go to achieve your heart's desire? In these ten tales of maddening lust Roald Dahl explores how our darkest impulses reveal who we really are.

Here you will read a story concerning wife swapping with a twist, hear of the aphrodisiac that drives men into a frenzy, discover the last act in a tale of jilted first love and discover the naked truth of art.

MADNESS
Tales of Fear and Unreason

Our greatest fear is of losing control – above all, of losing control of ourselves. In these ten unsettling tales of unexpected madness Roald Dahl explores what happens when we let go of our sanity.

Among other stories, you'll meet the husband with a jealous fixation on the family cat, the landlady who wants her guests to stay forever, the man whose taste for pork leads him astray and the wife with a pathological fear of being late.

THE COMPLETE ROALD DAHL SHORT STORIES VOL 1 & 2

'They are brutal, these stories, and yet you finish
reading each one with a smile, or maybe even a
hollow laugh, certainly a shiver of gratification,
because the conclusion always seems so right'
Charlie Higson

In these two volumes chronologically collecting all Roald Dahl's 55
published adult short stories, written between 1944 and 1988, and
introduced by Charlie Higson and Anthony Horowitz, we see Roald
Dahl's powerful and dark imagination pen some of the most unsettling
and disquieting tales ever written.

Whether you're young or old, once you've stepped into the brilliant,
troubling world of Roald Dahl, you'll never be the same again.

BOY

'An autobiography is a book a person writes about his own life and it is usually full of all sorts of boring details. This is not an autobiography. I would never write a history of myself. On the other hand, throughout my young days at school and just afterwards a number of things happened to me that I have never forgotten ...'

Boy is a funny, insightful and at times grotesque glimpse into the early life of Roald Dahl. We discover his experiences of the English public school system, the idyllic paradise of summer holidays in Norway, the pleasures (and pains) of the sweetshop, and how it is that he avoided being a Boazer.

This is the unadulterated childhood – sad and funny, macabre and delightful – which speaks of an age which vanished with the coming of the Second World War.

'A shimmering fabric of his yesterdays, the magic and the hurt' *Observer*

'As frightening and funny as his fiction' *The New York Times Book Review*

'Superbly written. A glimpse of a brilliant eccentric' *New Statesman*

GOING SOLO

'They did not think for one moment that they would find anything but a burnt-out fuselage and a charred skeleton, and they were astounded when they came upon my still-breathing body lying in the sand nearby.'

In 1938 Roald Dahl was fresh out of school and bound for his first job in Africa, hoping to find adventure far from home. However, he got far more excitement than he bargained for when the outbreak of the Second World War led him to join the RAF. His account of his experiences in Africa, crashing a plane in the Western Desert, rescue and recovery from his horrific injuries in Alexandria, flying a Hurricane as Greece fell to the Germans, and many other daring deeds, recreates a world as bizarre and unnerving as any he wrote about in his fiction.

'Very nearly as grotesque as his fiction. The same compulsive blend of wide-eyed innocence and fascination with danger and horror' *Evening Standard*

'A non-stop demonstration of expert raconteurship'
The New York Times Book Review

He just wanted a decent book to read ...

Not too much to ask, is it? It was in 1935 when Allen Lane, Managing Director of Bodley Head Publishers, stood on a platform at Exeter railway station looking for something good to read on his journey back to London. His choice was limited to popular magazines and poor-quality paperbacks – the same choice faced every day by the vast majority of readers, few of whom could afford hardbacks. Lane's disappointment and subsequent anger at the range of books generally available led him to found a company – and change the world.

'We believed in the existence in this country of a vast reading public for intelligent books at a low price, and staked everything on it'
Sir Allen Lane, 1902–1970, founder of Penguin Books

The quality paperback had arrived – and not just in bookshops. Lane was adamant that his Penguins should appear in chain stores and tobacconists, and should cost no more than a packet of cigarettes.

Reading habits (and cigarette prices) have changed since 1935, but Penguin still believes in publishing the best books for everybody to enjoy. We still believe that good design costs no more than bad design, and we still believe that quality books published passionately and responsibly make the world a better place.

So wherever you see the little bird – whether it's on a piece of prize-winning literary fiction or a celebrity autobiography, political tour de force or historical masterpiece, a serial-killer thriller, reference book, world classic or a piece of pure escapism – you can bet that it represents the very best that the genre has to offer.

Whatever you like to read – trust Penguin.